There's no DRM on this because frankly I don't like it, but if you pirated this book, maybe drop me a dime or so through PayPal or Patreon, unless you are too poor to do so. Be a decent human being, it's not like I'm swimming in cash.

Table of Contents

Titles in bold and cursive are exclusive to this book.

A Quick Foreword

By Gwydion JMF Weber

I am writing this while still high off having just finished this beast, long before the anxiety about how successful it may or may not be hits. All of these stories were written over the course of the past three years, but to me this collection is the result of 13 years of blood, sweat, tears, anxiety, and beating the odds.

I can count on one hand the people who genuinely believed in me, though I know there are many more out there that I have never met. To each and every one of you I would like to say: thank you so much. Your support got me through my darkest times, and I will be forever grateful for that.

It is true that I have written many more stories than just these, but I wanted my first collection to consist solely of stories that were not part of a larger universe, and that is what 34 Worlds is. It is also true that you can get 30 of these stories for free on the internet, but that's not why I published this collection.

I published this collection because I needed to prove to myself that I could do it, and here I am, doing it. If you are reading this text, you have purchased my book, and I cannot express how grateful I am for that.

The order of the stories here is entirely random. They do not follow the alphabet or their date of publication, they are not grouped by stories I wrote entirely on my own and stories I first put out on r/writingprompts. Some stories I like more than others, some stories I hate and am ashamed of, but people have assured me that I should let that stop me, because the ones I dislike the most tend to be some of the best pieces of work in my portfolio.

In that spirit, enjoy this book, come find me on YouTube

as Who Is Betty? and TheBurgerkrieg, and see you round friends.

The Call of the Sea

By Gwydion JMF Weber

Walking the Ringwall that encircled his city, the Vizier wished he could be up on the hill instead, sitting comfortably on the balcony of his mansion, drinking tea. The waves of the stormy sea hammered against the wall below, where they'd been eating into the fused stone for a thousand years.

The Vizier adjusted his headwrap as a particularly strong gust of wing threatened to take it away. The guard captain, an enormous woman clad in yellow steelglass plate, looked at him with concern. Though many years old, the ritual scars on her face were still red as fresh blood.

“Is His Excellency quite well?” she inquired.

“It's quite alright,” the Vizier responded. It was important not to appear squeamish in front of the soldiers, and he was doing his best to hide the fear reverberating through him like a gong. Even from the hill, where he could see past the Ringwall, days like these could drive shivers down his spine.

“This is the spot, Your Excellency.” The guard captain gestured toward a rounded platform protruding from the wall outward over the sea. It was barely large enough for single man to stand on, and lacked any kind of parapet. A lone guardsman with a golden halberd stood in defiance of the storm next to it.

The Vizier was apprehensive about approaching the platform. There were many of them along the Ringwall. Hoops of eversteel were attached to the sides of its openings, allowing daring guardsmen to rappel down.

Yet, in spite of its ordinariness, the son of the Politarch had chosen to jump into the sea from this spot. He hadn't done it from a spot that was easier to reach from the palace, and he hadn't chosen to do it from one that was furthest away either.

Of course, the palace was at the very centre of the city, on top of the hill. But not all roads were made equal, and not all were as convenient. The Politarch had suggested that she was somehow to blame, but in relation to her abode, this platform was as meaningless as any other.

The Vizier looked down into the city, seeing one of the three ports. In this weather, the water lock was closed, and the many hundred ships in the lagoon were safe from the storm. The Singing Frigates of the Sunwalkers and the Bone Caravels of the Bloodless Folk were moored side by side among the plethora of ships, respecting the neutrality of the city.

"Where is the closest stairwell?" The Vizier asked.

"Not far from here, Your Excellency. Only a few minutes of walking."

"Take me there," he commanded.

"Of course, Your Excellency," The guard captain bowed.

The Vizier stayed away as far as possible from the hole in the parapet as was unshameful. He noted that no other platforms appeared between this one and the stairwell, giving credence to the notion that the Prince had ascended here. It lead down to a small, snaking island dense with squat buildings hugging the side of the Ringwall.

"Your Excellency, the district at the foot of this stairwell is quite disreputable," the guard captain warned.

"That's why I have you." He made sure to give the woman a magnanimous smile. In truth, he would have waded into a sewer if it had meant getting off the Ringwall.

Ten soldiers in full armour could have run past each other on the stairwell, but the Vizier still found himself keeping to the Ringwall. Every time one of the guards confidently set foot on another step right by the edge, where one slip could lead to a fall many heartbeats long, his throat tightened.

When they arrived at the foot of the stairwell, the Vizier's legs had begun hurting. Usually he travelled around the city by rickshaw, and spent most of his time at home or in the palace. He'd become an old man, it seemed. His bones were cold and rickety, and his back fraught with pain.

The island at the foot of the stairwell was indeed a cesspit of filth. The coral bricks were porous and worn, the few roofs that were not thatched with palm leaves but wooden shingles were all in dire need of repair.

The locals, all but dressed in rags, stood still on the poorly paved roads, backing away into home entrances and whispering behind drawn curtains. It occurred to him that none of them had ever seen a vizier before. All of them averted their eyes when he looked at them, whether out of fear or shame he could not tell. Only a tall man with silvery skin and cat eyes met his gaze. He gave the Vizier an apologetic smile, then disappeared into a small crowd of bystanders.

Almost by the shore near the water lock, a building towered over the others. It was hardly pristine, but better maintained than the shacks around it. The smell of strong beer and sour wine mixed with urine and vomit. The innkeep, a fat man with arms like logs and shoulders like construction cranes, was throwing out early troublemakers with a whipping rod.

Obscenities the likes of which the Vizier had never even imagined possible flew out of his mouth as his wooden sandals clacked on the cobblestone. When the innkeep turned around and saw the Vizier, he at first didn't seem to register what he was looking at. Then, like a hinge, he collapsed, and began kissing the dirty ground before the Vizier's feet, mumbling apologies.

The Vizier knelt to put a gentle hand on the man's shoulder, prompting him to rise. “You've nothing to apologise for, my good man. Rowdy patrons require rowdy methods.”

“Yes Excellency, whatever you want.” The innkeep nodded profusely, tears of gratitude in his eyes. The Vizier was not sure what the man had expected. It was not a crime to curse while in the presence of a vizier.

“I'd like to inspect this establishment more closely,” the Vizier told the guard captain.

The woman frowned, but ordered two of her soldiers to go ahead and secure the interior.

The Vizier followed them, the innkeeper close on his tail before being held back a few paces by the guard captain.

The tavern was completely silent. Even the mechanical music box jingling away in the corner hit a silence between songs. There weren't many patrons at this early hour, but all of them looked at him with frozen emotions ranging from surprise to fear. A group of Bloodless Folk, pale, huge, and hairless, were the first to resume their carousing. Others followed, careful to keep the Vizier in sight.

The Cat-Eyed Man from earlier was sitting alone at a table in the back corner of the room. The Vizier wondered how he had gotten here so quickly. He was nursing a steaming mug of what smelled like mulled beer.

Much to the guard captain's frustration, the Vizier approached the Cat-Eyed Man without letting one of her underlings frisk him first, and took a seat on the creaking chair opposite to him. “You know why I am here.” It was a statement of fact, not a question.

“I know many things, Your Excellency. That is one of them.” Despite his friendly appearance, the Cat-Eyed Man's voice was dark and raspy. His accent was refined, like a scholar's might be, and didn't fit the surroundings at all.

“The Politarch's son. He was here last night, wasn't he?” the Vizier asked.

“And not for the first time, Your Excellency. He was a regular, even had a set of commoner's clothes so he could walk the streets safely without an escort.”

The Vizier nodded. The Prince had made a habit of shaking his tails whenever he left the palace. Because he always returned, the Politarch had soon stopped worrying. “Was there a reason for his continued patronage?”

“Certainly not the beer.” The Cat-Eyed Man grimaced as he took a swig. Either his manners needed work, or he didn't care about disrespecting the Vizier. “He had, shall we say, a *pearl* up in the gallery he was quite taken with.”

The Vizier looked up, finding a wide selection of nubile young girls timidly peering over the railings. “Did something occur?”

“Months ago. She was killed by disease. A shame, too. She was such a pretty young thing, like a princess from a distant land." The Cat-Eyed Man tilted his head. "The Prince continued to come after she passed, to drown his sorrows."

The Vizier leaned back in his chair, sadness spreading through his chest from the realisation of what had taken place. Young love could be fierce. Too fierce for some.

"No. That's not what happened." The Cat-Eyed Man spoke as though he could read the Vizier's thoughts.

Before he could inquire further, the fat innkeep appeared holding out a lavishly filigreed bottle of walnut liqueur from the Moonrock Isles. It looked to be as valuable as the rest of his inventory combined.

"Here, on the house, Excellency," he insisted.

The Vizier shook his head, smiling. "You owe me neither apology nor gratitude. I am not in need of drink. Lock that bottle back where it belongs."

The inkeeper bowed, then stomped off back to his counter.

"That man worships everyone who lives on the hill like they are living gods. To think he never knew whom he was serving breaks my heart," the Cat-Eyed Man said.

"What did you mean earlier?" The Vizier demanded.

"It has been said that, for a month or so, the Prince has been hearing the Call Of The Sea."

"That is a euphemism for suicidal ideation," the Vizier noted. He was beginning to lose patience.

"I assure you it is quite real, Your Excellency. Difficult to describe to someone who hasn't experienced it. Like a mother's embrace and a seductive moan at the same time, only felt in the heart, not heard." The Cat-Eyed Man's eyes trailed off into the distance for a moment.

"So you have experienced it?"

"I am experiencing it right now. It's why I live so close to the Ringwall. Moving further into the city causes me physical discomfort," the Cat-Eyed Man explained.

"So why haven't you thrown yourself into the sea?" the Vizier asked.

"Because I value living. There are certain substances that can keep her calls at bay, dull them or even entirely blur them out. The Prince was not one for deviating from his usual poisons." The

Cat-Eyed Man tapped the side of his mug.

"Still, that would clean up the reason for his death," the Vizier noted.

"Oh yes, definitely. But it's more than just a tragic chain of events. It's something to be concerned about." The Cat-Eyed Man had a wry smile on his lips.

"Explain."

"Hearing the call of the sea runs in the family, as it were, and it can do much more than just lure people to their deaths." The Cat-Eyed Man gestured toward the door. "The sea has been trying to claw its way into this city of ours since the Ringwall was raised. Her methods are insidious, as your guards will be able to attest to. It might be a good idea to keep the Politarch away from the Ringwall in the future. Who knows what the sea could convince our appointed protector to do."

"Drink up and come with me to the palace," the Vizier ordered.

The Cat-Eyed Man shook his head. "No, Your Excellency. I'd rather die than leave the shadow of the Ringwall ever again."

"I am not granting you a choice in the matter. Your services are being requisitioned. You will be compensated, but you cannot refuse."

"I already have." The grin on the Cat-Eyed Man's face was that of an untouchable victor. A droplet of blood came out of his nostril, followed by a light stream. Green foam formed in the corners of his mouth. One by one, his thick black hair went grey, individual strands at first, then whole patches at once.

The guard captain grabbed his chair and pushed it further back, putting herself between the Cat-Eyed Man and the Vizier. In her grasp, the Cat-Eyed Man keeled over, threw up bloody retch onto the floorboards, and died. As the light left his enigmatic eyes, he still had that victorious grin on his lips.

"Throw him into the sea," the Vizier ordered. "And get me a rickshaw for the palace."

The Crooked Spire

By Gwydion JMF Weber

Everything had started to go bad the day they allowed artists to become architects. They did everything wrong, and when Okhom Zaelek told them so, the response was "well then make it work," not "sorry, I was unaware of that."

A buildmaster by trade, trained at the prestigious Blue Academy, his portfolio included everything from small grain silos to palatial estates. Yet all formal education in structural engineering, bricklaying, roofing, carpentry, and half a dozen other competencies was apparently insufficient to trump the whims of a fat drunkard whose only skill was putting pen to paper to produce drawings.

Zaelek could do the same, only his drawings became useful aides to the workers under his command.

The sun was already halfway to its zenith when Zaelek was marching through the busy streets of Mankheda, passing peddlers, beggars, and carriages on his way to the Stone Garden District. He had no choice but to coat his embarrassment in fury. The angry *clack-clack* of his wooden shoes hitting the cobblestone drove people out of his way. Nobody tried to talk to him.

A sky column rose in the distance, disappearing into the heavens, holding up the sky.

Haasir Funtho's town house was an ode to opulence. It was insulting that the architect devised such impractical, even dangerous buildings for everyone else, but had limited the unorthodoxies of his own home to round windows encased in colourful mosaics. It was easy to hide your own insanity when it was located elsewhere.

Fuming, Zaelek brushed past the housekeeper when she opened the door and headed straight upstairs to Haasir's "recreational space." Upon opening the door, his nostrils were assaulted by the sour stench of sweat mixed with thinkersgrass.

Haasir Funtho himself lay sprawled on an expansive recliner, pipe in hand, his heavy belly rising and falling as he snored. Zaelek ripped open the heavy curtains, and the architect gave a startled scream at the sudden influx of sunlight.

"By the Archangel, what are you *doing*?" he gasped, his voice laced with terror.

"It is but one morning per week that you must be present at the building site, yet half the time you fail to appear at all!" Zaelek roared. "Have you no understanding of the delays this causes?"

"Is it Seventhday already?" Haasir frowned.

"Yes, it is, and the entire construction crew has been waiting for two hours on your arrival."

"Look, Master Okhom, I've already told you that you needn't involve me in your weekly inspections. Scheduling interrupts my creative process," Haasir offered.

Zaelek shook his head. "No, you must sign the appropriate documents to give your assurances that the project is not deviating from your plans."

"So bring them here, I'll put my signature under them, and we'll all be happy. I have full trust in your competence to follow my instructions." He grabbed the casket that kept his thinkersgrass to stuff himself a morning pipe.

"How can you know if everything is to your liking if you do not attend the inspection?" Zaelek asked.

"As I said, I trust you."

Zaelek had to bite his tongue not to hurl insults at the man. "It is improper. The implementation of an idea such as this requires the presence of the architect, preferably every hour of every day." He pointed at the drawings of Haasir's spire, strewn about over floorboards and couches. It was an impossible construction, taller than most buildings in the city, bent like a half-crescent, with a turret at its tip.

The turret was to be plated fully in bronze, and the round windows that were the architect's hallmark would be framed with heavy stonework of sea snakes and molluscs. The mere thought of it seemed laughable to Zaelek. It would never be able to support its own weight.

"Please don't demand such things, they agitate me. Sometimes I work so late into the night that your workers have already started their shifts when I go to sleep." The fat man shivered at the thought, lit the pipe and took a deep drag, then offering it to Zaelek.

"It is my hope, Master Haasir, that exposing you to the construction effort will finally reveal to you the folly of your grand vision," Zaelek admitted, tense with the anxiety of insulting a frequent guest at the court.

Haasir did not seem to mind. "The quantarch loves my grand vision, that's all that matters. Speaking of, It came to me that we should shape the turret to look like his eminence in solid gold. Picture it: The shining face of Quantarch Uzkhot the Implacable, tall as three men, watching over the city." He had that dreamer's glow in his eyes, the one that so frequently accompanied ridiculous ideas. "I considered making it only a gold coating, because of just how much gold weighs, but for the quantarch we will go for nothing but massive. Anything less would be an insult. You'll have to account for the added weight at the tip, of course."

"It cannot be done. The weight is already impossible to support." Zaelek's frustration was transforming into resignation, as it so often did.

"That's not true. I can see the tower in my head, arching over the city. It'll be glorious, trust me." Haasir waved Zaelek's words away. "But I'm open to discussion about the face. How about we talk about it over breakfast? Zina! Get two servings of shortbread and custard up here for me and Master Okhom,"

"You will do no such thing, Zina. Master Haasir, I cannot allow construction to be delayed any further. I *must* insist that you come with me *immediately*."

Haasir took his shortbread for the road.

“Are you sure you wouldn't like at least one?” he asked, already wheezing from the exertion of leaving his home.

“I have already broken fast, thank you.”

“It's really good shortbread, though. Zina knows this recipe from-” Haasir did not get to finish his sentence. A bone-shaking boom resounded through the street, like a thousand trumpets blaring at the same time. It seemed to come from all directions at once, but Zaelek knew it was coming from high up in the sky.

Everyone in the street stopped. The Heavenly Roar never preceded anything pleasant. Zaelek felt himself choking up with fear. Memories of his childhood returned. A red column of light larger than anything he'd ever seen pushing down on a field. When it went away, the village that has once been there was scorched to fine ash.

“Don't worry, this is not going to be too bad.” Haasir Funtho pointed at the sky, where a pitch black hole had appeared in the deep blue firmament. Several dots of light descended from it, plumes of smoke trailing behind them. Angels. The architect took another bite from his shortbread and stared upward with serene fascination.

“The angels are coming for us!” Zaelek screamed. “They've come to bring their judgement.”

“No, this is not how they do it.” Haasir shook his head. “Trust me, I've read a lot of scholarly works on angels. They don't bother coming down to destroy things, they can do that from up there, I'm sure you've heard the stories.”

“I've lived them, you fool.” Zaelek could not control himself. There were still times when he heard the sizzling in his nightmares, closing in, following him. But Haasir didn't need to know about any of that. Nothing good ever came from the angels.

In mere moments they were on the ground. Any hope that they might have been headed somewhere else was shattered when they landed on the pavement only a few paces ahead of them. Though they fell at impossible speed, their descent slowed abruptly a few ells above the ground, and the giants of shimmering metal landed soft as feathers.

They had smooth, humanoid shapes. The iridescent

material they were made from shone in a million colours. They had no solid head, only a fountain of light emanating from their neck, forming a seemingly solid shape of white radiance that could be barely detected, but never quite clearly discerned.

There were five of them, herding people into small groups, their footsteps making absolutely no sound at all. They did not speak, but everyone obeyed their commands. Every child in the entire world was taught one thing from birth: If you ever encounter an angel, offer them your right wrist. Most people never saw a single angel in their life, but it was the single piece of knowledge everyone agreed was necessary to survive. Zaelek bared his wrist. Tense with fear, he didn't even think about it. The voice of his first school teacher made him do it automatically.

People started approaching the angels, always one at a time, wrist extended. The giants shone a light on it, and then either sent them off into the street, or directed them toward a circle of blue light hovering above the ground. One man was sent to the circle, but his panic got the best of him. Instead of following the angel's instructions, he ran, and paid the price.

He hadn't taken three steps before his face turned into a mask of surprise, followed by agony. He fell to the ground, clutching his chest, lips parted in a silent scream. A bright light emanated from his mouth, eyes, and nostrils, then his ears and neck, until every pore of his skin glowed pure white. At the end there was nothing but a heap of light convulsing on the ground. The light disappeared, and a thin blanket of ash covered the cobblestones where the man had been.

One of the angels looked at Zaelek. He couldn't see the being's eyes, he just knew. It wanted him to approach. His legs were shivering, but he wasn't a man who gave in to fear. He commanded himself to step forward, his heart pounding like a sledgehammer.

The angel shone a light on his wrist, and an intricate shape of countless interlocking circles and lines appeared on it. It was the Mark. Every person had one, but in spite of the best efforts of brilliant scholars and inventors, only the angels could make them appear.

Then, the unthinkable happened. The angel directed

Zaelek toward the blue circle. This time he found it difficult to make his legs obey him, but he forced himself to step inside. He was not going to explode in white light.

Other people were already inside the circle, shivering, looking longingly at those who were sent back into the streets. People were looking down on them from their windows, most of them hiding behind curtains, unable to resist the spectacle.

When the angels called forth Haasir Funtho, the architect seemed utterly at ease, possibly even a little excited. What was wrong with that man?

A boyish grin appeared on his face when he was sent to the circle. He stood next to Zaelek, giddy with anticipation. “Oh this is fantastic,” he yelped, and finished his shortbread.

“We are going to be slaughtered,” said Zaelek. “This is it, I am going to die.”

“Nonsense. If the angels wanted you dead, you would be dead. No, this is an uncommon occurrence, but a known occurrence nonetheless. The angels come down, take a few people, then after a few hours they come back unharmed. Most of the time.”

“When I was a child, I saw an entire village burnt to cinders by the angels,” Zaelek admitted. He had never told anyone but his wife, and she'd had a hard time believing him. Everyone was terrified of the angels, but on some level they wanted them to be good. Zaelek knew better than that.

“Yes, I hear that can happen. Something terrible must have been going on in that village for such a drastic punishment.” Haasir shrugged. “It's not happening right now, so we are safe.”

“No, Master Haasir. We are cattle for the slaughter now.”

“I already told you, people get taken from time to time. They tend to return.”

“And what do they say happens to them up there?” Zaelek asked.

Haasir shrugged. “They can't talk about it. Physically, I mean, like you couldn't breathe air under water. It is not possible.”

That did not give Zaelek much comfort.

There must have been thirty people in the circle when the

angels abruptly stopped. For a moment they looked at each other idly. Then, Zaelek felt himself becoming light. There was no force acting on him, he simply felt himself become lighter and lighter, until he was completely weightless.

The others also began to float, and, aside from Haasir Funtho, all of them were as disconcerted by it as Zaelek was. A child was standing on the street, crying out for its mother, who was only an arm's length away from Zaelek.

The flickering circle of blue light rose, then thickened, growing into a translucent bubble the colour of robin eggs. Its occupants were lifted off the ground, and the sphere catapulted itself into the sky at breakneck speed, accompanied by the five angels.

The ground grew rapidly more distant, and the world below that had always seemed so large grew smaller and smaller. After only a few moments, Zaelek could have covered the great city of Mankheda with his thumb. How vast the rolling emerald hills were, how majestic the lakes and rivers. In the distance he could see the deep blue of the ocean, and the Mountains of Car, so tall no man had ever climbed them.

Then they were swallowed by the black hole in the sky.

Zaelek awoke surrounded by blinding white light. No, he was not surrounded. He wasn't at all. His body had disappeared, there was only his mind floating in the light. He knew he wasn't dead, somehow, just like he knew he wasn't dreaming, but not truly awake either.

What is your dread?

There was no voice, only words spoken without sound. Zaelek could feel the shadow of fear looming, but something was keeping it at bay.

What is your dread?

He didn't understand the question, but couldn't ask for clarification without a mouth. Saying the words in his mind seemed to have no effect.

What is your dread?

Images of angels appeared in his mind. That was his dread, but he did not feel afraid. It was like looking at a diagram of a building. All the information was there, but the material essence would only manifest once he had built it in the physical world.

What preoccupies you?

Had he answered the question, or had the voice simply given up and moved on? The answer was obvious: He wanted to know what was happening to him, and whether he would be returned down to the world. The terror attempted to move in closer, envelop him like a blanket, but the ethereal shield around him held firm.

What preoccupied you before you came here?

It couldn't have been the tone of voice, but something about the question *felt* annoyed. It must have been his imagination. Angels did not have emotions, so whichever beings they served could not have them either.

There was information in that thought. Zaelek realised that, much like he knew he wasn't dead, he also knew that the voice talking to him was not an angel, but something the angels served. No tale of folklore had ever mentioned such beings, yet he knew this with the same certainty he knew that a roll of paper could not hold up a man-sized rock.

What preoccupied you before you came here?

The spire, of course. Quantarch Uzkhot's cathedral to the great beyond, where he would be interred once his term ended. He needed to be on schedule, and Haasir Funtho's incompetence was interfering with that.

The white light disappeared, and Zaelek was floating incorporeally over Mankheda. Everything seemed like a rough facsimile. There were no people in the streets, and all surfaces seemed flat, without texture. Right by the Old Market, at the building site, stood the cathedral as Haasir envisioned it, his impossible crooked spire rising high above the rooftops.

The scene stood still for a moment, as if the world was waiting for Zaelek to do something. His mind did not accept what he was seeing. This tower could not exist, he decided. It snapped in an instant, the heavy head with the quantarch's face on it crashing through the roof shingles and into the central nave.

Zaelek could feel the presence of Haasir Funtho, even

though the fat architect was nowhere to be seen. He seemed to be disagreeing with his assessment about the tower's viability, and the whole spire came floating out of the cathedral, undoing all the damage it had caused on its way down, and reattaching itself to the impossible arch meant to hold it.

What a fool that man was. Yes, maybe his mind's eye could visualise such folly, but Zaelek was trained for practical matters, and this idea was untenable to him. The tower snapped again, and crashed into the apse. Moments later, it returned to its original position.

Zaelek insisted it crash again, and Haasir pulled it back up. Every time one asserted something, the other put forth the opposite, and the tower was caught in a state of constant back and forth, falling and being mended again.

It was impossible to know how many cycles passed. Time did not have much meaning here. Haasir was iron-willed as a mule, bit Zaelek knew he had reality on his side. Neither of them would give the other an inch. It was impossible to concede. Haasir was simply wrong, but Zaelek was too stubborn to see that it could be done.

How had that happened?

It felt as though he could not only see into Haasir's mind, but experience his thoughts. He understood the man's reasoning now, and it made sense, at least in his own head. Not in Zaelek's though. Haasir was a dreamer. Whether or not something was possible had little bearing on his assessment as to whether or not it should be done.

Zaelek stopped for a moment, deciding to shift the argument elsewhere. Whether the tower would be able to support its own weight was irrelevant, it would already fail at construction. The cathedral turned into a building site, invisible hands building the spire. It snapped later than it did with the head attached, but it did snap.

When it hit the ground, Zaelek realised something. They had been taken into the sky by angels, yet they were still arguing over a tower. How had that happened?

Zaelek knew that Haasir had come to the exact same conclusion. The city disappeared underneath them, blown away by a gust of wind, and the white light began to burn, shaping the world around them, putting pressure on their very souls.

This time around Zaelek woke up in his body, in the real world. He was still in the sky, but at least he was once again a man of flesh. He strained to open his eyes. It was as though his mind had woken up ahead of his body, and his extremities were only now following suit.

Cold vapour danced around him. He was floating a few feet above the ground over a mound of ever-shifting, quicksilver substance. The other abductees floated over mounds of their own, though all of them seemed to be fast asleep, occasionally twitching or making a subdued exclamation.

Above, faint light illuminated thin arches holding up a milky-white ceiling. The room they were being kept it was rectangular with rounded edges, and contained many more empty quicksilver mounds. Two angels were flanking the only entrance, utterly motionless.

Zaelek felt himself descending gently to the ground, the pool of quicksilver beneath his feet bubbling languidly as his wooden shoes clacked on the solid floor. He couldn't ascertain the material it was made of, only that it was grey like metal and smooth as his wife's skin had been when they were both much younger.

“I'm glad we got that sorted,” Haasir Funtho said. Zaelek turned around to see him standing half a dozen mounds to the left. “You caved in first, so technically I win the argument and you have to build my spire.” He said it with a grin, but Zaelek still had to swallow a gust of frustration.

“Why are we the only ones awake?” he asked instead.

“I couldn't even begin to guess.” Haasir shrugged. He didn't seem disturbed by the situation at all.

“What do we do?” Zaelek realised that he did not know how to even begin formulating a plan. Usually problems presented themselves with certain parameters, and he would fall back on his training to find the right approach for a solution. This fell very far outside his education.

“They don't seem to be paying us much mind.” Haasir

nodded toward the two angels by the exit. “Maybe we're supposed to go through there.”

Zaelek grabbed the fat architect's arm to stop him. “Are you mad? They could destroy us in an instant.”

“Don't you think they would have done that already?”

“What if this is the test? To see if we will be obedient prisoners?”

“I don't think we are being tested here, Master Okhom.” Haasir shrugged him off and walked confidently toward the exit. The two angels showed no reaction.

Zaelek followed a few paces behind, getting ready to return to his mound if Haasir suddenly burst into flames as he passed through the enormous doorway. Nothing of the sort happened. The angels simply let him pass.

As they moved forward, the corridor around them became darker and darker. Once again, Haasir seemed entirely unperturbed by this. Only when it was almost entirely dark did he stop.

“What is it?” Zaelek asked.

“I don't want to bump into a wall.”

“Walk with your arms outstretched.” Zaelek frowned. Was Haasir truly so caught up in fantasy that he could not deal with simple problems?

The floor disappeared, and the corridor was flooded with light. It came from below, from the world, its landscape small as a map, peacefully green, brown, and blue. Zaelek jumped toward the walls, where the floor was still solid. Haasir simply admired.

It took Zaelek a moment to realise that the floor had not in fact disappeared, but somehow become glass. They were quite literally standing in the sky, just on the surface of the dome over the world. He had never seen glass this clear before, not to mention this strong. He expected Haasir to break through at any moment.

“Incredible,” the architect said. “Simply incredible, for me to be able to witness this. Do you know how privileged we are, to be chosen by the angels?”

“I don't care! I want to go back home! Back down there, where I belong!” Zaelek screamed. The modicum of calm he'd felt disappeared, and the pure terror of his situation revealed itself. He was in the sky, taken by angels, with no way of returning home. He was utterly at the mercy of inscrutable beings he knew to be nothing but murderous.

“Let us go. There's still a lot of corridor left, but I do see a light at the end of it.” Haasir pointed ahead and began walking.

Zaelek followed, not knowing what else to do. He remained near the walls, where the floor was not made of glass. Even though he was seeing the fat architect walk on it, his mind still insisted that it would break apart under his feet after only a few steps.

It was a long walk. The clacking of Zaelek's shoes became the metronome for their trot. He was surprised that Haasir didn't seem the slightest bit out of breath.

There was no denying that something was drawing him to the end of the corridor. It was like a silent voice, beckoning him forth, promising something he wanted but didn't quite understand. It was a longing older than life itself, like something he might have felt in his mother's womb.

They arrived in a dome so gargantuan it should have collapsed under its own weight, but it wasn't the first thing that caught Zaelek's attention. Hovering in the centre was a fountain of diaphanous light, a ball of flares and shimmering beads spinning slowly around its own axis. It was like the head of an angel, but, as opposed to representing nothing, it represented everything.

Faces of people he knew and had never met, places that were important to him and places he had never seen, scripts, manuals, and diagrams, as well as arcane runes and foreign verses seemed to be contained in each and every tiny dot of light. A thousand emotions awoke in him, from primal fear to a feeling of all-encompassing love, but first and foremost a great respect for the entity standing before him.

“Greetings. I am the Archangel.” It spoke with the voices of every person that had ever lived.

“Oh great Archangel!” Haasir Funtho suddenly dropped to his knees, supplicating. “You have chosen us!”

“I have not. You have chosen yourselves, and presented

your great conflict to the Watchers. They approve of it."

"What does that mean?" Zaelek heard himself ask. Out of all the questions he had, this one seemed to be the most important.

"You will be allowed to resolve your conflict. A vote has been had on the matter."

"Is this really just about my tower?" Haasir Funtho sounded puzzled. "That seems a bit mundane."

"The Watchers have answered all of life's great questions. The mundane is all that intrigues them any more."

Zaelek couldn't help but feel a slight pang of satisfaction at the idea that whatever beings controlled the angels were concerned with practical problems. Those were the only problems worth solving, after all.

Haasir took a few steps back, his expression that of a thinker who had just been presented with a great revelation. He was confused, afraid, and excited all at the same time.

"And how are we supposed to 'resolve' our conflict?" Zaelek asked. He felt strangely at ease now that actionable questions could be asked.

"You will both be correct. Okhom Zaelek, it is indeed true that the construction of the spire would not be possible with your materials and techniques. Haasir Funtho, your vision would indeed be a wonder for the ages. The Watchers have decreed that you shall be able to build this spire."

"But how?" Zaelek frowned. "You just said yourself it was impossible!"

"This encounter is concluded."

Before he could say anything in response, Zaelek's vision went completely white, and he felt himself drifting away into unconsciousness.

It was night when Zaelek awoke at the exact spot where he'd been abducted. Looking around, he found that everyone else had made it back also, including Haasir Funtho, who was lying on his back, looking at the sky with a shocked expression on his face. Slowly, the others awoke, and people began emerging from the surrounding streets. The angels must have come back to deliver them. It was unsurprising that this had drawn a crowd.

“I know what to do now.” Haasir Funtho snapped back to his old self, rising with unexpected vigour.

For a brief moment, Zaelek didn't understand. Then it came back to him, information he had never learned. There would be a stash of a strange material at the building site, and he knew how to work it properly. It would be able to support Haasir's tower with ease.

“We'll do the gold-plated head, we just have to,” the fat architect insisted.

“Indeed.” The next words seemed stuck in Zaelek's throat. He wanted to tell Haasir about the knowledge that had been implanted in his mind by the Archangel, but couldn't. It was as though he needed to express them in a language he didn't know.

But Haasir Funtho understood. He smiled, cracked his knuckles. “Do you think you could still show me the site for inspection this late in the evening? I'd like to get this crooked spire built with as little delay as possible.”

Zaelek nodded. He very much liked the sound of that.

Cargo Samurai

By Gwydion JMF Weber

Though not the first to set foot on the red planet, the Japanese were the first to establish a permanent settlement here. Even today, ninety-three years after Igarashi Aki had planted the Nisshōki on the spot where Suchīrugāden, the largest city on Mars, would sprout over the decades, its traditions permeated every facet of Martian culture. Most famous in popular fiction of Earth, Mars, and beyond were the Cargo Samurai, the customs agents that protected Kasei from humanity's most dangerous invention – Firearms.

One of these men was Ivor Veltsmann, whose parents had sought refuge with the Red Mother when they were fleeing wars in their respective home countries. Like all Martian natives, he was tall. Very tall. His dispassionate brown eyes, and harsh, mask-like features gave him the appearance people expected from most fictional Cargo Samurai, and he knew it.

Today, he was employing his cool stoicism to properly screen a group of weary refugees, who had arrived in a battered tin can of a spaceship two days ago. The passengers were quiet, reserved, and nervous. But something was wrong with them. Ivor could feel it in his gut, and his gut wasn't known for its dishonesty.

That day, when he entered the small holding dome reserved for this particular vessel, he was greeted by the ship's pilot. He was short, even for an Earthling, and had green eyes behind which there seemed to be no soul. It was unusual, though not unheard of, for traffickers to actually land on Mars. Usually they dropped several containers in orbit for the stations to pick up.

Sometimes, the people in them suffocated long before they could be reeled to the safety of a space station. The fact that this particular trafficker had piloted the ship to a rough landing on the ground could only mean one thing: He was a refugee himself, fleeing from Earth authorities. It was all the same to Ivor, though he did have to consider whether such a potentially dangerous individual was to be allowed on Kasei.

"We've been waiting very long, Sir. Many hours," the trafficker informed him in an accent that was difficult to place. "These people are tired, they just want to begin their new life."

Ivor nodded, expressed his empathy for the situation, and ignored the man. His "customers" were an odd bunch. They were mostly young men, though a number of women were among them, and though they did seem weakened from a month-long journey through deep space, they seemed much more strong and vital than the usual mint of people seeking a new life on Mars. Their muscles seemed to have atrophied little, and their hawkish eyes were alert not out of fear, but out of discipline.

Ivor told his subordinates to fan out, form three queues, and catalogue each of the refugees with biometric scans and a collection of their personal details. With the information blockade that Earth governments had sanctioned Kasei with, they would not be able to search any police databases, but at least they would be registered in some system. In the meantime, he directed his attention toward their ship. Like any vessel designed to travel long distances in space, it was well shielded against all kinds of radiation, and, unfortunately, the magical scanning technology many of the poorly researched films and manga portrayed Cargo Samurai having access to did not exist. Thus, Ivor had to search the ship the old-fashioned way.

Inside, the reason for the fitness of the refugees became obvious. Not only did they have training equipment, but also access to ubiquitous amounts of dietary supplements. They were usually given to astronauts on deep-space deployment. Come to think of it, this vessel very much looked like something one would find patrolling the inner solar system. Ivor asked the trafficker inside.

"Why is there so much protein juice on board your ship?"

he asked.

"These people want to do manual labour. They think that, if they are strong like an Earth person should be, they will have an advantage finding work here," he explained sheepishly.

"If they had the money to purchase this type of transport, why did they not come here on one of the regular immigration ships?"

"It's not all that expensive, if you know the right people." The trafficker winked. "Besides, a ticket on those luxury liners is very expensive. I have good fares." He wasn't even trying to hide his less than honourable profession.

"Thank you. You may return to your passengers now," said Ivor, looking to the ground to find an activated e-reader. It was open on the seventh chapter of *Mars is for Men – Surviving on the Red Planet*, and elaborated on how one could extract water from several different types of icy rocks with jury-rigged equipment. The book gave Ivor pause, but did not surprise him.

The ever-nagging detective's instinct in the back of his mind did find something to be off. This room was not large enough. Of course, fuel tanks could be big, but not that big. For this apparent upper class of poor refugees, this space was simply too crammed. And then her saw it: A gap between two panels, unnoticeably thin save for the small spot where they didn't align right. A secret door, to a secret compartment.

He pressed down on it, half expecting it to be a proper cargo hold where he would find more muscle-building nutrient packs and personal effects. What he found instead made him freeze on the spot. This place was an arsenal. Land mines, hand grenades, and shaped charges could be found alongside SMGs, sniper and assault rifles, shotguns, pistols, and combat knives. There was also a sizeable collection of body armour, survival packs, combat scanners, thermal and night-vision goggles, portable pressure tents, and scouting drones. How could anyone be this brazen? This was both the largest and most poorly concealed attempt to smuggle firearms onto Mars of all time. Before Ivor could act, the cabin came to life, and a woman's voice began to speak.

"Hello there. You're probably wondering why we would

do something so stupid. After all, smuggling so many weapons, and soldiers who know how to wield them, past one of the legendary Cargo Samurai is supposed to be impossible. Well, it isn't for us."

Ivor pulled his com from his chest pocket.

"Right now, a thermonuclear warhead is headed for the Deimos Listening Post. It will impact in about thirty seconds, and kill all personnel stationed there. Yes, we do have a battleship stationed in Martian orbit, and we will not hesitate to use it. Today, you will have the chance to save hundreds of thousands of lives, because a second warhead is headed right for Phobos Terminal."

Ivor grunted. Phobos was the primary arrival and departure point for anyone travelling to Mars. Some called it the Ellis Island of the red planet. It was full of people.

"If your clear this vessel and the people in it, the nuke will be called off, and explode somewhere in deep space. They will then take over the sad excuse you have for a planetary government, and ensure a peaceful transition of power to the rightful authorities. Earth authorities."

"Kasei does not belong to you," said Ivor, his voice wavering with rage.

"It does now. If you fail to comply with our demands, we will start an invasion, targeting key infrastructure first. We will be ruthless in taking what is ours. The deaths on Phobos and Deimos will be nothing compared to what will be coming. All because you were too proud."

The voice let the words rest for half a moment.

"You have twenty seconds to comply."

The choice was obvious. There could be only one way – the hard way. Though many tears would be cried for the dead, his loyalty was to Kasei and its people, and its people wanted to be free. Taser in hand, Ivor marched outside and incapacitated the trafficker, who was chatting to one of his subordinates.

"Arrest them! Arrest them all!" he commanded. That very moment, the a-bomb hit Deimos Listening Post. Three-hundred-and-seventy-seven military personnel were vaporized in an instant."The moons need to be evacuated now! Nuclear weapons are headed their way! Earth is attacking!" In his subordinates, he was looking at perplexed faces. In the Earthling ground troops, he was looking at people who were switching to Plan B.

Despite being trained warriors, every single one of Ivor Veltsmann's unit died that day, including the Cargo Samurai himself. It was seven of them against thirty of the much stronger Earthlings. Thus began the first Great War for Mars.

Boreas Returned

By Gwydion JMF Weber

Erasmus hated going to Paris. Even at the height of summer, it was just fucking cold. The desolation was palpable. Outside the city centre, seeing anyone on the ice-covered streets was so rare that it was cause for concern when it did happen. Buildings, some once considered marvels of architectural beauty, were inhabited only by the Frost.

A train rolled on the Seine, its spiked wheels crackling the river's frozen surface. Ironically, it was easier to transport goods up to the world's northernmost city in winter, when the Seine froze all the way to the riverbed.

Much of what the train was transporting would be loaded straight onto one of the airships docked at the Eiffel Tower, for delivery to settlements as far north as Waterloo. Black balloons inhabited the skies.

A group of tourists huddled along the pier, taking pictures with their cell phone cameras. They could be distinguished from the locals by their lack of frigid torpor. Even beleaguered by ice, and after losing 70% of its population, Paris remained the tourist capital of the world. It had all been a matter or rebranding.

His phone rang. *He's in,* a text message from Giselle said, accompanied by an address.

Erasmus took a deep breath of chilly air, crossed himself, and walked down the stairwell into the *Musée d'Orsay* Métro station. He nodded to a group of gendarmes guarding the entrance. One of them nodded back. Erasmus knew how to move like law enforcement.

The *Métropolitain* hadn't seen trains in a long time. It was part of the Parisian underworld, alongside the legendary catacombs, extensive basements, and more recent excavations. When the Frost had arrived, they became the blood vessels of the city. The Métro tunnels were roads that could never freeze over.

The tracks had been covered, and trains been placed at economic and strategic locations, prime real estate for businesses and the police alike. Métro stations were important communal mall areas, their art-nouveau kept pristine by the city government as one of the last remaining landmarks of old Paris.

Down south, where Erasmus lived, many were under the impression that Paris was not hounded by the same overcrowding problems they suffered from. The assumption was that people simply lived in the many apartments the city had to offer.

In truth, only the wealthy could afford to live above the surface. Though a massive effort to insulate as many topside residential buildings as possible was ongoing, Paris often had more pressing issues to deal with.

Erasmus pushed past a bulk of people crowded around a kiosk selling baguettes, and made his way through the stairways and corridors toward *Solférino* station. An Imam of the *Manabudh* sect offered him a digital copy of his holy text at the first corner, and a young street musician was singing French folk songs underlaid with electronic beats on the next.

Crowds of commuters, all dressed appropriately for potential visits to the outside, pushed past each other, avoiding eye contact. Erasmus joined the stream of people disappearing into the tunnel under the white tiles of *Solférino*, and there was a little more breathing room.

The naked concrete walls were illuminated by powerful LEDs. Erasmus heard mumbled conversations, a crying child, and the laughter of a woman. It was hardly warm down in the tunnels, but at least it was a good bit above freezing.

Erasmus needed about twenty minutes to reach *Pasteur* station and enter the maze of tunnels that connected the district's basements. The crowd was different here. Businesspeople and tourists were replaced with scientists and scholars, sometimes even wearing lab coats as they moved from one research facility to another.

The laboratory Erasmus was interested in was located in a particularly hard to reach place, behind a series of separator doors and through a number of poorly lit hallways. Erasmus took the wrong turn a number of times. He had instructions, and turning on the navigation app on his phone would have been admitting defeat.

Erasmus knew that the door would be unlocked, but he regretted his decision not to ring the bell when he found himself suddenly confronted with the imposing frame and bared teeth of a big cat scrutinising him with all the consideration a predator would have for its lunch.

“Don't worry, it may look like a Bengal Tiger, but it behaves like a common housecat,” a raspy voice said. Wolfgang was standing behind an extensive counter, mixing chemicals in an Erlenmeyer flask. The last few years had not been kind to him.

“So it's unpredictable and potentially lethal?” Erasmus asked, finding that his legs refused to move.

“A gentle common housecat,” Wolfgang said. “The only danger really is that it could cuddle you to death.”

“This beast is at least two metres long,” Erasmus estimated. “That is still a real danger.”

“There are worse ways to die than being smothered with love by an extinct genus of feline. Well, formerly extinct.” Wolfgang put down the flask and made a low whistle. The tiger turned away from Erasmus and trotted over to its owner, who gave it a snack and sent it to an oversized cat bed. It obeyed without hesitation.

“Seems well-trained. You sure you didn't sneak some dog genes in there?” Erasmus asked, finally able to move again. Aftershocks of the experience were only now being processed as bursts of primal fear.

“You know, that's actually a very good idea. I hadn't considered that before.” Wolfgang scribbled on a notepad hanging on the wall.

“What are you doing, Wolfgang? I was told that you had fallen into a hole, but this is worse than I imagined,” Erasmus said.

“Eight years, and the first thing you do is lambaste me.

Not so much as a hello, not so much as an opportunity for me to inquire how the weather is down in Gibraltar," Wolfgang complained. "I thought we were friends, Erasmus."

"I tried to keep in touch. You never responded."

"Yeah, well, you know I don't like text conversations. The internet is too impersonal for relationships," said Wolfgang.

"Complete silence is even more impersonal." Erasmus knew it was pointless to belabour this. Wolfgang was not one to back away from his peculiarities. "Why are you resurrecting Bengal Tigers?" he asked instead.

"Because I can, of course. I am one of the wealthiest people in Paris. My crop strains are being used all over the world. Even with the meagre royalties I charge, I am in a position to do the research I want to do. Do you know how much biodiversity is locked away in digital gene vaults? Who knows what useful things we might find in there." Wolfgang did not move from behind his counter.

"And how is the Bengal Tiger going to help us survive out in the cold? How is he going to increase crop yields?" Erasmus asked.

Wolfgang shrugged. "Who knows? All great discoveries are made by accident."

Erasmus sighed. The situation was worse than he'd thought. "You're one of the greatest scientists alive. You could change the world, and you do this? The Lord gave you your intellect for a reason."

"Some would say I already have changed the world. I have earned the right to rest on my laurels. If your Lord sees fit for me to change the world again, he will have me stumble upon a great discovery." Wolfgang finally emerged from behind the counter, beckoning for Erasmus to follow him into the kitchen. "Who even told you where I live?"

"Who do you think?"

Wolfgang stood in place for a moment, his eyes darting to the ground, then immediately turning to his cupboards. "Do you want some tea? I'm out of coffee."

"No, thank you. What I want is for you to take a look at something." Erasmus produced a USB stick from his pocket.

“What is it?”

“It's from Namir. There are several roadblocks only you can overcome.”

“She cannot take a hint, can she?” Wolfgang shook his head. “There's a reason I did not respond to her e-mails. I am not interested in her little project.”

“Excuse me? Her *little* project?” Erasmus was baffled by his former friend's arrogance. “If she succeeds, she will change the world to a greater extent than any individual before her, and probably after her for hundreds of generations to come. She will become more important than you.”

“But why? What is the point?” Wolfgang filled up his electric kettle.

“To reverse the damage that the Inman Team did, of course. She will regulate *Stratobacillus boreas*. She will end the eternal winter, give humanity their world back!”

Wolfgang shook his head. “I know what she is doing. It's the why I don't understand.”

“What the *fuck* do you mean?” Who was he talking to? What had become of this man he used to call his best friend?

“What I mean is that nobody alive today remembers the world before the Frost. My grandfather was one of the last, and he was barely more than a child when *Stratobacillus boreas* was released. Even he lived to be over a hundred years old.” Wolfgang made a sweeping gesture toward his lab. “The world is fine. Yes, billions died, there was a crisis of unprecedented magnitude, but reversing the Frost will not bring back the dead. The Inman Team failed because they were pressed for time. The Siberian methane was being released. Another two years of research and the world would have been turned into Venus.”

“The Lord has given us the opportunity to fix their mistake!” Erasmus screamed. He was furious. When had Wolfgang turned so callous?

“But why would we? The world is fine. Science has continued to advance. We have adapted to living in the cold. We can do things today that people back then could not even imagine. Even assuming that Namir can properly regulate *Stratobacillus boreas* without making some mistake of her own and dooming us to live in the hellscape that the Inman Team prevented, why would we want to do that?"

"To reclaim the world we lost! We had dreams of Mars, Jupiter, the stars, even! Now all that remains are a bunch of skeletons that starved to death because we could no longer feed their expedition." Erasmus wanted to walk over there and choke him.

Wolfgang poured boiling water into a tall mug. "Who cares abut Mars? The people there are dead also. You know who isn't dead? All the people that would die from yet another massive shift in the parameters our species has to cope with. Think of the Saharan farmers. Do you think they want their land turning back into a scorched desert?"

"They would get new, fertile land. Do you know how bad the situation is down south? How crowded our cities are? The poor sleep standing up because their apartments cannot fit beds. There are so many of us that we literally breathe away each other's air."

"That sounds like the problem that Namir should be tackling," Wolfgang noted.

"She *is*! When the Frost leaves, all these problems will go away!" Erasmus could hear his heart pumping with unbridled rage.

"And what problems will replace them? Have you ever opened a history book? Frontiers are not good places to live. People who claim descendance from one group or another, organisations of ideology or necessity, all competing for the best lands, laying claim to memories none of them ever experienced. And who knows what ancient diseases will be thawed , what colonies of degenerates will be found having survived under the ice for generations?" Wolfgang shook his head. "No, the world is fine as it is. Humanity does not need another catastrophe."

"You're going to doom us all because you are afraid of what the future might bring?" Erasmus was struggling to contain his anger. It would not have been the first time he beat someone bloody for being stupid and morally bankrupt.

"I'm not afraid of anything. I'll be fine either way. I merely think it is a bad idea. You may think you want this, but you don't."

Wolfgang sounded utterly sure of himself.

"That's not your choice to make."

"Considering I am the only one who can help Namir with her problems, I think it very much is." Wolfgang smiled sardonically.

"For the record, I truly wish I hadn't come to this. I certainly didn't expect it to." With trained movements, Eramus grabbed into his jacket, and pulled a Walther PPK from his shoulder holster. "You will come down south with me. You will work on this project, or so help me the Lord I will end your life as you are willing to end ours."

Wolfgang's smile did not waver. "There's the man I travelled to Dublin with. Erasmus the mercenary."

"There's nothing funny about this. You know I can and will shoot to injure if you don't cooperate." Erasmus kept his eyes fixed on Wolfgang's.

"It's not so much funny as it is ironic."

Erasmus did not have the time to ask why. A massive weight threw itself onto his back. As an expert marksman, he did not pull the trigger. It occurred to him that maybe he should have.

He was lying face-down on the ground, two stilts bearing what seemed like tons pressing down on his shoulders. The Bengal tiger growled, its breath blowing hot on Erasmus' head. The agony he felt when the beast snapped it's jaw around his neck was unlike anything he'd experienced.

The razor-sharp teeth cut through his flesh like hot icicles, scraping over bone and cartilage for a moment. Then he felt something rip and snap, and he knew, rationally, that his spinal cord had been severed.

As his brain realised that it was no longer receiving signals, the next pull of the tiger's jaw took his head off his torso. For the briefest of moments, Erasmus experienced being a severed head.

It was strange.

Tintinnabulum

By Gwydion JMF Weber

Rusty was panting. He could feel the heat evaporating off his tongue, but it was not enough to generate anything remotely approaching comfort. For the past few months he'd kept to the shade, drunk lots of fluids loaded with chemical coolants, and worn ice packs on his body. None of it helped against the merciless sun of the Australian outback, even considering that Rusty's genetic archetype was the Rhodesian Ridgeback, a dog well adapted to torrid climates.

It was difficult to imagine how human sweat glands could cope with this heat, or how anyone could be so comfortable here that they would build a city around Uluru. But here it was, a small metropolis in the middle of the desert, rife with healers, mystics, and priests, claiming the rock as the focal point of their Aboriginal faith, their Christianity, or their ecocentrism.

Rusty was standing on a crossroads between fields of Outback Potatoes and solar panels, waiting. To the south-east he could see the crest of Uluru above the highrises of the city, and to the north-west the suburb of Yulara baked in the afternoon sun. A ceremony somewhere in the distance brought the smell of marijuana and the sound of didgeridoos. The occasional farming drone passed overhead, whirring quietly.

He knew that they were watching him, and he knew that they were making him wait to demonstrate their power, and to weaken his resolve. But when one wanted to get ahead in life, one had to suffer, and Rusty had suffered the climate of this place since last winter, when it had already been unbearable. The people he'd be dealing with were notoriously difficult to find. Remaining hidden was the most important part of their strategy.

The sound of tires on dirt. Rusty turned around. Two kilometres down the road, an SUV was approaching him. It was white, a bit dirty, and very much inconspicuous. It's electric motor was louder than it should have been, an older model. It stopped a hundred metres short of him, and two men climbed out, leaving the driver inside. Instead of approaching, they waved Rusty over to them.

One was clearly little more than a bodyguard, and judging by his smell, he had some reptile and rhino genes. He was gigantic and muscular, his eyes scanning the perimeter dispassionately. The other man was pure human, unusually light-skinned for the inhabitants of Uluru City, with wispy, dark blond hair, and cobalt eyes.

The human threw him a bottle, and Rusty caught it out of the air.

"Oh come on, I was hoping you'd catch it with your mouth!" The human complained.

"I have human hands, why not use them?" Rusty asked.

"Go on then, drink of the salubrious substance, dog." The human pointed at the bottle.

He opened the lid, smelled it. Water, mostly, and cold, too, but also the tiniest bit of Veritas. It was unfortunate, but he had prepared for this situation. All he could hope for was that he wouldn't overheat as the counterserum protected him from becoming a truth-speaking idiot. Rusty downed the bottle in a few drags, happy about the cold relief. He then threw it back, watching it land at the human's feet. "You're not Anna Flagrey," he noted.

"You thought you were gonna speak the big boss herself?" The human laughed. "Myopic, even for a dog. I'm her appraiser. I know what she wants, and I make all the deals."

"That wasn't what we agreed upon," Rusty complained.

"Show me the goods before I have some sense beaten into you, dog." The Appraiser did not sound like someone who played games.

Reluctantly, Rusty closed the distance between them, and opened his briefcase. Inside, packed in protective gel cushions, was a bronze figurine of a man carrying pails of water. His phallus was enormous, measuring a third of his body length, and there were eyelets on his joints through which bells could be attached. Oxidisation had turned the metal green, and covered it with encrustations protruding from the man's body like pest boils. “Roman Tintinnabulum, third century CE, stolen from the Naples Archaeological Museum ten months ago.”

Rusty could feel the Veritas doing its work on his brain. He was momentarily dizzy, and his tongue became distant, like a foreign entity connected to his body. His mouth was immediately drier as the counterserum lowered the production of saliva in order to achieve its goal.

The Appraiser carefully lifted the figurine out of the briefcase, inspecting it from all sides with keen interest. His retina flashed like a strobe light as he scanned, and presumably sent pictures of it to his master. “How the fuck does a dog become a master thief? I mean, you can't even see colours properly.”

“I have a human pair of eyes and visual cortex,” said Rusty. “I can see all the same colours you can.”

“If that's what they told you...” The Appraiser placed the Tintinnabulum back in the briefcase. “Your story checks out, even though I had not expected it to if I'm honest. But I have to ask: Why the fuck did you come all the way from Europe to sell this item to my boss in particular?”

“Believe it or not, there are not that many buyers in the market of ancient Roman wind chimes. There's a man in Iceland, but he would have reported me to the authorities, and a collector in India, but she's known to be a cheapskate and just generally interested in everything Roman, so the price would not have been as good as whatever I could get out of someone specifically interested in Tintinnabulae.”

“If they're so difficult to get rid off, why steal them in the first place?” The Appraiser asked.

“Well I didn't go to Naples to steal this thing specifically. If you checked my background, you'll know that a whole host of items was stolen that night,” Rusty explained.

The Appraiser nodded. “Okay, then. I'll take it.”

“No, no, no.” Rusty quickly laid his hand upon the

briefcase. “I was told I'd be meeting with Anna Flagrey, not some emissary. How do I even know you're really working for her?”

“You'll just have to trust me, mate.” The Appraiser shook his head. “She's not stayed anonymous for so long because she's cavalier with who she deals with, so I rather think you sell to me, or you're stuck with the Indian cunt. Your choice.”

Rusty took a deep breath, as if weighing his options. Even closing his mouth for a moment felt as though he was closing the door of the oven he was inside of. “Alright then, but I expect ten precent more than the agreed upon price.”

The Appraiser frowned. “Why the fuck would I do that, dog?”

“Because,” Rusty almost stumbled, feeling light-headed for a moment. The heat could overwhelm him at any second. “Because I am incurring a risk right here. There is no guarantee that you are actually working for Anna Flagrey, and I guaranteed that I would be selling the item to her, not a third party.”

“You fucking cunt.” The Appraiser shook his head. “How about, instead, I just have my friend here beat you to death and take the figurine off your dead body?”

The bodyguard moved forward, his dead eyes locking onto Rusty's, tensing for a punch that could probably decapitate him. Before the man could attack, The Appraiser raised his hand. His stare had gone glassy-eyed, distant, and he was nodding, listening to a voice only he could hear.

After a moment, the fog disappeared, and the Appraiser looked at Rusty with frustration. “Alright mate, you're getting your extra money. The boss sends her regards.”

Rusty almost didn't make it to his car. When he finally climbed in, the cool interior felt like a refrigerator, in the best possible way. He closed the door, and let his head droop onto his chest. The dry heat of the Outback came out of him like air from a pressure canister.

“Did they bite?” a voice asked over the speaker system.

“Yeah. They bought the figurine. Let's just hope you concealed your device properly,” Rusty responded. The words came out of him almost involuntarily.

"Trust me, they won't detect anything. Now come, we are expecting you at HQ." The line was cut. No "thank you"s, not "goodbye"s. Even when he was about to take down the biggest money laundering operation the world had ever seen, Rusty was only a dog to the humans.

Men with Yellow Eyes

By Gwydion JMF Weber

What was a man to do?

Philanthropy and power alone could not heal the sick, and all the physicians in the entire kingdom had been forced into service with the containment crews by royal decree. They were helping identify symptoms, teaching city watchmen how to check for telltale signs, and maintaining those horrifying suits. “The Yelloweyes” was what the commoners called the containment crews now, and soon that would be the name given to all the Queen's constables, as the Plague was the only crisis worth dealing with right now. Crime was running rampant, lewd public behaviour was no longer properly being dealt with. Waking up last morning, Lord Catton had seen a drunkard urinate on the street corner. Seeing such things might have been commonplace in the lower reaches of the city, but not from the window of his study. Merchants just a few blocks down from his home had petitioned him to do something about the thugs that had begun extorting protection money from them. These weren't coopers, tanners, and farmers, but painters, jewellers and spice merchants. His city was falling apart. Something had to be done.

Lord Catton stepped off the railwagon, surrounded by his escort of city watchmen. He could almost see the frowns behind the yellow glow of their visors, hear their minds asking why a man of his standing would visit a district as wretched and plague-ridden as this one, especially at this hour. But when Lord Catton asked for something, he was not second-guessed. Some aristocrats he knew got up to all kinds of senseless folly, and everybody went out of their way to accommodate them. It was only right he should get the same treatment.

The smell of sewage assaulted his nostrils. He hadn't experienced odours like this since the war. A wrinkling of the nose was the only reaction it would get. The watchmen seemed impressed at how unfazed he was, and said nothing as he descended the cobbled steps down to the checkpoint. Over a dozen Yelloweyes were standing watch around a set of waist-high metal barricades. Powerful spotlights illuminated the street, and anyone who looked even remotely sick and was trying to approach was warned once, and then shot with extreme prejudice. The plan was to keep the sick away from the railwagon stations, so that the Plague might be prevented from spreading throughout the city. A futile effort, really.

"Lord Catton, please. We have been instructed to allow you no passage," said a young watchman, stopping the noble's confident advance toward the checkpoint. It was clear he was uncomfortable denying Catton anything.

"And who, might I inquire, has given you such insolent instructions?" Catton asked, taking care to seem as intimidating as possible.

"The chief inspector, my Lord. He has telegraphed all checkpoints, banning you from any and all areas that might contain infected." The old dog was quick, Catton had to give him that. The original plan had been for him not to learn of his nightly excursion until it was too late. "He says that, as soon as the cure has been finished, he will give you a tour of whichever districts you like in person."

"Pah! A cure, ridiculous! Nobody is working on a cure, young man. The Queen has demanded an inoculation, a vaccine, because it will be easier to achieve. Who do you think will receive that vaccine, huh?" Catton asked, looking intently at the watchman's visor. "Us aristocrats, of course, is the answer. And what will happen to the commoners?"

The watchman needed a moment to respond.

"They will most likely perish, my Lord," he finally answered, unsure if he was stepping out of line.

"That is exactly correct. The commoners will suffer." Catton straightened himself to look even more exalted. "You will suffer. Your families will suffer. Though we may like to let you believe it is the other way around, this city could not function without its commoners. That is why I must do what I will do. Forgive me, oh my wise Queen, for I believe you have erred."

With the confidence of a powerful nobleman, Lord Catton walked through a gap in the barricades – only for the young watchman to step in his way.

"My Lord, please, I most humbly implore you. The chief inspector speaks with the authority of the Queen Majesty herself," he insisted.

Catton looked around. The other Yelloweyes were ready to jump at the occasion, though they were all very reluctant to disobey his orders directly. The chief inspector had a hand for placing loyal people in the right positions, that much was evident. He'd probably already anticipated Catton's plan. It was time to act. With a motion he'd used a thousand times over a decade prior, he unsheathed his sabre, and stepped backwards across the barricade. His weapon pointed at the Yelloweyes, he moved slowly. They might have been willing to step in his way, but attacking an aristocrat was a whole different matter, even if it was on royal orders. These were only commoners in bulky suits, after all.

The commotion had attracted quite a bit of attention, especially as there was a man involved who wore clothing that was worth more than any of the poor saps in this district would ever earn in their lifetime. Catton spotted a gaunt man peering around a nearby corner. Even in the twilight he could see the black blemishes on his skin. He was infected, no question.

"You, come here! I demand it!" he shouted. When the man only sank further into his corner, he added, "I am Lord Catton, and together we will cure this city! Come here, and I will shower you with gold." That did the trick. Even on the brink of death, the greed of poor commoners always exceeded their sense of caution. "Come quickly!"

The gaunt man picked up his pace, and Lord Catton used the sabre to inflict a nice, deep, bleeding cut onto his own forearm. The Yelloweyes shouted when they saw it, getting in motion to catch the vagrant before he could reach Lord Catton.

They would not shoot. The risk of hitting the man they were supposed to protect from himself was too high.

When the gaunt man arrived, he looked surprised when Catton cut his arm, too, and pressed the two together by grabbing a hold of his elbow. He could almost feel the Plague seeping into his veins through the commoner's contaminated blood. This was going to be a momentous occasion for centuries to come.

The Yelloweyes arrived, and, to his surprise, their leader tackled Lord Catton to the ground. Three others started beating the gaunt man to death. It was all the same to Catton. His goal had been accomplished.

"It's too late!" he exclaimed. "It's too late. Now, I have the plague. An aristocrat, one of the most powerful men in the Kingdom. They'll have to create a cure for everyone. There's no other choice now." Lying on the ground, the young watchman with the glowing, yellow visor still laying on top of him, Lord Catton laughed. There was nothing they could do now. They had to heal everyone.

Dias' Deal

By Gwydion JMF Weber

It was sickness and disease that Umeko wanted to fight, not the demons of someone else's past. But now, with Dias withholding the latest medicine shipment, she would have to deal with a situation she wasn't used to being in, and had never planned on entering.

The warm Kagoshima rain pattered onto her umbrella hat, and all around her commuters were headed for the ferry dock in one direction, and for the food concourse in the other. Her eyes lingered on a passing Caucasian man for a few moments, which her implant misinterpreted for interest. It told her he had features of Greek ancestry, his movement and momentum suggested a small frame and lean, muscular body, and that the clothes he was wearing indicated he had the income of a lower middle-class person.

With the slightest bit of anger, Umeko averted her eyes. She hated this implant, how it always told her everything she didn't want to know about everything her eyes lingered on. But she needed it, and she needed it right now more than ever. There was a red light blinking in the corner of her vision. The implant had detected someone, a man, Filipino, wiry and strong. He had a short ponytail and tattoos on his arms, accentuated by his khaki sleeveless shirt. Though drenched, he didn't seem to mind the rain much.

“Lady Sukuna?” he asked, inspecting her in a less than cavalier manner.

Umeko nodded, seeing that he was indeed unarmed, as agreed upon.

"You're with Dias?"

"Might be with you soon." His smile revealed a set of sharp, white teeth. The smile of a predator.

"Cut the crap. Where is my shipment?" Umeko knew that being assertive was the most important part of negotiating with criminals.

"In the city, ready to be picked up. If you meet his demands, that is. Otherwise you can kiss your profits good bye." He puckered his lips.

"I'm not doing this for profit," Umeko responded, irritated.

"You mean you don't have illegal drugs smuggled into your country at a hefty markup to make money? What kind of operation are you running here?"

"One that doesn't concern you." She'd already said too much. If Dias and his people found out what she did, it would not take them long to figure out who she really was. "What do you want?"

"Well, the guy Dias is buying from over in the fatherland has increased prices. He went out of his pocket to get the load here in time, because he knows how you are about schedules, but he'll need that paid for."

"How much?" Umeko knew he was lying. She knew the people he was buying the medicine from down in the Philippines. Hell, she co-owned the factory they were being produced in.

The contact shook his head.

"This time it's not about money. Dias is willing to take over the share this time around if you do him a favour. You know a man called Jett Stone? Tall, blond hair, black eyes? From New Zealand?" He posed the question as though he didn't already know the answer to it.

So it was about him. She damned herself for ever not listening to Jett. She should have gone with Yakuza smugglers instead. They were cheaper and had no beef with him, but then again there were their corporate ties...

"I need him. His skills are an integral part of my operation," she explained.

"He's just a doctor. Plenty of doctors in this city. Good ones, too, many looking to make some money. You'd do well to look into hiring someone new for his position."

"I'll pay double," Umeko decided. She was not going to lose her head pharmacist. "And not just double the usual price, but double the new price, which I will agree to pay henceforth."

The smuggler grinned.

"See, if you're running an operation not for profit but, apparently, for charity, you shouldn't be able to throw around money like you do. It begs the question: where do you get your funding from?"

There was another alarm on her iris screen. It was a message from Jett. *The stars have fallen into the green bosom of Mount Fuji.* Umeko tensed up. Images flashed through her mind, of her clinic being raided by police, of the countless poor who would die of terrible diseases because they had no access to the medicine they needed.

"One would theorize that you are the daughter of someone wealthy, and by that I mean very wealthy. And one might also be able to reach out to that person and tell them what you have been doing, in exchange for a lot of money, and the promise to lure you away from where the police is currently arresting all of your accomplices." His predatory grin widened.

Umeko turned around. She needed to get away, back to her clinic, but there, behind her, was a mountain of a man in a black uniform. Coming from the ramen shop to her right were two more, clad in the same uniform. Another three approached from behind her contact, who was backing away. *Tenshin Security.* Her father's men.

"Don't worry. No jail for you, pretty girl. You're too rich for that," the smuggler said as he turned around and passed between the men that had surrounded her.

"You're making a mistake! Dias is making a mistake! I'm good business!" she screamed, her heart pounding. "The only reason these drug imports are illegal is so Japanese Pharma has a monopoly on them! They're not harmful to anyone! I'm helping people!"

"You've cost your father a lot of money, Little Firefly," said a voice she knew all too well. Takeshi, or Old Samurai, as the other servants called him, was suddenly right there. "This could have ended very badly for you." She looked at the man who had watched over her childhood with nothing but spite in her eyes.

"You're a dog, a corporate slave." She spat at his face, hitting only his chest. "I hate you!"

Takeshi smiled and produced a small syringe from his pocket.

"Don't worry, Little Firefly," he said as he uncapped it. "It's straight back home for you."

Danesville

By Gwydion JMF Weber

Leclerc jumped from his dreamless sleep, drawing in air like a drowning man. The twin suns burned hard on his chest. It felt as though he'd spent the night dead, not just asleep. Squinting, he sat up and scanned his surroundings.

All around him were red rocks and coarse sand, and the occasional bushel of dark shrubbery rustled by the torrid wind. The air smelled of oxidized iron and burnt copper. There were no signs of civilisation. Leclerc was stranded in the desert.

To the south was a large rock formation, almost a misshapen mesa, that looked like a trumpeting megaphant. One of its tusks had been broken off since the last time Leclerc had been there, but he recognised it as the aptly named Megaphant Rock. His momentary panic abated. This was familiar territory.

Looking down at himself he realised that all he was wearing were canvas trousers and a pair of trekking sandals. The clothes were not his own, and surprisingly clean, almost fresh, not at all the outfit of a man who had spent the night out among the sands.

Leclerc felt excellent. Considering all he remembered from the night before was a blur of liquor in the Danesville saloon, this was lucky yet disconcerting. Instead of a headache he had a clear mind, instead of thirsty he was well-hydrated, and instead of hungry he was not even feeling the slightest bit peckish. When Leclerc rose to his feet, he realised that no searing pain had ripped through his knee. He'd had that problem for years. What in the rains had happened last night?

There was no point wasting time thinking about it now.

His tanned skin would save him from an immediate sunburn, but even so he'd have to move to the shade fast. More than once had he seen men cooked alive when the twin suns reached their zenith, and he was not interested in joining their ranks.

As he trekked toward Megaphant Rock, he reminisced. Oh what memories had been made in that place. A dozen ambushed caravans, mornings drinking cold milk and eating fresh fruit, days sampling the goods they would be selling to the pleasure house, and evenings of exotic cheeses and expensive wines. The Red Raptors Gang had been great while it lasted. Leclerc had spent his nights scouting on a rocket horse, driving traders into the ambush at Megaphant Rock. He'd made a name for himself back then. How he would love to have a rocket horse now.

There were shapes moving on the face of Megaphant Rock. People standing up high, keeping an eye on the perimeter. Excellent news, really. If they had been waiting to ambush a caravan, they would not have been as obvious, and if they wanted to keep him away, they would have shot him already. The most likely scenario was that they were traders themselves, looking out to protect the camp they had made for the day.

Megaphant Rock was distinctive and easy to find, had an inner courtyard that was well protected from dust storms, and a watering hole in the shallow caves. Ever since Leclerc and the Red Raptors Gang had been driven out, it had also been become very safe.

Driven out. Who had been driven out? Yesterday had not just been an ordinary night of drinking, Leclerc remembered. It had been a full gathering of the Silver Tree Council, that's why he had been in Danesville, not Dust's Edge where he ran the underground warehouses. There had been a dispute between two factions of the Council, one lead by Frank Baumann, and the other by Leclerc. Leclerc's side had won. Then had come the celebration, and then had come the pang of rifles and the smell of plasma. The others, Baumann, had sent mercenaries after them. But how had Leclerc ended up out here, a week's walk away from Danesville?

“Halt!” a voice commanded. He was a hundred paces away from Megaphant Rock now, and it seemed the traders were finally ready to acknowledge his existence. A broad-shouldered, middle-aged man emerged from the entrance to the formation's sheltered interior and marched toward him, one hand raised and the other on the butt of his rifle. Leclerc stopped, not wanting to alarm the man.

As the the guard came closer, it became clear how exceptional he was. He was clad in bronze metalloplast armour, not just partially, but from the tactical display hovering in front of his left eye to his heavy combat boots. On his hip was a collapsible antimatter rifle, probably capable of switching from sniper to shotgun mode and anything in between in a matter of seconds. There was a pistol of similar make strapped to his leg, and a grenade belt slung across his chest. It took Leclerc a moment to realise that that a chameleocloak cape was billowing in the wind behind him, changing colours at a speed that Leclerc had not even thought possible.

Whoever these people were, they were not scared of bandits. Gear like this only came from off-world, and if someone was wearing it head to toe, chances were high that they themselves were from off-world, too. Leclerc was beginning to think that coming here may not have been such a good idea.

"What is your name, stranger?" the off-worlder asked, his accent too refined for his brutish appearance.

"Leclerc. Jake Leclerc. I'm in a, … a bit of a problematic situation, as you can see," Leclerc responded.

The off-worlder nodded. "I am aware. How did you get into this problematic situation?"

"In all honesty I don't remember. I was out drinking last night, and had a couple too many."

"So it would seem." The off-worlder subvocalised into a laryngial microphone, then waited for a response. After a moment, he nodded, then gestured for Leclerc to follow him. "Today is your lucky day, Mister Leclerc. Madame Ding has decided to assist you."

Entering the shade was a relief for his skin, which no longer felt like it was being cooked. The smooth, wavy grain of the canyon walls made him feel like he had arrived home, and the slight echo of his footsteps reminded him of simpler times.

The guard who had greeted him was not the only off-world mercenary equipped with gear that Leclerc would have, and had, killed for. He spotted at least a dozen more men, and a few women, all sporting armour identical to the guard's. They were climbing the rock face toward elevated positions, reclining in the shade, and setting up equipment. They threw him curious glances, some even frowned. It otherwise seemed that, whatever he was doing here, it was none of their business. These people were working for someone, and that person often gave unusual orders, this much was clear.

In the courtyard of Megaphant Rock, a sandcrawler larger than most buildings Leclerc had been inside was parked next to a squat, grey personnel tank that presumably housed Madame Ding's security entourage. Her own rolling palace was stylish in a way only off-world things could afford to be, white and streamlined, with large, laminated windows.

Madame Ding carried herself with the grace of an empress. She beautiful was in the way only a woman of wealth and power could be, with smooth, cinnamon skin, and amber eyes speckled with bright yellow flecks. She wore the traditional layered garb of the dustwalker peoples that sometimes found their way up north from their usual routes, except hers was much cleaner, colourful, and made of fabrics so expensive that no dustwalker would ever have been able to afford them.

“Thank you, Commander Bryde,” she said to the man who had brought Leclerc in. She spoke with the same refined accent he did, and nothing like the dustwalkers. It was as though what she was wearing was a costume.

“I'll be there if you need me, Madame,” Commander Bryde responded, and marched off.

“Mister Leclerc, I must say you are an unexpected visitor. Surviving the desert in nothing but trousers is an impressive skill,” the woman said.

“It's my speciality. I've worked in the desert all my life, I'm a survivalist. If you take me along, I can work for you. I know all the secrets, all the safe places, and all the dangers of this area.” He also knew that, though not easy, looting a caravan like this would make him rich beyond imagining. "I would appreciate some clothes, though, if you can spare them. I promise I will earn them out."

"Well I'm glad to see you don't believe I took you in out of the kindness of my heart. You will work for me, and you will work hard." Madame Ding looked him up and down. "Though I'm afraid I can't get you any clothes right now. Those would only hinder you in your work."

Leclerc gave her a roguish grin, understanding. This was getting better by the minute. His almost preternatural charm had been one of the driving forces behind his career, and Madame Ding was making it easy for him. In a few days she would be so addicted to his attention that he would be able to make her do anything he wanted.

"I'm happy to be of service, Madame Ding."

"Oh please, do call me Tatiana. And now come, I'm feeling very womanly."

Heaven was a real place, and Leclerc had entered it. Tatiana's sandcrawler had three decks, though with how open and interconnected they were it was difficult to tell where one ended and the other began. It was an exercise in understated luxury. Plaswood floors moulded themselves to the shape of his feet as he moved over them, art was on display that he didn't understand beyond the fact that it was expensive, and an android butler waited to serve up every amenity Leclerc could dream of.

The vehicle had full atmospheric and temperature control of its interior, and any type of environment could be replicated down to the sound and vista through the windows. Leclerc had never been in a landscape of ice before, though he knew that they existed very far to the north for short periods of the year. After their first session, Tatiana had shown him what it looked like, along with some places so alien he could scarcely take them all in.

Gardens of tubular plants in bright shades of red springing from violet soil overgrown with pulsating lattices. Birds the size of megaphants gliding across the starry night sky, illuminated by strange lights dancing eerily above. A forest of fleshy trees connected by thick strands of red liquid.

After only a few minutes, Tatiana had decided to make use of him again, though to Leclerc it did not feel like work. The woman knew things and did things that no other woman had ever done to him before, and Leclerc had sampled a lot of women. Best of all, he never got tired. The butler simply gave him a sweet drink of water, and he was ready to go at it again.

"You're starfolk, aren't you?" Leclerc asked after having left the bed for the third time today.

"Isn't all folk starfolk, really?" Tatiana responded.

Leclerc did not understand what she meant by that, but did not want to look stupid. "What are you doing here?"

"I'm waiting for a friend of mine. He got caught up, but he should be here tonight."

"I mean what are you doing on this world?" Leclerc specified.

"Leisure." Tatiana reclined in an armchair that perfectly fit her contour. "I am a big game hunter of sorts."

"There's not a lot of big game to be had around these parts, I'll tell you that much," said Leclerc. "There's duneskitters south of here, in The Dust, and the Bristle Savannah up north has a lot of megaphants passing through it at this time of the year."

"Trust me, Jake, I am exactly where I want to be." Tatiana slapped his butt. "Now do speak to the butler, I want you in a tailored suit when my friend arrives for dinner."

Suits had never been very comfortable. They were delicate, clunky pieces of attire that one wore to events one did not want to attend for reasons one did not entirely understand. What did a fallen brother in arms have to gain if Leclerc kept scratching his neck at his funeral?

This was different. The suit the android butler had manufactured for him was made of some sort of artificial silk, keeping him cool in the heat. The chalk white dress shirt scratched even less than his most worn-out and beloved tops. He might as well have been naked for all the difference it made. The black jacket was not heavy, constraining, or too padded on the shoulders, but just as well-fitted as the shirt. If Leclerc walked into town like this, he'd be gutted in a street corner in a matter of seconds.

Tatiana's friend arrived just after sunset in a sandcrawler very similar to her own, complete with its own security detail. He was tall and lanky, with piercing green eyes and an aquiline nose. His black hair was combed back with pomade, and both his hands were heavy with rings so valuable that each could buy a mansion. Like Leclerc, he was wearing a suit, only his was midnight blue, and his shirt was black as coal.

“Jake Leclerc, meet my friend, Erol Fox.” Tatiana was wearing a slim but not skin tight cream-coloured dress that, through some kind of starfolk technology, rippled as though its surface were liquid with every movement.

Leclerc extended his hand and gave Fox a cocky grin. “Pleasure to meet you.”

Mister Fox shook Leclerc's hand. “The pleasure is all mine,” he said, but the resentment in his eyes told a different story. He threw Tatiana an annoyed glance, and she replied with a grin of her own.

So Fox was here because he was into Tatiana, which she was clearly aware of. To make her lack of interest abundantly clear, she had brought Leclerc into the picture. If this morning someone had told him that, by the end of the night, he would stand higher in the pecking order than a starfolk man, he would have laughed at them. But here he was, the lover of a woman who could have also had a man of nigh infinite means.

Dinner was served on the terrace extending from the sandcrawler's highest deck. Megaphant Rock was radiating heat onto it, and they had a view of the vast desert ahead through a large gap in the stone. A gentle breeze and the chirping of crickets filled the air.

Tatiana sat in the middle, while Fox and Leclerc took seats perpendicular to her, and opposite to each other. As an appetizer, the butler served little green balls of what looked like dough, but tasted sweet and sour at the same time. They came with a smoky caramel sauce that Leclerc enjoyed immensely.

“I see you've already gotten your spoils,” Mister Fox commented, pointing at Leclerc with his fork.

"As I do every time, Erol. And you complain, as you do every time," the woman responded.

"I'm just pointing out that he might be dangerous. Insurance doesn't help when you're dead. I should know, I sell it."

Leclerc gave Fox another sardonic grin. The man had looked right through him, but Tatiana, taken as she was with her strapping outlaw, had not.

"Well, what can I say. I like dangerous men," she said, giving Leclerc a wink. Being starfolk, most of her wealth was forever outside his reach, but that didn't mean he could not devise a way to take everything she had brought down to the planet with her.

"Mister Leclerc, if I may, what is it you do for a living?" Fox asked.

"Oh, a bit of this and a bit of that," Leclerc responded, pretending like his accumulated wealth compared to whatever Fox considered pocket change. "I'm a man of many talents, as one needs to be to survive out here. Tatiana hired me for a few of them." He winked.

"It must be exciting to be a jack-of-all-trades," Tatiana said. "Me, I would be happy to get a little respite from mining stars for their base elements, but that is what I'm best at."

Fox raised an eyebrow. "How much is she paying you, exactly?"

"Shelter and passage, that's all I need." Also everything he could loot off her and her guards once he had found an appropriate trap and gotten his band back together.

"So we are going to Danesville?" Fox asked Tatiana. "I figured as much when you asked me to meet you here. Do we really have to?"

This gave Leclerc pause. How did Fox know he had come from Danesville? How did he know he wanted to get back there when the smoke had cleared? How did starfolk even know the name of an outlaw town in the middle of the desert at all?

"Of course we're going to Danesville. I go to Danesville every time I'm, here, and I always enjoy it immensely," Tatiana responded. This, too, was weird. Leclerc had never heard of any starfolk that visited Danesville, but then she did have a penchant for costumes, so maybe she had come disguised as a dustwalker.

The android butler served the next course, a blue steak with the consistency of beef, but skin like chicken. It tasted like pickled cabbage, the meat juice having an onionlike note. Though he had never tasted anything like it, Leclerc pretended like this was the most normal thing in the world.

"Danesville is played-out, boring, and full of moralists," Fox said. "I realise the excitement it may have once generated, but that was so long ago I can scarcely remember it."

"Danesville is a timeless classic, Erol, you just can't appreciate the subtleties of it." Tatiana turned to Leclerc. "Jake, being a local, you probably know all about Danesville, don't you?"

"Oh yes, I've been there from time to time, comes with the territory, quite literally. Very dangerous place, full of unsavoury folk." It was best that he not give them too much of a reason to suspect his involvement with any form of banditry. As far as Tatiana was concerned, he was just an honest guide who'd had a little too much to drink. Identifying himself as a gangster would destroy the allure that attracted her to him.

"So you wouldn't recommend it?" asked Mister Fox.

"Well, if you are up for seeing the sights, it's definitely something you have to work your way up towards. If you want my advice, I recommend visiting a few other settlements first, to test if you can withstand the danger." It would also give Leclerc time to learn more about Tatiana and her security detail, and make contact with some people who might help him set up an ambush worthy of her defences. Barry Hobbs over in Salt Pit would probably be able to get some high-end weapons on a loan, and Mister Buttercup up in Elmrot could mobilise a small army of men capable of using them.

"I've seen all of them, none are as exciting as Danesville," Tatiana said, squashing Leclerc's plans. "We'll also have to move fast. Things are getting hot over there, from what I hear."

So news of what happened had already travelled to her. Leclerc decided to try and gleam some information from her later. At this point he did not consider it unreasonable to assume that she knew more about the current state of Danesville than he did.

After dinner was over, Mister Fox returned to his own sandcrawler, and the vehicles turned into motion. They were crossing the desert at a rapid pace, and Tatiana had demanded Leclerc take her on the dinner table. A hydraulic system compensated for the rough terrain so perfectly that the terrace was even at all times as Tatiana screamed into the night.

Afterwards, Leclerc had remained outside, watching the desert pass him by. The android butler had been very forthcoming at his request for a glass of moonshine, though this stuff was not nearly as strong as anything he was used to.

Something was definitely off about this whole situation. As long as he was with Tatiana and her security detail, he would not be harmed in Danesville. If the Baumann faction had truly driven out his own last night, then they would surely still be looking for him.

But even if they pointed him out on the street, what was the worst that could happen? He had become the companion to a starfolk woman, and she clearly relished his identity as a rogue. Who was Tatiana to concern herself with the schemes of Frank Baumann?

But then who was she to concern herself with the schemes of Jake Leclerc? He was planning this grand caper for which he would need a lot of support and a lot of manpower, but did not even know the state of his network.

On any other caravan he would have tried to use their communicators to call up some trusted individuals, then covered his tracks. But risking such a thing on a starfolk sandcrawler was much too risky. He was able to fool them in the wilds of the desert, but technology was the one thing he could not hope to ever beat them at.

“I hope you're not getting soft on me, Jake.” Tatiana was standing in the doorway to the terrace, wearing nothing but a white sheet draped over her shoulders. “I'm too excited to fall asleep, and I want you to help me with that.”

Danesville was both the same as always and completely different at the same time. Located by a geyser spring in one of the greener patches of the desert, it seemed many of the brick-and-wood buildings had taken fire in the battle. Many of the town's characteristic blue-painted walls had plasma scorches and bullet holes in them. The Silver Tree in the town centre had been on fire at some point, as evidenced by burnt and fallen branches.

Brannigan's Fort was the only structure that had been completely destroyed, and Leclerc was unsurprised by this. The building had contained all the secrets, garrison, storage, and administration of the Silver Tree Council, and the Baumann faction had wanted access to it. It appeared Leclerc's comrades had been valiant in their defence, so much so that Baumann saw no other option but to raze the place instead of taking it as a prize.

"Do you want to see something?" Tatiana asked. She wore a wide dress and corsage flaunting delicate lacework and vibrant colours, as the wealthier ladies of Danesville enjoyed. Much like her dustwalker attire, it was too clean, too perfect, and to stylised to seem real.

She'd forced Leclerc into a similarly ridiculous outfit, black jeans, and a jacket with silver trims, as well as a wide-brimmed hat, and pointed boots with small stars on metal sticks at the heel. Leclerc had never seen such strange footwear before, but then starfolk did have a weakness for vanity.

"I don't think there's anything about you I haven't seen," Leclerc responded, and gave Tatiana a wink.

She grinned, and raised an eyebrow. "You are a dirty man with dirty thoughts, Jake. But that's not what I mean." Tatiana handed him a pair of black binoculars. "Have a look around."

"I have very good eyes," Leclerc insisted.

"Not this good." Tatiana shook her head.

Leclerc looked through the binoculars, and could not believe what he saw. Behind the green tinge of the lenses, he found that Danesville was surrounded by dozens of luxury sandcrawlers just like Tatiana's. When he took away the binoculars, it was as though they weren't there, but when he put them back on, they were in the exact same spots.

"They're cloaked, so as to not break the immersion," Tatiana explained. "If you get within ten metres of one, you'll be able to see it. We wouldn't want people bumping into these things, after all."

There were rumours of starfolk having technology that could make things invisible, truly invisible, much better than chameleocloak. Leclerc had never believed them. It was crazy talk, spacer yarn spun to make the starfolk out to be more godlike than they actually were. Everything that existed could also be seen, that was a simple fact of life. Or at least it had been, until now.

Leclerc felt his knees getting weak momentarily. It was confusing. He had not felt like this in many years. "What in the rains is going on here?" he asked, looking at Tatiana, who had an amused expression on her face. "Are you in league with Baumann?"

"Baumann?" She gave a snorting laugh. "Ah Baumann, what an unsavoury character he was. No, Baumann is dead. It's all about you this time." For some reason, Tatiana sounded nostalgic.

"But you know Baumann? Why does a starfolk know Baumann?" Leclerc was holding on to the terrace railings. "Did you loan him the money to get those mercenaries? Some of them looked like they were from off-world."

"Oh my sweet Jake, this will be such fun." She moved into the sandcrawler, beckoning for him to follow. "Come, let's go into town. You'll see that it all makes sense there."

Inside Danesville, Leclerc was shocked to find that Tatiana and her fake attire were anything but out of place. Half the people here looked like they were only pretending to be from this world, and that could only be because they were starfolk playing dress-up. Even their bodyguards, often just one or two, but still easily detectable, wore costumes.

How had he never heard of something like this happening before? The Danesville natives, some of whom he recognised by face, but all of which were discernible by their authenticity, mostly treated the parade of strangers strolling through town with the same suspicion he did. Surely this was unprecedented, most likely on the entire planet, because otherwise he would at least have heard rumours of it.

Tatiana had joined up with Mister Fox, who was wearing a

bejewelled grey suit that was making the least effort possible to fit in. His two bodyguards were dressed in uniforms like the one Leclerc's grandfather, who had fought in the Third Water War, had worn to special events. Tatiana herself was accompanied by two of her security detail, both dressed like third-rate bandits. Commander Bryde was nowhere to be seen.

“Oh look, it's Faisal Totak,” Tatiana said, pointing at a dark-skinned man in a sky blue travel coat.

“Please don't draw his attention, I haven't seen him in twenty years and those have not been enough to recover from his drivelling,” Mister Fox said.

“Erol, the quality of his starships is why people buy insurance for when they break down. You should be happy about all the business he brings in,” Tatiana scolded.

“His rustbuckets break down, I get to pay out policies. So no, his business is not appreciated.” Fox spat on the ground.

They entered the town square, what remained of the Silver Tree at its centre. The businesses around were in a much better state of repair than Leclerc had expected, almost as though they had been fixed back up as soon as the fighting was done.

Tatiana lead them over to the *Deep Vault Bank*, which, as always, advertised *unmatched rates, perfect discretion, and planetary services* underneath its cast-iron sign. It was protected by the Silver Tree Council, and was also where Leclerc and many other bandits had stored part of their fortune as a torrid day fund.

“Do go talk to Faisal, Erol. I don't think you will like the bank very much,” Tatiana said to Mister Fox.

“I'd rather shoot myself in the head.” He tapped one of his guards on the shoulder. “I think I'll go to the casino instead, if you don't mind.”

“Suit yourself,” Tatiana said.

“Mister Leclerc, I'll see you again soon enough,” Mister Fox said, extending his hand.

After a moment's hesitation, Leclerc shook it. “I sure do hope so.”

A grin on her face, Tatiana took Leclerc by the wrist and dragged him into the bank. Inside, Old Cato's fat, pale face was behind the counter. His ever-present frown deepened when they came in.

“Leclerc? Where the rain have you been?” He snorted a spoonful of tobacco. “I haven't seen you in town for a long time.”

“What do you mean? I deposited some cash here last week,” Leclerc insisted.

“You most certainly did not.” Old Cato shook his head.

“I told you this would all make sense soon, Jake. Don't worry about it.” Tatiana put a hand calmingly on his chest. “Now, I should very much like to get into vault number six,” she said to Old Cato.

“Yes, you should,” he responded, sounding a little surprised. He unlocked the heavy metal grate in front of the stairway that would lead them underground.

“You two stay here, make sure we don't get any visitors,” Tatiana said to her guards.

“Please, follow me.” Old Cato jangled his keys.

The *Deep Vault Bank* had its name for a reason. It occupied most of the dense but extensive cave system underneath Danesville, sealed off from the parts of it that were underneath Brannigan's Fort, or private households. The dark orange rock smelled of dirt and blood, and was sparsely illuminated in the white light of LED glowspheres covered in dust.

Heavy doors of wood framed in steel and covered with rock tiles were set into the walls of the labyrinthine tunnels at irregular intervals, and Old Cato opened the occasional steel grate with a thumbprint. The vaults were not marked or in chronological order, and only Old Cato knew the location of each individual vault, making it more difficult for potential thieves to target a specific one. Of course that would require them to get into the tunnels in the first place, which, even in the town that played home to one of the great bandit associations, nobody had ever accomplished.

Vault number six was down half a dozen stairways and twoscore twists and turns. Old Cato used a faded keycard to unlock the first stage of the door, then let Tatiana forward to do the rest. She lowered her eye to a hidden retinal scanner, and the door unlocked with a click.

"I didn't know you had access to this kind of security," Leclerc said to Old Cato.

"You don't pay enough to get one of the good vaults," the banker responded. "I will leave you to it now," he said to Tatiana, and turned around. "If you want back out just shout for me."

"Thank you," Tatiana said, and waited for Old Cato to have walked around the corner. "So, Jake, are you ready for some answers?"

Leclerc did not know what to say. "I guess so."

Smiling, Tatiana pushed open the heavy vault door like it was made of foam, and stepped inside, beckoning Leclerc to follow.

It was not what he had expected, though he was not sure what that had been in the first place. What he found were pictures, racks upon racks of pictures, framed in metal and arranged in columns. Most of them were of the desert, many of Danesville, but he also found some from The Dust, and the Bristle Savannah, and places he had never seen before.

There was one series of pictures shot in an area that was covered in snow. At the bottom were mostly landscape shots, vast plains of ice framed by black mountains. Above that were pictures of a man standing atop what looked to be a type of sandcrawler, only adapted for ice, and definitely not of the luxurious kind the starfolk had access to. He had a stern face with narrow eyes and an ugly scar across his nose. White crystals hung in his wispy beard.

There were pictures of him with other men and women, sitting around a fire outside a cave; one where he stood on a rocky precipice, aiming at something with a sniper rifle; one where he was in a stuffy ball room, dancing with a woman. It took Leclerc a moment to recognise her as Tatiana.

The picture at the very top was of that same man, sitting in a chair, dark blood flowing from his throat to the white snow on the ground. Tatiana was standing behind him, a razor in her hand, smiling. *Quoram Eskel, The Ice Wraith, #3*, was emblazoned in the frame above the picture.

All the other series were the same. Landscape shots at the bottom, pictures of men or women above that, and finally them being killed by Tatiana. *Bloody Colin Fint, #5*, *Casimir Jones, The Laughing Reaper, #1*, *Leonore Pirdole, Witch of the Wandering Dune, #2*. Leclerc had never heard of most of these people, until he saw a name that made his blood freeze. *Frank Baumann, The Plasma Kingmaker, #8*, *Red Yvette Noble, #1*, *Malcolm Manhunter, #5*.

"Some of these people are legends, they've been dead for decades, if not centuries," said Leclerc. Then he spotted something that sent another shiver down his spine.

There was a second series for *Quoram Eskel, The Ice Wraith*, only this one was marked *#2* instead of *#3*. He was still dead in the top picture, but instead of having had his throat cut, he was hanging from the neck by a chandelier, Tatiana posing next to his dead body.

"What in all rains is this?" Leclerc asked. He could barely speak. It felt as though his breath was wheezing out of his lungs, unwilling to form words.

"I think you will find this one particularly interesting," said Tatiana, who had closed the door behind them. Leclerc had not even noticed.

He walked over to the rack she was pointing at, only to find that it was about another person he knew very well – himself. This series focused mainly on Danesville, and it ended in him laying face-down in the street, bullet holes in his back, and Tatiana standing next to his corpse, a hunting rifle in hand. *Jake Leclerc, Ghost of Megaphant Rock, #9*, it said.

Leclerc stepped back, bumping into another rack of pictures. He spun around, feeling his throat tighten as fear grabbed a hold of him. This one was him too, only *#3*, where Tatiana had beheaded him with a sword out in the desert. "What is this?" he repeated. The world around him began to spin.

"This is the third time I killed you, Jake. And that over there was the ninth. Today is going to be the thirteenth," Tatiana said, taking a slow step toward him, a smile on her face.

Leclerc retreated instinctively, running backward down the aisle, stopping when he bumped into another rack of pictures. He could not turn around to look at them. His eyes were fixed on Tatiana, who was patiently moving toward him.

"Do you know how difficult it is to create a living, breathing world with rich, realistic lore?" she asked. Leclerc had no idea what she was talking about. "It's impossible. Too much work and brainpower required for a single person, too difficult to organise for a team, and too creative for a machine. So what does one do?" She tapped on one of the picture frames with a fingernail. "One let's the lore write itself."

A mischievous grin on her face, Tatiana began to take off her fancy dress, still pacing slowly as she walked toward Leclerc. "Six centuries of history have been recorded in this system, every world, every continent, every territory, every town. From the beginning of your life to its premature end at the hands of Frank Baumann's mercenaries, your brain was recorded, as were the brains of everyone you have ever heard about or known." She dropped the dress on the ground, now wearing nothing but the underlying corsage. "Do you know how much material a team of creative geniuses can get out of that? A whole star system, every planet inhabited, everything recorded. They sometimes nudged history in a more interesting direction, but then they also switch up the details every season."

"Why are you doing this?" Leclerc asked, trying and failing to move back further. He had never felt this kind of fear before.

"Because you are special, Jake. You are the one that got away, the one I killed twelve times but still did not get everything out of." She opened the corsage, dropping it like a shell. "Every single person in this room I was able to seduce, some of them multiple times, but not you. You always got the drop on me, or were otherwise unreachable, and that it was makes you so intriguing." Tatiana stopped when she was standing right in front of him. She was naked, and terrifying. "I was tired of failing to get you, so I called up a few friends on the creative team, and they agreed to deploy you late into the season, at a spot where I would be able to find you. After all, my company sold them most of the mass they needed to build their planets." She knelt down to his level, biting her lip. "And I have to say, the wait has been worth it."

Tatiana's breath was hot on Leclerc's face as she leaned

over him, pressing her body against his. "And now I will have you one last time, and experience the ecstasy of taking your life, knowing that your character will never be deployed again."

Leclerc tried to yank himself free, but felt cold metal on his temple. There must have been a gun behind him all this time, and Tatiana had just taken it. The column of pictures moved away behind him, and strong hands grabbed Leclerc, raising him to his feet, arms locking around his chest. He could not see them, only feel them. They were invisible.

Tatiana grabbed a syringe with a clear liquid in it, and Leclerc knew instinctively that it was the same sweet water that the android butler had always offered when Tatiana wanted him. She buried it in his arm, and the effects were immediate. Tatiana grinned, placing the gun back on his temple. "Oh, how I love doing this."

When the final echoes of Madame Ding's screams had faded, the man holding up Jake Leclerc's lifeless body stopped being invisible. He was clad in bronze body armour. It was dirty where some of Leclerc's upper skull had spread, but not nearly as covered as Madame Ding's naked body. She seemed to relish it.

"Thank you, Commander Bryde. If you would be so kind as to take my victory picture."

"No clothes?" Commander Bryde asked.

Madame Ding raised an eyebrow. "What, are we going to pretend like we are civilised now. Just take the picture. Erol is probably bored to death in that dreadful casino."

Good Men

By Gwydion JMF Weber

There was once a good man. He loved his wife and children, and worked hard to give them the best life possible. Whenever his spouse was worried, he listened to her concerns, even if sometimes he considered them petty. Every time she cooked for him, he let her know how much he loved the food, and how much he loved her.

When his children had trouble with their homework, he helped them as often as he could. When his mother needed a handyman to fix something that was broken in her house, he would drive over and help her, enjoying the crusty apple pie of his childhood.

He was a good neighbour, a trustworthy fellow, and a reliable friend. When his country was attacked by the most insidious of threats, he left his lucrative profession to enlist, because he wanted to protect his family, his neighbourhood, and his nation.

He fought in battle, never enjoying the taking of life but understanding the necessity of defending oneself. When he was reassigned to a military compound, he was able to relocate his family there. It was sad that he had to pull his children away from the environment they knew, but the school here was excellent.

Dealing with prisoners of war was difficult, and required commitment by those of the strongest moral fibre. Still, the good man was glad when they reassigned him to exterminating the vermin, even if it required the handling of dangerous gas.

The good man, having become a respected officer, died when the enemy stormed the compound he and his family inhabited, falling to the bayonet of a young man who was himself good.

The good man had come to this foreign land in response to an invasion of his own country. Disgusting things had been done to him and his people by the foreigners. Rape, murder, genocide were only a few of the items on the list of atrocities committed, and though the good man had lived far away from all this horror, he, unlike many of his friends, had been happy to be drafted for military service.

The people of this land believed terrible things. Mutual respect, fairness, and camaraderie were foreign concepts to them. They had no solidarity for the underprivileged, and adored their oppressors instead of giving power to those who would liberate them from their yoke.

The war had been difficult, but his people had been victorious. Having seen the horrors committed by the foreigners, the good man realised that ideas such as theirs must never be allowed to take root in his own country, lest they corrupt the good thing they had built there. It was his duty to protect his family, friends, and everyone else from the festering influence that these lies could have on them, because he had seen the horrors they would cause, and he wished that no one else would have to face such trauma.

Being a good man, he took upon himself the task of overseeing the internment of those who would threaten the stability of the system he served. It was not the kind of work he enjoyed, but that was a sacrifice he was willing to make for the people he loved. With every new prisoner sent into his camp, he had hope that they could be converted from their corruption.

Alas, almost none of them were, and most died toiling in the mines and fields. The good man saw no reason why his fellow comrades should shoulder the cost of keeping those alive who would to them harm with their ideas, and thus he approved.

One day, the good man was sent to another foreign land, as part of a grand plan to fight a much darker kind of corruption, one that had always eaten at the borders of his own country. It was a place of hot deserts and frigid mountain ranges, and the locals, animated by this foreign corruption, refused to understand the good man's reason for being there.

Only months after his arrival, he was killed while surveying a field, by a sniper who was himself a good man.

The good man was protecting his country from these heathen invaders. Not only did he have a family to protect, with his own body if necessary, but a clergy to serve. God had given him and many others a divine mission, and it was a mission any good man would be willing to fulfil.

It was a righteous thing, a liberation he would do his part in bringing to the world, so everyone could live in the glory of God, and nobody would have to suffer as the heathens did. Heathens like these invaders, who had come to his country to oppress his people, and to exterminate their faith in God.

Feeling happy about having killed one of the commanders of these alien tyrants, he went home to his wife, and took her as God commanded, for she was his property, to cherish and do with as he pleased. After all, he would die for her safety at any moment. Years ago, she would have protested his advances, but after decades of being taken by her husband, the good man, the woman had even stopped crying.

She gave the good man seven sons and four daughters, all of which required shepherding and discipline so they would learn the right path to God, and become the upstanding, pious people the good man hoped that they would become. To this end, the good man beat his children with a rod, as his father had done to him, and his grandfather had done to his father. He knew why the children cried, and remembered having cried himself, but he understood now that this was the only way to instil good, moral values in his offspring.

Over the years, the good man killed many more of the invaders, taking their spoils and giving them to the poor. Eventually they were driven out, as God had promised they would, and the good man was optimistic.

He knew, however, that the people who had armed him in the first place were themselves heathens, and just as evil as the invaders. They had exploited the good man and his friends for their own nefarious purposes, and though those had been aligned with the holy will of God at the time, that time was now over. The good man resolved to meet with the leader of the foreigners who had given him weapons, determined to assassinate him and end his manipulation of the land and people he had sworn to protect.

But he was killed before he could ever draw his own gun by someone who had seen through his ruse, and was himself a good man.

The good man was not even a killer, but a healer by training. He had saved a great many lives on the battlefield. Once, in the war, his hospital tent had been full of wounded soldiers when it came under enemy fire. The good man himself had, at grave risk to his own body, picked up a rifle and beaten back the enemy through sheer force of bravery.

Ever since that day, he had known that God would protect him if he would only live by his laws and do his will. He returned to his own country a hero, but instead of resting on his laurels, he continued his dedication to saving lives by teaching the next generation of medical professionals.

Thanks to his relentless work ethic and patience, many more students persevered under him than anyone else, because the good man had an eye for spotting their brilliance even when others did not. Many of his students went on to become important doctors in their own fields, but they always came back to their mentor for advice, which the good man was happy to give.

But a shadow was cast over his life one day. His son, once a god-fearing young man who had grown up to be everything his father had wanted him to become, and who on any other day would have filled the good man's heart with pride, had revealed a terrible secret. Even though he was a man, he wanted to take no wife, but instead to live with a man, maybe even make him his husband if the laws of the land would ever allow it.

The good man comforted his wife as she cried, but truly knew that he only had himself to blame. Yes, he had always followed the laws of God, but he'd spent so much time abroad that his son had practically been raised by his mother and grandmother alone. Without a strong fatherly influence in his life, was it a surprise that he had become a homosexual?

Anxious to correct his mistake, not wanting his beloved son damned to hell, the good man set out to do what he did best –

to heal his son of this sickness that had taken root inside his soul. Many nights did the good man spend searching for a cure, treating with professional colleagues and clergymen of great repute.

In the end, the cure he found was not one he wished to administer, but the only one that was proven to work. With a heavy heart, the good man collected some of his closets friends and intercepted his son, whom he loved dearly, on his way to work.

It was difficult to undress, weigh, and measure the struggling man even after he had been strapped down, but everything had to be done in accordance to proper medical procedure, lest his son suffer any ill side effects. Carefully, the good man placed the electrodes on his son's chest, made sure the right voltage was selected, and sent shocks through his body.

Some hours later, the son he loved so dearly was dead, and the good man, consumed by grief and guilt about his own failing to save his son, drank until the sun rose again in the morning, got the handgun from his desk, and took his own life.

The Blind Huntsman

By Gwydion JMF Weber

Of all the predators that roam this world, the Blind Huntsman is the most cunning.

Clifford Curtis sat in a rusted sedan, sipping saccharin-sweetened earl grey from a thermos flask. On the highway, a river of red lights slowly flowed into the city, while a trickling stream of white lights came out of it. Strings of pale, turquoise steam rose from the houses, highrises and parks, coalescing into a hybrid mixture of fog and clouds hovering ominously overhead, sparkling faintly in the moonlight. It was from this embankment of haze that the Blind Huntsman would emerge.

"Are you even listening to me?" Erasmus asked. The skull chattered his teeth as he spoke. An unnecessary sound, generated solely to gain Clifford's attention. Erasmus was set inside a specialised compartment at the centre of the dashboard, just above the radio, and secured with a strip of Velcro tape glued to his jaw. On his forehead, the shape of a crucifix was carved into the unusually white bone, painted gold with a silver rim. Two balls of obsidian rolled around freely in the eye sockets, the dots of light that represented pupils now focused on the man in the driver's seat.

"Sorry mate, I was lost in thought for a moment there," Clifford responded. "What was it you said?"

"I said: You should stop drinking so much tea, it'll make your teeth go yellow, and then some poor bastard will have to spend centuries inside a vessel with tainted headlights." Erasmus showed off his gleaming white biters.

"Don't assume everyone is as vain as you, mate. You also

might wish to focus on our task at hand," said Clifford, demonstratively taking another big gulp of his earl grey.

"Oh, you mean like you're doing by getting lost in thought? Right now, the Huntsman is up *there*, so save your introspection for when you need it. This type of lapse in attention could cost you your life on a night like this, and the way things stand right now, the Lord will not have mercy on your soul," the skull lectured.

"Here we go again," Clifford rolled his eyes.

"Oh yes, we do. You regularly fornicate with married *and* unmarried women, you sleep in every day, regardless of whether or not you had the night shift, you never give anything to charity, and you haven't been inside a church for years!" If Erasmus were capable of spitting, he might have.

"All allegations for which you have no evidence, though I will freely admit that I don't attend the Sunday service, because I do not believe that God cares. Besides, it's easy for you to be a puritan. I have bodily needs." In truth Clifford was tired of having this argument every time they were out on duty, but it was a better way to pass the time than sitting in silence.

"Descent at sector three forty-five," the dispatch woman's voice said over the radio. *"No guarantees, but it's probably him."*

Clifford checked the coordinates against a map of the city to see where the Huntsman was descending, then looked at the spot through his binoculars. Though there wasn't yet a vortex forming, he could see the tiny bolts of static electricity discharging around where it would appear. Without the binoculars he would not have been able to see them, not only because of the distance, but simply because his human eyes could not see everything that was going on.

"This is Sentinel Two, we have it. Driving over there now," Clifford spoke into the radio.

"They're getting better at detecting it early," Erasmus commented. Both of his pupils had disappeared as he had fixed his gaze on the forming vortex. One of them rolled back, looking at Clifford. "We'll finish this conversation," the skull announced.

"That's what you always say." Clifford turned the key and rolled onto the road. It was time to earn his living.

The Blind Huntsman was about to come down on a quaint little neighbourhood of family homes differentiated only by minor details. One had windows with blue plastic frames, instead of the usual white, while another had the dark bricks around its entrance painted a lighter shade of brown than its neighbours. There were different fences, fountains, and cars parked in the driveways, but it was all superficial. Road signs were the only way to make sure one wasn't actually in an adjacent street.

When they arrived, the vortex had become discernible, and the discharge lightning, had Clifford been able to perceive it, would have turned from a prickling of mint green to a crescendo of bright orange. There was a convenience store at an intersection near the point of descent. Clifford decided to take a look inside, just to be sure.

As expected they sold everyday supplies, from candy bars, to pencils, to soulstones. Also as expected, they sold a wide selection of coffee, black tea, and other caffeinated drinks. Both the shelves and the refrigerators were very close to empty.

Exact pay or credit card only during night shift, said a sign right by the cash register. Nobody was manning it. The owner must have gone home very early. Instead of a human cashier, Clifford was greeted by a skull located in a secure cage right above a rack of glowing eggs and chewing gum. It was painted sky blue, with little dots of black and yellow around the eyes and mouth, and spoke with an androgynous voice that might have been a man's, woman's, or even a child's.

“You need to get your wares to the cash register if you want to buy them. I can't fetch them for ya,” it said. The blue slits shimmering in its eye sockets narrowed.

“Good evening to you as well,” Clifford answered, flashing his gold-rimmed ID card. “May I see your sales records for tonight?”

“No, but you may speak to them,” said the skull. “At what time should I start?”

Clifford frowned for a moment. They were supposed to have these in paper, but it might make the tedium of going through the books a tad easier. “Did you sell a higher volume of stimulants than usual today? I'm talking mainly caffeine, but also guarana powder and energy drinks."

The skull's glowing eye slits lost contour for a moment, then returned into focus. "Now that you mention it, yes, we did sell a lot of all that today," it said, a note of surprise in its voice.

"You're supposed to report these things, especially on a night where the Huntsman is predicted to come out," Clifford complained. Had the Office been unable to spot the point of descent as early as they did, the Blind Huntsman could have already been wreaking havoc on this neighbourhood. People subconsciously preparing to avoid sleep was the best early warning system, but it required the public to cooperate.

"Is the Huntsman coming out tonight?" The skull sounded genuinely surprised.

"Have you looked outside?"

The skull's eyes became a bright red as its vision penetrated the walls of the store. "Oh," it finally said. "Well, me not sleeping means that I don't think about the Blind Hunstman all too much, to be honest."

"That's no excuse. This is a massive public safety code violation! We could have proofed the neighbourhood and set a trap. Now, people are in danger," Clifford explained. It was always irritating to have to elucidate on these things to those who should know better.

"Well, the affairs of people are hardly affairs of mine," the skull responded. "Now, are you here to bother me, or will you actually purchase something from the store? We *are* licensed resellers of Chocolate, you know..."

"Do you really think someone who works for the Office would go on duty without Chocolate in his pocket?" Clifford was incredulous.

"I thought you might have run out, from all the hard work you do. Now be gone, I have business to attend to." With that spiteful remark, the glow disappeared from the skull's eyes.

Outside, the vortex was now almost fully formed. Clifford felt his limbs become heavy. His heart rate slowed as a deep calm spread through his body. It was time. The Blind Huntsman was about to emerge. He observed people turning off the lights in their homes as they were befallen by a sudden onset of tiredness, oblivious to the danger lurking above. It was always like this. Whenever the Blind Huntsman begins to manifest, people rest peacefully and forget about the danger.

Clifford slouched against the sedan. It required all his strength to pull the door open and sit down in the driver's seat. The fabric was warm and comfortable, and it felt as though it were heated somehow. Strange. It wasn't like the Office to have such a fancy feature installed. He blinked, leaned back, and got ready to sink into the soft embrace of sleep.

"Come on, you amateur!" a voice called out. "When the Huntsman works fast, you need to work faster!" Clifford recognised it as belonging to Erasmus, but wasn't quite certain of what he'd just said. It was time to sleep, not work. Work was tiresome. "Wake! Up!" Erasmus shouted. "Do *not* fall asleep. You will *die*!"

That startled Clifford somewhat. A dull surrogate of fear made him a little more aware of the situation. He was in his car, falling asleep. But he couldn't fall asleep, he was on duty. Sleeping on duty was dangerous. Lethargically, he raised his arm and opened a little compartment between the gearbox and the handbrake. He produced a small syringe filled with a milky grey substance, strained to uncap it, and plunged it into his arm. The injection happened almost on its own. Good. He was done. He could sleep now.

Clifford jolted awake with a wheezing breath. He pulled the syringe out of his arm and hastily put on a plaster. That had been a close call.

"Thank you Lord for protecting this fool!" said Erasmus with genuine elation. "Thank you oh Lord, for he is not worthy of your favour."

He needed a moment to clear his vision. A lethal amount of neurostimulants was coursing through his veins. On any other day, his heart would have exploded. Tonight, this injection gave him an hour of being awake in the Blind Huntsman's prowling grounds.

"He's coming," said Erasmus, his eyes directed upwards.

And indeed, peering through his binoculars, Clifford saw a snake of liquid shadow drag itself out of the vapour vortex above, becoming a streak of pure black writhing across the sky. It moved quickly, hovering, twisting, turning, and changing directions erratically.

"Can you find a pattern?" asked Clifford, putting aside the binoculars. He could only see the fading vortex above them now.

"No, but he does seem confused, I suppose," Erasmus responded. "I'm not sure why, but he hasn't honed in on anything yet. Oh, wait, he's on the move." The skull's eyes followed the path of the Blind Huntsman.

Clifford turned the key and started the car, following Erasmus' directions. It wasn't long until he came back to a halt. "Looks like he's found his first victim," the skull said. "Though he still seems a bit jittery. Be careful in there."

Not waiting for his partner to elucidate, Clifford got out of the car and approached the house Erasmus had pointed him towards. It was a perfectly normal, two-storied family home with a red door, lace curtains, and a stone fountain. Using the skeleton key that every agent of the Office possessed, he entered. Through his binoculars, he saw the black mass swirling above the head of a man in his mid forties, who had fallen asleep at the living room table, his head lying on a stack of documents next to his laptop. Indeed, the Huntsman was not behaving as usual. Instead of direct, methodical movements he seemed hesitant, tentacles moving as though they were looking around.

So long as Clifford wasn't asleep, the Blind Huntsman could not perceive him. However, he was about to make himself a lot more vulnerable. As the darkness enveloped the sleeping man, Clifford put away the binoculars and produced a small packet of Chocolate from his breast pocket. He removed the star-spangled black wrapper, revealing a flat bar of an ambergris-coloured substance, dotted with black and white spots, like rice puffs. It split into two roughly thumb-sized pieces. Clifford placed one in the mouth of the sleeper, and ingested the other one himself. The Chocolate sizzled like sherbet powder in his mouth, and flowed down his gullet like a living thing that wanted to be consumed.

After taking a breath, Clifford lied flat on his back next to the man. “Here we go,” he said, and closed his eyes.

He came to in a park. There were dogs crawling up trees with crimson leaves, jumping around in the branches like goats. The distant cityscape surrounding it was flat and poorly defined, like a set in a low budget film. The Dreamer was easy to spot. A grown man and a little boy at the same time, he was sitting in an octagonal sandbox, playing with wooden blocks. He was attempting to build a tower, but every time he tried to place the fourth block on top, it turned into a ball and rolled away, felling the entire edifice.

Clifford brought the world around him into focus. He was not truly asleep. He could feel himself lying on the floor of the man's living room, and regretted not having taken the time to grab a pillow from the couch. The back of his head was already hurting.

The Blind Huntsman would be more of a challenge. It could be any element of this dream until it chose to reveal itself, and at that point it would most likely be too late. Clifford approached the problem strategically, working outward from the elements closest to the Dreamer, which were also the most stable ones. He peeled back the layers of the buildings blocks, lost his gaze in them. If the Dreamer did this, he would change the dream, but not Clifford. He was merely a visitor here.

There was a skull on one edge of the sandbox, staring with big, empty eye sockets. It was new, and he needed a moment to remember why it was here. Clifford pictured a golden crucifix on the skull's forehead, and big, obsidian marbles for eyeballs. With much mental effort, the cranium changed in appearance, until the transformation began happening on its own. Like an oil painting under a blow drier, the skull melted, and formed a humanoid shape sitting in the sandbox. The Dreamer seemed blissfully unaware of this process. Finally, a Teutonic Knight, clad in full armour and with a winged helmet on his head, rose. Every wrinkle in his coat, every kink in his mail, and every bit of chipped-off paint was visible and well-defined, making him stand out against the fleeting nature of the dreamscape.

“Took you long enough,” Erasmus complained. “Have you

found him yet?"

"Yeah, he's in that rabbit over there," Clifford responded.

Erasmus spun around, twirling his blade, only to pause. "There is no rabbit over there." He was quiet for a moment. "Ah, yes. Humour. You ought to take this more seriously."

"How could I, when the best example of how 'taking things seriously' sucks the joy out of everyone's life is sitting in my dashboard." Clifford continued his scan, analysing the blocks, the sand, the little plastic excavator, even the planks of the sandbox. They were all what they appeared to be.

The Dreamer startled. Something had grabbed his attention, but Clifford could not see what it was yet. A young girl materialised out of nothing, sitting in a sandbox of her own. She was playing with a doll house bearing a striking similarity to the man's home. The dolls she was playing with appeared to be the Dreamer and his family. Focusing on each individually, Clifford noted that, though their composition was different, more recent than the original elements of the dream, they were not the Blind Huntsman.

The Dreamer stepped out of his own sandbox to approach the girl, but slipped and fell several times on the short way there. Embarrassment filled the air, and laughter could be heard coming from an unseen group of children. The little girl ignored the Dreamer.

The ground around him oscillated between concrete, dirt, and grey bricks. "Are you having any ideas?" Clifford asked Erasmus.

"I've never prided myself on creativity," the Teutonic Knight responded, "but, judging from experience, the Blind Huntsman already knows you are here, so he will try to exhaust you by being patient."

"Let him try."

The Dreamer had entered the girl's sandbox, and was trying to get her attention, only for her to turn away from him with deliberation and continue playing with his family. Clifford could feel him shouting incoherently, believing that he was making sense, but in truth merely uttering sound. Finally, the little girl took the doll that was supposed to represent him, and threw it into his face, laughing.

The ground of the dreamscape shook from the impact. Clifford almost fell over, but managed to catch himself at the last moment. They were in a different place now, a desert, and the Dreamer was no longer a little boy, but a man-sized version of his own plastic doll. He was thirsty, and in desperate need of drink, but the bottle of cool, refreshing water in his hand simply drained through his plastic joints.

Mirages hovered over the sand all around them. They dissipated the moment Clifford tried to focus on them, and he couldn't even tell what they were supposed to represent. “Bloody hell,” he complained. This was a perfect environment for the Huntsman.

“Clifford!” Erasmus shouted. “Over there!” the Teutonic Knight was pointing at a tiny figure in the distance. It was a man on a camel, clad in black Tuareg garb. He had a rifle in his hands. It took only a moment of focus to determine it – this was the Blind Huntsman.

The ground under Clifford's feet gave way, and before he knew it he was waist-deep in quicksand. The Dreamer was walking off, and the Huntsman was riding their way. Clifford tried desperately to wriggle himself out of the pit, but the more he struggled, the deeper he sank, until eventually the quicksand was up to his chest. All he could do was damn the creators of children's cartoons that had made quicksand such an omnipresent obstacle ingrained in the subconscious of so many people. He looked over to Erasmus, who seemed to be in a similar pickle.

The Blind Huntsman passed them on his camel. Though its eyes were grey like those of a blind man, it looked at Clifford directly. A sardonic grin shaped its lips as the Tuareg rode past, approaching the Dreamer from behind.

It tapped the man on the shoulder, offering him a seat on the camel. Clifford began to shout. “No! Don't do it! Run!” He knew it was pointless. The Dreamer could hear neither him nor Erasmus. In a final act of desperation, Clifford tried to push himself out of the quicksand, grabbing handfuls of desert in the process. It only dragged him deeper into the pit, until the sand was right up to his neck.

The Dreamer smiled when the Blind Huntsman offered him a bottle of water that he could drink. The desert seemed less parched for a moment, the mysterious dunes almost inviting and full of promise. He jumped onto the back of the camel, thanking the rider for his kindness. It was the last thing he would ever do.

The Blind Huntsman's torso turned around completely. Where once had been the face of a kindly old Tuareg was now a black maw tearing at the fringes of reality itself. The world shook as it sucked up parts of the dream around it. The Dreamer screamed, but it was too late. Slowly at first, he was torn apart by the maw's suction. Like a black hole, it pulled in the Dreamer fibre by fibre, until eventually it pulled him in all at once.

The dreamscape shattered.

Clifford woke up on the floor. The Dreamer was having wild spasms in his chair, convulsing in agony, not making a sound. Blood was coming from his eyes, nose, and ears, until suddenly all movement ceased and he fell out of his chair. He was dead.

"Fuck!" Clifford cursed. "Fuck, fuck, fuck!" It wasn't his first dead Dreamer, not even his fiftieth, but he knew he would be agonising over this one for months. Through his binoculars he could see the Blind Huntsman hover above its victim for a moment before escaping through the back door, a snake of black smoke diffusing through the mosquito net.

It was locked, and Clifford's skeleton key did not fit. He leaned back and kicked it open. There was not time to go any way but the direct way. Outside, the Huntsman flew over the hedge and into and adjacent garden. Clifford grabbed a shovel and tore down an old piece of fencing. The rotted wood gave way easily, and he found himself in an area fashioned after a forest grove. All around him, fireflies danced in the moonlight.

There was a young girl lying on the ground, her chest rising and falling with calm breaths. She looked happy, even as the Blind Huntsman entered her mind. Clifford took out another piece of Chocolate, broke it, placed half in the girl's mouth and lay down next to her.

For a moment he thought that it somehow hadn't worked. He was still lying on the ground in this grove-styled garden. The fireflies were still dancing. But they were dancing in an unreal manner, forming complex patterns, flying in little colonnades, and sparkling in a thousand colours. He heard the little girl laugh as she chased them.

Clifford got to his feet and looked around. Though the surroundings of this dream were similar to the garden, this was actually a brightly illuminated forest, like one might find in a fairytale. There was a castle on a hill far away in the distance, and a white stag with silver horns trotted around a nearby pond. Clifford focused on it immediately, trying to strip away the layers, but it was just that – a stag.

He fell back into his usual pattern, identifying the different groups of fireflies as individual dream objects with a hierarchy. Those the Dreamer was paying attention to were smaller, more detailed groups, while the ones in the background were just tiny dots of light.

Clifford stumbled over a rock in the floor. It was a skull, and he repeated the process of materialising Erasmus in the dream. Once again, the sheer detail of the Knight seemed out of place somehow.

"Ah yes, the simple dreams of childhood," he said. "Can you imagine anything more beautiful than this?"

"Maybe if there wasn't a monster in these woods I would appreciate it more," Clifford responded. He'd gone over to focusing on the trees, one by one, which, in a forest, was an exhausting task. But it proved to be a worthwhile one.

As one of the trees became translucent under his gaze, Clifford spotted a figure behind it. It was a man dressed like a medieval forester, holding a hunting bow. A bandage covered his eyes. The Blind Huntsman reacted immediately, materialising an arrow in its hand and shooting at the girl with implacable speed and precision.

The only thing Clifford could do was throw himself into the line of fire. He howled as the arrow penetrated his chest and bored through his lung. It was a sharp, burning sensation. Wood splinters dug through his flesh like razor-bladed maggots, and his breath was taken away. This was how the little girl imagined being shot by an arrow felt like.

Better him than her. That was a fact. Even though Clifford would have phantom pains for a few days, his soul could only be hurt in his own dream. This was not his own dream.

"I will vanquish you in the name of the Lord!" Erasmus shouted as he charged. For a man wearing heavy armour, he moved with remarkable speed, brandishing his blade with holy self-righteousness.

Instead of bracing for a fight, the Blind Huntsman simply sprinted up the tree and jumped into the sky, knocking another arrow aimed at the girl. That was the problem with children's dreams: things that were often impossible in the more rigid minds of adults were very much realistic here.

Clifford looked over to the Dreamer. She had no idea what was going on, too lost in playing with her fireflies to care. Gritting his teeth, Clifford once again jumped between her and the Blind Huntsman's arrow. This time it struck his abdomen, and though the pain was less sharp, it had a dull, hot quality to it that made it very distracting.

The Huntsman landed only a few metres away, knocking another arrow, but Clifford ran at it with his arms raised, dead set on tackling it. The arrow was let loose and pierced through Clifford's clavicle. It felt as though his torso was being split in two, a lightning strike of hot steel ripping him apart at the neck.

Through the haze of white hot pain, Clifford saw Erasmus once again charging toward the Huntsman. Instead of taking another shot at the girl, it ran, whistled, and jumped on the back of the white stag. The animal carried it away into the trees, where it disappeared into a distant mist. The battle was won, but the monster was not yet ejected.

Erasmus was breathing heavily behind his visor. "I'd say that the devil will have him, but he *is* the devil," he complained.

The dreamscape changed. Beneath their feet, the ground shifted away, forming a funnel of grass around a hole right where the little girl was standing. Pumpkins began to rain from the sky as Clifford and Erasmus rolled toward the centre. Their carved faces were evil and twisted, and they cackled like demons.

Clifford tumbled through the hole, falling through a seemingly endless bank of black clouds. He lost sight of Erasmus as he spun, and when he looked back up the Teutonic Knight was gone. Up ahead, the little girl was crying. Her dream had just turned into a nightmare. For Clifford it was a relief. The changing of the dreamscape had removed the arrows stuck in his body. Though they left a painful aftertaste, he no longer felt like a pin cushion.

They came up hard on a bouncing castle. It was made of inflated rubber and plastic, even had the right colour scheme, but was the size and shape of a real castle, or at least what the little girl believed a real castle to look like. She seemed momentarily surprised at the sudden reversal of her fate, but also curious at this new environment.

Erasmus landed somewhere behind them, almost ripping through the fabric, but getting to his feet eventually. Clifford had no choice but to follow the girl and hope the knight would not lose them.

The great doors of the castle opened, revealing a warmly lit interior. A platoon of heavy chandeliers hung from the ceiling, swinging back and forth in unison. Servants in red uniforms all bowed before the Dreamer as though she were the princess herself, and she seemed as surprised at this fact as anyone.

The clangour of metal on stone behind them told Clifford that Erasmus had entered the castle proper. His first thought was that the knight had crossed the distance quickly by bouncing, but then he remembered that Erasmus was about as inventive as a pot of earl grey. He'd have to ask him later.

Making sounds of delight, the little girl walked deeper into the castle, a mechanical bow going through the rows of servants like a wave as she passed them. A crystal stood at the end of the hall, at least seven storeys tall and glowing with the light of a hearth. It was the colour of light amber.

Clifford was so captivated by this that, for a moment, he didn't keep his eyes on the girl. Suddenly, she was gone, as though swallowed by the ground.

“Fuck!” he shouted, looking around frantically, scanning the environment for clues as to where she could have gone. “Did you see where she went?” he asked, expecting a snappy retort from Erasmus.

The knight said nothing.

Clifford focused the spot where the Dreamer had been standing just a moment ago, but it was real, solid, and impenetrable. How could she have disappeared like that? “Shit, fuck, shit, cunt,” he murmured. He hadn't lost track of a Dreamer in years.

It was more coincidence than deliberation that Clifford turned around at exactly the right time to see Erasmus' sword come crashing down on him. He jumped back at the very last second, so that only the tip of the blade cut through his pectoral muscle. He understood the situation faster than he would have expected. Behind the Teutonic Knight's visor, instead of the usual faint outline of a nose and eyes, there was nothing but pure blackness. This was not Erasmus. This was the Blind Huntsman.

Before Clifford could ask himself why the monster was attack him, not the Dreamer, the sword was rammed through his heart as the Huntsman moved his arm in an anatomically impossible jerk. He felt his body freeze, go limp, as his life force was drained into the blade. The knight's armour parted at the neck, revealing the Blind Huntsman's gargantuan maw.

It had all been a game. There was no little girl, possibly no man in his house, either. From the beginning, the trap had been laid for *him*. The Blind Huntsman was not usually one for personal feuds, but considering how often Clifford had cut short its fun in the past, he was not surprised that it had made an exception.

He slipped off the sword. Clifford hit the ground, unable to move.

“Foul creature! The Lord is with me!” Erasmus had tackled the Blind Huntsman just as it was about to consume Clifford. “You will perish on the tip of my blade, impostor!” The two knights were a whirlwind of metal. The singing and clanging of their blades was enough for a whole battlefield, so fast were their movements.

Erasmus cut at the Huntsman's shield with such force that he sent his opponent tumbling backward. He parried a retaliation blow with his shield, then went for a rapid stab at his enemy's neck. The sword pierced mail and gambeson like it was butter.

“In the name of the Lord, you are destroyed!” Erasmus roared.

The Blind Huntsman turned into a maelstrom of darkness around the blade. His maw reappeared, but it was filamentous, weak, fading. The room was filled with an omnipresent, bone-chilling wail. It bored into Clifford's head like the cries of a million banshees. A white light filled the castle, too bright to see anything through it.

“It is the will of the Lord that you be eternally banished to *hell*!” was the last Clifford heard before the light engulfed all.

He awoke on the floor of the first Dreamer's house. The man was dead. The Huntsman truly had taken him. Groaning from the pain of his invisible wounds, Clifford rose to his feet and ran outside.

There was a fire in his car, emanating from the dashboard. It was Erasmus. The skull was ablaze with holy flame.

The Orange Tower

By Gwydion JMF Weber

On the other side, it was the entrance to what many called "The Dark Land." To Dexine, who saw the sun wander across the sky every day, this name had always sounded a bit stupid. Until the day she'd met her first Suiter, that is. As it turned out, Suiters often said things that had nothing to do with what was actually there, and held on to their figures of speech even after being proven wrong. Strange folk, the people from the other side of The Wall, but quite agreeable if one could get used to them, and quite open-handed if one was a guide.

The group that Maksim was leading out of the Shadow Gate today was large. More than a dozen people, clad in tight-fitting suits of soft rubber, their heads enclosed in rebreather helmets with reflective visors. It could be quite difficult to tell them apart sometimes, especially if they were all wearing the same colour, but this group seemed to be wildly varied. Though two of them wore suits the colour of cantaloupes, one was much taller than the other. Three small, six-wheeled vehicles followed the group like packing mules, carrying their equipment.

"Look, that one, the one in the blue? That's Worthington," Bayles explained. "My grandpapa worked with him. One of his first tours, they met, and Worthington has only ever come here if grandpapa was the guide. Or papa, later. And me, now."

"If he worked with your grandpapa, how old is this Worthington?"

Bayles shrugged.

"Don't know, don't need to know. The point is, you need to behave. No shenanigans."

"I never do shenanigans," Dexine objected.

"Well, it's what my papa used to say whenever we went with Worthington, so it has to be important."

"Mister Bayles. It's a pleasure, as always. I've been away from here for too long." Worthington said words in a strange manner, as Suiters often did, but his speech seemed especially important, and laden with meaning somehow.

"Pleasure is all mine, Mister Worthington," Bayles repeated, adhering to Suiter etiquette. He was not the owner of all pleasure in existence, and Dexine doubted pleasure was even a thing that one could own. "This here is my friend, Dexine. She knows the place you wanna go better than I do, so I'm having her tag along."

"Excellent. I've always placed great importance on appropriate expertise," Worthington explained. Bayles nodded, and it was clear to Dexine that he hadn't understood a word of what his patron just said. She did, though.

"The appropriate expertise is in my property, Mister Worthington," she said.

For some reason, the man in the blue suit started laughing.

"I have no doubt about it,"

After a short chat with Maksim, who had been paid with a high-capacity water purifier, they learned that it was the first trip to this side of The Wall for many of the Suiters. Dexine wasn't sure if the Vipertail Slopes were the best place for a first-timer, but then it seemed that Suiters were completely indestructible, and the Stingtongues were hibernating anyway. After that, it was straight off, into the wild.

It soon became clear that Worthington was experienced with the terrain. Unlike the first-timers, he had no problems navigating the bog without stepping into sinkholes, and didn't recoil from every Stinkbat and Bladderfly. Dexine paid special attention to the women among the Suiters, who were the most prone to jumping at anything they were scared of. She neglected to tell them that Stinkbats and Bladderflies were the friendliest of creatures around to avoid a panic. Ominous shadows stalked around the periphery of the group, and Dexine knew they would claw at anyone who got separated from it. Thus, keeping them all together was the most important thing.

It took two days to get to the Vipertail Slopes. The Suiters, as they did, needed many hours of sleep every night, and they had to lie down for it. They sure were peculiar folk. Meanwhile, Dexine and Bayles slept while walking the perimeter every night. When they finally arrived in the dry, grass-covered Vipertail Slopes, many of the Suiters seemed much more at ease, even though it should have been the other way around. Razorweed and Skysharks were much more dangerous than anything out in the bog.

That night, Worthington sat Dexine down for a chat.

"I'm afraid I've not been entirely open with you, Miss Dexine." He sounded more apologetic than afraid. "You've been left under the impression that we wanted a tour of the Vipertail Slopes, but that is not true. We actually want you to safely lead us to a specific location."

Dexine clenched her jaw. There was only one location in the Slopes that the Suiters had a name for.

"I believe you call it 'The Orange Tower'?" Worthington asked.

"Can't take you," said Dexine. "Nobody can go to Orange Tower. It's where the Skysharks come from." She shivered at the thought of whirring metal blades inside a maw descending from the sky.

"I can assure you that the Skysharks, as you call them, will not be a problem." He produced two hand-sized discs from his back pocket. "Take one of these, and give the other to Mister Bayles. They will identify you as friendlies to the Skysharks. We have them in our suits."

Dexine kept her hands away from the tech.

"Can't take rewards before doing the job," she noted.

Worthington chuckled.

"Look at them as a gift. A woman in your line of work will probably find them very useful." Now that was an accurate statement. If they worked.

"Why do you want to go to Orange Tower?"

"I'm afraid you wouldn't understand even if I told you. It was never planned for anyone to go there, but alas, circumstances have changed." The Suiter sighed and left it at that cryptic statement.

Despite their new tech, Dexine and Bayles were still terrified of their approach to the Orange Tower. A route was easy enough to find, far away from any holes in the ground, where no hands would break through the dirt and drag people down. Dexine knew how to avoid them even around here, in Skyshark territory. With a tech rope as thin as her pinky finger, she was able to let the whole group of Suiters down into the basin where the Orange Tower stood. A huge cylinder, perfectly smooth and devoid of windows, Skysharks going in and out of an invisible hole at the top. It was terrifying.

When Worthington stepped before it and made a series of hand gestures, the wall of the Orange Tower simply split like a doorway, and allowed everyone inside. Dexine had no intention of following. Bad enough that she had to go to the nest of the Skysharks. She certainly wouldn't go inside of it. But Worthington insisted that it was much safer, and, seeing as the Suiters were all eager to get in, Dexine and Bayles followed.

It turned out that the Orange Tower was exactly that – a tower. It had rooms in it, with seats, benches, tables, shelves, and blinking lights on the walls. For first-timers, the Suiters seemed awfully familiar with the Orange Tower, immediately getting to work doing whatever Suiter things they did. Once, she'd guided a group of Suiters who literally just filled a few bottles with water from several ponds and bogs, then returned home and rewarded her with a packet of neurostimulants. In here, things didn't make much more sense. Some of the Suiters were ripping out panels of blinking light from the walls and replacing them with new ones, others were pressing buttons on a vast array of consoles, and even others were assembling something she'd always heard of, but never actually seen in action: firearms.

At some point, Dexine and Bayles were simply told to go upstairs, sit down, and stop standing around. Dexine was happy to comply. The upstairs was much simpler than the rooms with the blinking lights, and she hadn't even been to the downstairs. Not allowed, they told her. Instead, she sat on a soft bench and looked at the Skysharks float around the tower through a huge window that could not be seen from the outside. It was fascinating. She was suddenly no longer scared of them, just like that, and they even seemed strangely beautiful to her.

That night, when all the Suiters were sleeping, Dexine was awake. They expected her to sleep like they did, but she didn't. Driven by something she could not quite explain, Dexine silently slipped off her sleeping bench and snuck downstairs, where a single Suiter was sitting at a desk, his head resting between his hands, struggling to stay awake. Without making a sound, her feet carried her to the basement ladder. She knew she should be terrified, and on some level she was, but Dexine was an explorer, and telling her that there were places she wasn't supposed to go had always prompted her to go there.

There was nobody down here, either, only a big, round room with a cage in the middle. A wide array of guns and other equipment was laying around on the floor, ready to be used the following day. One side of the cage seemed to be missing, so, just to test it out, Dexine stepped inside. She immediately regretted her decision. With a loud clacking noise, the cage fell down into the darkness, turning on some lights of its own. Then, it began its slow descent. Over the following moments, Dexine felt herself get lighter and lighter, and had trouble telling where up and down was. Eventually, what had once been the ceiling became the ground, as the whole cage turned upside-down. It was the strangest thing she'd ever experienced, but she had no fear. After a few more moments, the cage appeared in a room similar to the one inside the Orange Tower, only this one was devoid of weapons. When she went upstairs, Dexine found that it, too, was identical. On the level above that, she saw something she could not comprehend.

Strange enough that the Skysharks didn't attack Suiters, and that the floor had turned to ceiling. But this had Dexine frozen in place, unable to understand what was happening on the other side of the huge window.

It was a wilderness, similar to the one that was her home. But this one was different. Instead of in a basin, the Orange Tower was on a hill, overlooking shallow waters of a blue so intense she had never imagined it could actually be real. It was so clear that she could see tiny fish swim around inside it, and birds stalk through the mud. The water stretched to the horizon, where Dexine could see several plumes of smoke rise into the heavens. And the heavens, the firmament, it was even stranger than all the other things. Whereas it had been the dead of night just moments before, on the other side, up here, it was the middle of the day.

"This is my mistake," said the familiar voice of Worthington behind her. "I apologise, Miss Dexine. You were never intended to see this." He had a gun in his hand.

Firstborn

By Gwydion JMF Weber

The name Aglain Finnegal had rattled around Andromeda's head for as long as she could remember. All she knew about him was that he was a wizard from Earth, and that he was her father. But that was about to change today, and she could barely take the anticipation.

The hooves of her winged horse thumped rhythmically on the shimmering clouds. Willows, their leaves made of colourful glass, swayed gently in the solar wind. Ahead, a vortex of liquid firmament swirled around the ethereal starbridge. On the other side, a winding road lead to the majestic palace of the faerie court, its crystalline spires radiating serene beauty.

Andromeda hadn't seen the palace since she was thirteen, and now that she was twenty-one, she seemed even less capable of comprehending its elegance. Parts of it seemed out of focus even when she looked at them, while others flickered in and out of existence at random. It was one of the disadvantages of being human in the land of the faerie.

“Don't slow down now, this forest is swarming with egregore thieves,” said Uwayn as he rode past her. The faerie lord was tall, blond, and clad in nacreous armour. His eyes were the same shade of gold as the unicorn he was riding, and his ears were sagging trumpets, the hallmark of his clan.

“Of course, My Lord.” Andromeda picked up her pace.

“My Lord? All this excitement is really getting to you, my dear.” Uwayn laughed.

“Sorry, I just can't wait to meet my father.” Andromeda felt a slight tug at her stomach as she lead her horse to the starbridge. A thousand suns churned around her, being pulled apart like noodles and pressed down like pancakes.

Uwayn gently touched her shoulder, and she felt the cold, unpleasant tingling sensation she was so familiar with. She gritted her teeth, waiting for it to be over. Uwayn, his hand glowing, sent a flare of light through the starbridge, stabilising its contours, making it safe to travel.

The entourage passed the starbridge in an orderly fashion, then stood still on the other end for a moment, marvelling at the plane the faerie King and Queen inhabited.

The sky shone midnight blue, stars sparkling in spiralling constellations. Glowing crimson fruit hung from stately trees with dark leaves, wooden vipers coiled around their branches, protecting them from brave little squirrels. The song of a faerie maiden resounded from everywhere at once, its beauty chilling Andromeda to the bone.

Lord Uwayn and his golden unicorn took the lead, parading down the winding path with a regal swagger, followed by a bulky red sugarhorn carrying a chest of gifts on its back. Andromeda followed alongside Lady Caramyl, Uwayn's wife, and her godmother. Flowers sprouted from her white hair, and her smile revealed a set of filed teeth sharp as razor blades.

Uwayn may have been the one wearing the armour, but whenever ceremonial combat was required, it was Caramyl who fought for the clan. Her prowess in the arena was legendary, and Andromeda had watched her fight a thousand foes and one.

"Are you looking forward to finally meeting your father?" she asked, her voice motherly, smooth as velvet.

"I wonder if he is as excited as I am. I'm his firstborn child, that must mean a lot, no?"

"It most certainly does to us." There was a painful note in that, but Andromeda did not get the chance to ask about it.

The path was joining another at a fork in the road, and galloping hooves could be heard in the distance to their right. Uwayn commanded the entourage to stop. There was no reason to get trampled by the stampede of whoever was coming around that corner.

After a few moments, a white stag galloped around the

bend, mounted by a faerie lord with pitch black skin and bloodied brambles for hair. Behind him, a dark convoy emerged. The members of his clan looked much like him, but most of his entourage was comprised of bulky ogres clad in dark steel armour, riding on the backs of bears.

"You didn't need to bring an army, Ritskarr!" Lord Uwayn shouted mockingly.

"My plane is distant, and the road is dangerous." Ritstkarr signalled for his entourage to slow down. "And I don't have my wife fight for me. It's unseemly."

Lord Ritskarr's wife, Lady Ekmeid, pulled up next to her husband on a slightly smaller stag of her own, not saying a word. A milky white dress contrasted her black skin, and a thick veil covered her face. Andromeda had been told that she never removed it except when she was alone with her husband.

Caramyl flashed the ogres a confident smile, which they reciprocated with a growl. There were eight of them and one of her, but Andromeda still liked her chances. The ogres of her home plane were faster and more slender, but her godmother could still dance around a dozen of them blindfolded.

"What brings you to the court?" Uwayn asked.

"You're not the only ones who have business with the wizard. He is a well-connected man, this Aglain Finnegal."

"What do you know about my father?" Andromeda blurted out.

"Do not speak to me unless spoken to, Ward." Lord Ritskarr didn't even look at her. "You spoil this human child, Uwayn, as you always do. Last time I was given a firstborn by the court, he didn't make it to twenty-one."

"That's why they don't give you Wards any more." Uwayn shrugged. "I'd ask you to join us, but I know you are going to refuse, so go on, get back to stampeding." He gestured down the path to the faerie court.

"You know me well, old friend." Lord Ritskarr bared his lupine fangs, then broke his stag back into gallop. His ogres roared war cries as they passed.

"I'll never understand that woman," Lady Caramyl said when they had disappeared over the horizon.

"Don't pass judgement on the savages, my beloved," Uwayn joked. "They don't know any better."

They arrived at the palace two hours later. Centaurs in gleaming plate guarded a marble bridge leading to the wide open gates. Statues of flagon bearers were pouring endless streams of water into the moat.

Andromeda could hear music, but was unable to grasp any of the notes. Any other mortal would have been entranced by the faerie song, made docile and open to suggestion, but she was under Lord Uwayn's protection.

The centaurs in the courtyard formed an honour guard as their caravan entered, and an elderly human dressed in fine regalia circumflexed with a level of flexibility that his old bones should not have allowed for. Andromeda knew him only as the Chamberlain.

"Lord Uwayn, Lady Caramyl, welcome to the Court of Sidhe. Your house is in good favours, and your visit has been expected."

"We thank the royal Sidhe for their grace and hospitality, Chamberlain." Uwayn nodded, and the Chamberlain rose back to his full height. Andromeda had forgotten how tall he was. "I take it we are not the only guests of the court?" He nodded toward the diverse assortment of mounts standing by the stables.

"The court always has guests, Your Highness."

Stablehands with shimmering wings fluttered over to tend to their horses as they dismounted. They ignored the riders as though they didn't even exist, and the animals obeyed them as though they had known them their entire lives. Ogres with clean skin and aristocratic scowls picked up the luggage, taking special care with the gift chest.

The Chamberlain lead the way through the splendid halls of the palace. The floor tiles were inlaid with amber and emerald, melting together in a complex floral pattern. Sconces were mounted on the walls, shards of glowing crystal floating inside them. Courtiers dressed in elegant robes observed them while engaged in hushed conversations.

The King and Queen were already waiting for them. A

massive figure clad in green sat on a thorny throne, their skin spirals of black and white. Four eyes, two of them green, the other two red, scrutinised Lord Uwayn and his entourage. A crown of iron and silver sat on their head, soft billows of smoke emanating from it.

Andromeda was so busy scanning the gallery for signs of her father that she almost forgot to bow. She didn't care how much of an honour it was to be standing in front of the King and Queen. Her entire body was tingling with anticipation.

"Lord Uwayn. You have brought us gifts." The King and Queen spoke with two voices at once. One male, one female, both beautiful.

"I have indeed, Your Majesties." The ogres carried the chest forward, and Uwayn opened it with a snip of his fingers. Inside, a thick, milky-yellow liquid flowed. "Honey, from our wild fields."

"We accept your gift. Ward Andromeda, step forth."

Andromeda's legs did not respond for a moment, then she almost stumbled. The excitement was like a spring pulling her intestines together while at the same time pulling them apart. She was seconds away from seeing her father, the man she had dreamed about meeting for twenty-one years.

"Magus Aglain, step forth."

A man emerged from the crowd of onlookers, and Andromeda could have sworn that he had not been standing in that exact spot moments earlier. If he had, she would have noticed him. Unlike all the other courtiers, who were dressed in their finest apparel, he wore a brown plaid suit and a matching beret. His hair was black, his eyes dark, and he was grinning like an idiot.

"My daughter. My beautiful firstborn daughter. I have spent two decades missing you."

"Father..." was all Andromeda managed to whisper.

"Magus Aglain, this reunion is happening upon your request. Your time to speak is now."

"Your Majesties, Lord Uwayn, Lady Caramyl, I humbly beg for my firstborn child to be returned to me."

Whatever whispers there might have been in the throne

room were gone. There was nothing but shocked silence. Andromeda needed a moment to comprehend what he had just asked. It was an impossible request, and she would never have expected it. Even the King and Queen seemed unsure how to respond.

"Ward Andromeda was given to us in exchange for an entire library of arcane knowledge. She was awarded to Lord Uwayn for his house's service to the Court of Sidhe. How do you justify this request, Magus Aglain?"

"My country had a revolution recently, and my power helped drive out the English. It was a great honour, being able to fight our oppressors in the name of Irish freedom. But then I turned around, saw the country I had helped liberate, and found it devoid of anything I love. A father needs his children, wizard or no."

Andromeda looked over to Uwayn and Caramyl. Both of them were frowning. She was unsure how to feel about the situation herself. On one hand she had always wanted to meet her father, of course. But leaving the realms of the faerie with him? Going to the Earth? She would have to leave behind everything she knew and loved. Whatever country he was speaking of, Andromeda knew it only from strange tales.

"Your appeal is condemned, and your request is denied, Magus Aglain," the King and Queen declared.

A gasp went through the courtiers. Andromeda turned around to find that it wasn't because of what the King and Queen said, but because Lord Ritskarr had stepped forward.

"Your Majesties, as a high lord of the faerie and attendant at the Court of Sidhe, I support the request of Magus Aglain and seek to put it forth as an official motion."

The King and Queen looked at Lord Ritskarr for several long moments, then nodded. *"Your motion will be entertained, Lord Ritskarr. Proceedings shall began within one cycle of the sun. Magus Aglain, for your audacity you will be held in captivity until a decision is reached."*

Everything happened very fast. Two centaur guardsmen trotted forward and flanked her father. He raised his hands, showing them that he would not resist. As he was lead away, he looked back at Andromeda. “I love you, my firstborn daughter, and I will free you from your gilded prison.”

Andromeda did not know how to respond.

Their chambers were located in one of the palace's countless towers. Andromeda was sinking into a mountain of pillows, staring at the pixies dancing up near the ceiling.

“We walked into a trap. I don't know what kind of trap, why it was set, or who definitively set it, for that matter. I don't even know if it's closed yet. This is a nightmare.” Uwayn was pacing up and down the room. Lady Caramyl followed him with her eyes.

Andromeda had never even considered any of this. Her father had given her to the Court of Sidhe, she was a Ward of the faerie. That was how it was, and it couldn't be any other way. There were other Wards, and none of them had ever returned to their parents.

“We might not be the target of this at all, though considering the … disagreements we have had with Ritskarr in the past that is unlikely. The question is what he hopes to gain from this. He wouldn't endanger his relationship with the King and Queen simply out of petty scorn, would he?” Uwayn kept thinking out loud. Caramyl continued watching him.

As a child, Andromeda had read about humans on the Earth, and the scorn with which the idea of a parent giving away their child was treated. Lady Caramyl had to sit by her bed for an entire week before she finally stopped crying herself to sleep.

“This was not a spontaneous act. Aglain and Ristkarr planned this in advance, and if I know one thing about him is that he has no respect for love. He would never work with a man so weak that he would love someone, even a wizard as powerful as Aglain Finnegal.”

For years, the only reason Andromeda had wanted to meet her father was to confront him about not having loved her. But she was past that now. She was an adult, and she understood why people made compromises. How could it be anything but an act of love to give her to Uwayn and Caramyl?

“We can't leave, that much is a given. If this is some kind

of trap against us, they will attempt to ensnare us as quickly as possible. Lord Ritskarr sits in the Winter Tower. If I send spies and they get caught, it'll be the end of them."

Of course he had not given her to Uwayn and Caramyl directly. He'd given her to the King and Queen, and they had awarded her to one of their retainers. She could have ended up going to Lord Ritskarr. She would be dead by now if that had happened.

"I *could* intercept communications between Aglain and Ristkarr, but if all this was planned out in advance, the only thing that might achieve would be to open myself up to false information. Ritskarr hides his cunning behind brutality, Aglain hides it behind more cunning. Nothing is certain."

"I need to speak with my father." Andromeda felt herself sitting up. "Do you think the King and Queen will let me see him in his cell?"

"Of course, but why? Do you think you can gleam his true intentions?"

Uwayn's words hurt, and Andromeda couldn't even tell why. He had spoken to her like he would a servant, not a Ward.

"I don't care what his true intentions are. I only wish to speak with him."

Uwayn did not look like he understood.

"Of course, dear," said Lady Caramyl. "Shall I accompany you?"

"I'd rather be alone with him," Andromeda insisted.

"I understand." Caramyl gave her a warm smile. She was her Ward, not her servant.

Her father was being held in an iron cage decorated with silver scrollwork. Glowing runes of power and other magical symbols surrounded it, pulsating softly. Crimson-scaled lizards stalked circles around him under the watchful eyes of no fewer than eight centaur guards. The lizards seemed quite disinterested in Andromeda.

"Don't worry about all this, my beloved daughter. The King and Queen are just being careful. This is the only cell they have that could hold me." Her father was smiling. The fact that this man, whom she had never met, seemed to care so much for her warmed Andromeda's heart.

"I'm sorry they put you in here," she said, carefully.

"It's quite alright, I knew it was going to happen. The King and Queen like their procedures, and I transgressed. When the proceedings are over they will let me go, and you will be coming with me."

"Why are you doing this?" She didn't know how else to ask.

"Because you're my daughter, Andromeda. Giving you away was the gravest mistake of my life. I was happy when you ended up going to Lord Uwayn and Lady Caramyl. I truly was, even if I told myself that I didn't care. They among the kindest of the faerie."

"So you didn't know? Whom I'd be awarded to?"

Her father looked to the floor. "No, unfortunately. I did not. Words cannot express how sorry I am for that, but I was a much younger, stupider man back then."

"I could have ended up with Lord Ristkarr," Andromeda accused.

Aglain Finnegal nodded. "Yes, you could have, and I would not have been able to forgive myself. In truth, Ritskarr is far less of a villain as he makes himself out to be. Of the faerie lords who partake in the Wild Hunt, he is the most gentle."

The mention of the Wild Hunt drove a shiver down her spine. It was the darkest of faerie traditions, a relic of a time from before the Court of Sidhe. Most had forsaken it, and those who still engaged in it were considered barbaric.

"He kills his Wards, you know. That doesn't sound very gentle to me."

Her father frowned. "So do Uwayn and Caramyl."

Andromeda froze.

"Didn't they tell you? Every time they tap you for power, a part of your vital essence is drained away. That is why the faerie take Wards. The firstborn children of wizards are reservoirs of great power. Uwayn and Caramyl see you as more than that. Ristkarr does not."

It was like his words had ripped a hole in her chest. "No."

The word was more a reflex than anything else. That couldn't be true, obviously. Uwayn and Caramyl loved her.

"This is so very like them. Gentle to the point of lying." Her father scoffed and shook his head. "Why do you think so many Wards die young?"

"Because most other faerie lords drain them. Uwayn and Caramyl merely absorb the radiance of my power. Like a plant taking in sunlight." Andromeda knew this like she knew her own name.

"So that's what they told you. Traditional, as lies go, but it's not true. They are patient with your vital essence, always giving it a little time to recover. It lasts longer that way, but eventually your sun will go dark, and you will die."

"Stop lying to me!" Andromeda screamed. A flash went through the room, her voice bouncing off the walls in an echo much more powerful than it should have been. The lizards stopped for a moment, then resumed their pacing.

"There it is, the spark. You have it."

Andromeda was perplexed by the sudden change of subject. "What?"

"You're a wizard, Andromeda. You're a wizard's daughter that is also a wizard herself. Do you realise how rare that is? How much power you have? Power they don't even know about. How could they, glorified vampires that they are." There was genuine contempt in Aglain's voice.

It was too much. Clenching her jaw, and without saying another word, Andromeda stormed off. Her father was pleading behind her, but the blood rushing in her ears was so loud that she didn't even understand the words.

"Are you killing me?" It was the first thing she said when she stormed into the room, where Uwayn was still pacing in front of Caramyl.

"What are you talking about, dear?" Caramyl asked.

"Are you killing me? When you absorb my power, are you taking away my vital essence?"

"Did Aglain tell you this?" Lord Uwayn's face was inscrutable.

“Please answer my question,” Andromeda insisted.

“Of course not, dear.” Lady Caramyl slipped off her chair and approached her. “We've explained to you how it works. It's not like that.”

“Stay away from me.” Andromeda lifted her hand, and Caramyl stopped dead in her tracks, looking confused.

“Andromeda please, calm down.” Uwayn's smile was warm and genuine. “I know this must all be very difficult for you, but we love you. You're our Ward, there's no one we care more about.”

He no longer looked like the faerie lord that had raised her from childhood. Both of them, the closest thing she had to parents, were no longer familiar faces. Even though they were all she had known her entire life. Suddenly they were alien creatures, strangers, beings she would never have anything in common with.

“All these years, why did you lie to me?”

“We didn't” Caramyl insisted.

“It's Aglain who is the liar here,” said Uwayn.

“I don't believe you any more,” Andromeda decided. Once again she turned around and ran off, into the bowels of the palace.

If the Court of Sidhe had followed no logic on the outside, its vast interior was even worse. Andromeda ran down a spiral staircase around and upward-flowing column of water, past a rapidly spinning cherry tree, and through a tunnel made of gnarled vines twisting past each other.

Birds with insect wings and shining carapaces extracted nectar from trumpet-shaped flowers in a round greenhouse. The closer she walked toward the centre, where a liquid statue danced elegantly, the darker her surroundings became, and the plants began to glow with their own light.

She sat down on a stone bench by the foot of the dancing figure, breathing heavily. Her heart was beating fast. Could she believe anyone any more? Could she even trust herself? One voice in her mind told her that Uwayn and Caramyl loved her, like they always had. Another told her that she had no choice but to stay with them, because they were the only ones that would have her.

Other voices trusted Aglain, feeling a deep connection to the man. He was, after all, her father, a bond which transcended space and time. But did it really, or was that just another of Uwayn's lies?

Something stirred inside her. It was a feeling, nothing she heard or saw, just something she knew. They were coming for her. Uwayn's guards were nearby, and headed for this very garden. In a few moments they would enter through the door to her left, and the only way to escape was if she went right. She didn't question it. Even in all the uncertainty, she trusted this new sense of hers.

Bowls with various tinctures in them floated around a long corridor. Sometimes they would collide, break apart, and mix into two entirely different new bowls. A column of light carried her upward, depositing her gently on a marble balcony. A group of courtiers were drinking wine out of baubles in the next room, giving her strange looks but otherwise leaving her in peace.

It was in a garden where the trees were made of granite that she finally came to rest. The stars above were framed by the walls and towers of the palace. The air was cool. This must be very high up. The silence made her feel truly alone, as she wanted to be right this moment.

Why had Lord Ristkarr come here to support her father? What was his stake in all of this?

“Jealousy.” The voice was a cold whisper. Lady Ekmeid's dress shone pale blue in the moonlight. Her black skin seemed almost translucent. The veil over her face wallowed in a gust of wind.

“How did you sneak up on me?” Andromeda asked. Already she felt betrayed by her alleged faerie detection sense.

“I am powerful in subtle ways, Andromeda. But to answer your question, Ritskarr is working with your father out of jealousy. The spark of magic that you have? The King and Queen must have sensed it when they awarded you. He did not mind it at the time, but now that he knows, he thinks that you should have been awarded to us.”

“Why?” She knew Lord Ristkarr was proud, but this seemed plain arrogant.

“The Lords of the Wild Hunt opposed the Sidhe for a long

time. My husband risked much by siding with the King and Queen. The fact that the most powerful Firstborn in many decades was awarded to a middling lord insults him, but he will never oppose the Sidhe directly. Ritskarr may be impulsive, but he has never picked a fight he knew he couldn't win."

"Why are you telling me all these things? Aren't you betraying your husband?"

Lady Ekmeid coughed. It took Andromeda a moment to realise that this had actually been a laugh. "I can't change anything. I merely want you to be aware that you are not the agent of your own fate. Nobody is. Everything is driven by an external force, even the King and Queen do not make their own decisions. It doesn't matter if you want to be with your father, Uwayn, or somewhere else entirely. Somewhere in the future, that decision has already been made."

Andromeda said nothing. Somehow she had expected that knowing more about the situation at hand would help her in some way. Instead it had made everything more complicated. She stared at the motionless Lady Ekmeid. "What do I do?" she finally asked.

"Sleep here. Nobody will come for you. Tomorrow, the proceedings will take place. Whatever you decide to do, it has already been written."

The throne room was tense. Courtiers peered at Andromeda as they held hushed conversations. She moved along the pews and tables, all eyes following her. Uwayn and Caramyl looked at her from a booth that had been erected on the dais, eyes filled with sorrow and relief.

Another booth had been erected on the opposite side. Her father was in it, wearing heavy shackles of rune-emblazoned iron. Lord Ritskarr sat behind him, without Lady Ekmeid. She was sitting in the front row.

A centaur guard directed Andromeda to a third booth, where she would be sitting perpendicular to the King and Queen. Their four eyes looked at her without expression as she took her seat. These proceedings may have been about her, but she had no say in them.

"We open the proceedings regarding Ward Andromeda, considering the request of her father, Magus Aglain, as supported by Lord Ritskarr," their dual voice spoke. *"Magus Aglain, you are free to make your case."*

Her father rose, giving Andromeda a solemn look. For a moment he was quiet, as if wanting to give the entire room time to focus their attention on him. "Your Majesties, I am aware that my case is a weak one. Instead of making an argument, I would like to yield this time to the good Lord Ristkarr."

Gasps, frowns, cries of indignation. Andromeda did not know what the courtiers had expected, but it must have not been this.

As Aglain sat down, Ritskarr rose. "Your Majesties, as a Lord of the Wild Hunt I call to the accord the Court of Sidhe has with those of my creed. I hereby invoke the ancient right of trial by combat."

Uproar in the crowd. Some of the courtiers rose and shouted abuse at Ritskarr for invoking such an archaic practice, others laughed at him, whereas even others demanded he be stripped of his titles, knowing that not even the King and Queen were capable of such a thing.

"Trial by combat as per the Wild Hunt Accord is permitted only between Lords of the Wild Hunt!" Uwayn protested.

Andromeda bobbed her leg up and down. None of this made sense, and it most definitely was not right. She cleared her throat, unsure what she would even say, but nobody paid any attention to her.

"Your objection is upheld, Lord Uwayn. A trial by combat will not happen if both parties do not agree to it," the King and Queen decided.

"We expressly do not agree to it," Uwayn emphasized. Caramyl tapped him on the shoulder, whispering something in his ear. He simply shook his head, giving his own whispered response.

"What sacrifice would you require to interpret the Wild Hunt Accord in a way that is favourable to Lord Ritskarr's case?" Aglain asked.

"And grant legal hegemony to those savages?" Uwayn

roared. "How *dare* you insult the Court of Sidhe? Your Majesties, I request this man be punished for his lack of respect."

"No, stop!" Andromeda heard herself say. "Stop fighting over me, I don't want any of this!" This was all going horribly awry. Yes, Uwayn and Caramyl may have lied to her, or it could have been her father, but there was no reason for anyone to die over her.

Nobody paid any attention to her shouting.

"No sacrifice you would be willing to make would persuade us in this way, Magus Aglain," the King and Queen said.

"You'd be surprised how much a father would sacrifice for his daughter, Your Majesties. I would be willing to lay down my very life. I would let you absorb my vital essence." There was laughter.

She rose, screaming. "Stop this right now, I want to say something!" Once again, nobody paid attention to her. Her voice sounded distorted even to herself, not echoing as much as it should have in this cavernous hall. Something invisible was surrounding her booth like a mantle of silence.

"You would die immediately from such a sacrifice, Magus Aglain, with no ability to have Ward Andromeda as a daughter in the human tradition."

"Then I would bequeath her upon Lord Ristkarr as a Ward instead, that he may help her become the powerful wizard she is meant to be."

That could not be right. It was the opposite of everything he'd asked for, which meant that he must have been lying from the start. He was not a loving father, and it had never been his intention to take Andromeda back. But then, why was he willing to sacrifice himself?

Andromeda pushed against the force surrounding her, screaming at the top of her lungs for everything to stop. The weave of the silence spell gave in ever so slightly, but not enough to break. It was powerful, and Andromeda had no way of estimating just how powerful, not to mention what the best way was to break it, if it could be broken at all.

"Your Majesties, this is clearly a ploy! There is no

precedent for this!" Lord Uwayn complained.

The King and Queen nodded, their four eyes inspecting Andromeda's father. *"Your sacrifice is granted. In exchange, Lord Ritskarr shall receive his right to trial by combat."*

In spite of Uwayn's objections, it all began immediately. The King and Queen raised their left hand, and strands of light began emanating from Aglain's body.

Andromeda had to stop this. This was insanity, and there was no way she would be a part of it. She pushed even harder, feeling the strain of the spell as it tightened around her. Something inside her flared up, a blazing spark, the magical power of her soul. The same cold, unpleasant tingle as when Uwayn took her power washed over her, but this time she was the one controlling it.

The stream of vital essence leaving Aglain's body became broader and brighter. His body began sinking, and the smile on his face became broader and broader. Sparks of his essence darted around the King and Queen's arm.

Andromeda's power built, her fingertips sparkling with energy. When she felt like she was about to lose consciousness, she pushed again, and the spell ripped apart, shattered, and collapsed all at the same time. A wave of blue force washed over everyone in the throne room, pushing back some of the courtiers closest to her.

But it was too late. The stream of Aglain's essence had already slowed to a trickle, and what had been a man in his prime only moments earlier was now a decrepit old mummy. Her father was dead.

Then everything happened at once.

The King and Queen looked down at Aglain's body, confused, then dazed. For the first time, their face made an expression, and it was one of abject horror.

A cool wind rushed through the throne room, bringing autumn leaves and the sound of clacking hooves. A blood-churning screech came from the door, and a cavalcade of faerie lords rode in on elks and reindeer. The Wild Hunt had arrived.

Ritskarr darted from his position behind the dead Aglain, a sword of frozen iron casting billows of frost in his hand. In one leap, he reached all across the dais and sliced at Uwayn, who was busy staring at the King and Queen.

A blade of gleaming copper blocked the sword's path. Lady Caramyl parried the strike with her right, and immediately retaliated with the blade she had in her left. Ristkarr jumped back, evading her blow, and assumed a defensive stance.

Andromeda stood there, unsure what to do. A moment ago, everyone had been staring at her. Now it was pandemonium. Nobody knew what to do, but everybody was doing something.

The Wild Hunt cavalry had decapitated half the centaur guards before they could mount anything resembling a defence. The pale riders used sickles made of bone that cut through the gleaming plate like it was made of butter.

A handful of courtiers implored the King and Queen to do something, but Their Majesties were melting. Still caught in shock and surprise, their flesh liquefied, began sliding off their bones. The crown of iron and silver set fire to their scalp.

Ristkarr and Caramyl danced around each other with force and grace. She was a whirlwind of singing copper, he a vortex of cold iron. Every time she almost struck a blow, Ritskarr disappeared into a cloud of dead leaves, only to strike at her back a fraction of a moment later. Caramyl always parried with her off hand.

Andromeda looked for Lady Ekmeid, but she was nowhere to be seen. She did, however, see Ristkarr's ogres, armed to the teeth, charging for Lady Caramyl. She knew what she had to do, even though she was not certain how to do it.

She jumped, tapping into her vital essence, and landed right in the path of the confused ogres. Not the least bit discouraged, their leader laughed at her and charged with a rusty blade. Before she knew it, Andromeda had parried it with her hand. The ogre could not fathom what he'd just witnessed. She punched him in the chest, a soft glow emanating from her fist. He stumbled backward, gasping, then fell, and began to burn.

Behind her, Andromeda could hear the clang of metal on metal as Ristkarr and Caramyl continued their duel. For a moment she considered picking up the dead ogre's sword, but remembered that she had no idea how to handle a blade.

The ogres did not give her any more time to deliberate. All at once, they attacked, swords crashing down on her with cries for blood. Andromeda knew she could not parry them all. Instead, she simply walked through her attackers. It was as easy as passing through a doorway. One moment she was material, then she was a shadow, and then back to being flesh and blood again.

Before the ogres could turn back around to her, she clapped, and they were blasted in all directions by a gust of wind. One of them almost hit Ritskarr, who evaded at the last moment, leaving an opening that that Caramyl exploited without mercy. Her onslaught would have cut anyone else to pieces, but Ritskarr was a formidable opponent. She drove him back several paces, but did not land a single blow.

Andromeda wanted to intervene, but something else caught her attention. On the dais, sitting on the thorny throne, watching the spectacle with poised interest, was none other than her father. Aglain Finnegal had the crown on his head, but it did not burn like it had the King and Queen of Sidhe. It simply rested there, radiating authority.

Lord Uwayn was shouting at him, but he didn't seem to care.

A scream and a ripping sound turned her eyes back to the duel. Ritskarr had, in one arcing motion, cut open Caramyl from navel to throat. One of her blades was stuck in his shoulder, the other in his leg, but the life was flowing out of Caramyl, and that was all that mattered.

"No!" Andromeda and Uwayn screamed in unison.

Her father snapped his fingers, and Lord Uwayn burst into flames. Another snap, and all the centaur guards fell over, dead. Whatever defence they had mounted against the Wild Hunt was broken, and courtiers were being slaughtered left and right.

Andromeda stood there, motionless, empty, uncertain. She'd been too late. Her indecision had paralysed her. Now the only people she'd ever loved were dead.

Lord Ritskarr pulled Caramyl's blades from his body and looked at Aglain, still sitting on the throne like nothing of note was happening around him. He removed the crown from his head and tossed it at Ritskarr's feet. "Your end of the bargain," he said.

Ritskarr brought his blade down, and it smashed into a thousand pieces. “Never again shall the Wild Hunt be ruled by a crown of iron and silver,” he declared. There were shouts of approval.

“But you will be ruled by a king made of flesh,” Aglain added, a sardonic grin on his face.

“What?” Ritskarr stared at Aglain in disbelief, raising his blade.

“Please, Ritskarr, you knew this was coming. I have absorbed the power of the King and Queen of Sidhe. You are faerie. You can't hurt me. This is why you needed me to kill them.”

“You were supposed to take their power and leave. That was your reward,” Ritskarr growled.

“And then what? Return to Earth with its petty squabbles and crumbling empires? I'd much rather rule over the greatest realm there ever was.”

In the silence that followed, Andromeda made her decision. Ritskarr had killed Lady Caramyl, but she knew who had really been pulling the strings. She knew who was responsible, and it enraged her. She felt power surging inside her, blazing embers that burst into a mighty bonfire, consuming her, giving her power.

“Father,” She simply said.

“Yes, child?” Aglain's eyes were cold, devoid of any fatherly affection.

“Die.”

All the power left her body at once. Andromeda felt like her skin was burning, and her insides were being ripped apart. A single strike of lightning burst forth from her, and hit Aglain Finnegal in the chest. This man had taken everything from her, and he deserved to be destroyed.

As her father screamed in a fountain of white flame, Andromeda collapsed onto the ground. She looked down on herself, finding that her skin was wrinkled, and the joints of her fingers thick with gout. She was suddenly old, and so very tired.

Letting herself go on the steps to the dais, she could spotted Lady Ekmeid standing in the upper gallery, looking down at her. Even though she could not see through the veil, she knew that she was smiling.

The Merchant of Wishes

By Gwydion JMF Weber

Vilim had seen the Outside before. He'd even seen it from the Command Bridge, on that beautiful day when his class of officer cadets had visited it. He'd even talked to the Captain, the man in charge of making sure the Lumberer stayed its course. It had been more stammering on his part, so awestruck was he that the Captain would actually exchange a few words with him.

Right now, deep below, beneath the creaking struts, jumping coils, singing cables, pumping levers, and turning cogs, Vilim could see the ground itself, the surface the Lumberer walked on to escape the Great Fire. There was nothing in between him and the Outside but moving parts. Not even a sheet of glass separated him from it, only distance. If Vilim fell off the narrow beam of steel he was standing on, he would fall right out of the belly of the Lumberer, and be smashed on the ice-covered rocks below.

It was terrifying and fascinating at the same time. Nothing was supposed to fall out of the Lumberer. Only the most unusable of garbage, waste materials recycled a hundred times, were dumped to be consumed by the Great Fire. Anything that had any use at all remained aboard.

If Vilim were to fall, the waste would be unfathomable. He was a young man, healthy and able-bodied, clever and of steady hand. Many resources had been used to train him, more than almost everyone else. He was a junior officer, an Assistant Underchief, proud of his red uniform and the respect it commanded. It was made of the smoothest, most insulating fabrics. Only the wealthiest could get clothes this comfortable. Even if Vilim could be spared, his uniform could not.

A giant pendulum swung by him only an arm's length

away. Two Clambermen, who had been holding on to its handle, jumped off to a crooked beam above Vilim's head. They were shorter than regular people, and covered in rust-coloured fur. Clambermen could only be found down here in the belly of the Lumberer. Most people didn't even know they existed.

After stopping for a moment to glance at Vilim, they leaped, grabbed hold of a thick cable, and climbed away into the darkness. They understood everything about repairing machines, but were too dull to understand that Vilim should not have been here.

"I did not think you would actually come." The voice was that of an old man, or possibly woman, marred by decades of chimney smoke. Vilim stumbled backward, almost falling off and into the Outside. A figure emerged behind a tank that he was sure nobody had been behind when he passed it earlier.

The Merchant of Wishes was large, much taller than Vilim, even bent over the way he was. Clad in a tattered coat of brown wool, his body and face were shrouded in darkness that not even the dim lantern he was holding in his hand could penetrate. His bare, ashen-white feet were larger than Vilim's head.

"Are you him?" Vilim asked. He knew this could be no one else, but he just had to be sure.

"Him who?" the Merchant of Wishes responded. "If by him you mean the man who will take your aspirations and turn them into something immediate, then him you have found."

"What is your name?" Vilim asked, not because he wanted to know, but because he suddenly didn't know what to say. The Merchant of Wishes was supposed to be a story, a last resort he had turned to in his desperation. He had already declared himself insane for interpreting the series of metallic beats he'd received in response to his own hammering onto the bedroom wall as a message. The fact that it had been real was more than a little unexpected.

"My name?" The Merchant of Wishes chuckled. "I could sell it to you for a price you would be unable to pay. Only a child of the Lumberer could make such a ridiculous suggestion."

Vilim was confused. There was no-one outside the Lumberer, so wasn't everyone a child of the Lumberer? "I want to become a Bridge Officer. I was third best in my class, but I was assigned to the Foundry instead."

"Foundry Officers are well respected, are they not? The Foundry Marshal is the second most powerful man aboard the Lumberer," The Merchant of Wishes said.

"But I want to be the Captain. When I was a boy, I had a dream that I would be Captain, and that dream needs to come true," Vilim insisted.

"So your real wish is not to become a Bridge Officer, but to become Captain. There is a difference, you know. Any officer can become Captain, such is the law. There have been Captains in the past who were Foundry Officers," the Merchant offered.

"That has not happened in over a hundred years," Vilim protested. "It will never happen to me!"

"I see." The Merchant of Wishes scratched his own chest. It sounded like metal bolts scraping over sandpaper. "What are you willing to trade for that wish?"

Vilim paused. He knew such a question was bound to come up, but he simply couldn't imagine what the Merchant of Wishes could desire. "Anything," he simply said, hoping that the Merchant would specify.

"Well that's a bit much," he said. "Say I make you Captain tomorrow, and in fifty years, when you are old a withered, a day away from your own death, I tell you to turn the Lumberer around and walk it into the Great Fire. Would you do that?"

If he was going to die anyway, and this would have given him the Captaincy for an entire lifetime, wasn't it worth it? It would be terrible for sure, but Vilim would no longer be alive for that. "Yes, I would do anything."

The Merchant of Wishes nodded. "It is as I thought, then." He lifted his lamp, and fingered around its bottom. It began emitting a bright, green light, blinding Vilim for a moment. He fell backward, onto the cold steel of the beam.

"Many young men set on becoming Captain choose the path of the Bridge Officer. Some become desperate, and ask me to help them." The Merchant of Wishes stepped closer.

It was as though a thousand needles pricked out from beneath his skin, boring through it like seedlings through dirt.

Vilim pulled back his sleeve to find that his arm was now covered in rust-red fur.

"You certainly are one of these men, but you do not have what it takes to be a Captain."

Vilim's back hurt. It was as though he was being pressed forward. Standing up was torturous, and took excruciating effort. At the same time, the twilight of the Lumberer's belly became bright, and its vastness apparent. The sheer extent of it, the intricacy, the beauty of all the machines working together.

And suddenly, he could comprehend them. Not just the individual pieces of this puzzle, but the whole, and the position of every cog in it. Every lever turned, every cable pulled, every flywheel spun, he understood how it all fit together, how it all *worked*.

"The Lumberer deserves better than you," the giant standing in front of Vilim said. For a moment, he understood the words, but then it was like waking up from a dream, and they became little more than sounds.

He heard the whistling of a pipe, not louder, yet somehow more prominent than all the other sounds around. If pressure was not released soon, the pipe would burst, and a chain reaction would begin that could lead to the breakdown of the entire machine. With great urgency, he jumped downward onto a turning lever, then over to a shaking gangway, heading for the right valve to turn.

Free-For-All

By Gwydion JMF Weber

The Chelmsford Riverside Free-For-All was one of the oldest Gunbrawl events in the country. It had never been as large as the Walworth Carnagefest or as exclusive as the Warport on Portsmouth, but it had seen a steady string of good fights for almost three decades.

Lano had always wanted to go, but with it being in the Outer District Belt of the Greater London Area, it was a bit of a hassle to get to, and something always came up that prompted him to stay down in Croydon. Not this year. This year was special.

"Any news about him?" he asked.

"Nothing. There's a post about going on a trip, I suppose," Mycah responded.

"Obviously. That was up three hours ago." Lano looked at the small crowds of players walking through the city centre. Tags were popping up over their heads, colour-coded and framed according to the prestige levels associated with them.

Some obvious players had not turned theirs one yet, so they were not showing up in the Aug, and if Peregrine did show up, chances are he would be using a throwaway tag. Open Deathmatches like Chelmsford could be wild, and everybody would be gunning for him anyway.

"You sure he was gonna show up today?" Mycah asked, his left eye glazed orange as he was looking at media feeds.

"Well, that was the rumour," Lano responded.

"There's three days of games, six games a day," Mycah noted. "I can't afford eighteen tickets."

“You don't have to. Maybe we'll meet him down in the street.” Lano was hopeful. Peregrine was the best player in all of Britain, uncontested, and number 3 on DorothyGaruda's Top 10 International Gunbrawl Pros list. The only people better than him in the entire world were MunGan, captain of the Shenzen Shamans, and Kalefurrnia, who was just a freak of nature. Just last week, he'd taken Yhläinen by surprise with a flipshot. Nobody had ever taken Ylhäinen by surprise. Ever.

“First game starts in an hour,” said Mycah. “You wanna grab a bite to eat before we get in there?”

Lano shrugged. “Yeh.” Maybe they would run into Peregrine at the café.

He slotted in the burnchip. This was amazing. Lano had the fifth-highest kill count of anyone in the game right now. Mycah was on number 12. If Peregrine was watching this game, he'd be reading Lano's *real* tag right now. Peering over the barricade, he saw a tiny camera drone hovering above the converted parking lot, lens on him. Maybe Peregrine was actually *seeing* him right now.

There was a whole group of players behind a wrecked car, just protected enough from Lano so that he couldn't hit them, but they could take potshots at him. The moment one of them scored a kill on him, they would immediately turn on each other. Lano was determined not to let it come to that.

Holding his breath, he targeted a mirror right behind the players camping him. His bright red, full auto *Loyalist* was equipped with bouncer rounds, and the burnchip he'd just slotted in would quadruple his rate of fire when activated. He'd also picked up a blue slidewall earlier, which could pas through solid objects, and combined it with a yellow one, which could bend. If he wanted to pull this off, timing would be crucial.

As the players, unsuspecting of anything, continued taking opportunistic shots and missing, Lano carefully shaped the green slidewall with his fingers, then flicked it over, its vague outlines flying across the parking lot and through the car. Just when it was past, he turned it on. The virtual semicircle stopped and became visible to the campers. When they realised what was about to happen, it was already too late.

Lano clicked on the burnchip and fired on the mirror. His bouncer rounds were reflected and shot right into the slidewall. In 2 seconds, he'd fired 200 rounds, all of which were low damage, but now bouncing back and forth inside the slidewall, hitting the campers again and again.

The tags above their heads went grey, little skulls appearing to either side of them. Shouting angrily, they stormed off to get rezzpacks. Lano would probably be seeing them later. He threw a wink at the camera drone. Granmer's Crookpot was a legendary move of emergent gameplay invented by one of Peregrine's legendary idols.

Lano had climbed to second place in the rankings, but that didn't matter. Even if Peregrine hadn't been watching thus far, now he was surely paying attention.

Quickly scanning his surroundings, Lano advanced underneath the passing road, toward the Lidl. There had once been a time where no company would even touch Gunbrawl with five metre pincers. Now they had closed the store and decorated it like a post-apocalyptic wasteland for the event.

Movement out of the corner of his eye. Lano spun and pulled the trigger, not even thinking. A guy in an almost retro-futuristic black trenchcoat recoiled as his name tag turned grey. He carried a *Lombovozh-47*. Lano laughed as he pointed at the gun. This guy was a joker, not really interested in winning, but trotting out his meme rifle.

At first, Lano thought the guy was laughing with him. He pointed the muzzle of the *Lombovozh* at his chest and pulled the trigger. Because he was dead, no bullets came out. Or at least that was what should have happened.

There was a flash, different than the virtual effect Lano was used to. Three punches to his chest, and suddenly his vision was blurred. Lano stumbled backward, feeling his legs give out from under him. What was happening?

"DI Kaczmarek, this is my colleague DI Williams." Greg held up his badge before the two local bobbies.

The tallest of them nodded and opened the way. All of

them were on high alert, carrying light submachine guns. "Sergeant Davies is waiting for you," the bobby said, pointing to a lanky man in blue briefs and with an imprinted neon shirt shouting orders at uniformed officers.

"Must have not been on duty," Rich noted as they jogged over to him.

"You think?" said Greg.

Davies turned to them just before Greg would have said something to get his attention. "Rapid Profiling?" he simply asked.

"That's us." said Rich.

"Thank fuck you're here, this shit is getting out of hand." Davies pointed in the vague direction of the city. "Shooter is still at large, seventeen dead, another twenty-six injured. We got three TFU's standing by, but the cunt just slipped away. We need a profile immediately."

"Not how that works, mate," Rich informed. "We got male, early twenties, black trenchcoat. He was using a *Lombovozh-47*, which is weird."

"Why?" asked Davies.

"Because it's a terrible gun. It's bulky, and though it abides by all the rules so you could play it in any game format, nobody does," Greg explained. "It was fashioned after the AK-47, design-wise."

"I thought these thing weren't supposed to shoot bullets!" Davies complained.

"They're not even guns, they're computers. The muzzles are closed, there's no firing mechanisms in there, no bullets, just circuitry and sensors. It's all virtual." Greg pointed at the gun of a teenage boy lying dead on his back in front of the Lidl. SOCO was swarming all over him.

"I fucking know it's all virtual. I want to know how the fuck he got a real fucking gun into a fucking AR shooting event," Davies spat.

"He's good with technology, that's for sure. Probably a machining hobby of some kind, and access to some high-class 3d printers," said Rich. "Because the *Lombovozh* is so big, I could imagine someone converting it into a gun. The question is how they spoofed the signal to get it on the battlefield."

"This is definitely someone with liberal access to university faculties," Greg decided. "High intelligence and education, obviously asocial, probably reclusive and engaged with action cinema from the early century, maybe fascinated with American massacres. He had a bad time at school and hoped uni would be better, but it wasn't. He does like it more than school though, otherwise he would have attacked there."

"Where are you getting all this from?" asked Davies.

"He wore a black trenchcoat," said Rich.

Greg pulled up the known route of the shooter across the battlefield. He'd spent the first ten minutes of the game just wandering, using a different weapon, one that actually functioned for Gunbrawl. He'd been at the bottom of the field, using the throwaway tag *GrimmestReaper667*. Definitely a retro edgelord.

"There hasn't been a mass shooting in England since 2022," said Davies before turning his attention back to his officers.

"There's a technical college in Writtle, maybe he's headed there," said Rich.

"No, school theory." Greg snapped his fingers. "Cross-reference student databases. Local area, victim of bullying, tech student, interested in retro cinema, offensive and sometimes ironically self-deprecating sense of humour." After a few seconds of processing, several stacks of images with files appeared before Greg's eyes. "Obviously limit by age range, currently late teens, early twenties, white, possibly mixed race." That narrowed it down to three.

"It's that one," said Rich, who was sharing his Aug workspace. He was pointing at Henry Treanor, a twenty-year-old born and raised in Chelmsford. His slim facial features did not match with the game footage.

"Looks completely different." Greg shook his head.

"That can be altered, easily. Biometric cameras have been consistently fooled for years now, and when you run around like that, people assume it's a costume, so if anybody notices the plastic applications on your face, they won't think it's suspicious," Rich pointed out.

“Could be, but why him specifically?” Greg gestured over to the profiles of Nox Fauver and Tyrion Emin. “These other two could have altered their features just as well.”

“Sure, but Emin is obviously from a nerdy household, so he would have gotten validation from his parents if he had been an outcast in school, and Fauver is just too tall.” Rich shrugged. “I'm not excluding either of them definitively, but if I had to bet, and I do, then I'd say it's Treanor.”

Greg pressed Henry Treanor's image to unfold his full profile. He was indeed enrolled at the technical college in neighbouring Writtle, and his usual Gunbrawl tag was *LordOfDeath*, which was no less edgy than *GrimmestReaper667*. “Sergeant Davies, the shooter will be heading for Great Baddow High School. You should at least send one TFU there.”

“It's fucking Saturday evening!” Davies roared. “No fucking school on Saturdays! Or evenings!”

Greg opened the file on the high school, and navigated to the itinerary. “Theatre club's putting on Hamlet right now,” he informed Davies. A note popped up. The system had discovered that Henry Treanor had been part of the drama club during his time at Great Baddow, but only the first year. “Good find,” he said to the soulless algorithm.

“Yeah, he's definitely going back to school,” Rich agreed.

The TFUs had already encircled Great Baddow High School when Greg and Rich arrived with Sergeant Davies. They had been given firearms and ballistic vests, and were holding back between the heavily armed tactical units approaching the theatre building over an open field.

Scout drones hovered above their heads and between school buildings, outlined in their Aug, but camouflaged for everyone else. A minimap was displayed in the lower-left corner of their field of vision, and a translucent isometric floor plan was overlayed on the buildings.

“Reception area clear, no sign of MCA,” somebody said over TacVoice.

“If you fucked this profile up and the cunt is shooting up some other place in town...” Sergeant Davies mumbled so quietly only Greg and Rich could hear it.

"I'm confident he's gonna be here," said Rich. "The profile is-"

Shots, bullets whirring through the air over their heads. Greg felt a gust of wind as something passed by his face. The sod next to his foot blew up as it was struck.

"Get down, down, down!" The TFU leader shouted.

Greg fell flat on the ground, gun in hand, looking into where he believed the bullets had come from. There was a treeline with two clearings. One of them had several police vehicles parked in it. It had been their entry point onto school property. The other was a few houses away, poorly lit, and an excellent vantage point.

There was a figure moving in the trees. A man wearing a trenchcoat. Greg fired once, twice, and the man jerked away behind a tree.

"Hold fire!" Sergeant Davies roared. "Those are civilian residences you twat!"

A cold shower ran over Greg's back. They were ten officers, lying in an open field, against a single shooter in good cover that they were not allowed to shoot at. The fact that he just had might even cost him his job.

Rich howled. He was writhing on the ground, holding his leg. "He got me! The bloody fucker got me!" A dark pool was rapidly spreading out from his thigh.

One of the TFU officers jumped over Greg and lay down next to Rich. "Hold still," he demanded. "Keep pressure on the wound," he then instructed.

"What is it?" asked Greg.

"Hit the femoral artery," was the response.

"We need immediate medical assistance!" Greg shouted into TacVoice. "Officer down!"

"Belay!" said Davies, then looked at Greg. "We're alone out here. Nobody can cross that space without getting shot by that madman."

The TFU deployed two ballistic shields in front of Rich, and Greg rolled over the ground to be covered by them.

"He'll die in a minute! Look at the blood!" The pool was

spreading at an alarming rate.

"This is a trap," whispered Rich. "He was never interested in the theatre group, he wanted us."

Greg nodded. He was making the connections in his own head now.

"What the fuck are you on about," Davies hissed.

"His obsession with the early century, possibly the nineties also. Mass shootings were common back then, but were always eventually stopped by police. He wanted to one-up them," Greg explained.

Shots clanked against the ballistic shields.

"Team Three will be in position in 90 seconds. They'll have a clear shot," The TFU leader said.

"Rich is fucking bleeding out! He'll be dead by then!" Greg aimed at the shooter, but Davies slammed his wrists into the ground.

"Fucking stop! No civilian casualties!"

The TFU medic was working fast to apply a compress, but bullets kept zipping by his head.

"Will he make it?" Greg asked.

There was no response.

"Fuck this." Greg jumped up and ran. He sprinted diagonally to the line of fire. Whatever weapon the shooter had improvised, it seemed to be no better then spray-n-pray. Rich had been an unlucky shot. There would be no second unlucky shot.

Blades of grass were flung in his face as the sod around him was ravaged. Davies roared behind him, but he did not understand a word of what the sergeant was saying. A hot pain cut across his shoulder blade. There was no impact, only a slice. He might have been hit, he might not. Greg did not care. He kept on running.

A tree. He pressed his back against it, breathing heavily. Pain ran through his shoulder, but it was manageable. Or maybe it wasn't. There was a lot of adrenaline in his system, so did it really matter?

The next step would be crucial. The shooter had the rifle aimed at the tree, but was not firing. He was standing twenty metres away, by a tree of his own, his line of fire funnelled over a pedestrian path. Depending on which side Greg emerged from, he might be dead in a second.

But Rich was bleeding out on that field. He had to do something.

Greg screamed. Bullets flew past the right side of the tree. He emerged from the left, firing repeatedly at the assailant. The trenchcoat winced in pain as he collapsed. His rifle clattered on the ground. Greg put three more rounds in him, just to be sure.

"MCA is down, I repeat, MCA is down," he said into TacVoice.

Without waiting for confirmation, paramedics rushed across the open field toward the TFU. The shooter was dead, and Rich was going to make it.

"You're a fucking madman, Kaczmarek," Sergeant Davies said. He did not sound angry, but genuinely impressed. "This might cost you your badge, but you're a legend in my book."

Greg collapsed against the tree, panting. He dropped his gun in the grass, and looked down the road. Paramedics rushed to him, examined his shoulder. As the adrenaline receded, it all became a blur.

The Flying Bus

By Gwydion JMF Weber

Some people thought flying a bus was an easy job. It was anything but. The engines weren't even the problem. They were heavy-duty American craftsmanship, powerful as dragons and precise as a surgeon's scalpel. Horace couldn't recall a single delay to his commands, and they took even the harshest hairpins and emergency reversals without so much as a wince. It wasn't the gravity mesh either, though that one did provide difficulties for some cadets. Smiling, Horace remembered overdriving the energy input on his first training flight, making the mesh howl beneath his feet, and the wings strain under the sudden upward force. These days handling it was second nature to him. The mesh was as responsive as the engines, if not more so.

No, the real issue with flying a bus was the people. His father had driven passengers around at the ground level back in his heyday, and he had some crazy stories to tell. None of them compared to the strange occurrences Horace witnessed every week. There was something about being trapped in a metal box high up in the sky that made people go mad. It didn't happen on large planes, as far as he could tell, and Horace believed that it had to do with the confinement. Planes were large enough for cocktail bars and swimming pools. In a bus, people had seats. That was it.

He was on Hyston Plateau, waiting for passengers to leave as others boarded. Horace loved these skyscraper platforms – they were easy to land on and depart from, and they had ticket boys handling the passengers. Things always went smooth up here. It was a group of businessmen that caught his eye. Laid back, laughing, clad in expensive suits, carrying suitcases. Most of them had salt-and-pepper hair, though there were a few silver foxes among them. They looked unreal, like actors from a movie, not the exhausted office drones he shipped across the skies every day. They were executives, cream of the crop, wealthy enough to employ their of chauffeurs. Why they were taking the bus, Horace could only guess.

The chaos began when they opened a bottle of champagne. Drinking a few drops on the bus was no problem, but popping a cork in a tin can was dangerous business.

"Gentlemen, please contain yourselves. Don't throw things on the bus," he spoke into the intercom. A dismissive "Yeah, yeah," was all he got in response, but they didn't pop any more corks. Of course, they only had one bottle of champagne with them, so they couldn't have done it again if they wanted to.

Things went messy again after Horace took off from South Garden Square, where a group of young, attractive girls joined them. College students, from the look of them, and dressed in the promiscuous manner the youngsters of today had chosen to rebel with. Modest, compared to the mint of people Horace encountered during his night shifts. The executives caught sight of them immediately, lions locking onto a herd of gazelles. At first it was some jokes, a few naughty compliments. The girls were giggling, enjoying the attention. Horace had better things to do. The spaces in this section of Midtown were narrow, and always crowded at this hour of the afternoon. He passed beneath a suspension bridge stretched between two buildings, part of the skybridge network for pedestrians and automobiles. A long-range triple decker bus and a taxi bird passed too close below him. Shaking his head, Horace looked in the mirror to see the executives crowding the girls. This wasn't anything unusual per se, but the students did look a little uncomfortable at the older men's physical advances.

Horace decided to let it rest for now. He wasn't out of Midtown yet, and the next stop required him to slot into the middle of a skyscraper. It wasn't difficult, but it required concentration. After he landed, some people got out, others got it, but both the girls and the suits stayed. Halfway to the next stop, one of the students shouted "Stop it!" at one of the silver foxes, and it wasn't the playful kind of rejection.

"You never been with an older man before?" the executive said in response. "I got money, and I know how to show you a good time. Experience and all that." His friends laughed.

"Is everything OK back there?" asked Horace through the intercom.

"Yeah, bus boy! Everything is fine, get back to flying!" the executive yelled.

"Actually, I feel very uncomfortable back here, Sir," the girl who had just been accosted said. "I've asked them to go away, but they wont listen."

"Gentlemen, please do leave those young ladies alone," Horace demanded.

"Or what?" asked the senior executive, getting to his feet. Cockiness on his face, he walked up to the cockpit. "What are you gonna do? Kick us off the bus?"

"Sir, if you don't calm down and return to your seat, that is what I'll have to do," Horace responded, keeping an eye on the airspace in front of him.

"Why don't we throw you out instead?" the executive said. His friends had come to the front now, and Horace had to slightly rebalance the mesh to accommodate for the sudden shift in weight. "Ya hear me, bus boy? Why don't you leave? We own your company, after all."

Horace shook his head, frowning. "Buses are owned by the city. You don't like like politicians to me."

The executives broke out into laughter. "No, you dumbass, they don't any more. We signed the deal three hours ago, you boys are getting privatised! And we get to be your owners. Why do you think we're even on this shitbird in the first place?"

Horace shook his head with confusion. "Gentlemen, please do sit down, or I will be forced to perform an emergency landing to remove you from the bus, which will result in a fine for you."

They laughed again. This clearly hadn't been their first bottle of champagne that day. Horace noted in the corner of his eye that one of them had stepped a little too close to the door, but he was too focused in navigating to do anything about it.

"First order of business," the lead executive said, "you're fired, and seeing as you're on the bus without a ticket, I'll have to ask you to step off the vehicle."

Horace had no idea how the junior executive knew how to perform a mid-flight emergency door-opening, but he did, and the doors opened. Reflexively, Horace hit the "close doors" button, but it did not work, as was intended.

"Come on, step off," the senior executive said. "I wont repeat myself." There was a click, followed by silence. Horace turned to see a gun in the man's hand. "Come on, bus boy. You know how to fly."

His friends had stopped laughing the moment the executive pulled the firearm. They looked a bit nervous now, unsure if following their ringleader was such a good idea, but unwilling to break from the group. Horace slowed the bus. The emergency lights were already blinking, signalling to other pilots that something was wrong.

"Are you sure this is a good idea, Roy?" One of the younger executives asked.

"You wanna jump out with him, Glover," was the response. "You're a weakling, that's why you're never gonna go anywhere on your own. Be glad I pulled you up this far."

Horace spoke slowly, trying to stay calm. "Please, Sir, put down the weapon. You do not know how to operate this vehicle."

There was a twitch of doubt on the man's face, his rational mind pointing out the stupidity of what he was currently doing. Instead of backing off, he decided to double down. "You wanna test me, asshole? I'll figure it out. Can't be that difficult if you can do it." He held the gun closer the Horace's back. "Come on now, get up, bus boy."

His next moves would be crucial, Horace knew. He was in a lower air lane, going slow. Other vehicles were giving him a wide berth. He rose, stepped aside, still facing forward, and slowly turned sideways toward the door.

"Yeah, that's my bus boy. Now get down there."

Horace moved forward, turned mid-step, spun away, and grabbed the man's hand. A shot discharged. The window shattered. The executive had a shocked expression on his face as Horace ripped his gun away and punched him in the mouth. He fell backwards, into the other executives, who moved around in a panic, pushing each other away. One of them screamed. It was the junior who opened the door. He had fallen out, and was holding onto the bottom step with one hand. His screams of terror would haunt Horace for the rest of his life.

"Hold him down!" Horace commanded the other executives, referring to their pack leader, and jumped down to the door to grab a hold of the man's arm. It was too late. He slipped off before Horace could grab a hold of him, his howls of terror disappearing into the chasm of skyscrapers. Horace had no time for shock. With the presence of mind of a veteran soldier, he undid the security lock, jumped back into the driver's seat, and closed the door. The old executive's gun sat on the dashboard, sliding back and forth, but kept inside by the small gap between it and the blown-out window. Horace grabbed it as he accelerated and found a place for his emergency landing.

"Fuck! Let go of me!" the senior executive shouted behind him as he presumably realised how much he'd just destroyed his own life.

Horace set the bus down gently on the terrace of a highrise, keeping the mesh running to reduce the vehicle's weight. The police arrived soon after, and arrested the executive. The other passengers were evacuated onto another emergency bus. As Horace lifted off to fly his own vehicle to the depot, he was unsure if what had just happened was real or not.

He was not fired after all.

Licensed Sales

By Gwydion JMF Weber

The lone stall bobbed up and down as the pontoon was hit by the bow wave of a cargo superliner passing in the distance. The tiny bottles lining the shelves clinked together, but the lights inside them remained undisturbed. They came in all colours, hues, and shapes. A dancing flame of robin blue stood between a cylinder of faintly glowing olive smoke, and a bright, scarlet orb bouncing frantically in its vial.

Siobhan sat in her plastic folding chair, grey hair bound together in a ponytail, back aching. A tiny stereo next to the register was playing Irish folk music, barely loud enough to be heard over the creaking of the float. Beyond the skyscrapers of the city centre, the last rosy-orange rim of sunlight was becoming thinner and thinner.

She turned around, looking at the open ocean, speckled with congregations of small boats, drifting pontoons, and several cruise ships straddling the horizon. "There's a storm coming in," she said, looking at Cliff.

The young man, who was leaning against a streetlight, stopped playing with his straight razor. He wore faded jeans, a frayed shirt, and a rotting leather jacket. His lips were pierced together with a small padlock. He gave Siobhan a solemn nod and began extending the tarpaulin to protect the wares.

A figure emerged from the shadows down the street. Most people would have noticed his distinctive apparel, but even from far away, Siobhan recognised him by his sagacious eyes. He wore an old-fashioned black suit and a top hat. The gold chain of his pocket watch gleamed in the lantern light, and his walking stick clacked rhythmically upon the ground.

"Doctor Nagata," Siobhan greeted when the man approached her stall. "We haven't seen you here in a while."

"My dear Siobhan, you look younger and more beautiful than ever." Nagata gave her a smile and a slight bow. "Have you been perusing your own wares?"

Siobhan giggled, letting him believe that his flattery was having any effect. "We don't carry *that* kind of soul," she lied. "You never know if they come from legitimate sources."

"They so rarely do," Doctor Nagata agreed. "I've come here dead-set on spending my money, so what do you have for me?"

"That depends on what you need. We have a middle-aged father of six who died in a car crash last week," Siobhan said.

The sentence wasn't even finished when Cliff was already getting the right bottle from the shelf and handed it to Nagata. Inside was a heavy, grey fog that filled only the lower half of the vial. A dense patch of what looked like a coiled worm clung to the bottom.

"Worn-out and depressed," Nagata observed. "I can't give this to my patients, not if I want to cure them."

Siobhan forced herself to smile. She knew full-well that his "patients" were not always looking to be fixed. He had purchased souls in a much worse state from her before. "This is a young woman, some would describe her as a social butterfly. Died of a drug overdose, poor thing, but it's made her more invigorating."

Cliff handed the doctor a vial containing a cyclone of pink lightning bolts flashing through a light rose mist.

Nagata inspected it with a wistful look, then gave it back immediately. "I'm sorry, Siobhan, but I really cannot engage in our usual dance tonight. Time is pressing."

The hair on Siobhan's back rose. She scanned her surroundings, looking for something out of the ordinary. Men were laughing and drinking beer on a fishing cutter moving slowly toward the port nearby, a vagrant was peering over the roof of a nearby warehouse, and a late-night delivery van was passing by on the road.

"If only you told me what you were looking for, Doctor, then I could provide it," she said carefully. She didn't know what, but something was wrong.

Cliff seemed to notice her agitation, touching the pocket of his jacket where the straight razor was stowed.

Doctor Nagata seemed fully at ease. "I suppose I do want to do a *little* bit of dancing," he admitted. "I have a lot of money, and not a lot of space to carry things home in."

That made Siobhan even more nervous. Nagata was the opposite of acerbic on the best of days, but today it sounded like he was deliberately avoiding being forthright about something.

The fishing boat was not speeding up, and it would take a while to pass them by. The vagrant on the roof was still watching. The delivery driver had not returned to his van.

"There's a schizophrenic woman on offer. She lived at the clinic, passed from a heart attack about a month ago," she said carefully, to see if Nagata would decline.

In the bottle Cliff took off the shelf, several small spheres of different colours were orbiting a diaphanous filament of bright light, prodding it with little shocks. He didn't even have to hand it to Nagata before Siobhan's suspicions were confirmed.

"No, thank you, but that is not the kind of soul I am looking for."

"In that case, I don't think I can help you." Siobhan threw her hands up apologetically. She knew exactly what he wanted, but she was no fool. Unless he asked for it specifically, she would not give it to him.

A crack appeared in Nagata's mask. He looked over to the fishing boat, a nervous flash in his eyes. The vessel was now passing by the stall, and was slowing down ever so slightly. "Siobhan, my dear, we have known each other for a long time..." he began.

"Not long enough for me to be able to read your thoughts, good Doctor." Siobhan smiled, but they both knew it was over.

There was a moment of loaded silence. Cliff swallowed audibly, the padlock on his lips flashing in the light.

The delivery van was first. Its doors swung open with force, and half a dozen men in black uniforms jumped out, pistols pointed at Siobhan and her stall. The vagrant on the roof suddenly had a sniper rifle, and positioned himself visibly. Last came the fishing cutter, doing a sharp turn toward the pontoon and spilling another half dozen officers onto it.

"I'm sorry, Siobhan, my dear, but they caught me." Nagata bowed. His forehead was almost touching his knees. "I had to cooperate. My family cannot be without a father."

"Traitorious pig," Siobhan hissed, raising her hands and getting up from her chair slowly.

One of the officers stepped forward. He wore a long coat and an inspector's cap. "Show us the contraband!" he shouted, pointing at Cliff.

"Sir, I am sorry, but I do not know what you are talking about." Siobhan accentuated each word.

"Don't lie to me, ghostmonger! Where's the key?" The officer demanded.

"I wouldn't know. Do you mean the key to my flat? My car? My register?" Siobhan did not move a muscle.

Frustrated, the inspector came around the counter. "Step back!" he commanded, pointing for Siobhan and Cliff to go to different corners of the stall. He pressed the button that would open the cash register, and pulled the whole drawer out as far as possible with much more force than was necessary.

A surly expression on his face, he rummaged through the hodgepodge of coins, caps, cards, bills, and gems for a few seconds before victoriously holding up a small key. "There you are," he whispered.

Cliff's jaw trembled. The young man's eyes were gaining a sadistic gleam, and his arms were dropping slowly.

Siobhan stared at him so hard that he looked over, and the murder in his eyes was replaced by fear. If he snapped now, it wouldn't end well for him, and he knew it.

The inspector walked over to Cliff and grabbed his jaw with a vicelike grip. Carefully, he inserted the key into the padlock, turned it, and removed it from Cliff's lips. "Open your mouth," he demanded.

The young man obliged, hesitantly, and the officer inspected him with a small flashlight.

After a few moments, he turned it off, and looked at Siobhan with blank hatred. “It's empty,” he finally said. Gesticulating, he turned around to the rest of his squad. “I said it's *empty*! This is over, everybody go back to your stations.” With a final glance at Siobhan, he added “one day, ghostmonger, I will get you.”

It took a mere minute for the officers to vacate the pontoon, slinking off with lowered heads. Siobhan gave Cliff a careful look. “We need to close up shop,” she said. “That was a psychotic murderer you just swallowed, and we need to get him out of you before he takes over.”

Cliff nodded, sweat running down his face. His eyelid was twitching with homicidal rage. Hopefully they would make it in time.

Seeing Shadows

By Gwydion JMF Weber

Everyone was out. From his narrow balcony, Andrej could see at least a hundred souls wandering through the night, their bodies an ever-shifting but always humanoid mass of shadow. Looking down, he saw the street below glowing. No wonder the souls wouldn't stay in the ground. To them, the rooftops and fire escapes had to be a fresh breeze in the desert.

Andrej peered across the street, spotting his neighbour Jegor at his window, smoking a cigarette. Souls crowded the apartment behind him, surrounding the piano, where Jegor's wife was serenading them with Rachmaninov. Andrej gave his neighbour a nod, and Jegor greeted back, a broad grin on his face. As the spirits were entranced by the music, he was sapping their essence with one of his strange contraptions. It looked like a blend between a vacuum cleaner and an electric kettle. The old man would make a good buck on the black market.

The smell from below was a mixture of gasoline, rosemary, and rain. Andrej quite enjoyed it, though with how frequent the streets were glowing these past few weeks, it was wearing out its momentousness. He wondered what caused the souls to rise from the ground so often this summer. The world wasn't much more troubled than ever, no major changes had affected the city, and there was nothing significant going on. He'd been taught that the streets always glowed most in times of great stress or impending doom, but it seemed as though that was an old wives' tale. Come to think of it, his grandmother had taught him that.

Perched atop the roof of Jegor's building, Andrej spotted a

soul that stood out to him. The dark shape was squatting next to an old satellite dish, looking at him. It was strange indeed, unusual to the point of being unsettling. Normally one would have trouble grabbing the attention of a spirit for more than a moment. Yet there it was, its features shifting ever so slightly under the light smog, observing Andrej as though he were some great work of art. He did work at a museum, and he knew how crowded with souls its halls had to be right now. Maybe some of whatever spiritual pheromones made great works of art so attractive had stuck to him today. Andrej stepped inside to make himself a cup of tea.

When he came back out again, there were three souls standing on that rooftop. They were all looking at him, it was unmistakeable. Andrej glanced behind himself, above and below, into adjacent windows. They were all dark. The occupants were either not home, or asleep. There was an ounce of fear in his stomach. He looked over to Jegor, who was blissfully ignorant of the strange events taking place above his head. If Andrej shouted across the street to ask for help, the spirits listening to Jegor's wife play might disperse, and the old man would become angry. It was out of the question.

Andrej scanned the rest of the neighbourhood. It seemed as though the spirits on Jegor's roof were not the only ones watching him. All around, small crowds of black haze had gathered, staring at him. What in God's name was the matter? Why was he so interesting all of a sudden? He flinched when one of the souls began its approach. It was a young girl, walking along the phone line between Jegor's building and his, sure-footed as an equilibrist. Panic rose in him. This was too much.

Shaking, he retreated into his flat, closing the balcony door, and completing the hermetic seal that protected his home. No soul would enter here, and when the sun dispersed their nebulous figures in the morning, he would go over and ask Jegor if he knew what this meant. With trembling hands, he set down his cup of tea, only to almost jump out of his skin again when he saw a small notecard on his counter top. The word “Hello” was printed on it in cursive letters. A frown on his face, Andrej picked it up and turned it around. “I'm hoping the police will go public after this one." it said.

Frightened, Andrej spun around, only to stare into the face of a pig. A cheap plastic mask, burning mania peering through its eyeholes, was only centimetres from his face. He didn't even feel the razor slash his throat. Only when a torrent of warm liquid started flowing from it did he begin to understand how he'd just been killed. His murderer took a step back as he fell over, going to his knees to look into Andrej's eyes as he bled out. This could not happen again. He had to follow this person, warn their next victim.

Clutching his throat, Andrej sat on an air conditioning unit. A nurse had just returned from the late shift, and was hanging up her coat. The streets were glowing. He had to warn her.

Franz Josef Land

By Gwydion JMF Weber

Snow crunched under Erik's polar boots. His heavy breath condensing in the frigid air, he trudged down the slope, following the young Russian. The night sky was alight with aurora borealis, projecting eerie shadows onto the white blanket covering Graham Bell Island. No wonder the Russians were seeing things that weren't real.

"Right here, over there," young Kostja said. He had climbed atop a cylinder of poured concrete, and was pointing to a spot near the frozen shore. It would have been impossible to make out where land ended and ocean began under the ice and snow, but a projection of the island's shoreline was visible in bright red on Erik's retina.

"Right over there is where you saw … a wolf?" Erik asked.

Kostja shook his head. "Ghost wolf, not real wolf. It stand there and disappear, like smoke taken away by wind."

"Just one?" Erik zoomed in on the spot by grabbing the edges of the area he wanted to see and mimicking a pulling motion. There were no paw prints. Unsurprising, considering that there were no wolves on this island, or anything else larger than a bird, really, and even those had left for the winter.

"Yes, one," Kostja insisted.

"Don't wolves normally hunt in packs?" Erik asked.

"Maybe ghost wolf don't." Kostja shrugged, as though that had been an unreasonable question.

Erik tapped the upper edge of his field of vision, returning it to normal. "Or, maybe, there is no such thing as a ghost wolf." He heard the ringing of an old telephone in his ear. He held up his hand to shut Kostja up before he could respond, and picked up the call. "This is Osberg."

The clean-shaven visage of Sigmund Lied appeared in a little window in the lower left corner of his vision. He was comfortably sitting in the corporate offices in Tromsø, a big, steaming mug sitting next to him on the desk. *"Hoy, how are things up there?"* he asked.

"As usual," Erik responded. "The Russians are superstitious. Now they think they are seeing ghost wolves."

"Those islands do things to your mind, I tell you." Sigmund Lied took a sip from his cup, then shook his head. *"You should have put in for Svalbard."*

"I like it here," Erik responded. "What is it?"

"You have an emergency landing coming in. Cargo plane, don't want to fly into the blizzard," Lied explained.

"I have a ship coming in tonight. Everyone is working on unfreezing the dock. If I put them on the airfield, the Japanese will not be happy," lamented Erik.

"The plane is equipped for arctic operations," Sigmund insisted. *"All you have to do is compress the snow."*

Erik shook his head. "We weren't supposed to see a plane for another month."

"And now you'll have one landing in three hours. Isn't that exciting?" Sigmund reclined in his chair. *"This is a very important client, and they're paying a lot for this blunder in their planning. They're going to be landing no matter what, all you have to do is make sure they do not die on the process."*

Erik sighed. "When the Japanese are angry tomorrow, I will tell their captain that you are responsible," he decided.

"Feel free," Sigmund responded, smiling. *"Now please excuse me, I have other calls to make."*

Erik hung up, and looked at Kostja. "Come, we need to wake the night shift. There is emergency work to be done."

"What about ghost wolf?" Kostja asked.

"Has it attacked anyone?" Erik gestured to the spot where the young Russian claimed to have seen the animal.

"No," the young may responded.

"Well then we have nothing to fear from it."

Three hours later, the plane was already beginning its final descent when the last compressor rolled off the airfield. The night shift had not taken well to being woken so early, and only the promise of triple hourly pay had blunted their anger. Erik had also given them a bottle of peppermint vodka from his personal storage, which they were indulging in downstairs.

He was standing in the traffic control tower, looking back and forth between the assortment of screens and the white landing strip illuminated by floodlights. Clouds had darkened the aurora borealis, and brought the kind of light but chaotic snowfall that was usually the harbinger of a particularly nasty blizzard.

The plane set down with a trudge in the distance. As it approached, Erik could see that it was a beast of a machine, its unpainted hull shining like chrome, and the four airjets on each wing glowing orange with heat. Sigmund had not been joking when he said that it was optimised for arctic operations. Those things would melt in warmer climates.

It rolled onto the taxiway, around the control tower, and onto the somewhat sheltered parking space of the logistics complex. It was so large that even the three-story building only reached up to half its size. The wings almost stretched over the entire lot.

A hatch opened beneath the cockpit, and a ladder was dropped out of it. Two black-clad figures climbed down onto the snow-covered tarmac, shook hands with a member of the ground crew, and moved toward the building. Behind them, the ladder was pulled up, and the hatch closed.

Jazz music was playing in the guest lounge. Posters of tropical landscapes hung on the walls, and the heated floor allowed for barefoot walking. A short, blond woman was sitting in an armchair, stretching her legs. There was no sign of the other person she had come in with.

"Hello, Miss Fredric," Erik said, her sparse visitor information displayed on his retina. She paid well, but also liked to keep her privacy, it seemed.

"Ah, you must be the station manager!" The woman jumped to her feet, a warm smile on her face. She spoke with a refined English accent, the kind one heard almost exclusively in movies. “Your colleague warned us that you would want a word. Martha Fredric, pleasure to meet you.”

Erik shook her hand. “Erik Osberg, just here to check if everything is okay.”

“Oh it's really quite good. Nice place you built up here.” She nodded over to the posters. “Add some ocean sounds and the escapism would be complete.”

“Some people don't like it,” Erik admitted. “You don't work the Arctic trade routes if you are not a fan of snow and ice.” He waited for a moment, unsure of how to say what he wanted to say. There were unspoken rules and protocols for the denizens of the Arctic, and he was confused as to why the owner this particular plane would be unfamiliar with them. “So listen, we have a lot of rooms here, and it is recommended that you get the rest of your crew from the plane to spend the night in safety.”

“Oh everyone's here,” a rough, voice with a musical Irish accent declared. It belonged to a tall man with grey hair and a thick moustache. He looked to be in his fifties, but in excellent shape. Cups of tea steamed in his hands.

“You two pilot this plane alone? Without extra crew I mean?” Erik asked.

“I pilot it,” Martha Fredric informed. “This is Clive O'Banyon, he does logistics and security.” She took one of the cups off the old man.

“You want some tea, Mister Osberg?” Clive O'Banyon asked. “It's exceptional Earl Grey. Brought it myself.”

“No, thank you, and please do call me Erik.” He gave them a smile. “Well, if it really is only you two, I am sorry for interrupting and will leave you to enjoy your time off.”

“Oh it's really no imposition,” said Martha Fredric.

“And do feel free to change your mind about the tea,” Clive O'Banyon added.

“He is crazy in the head, what am I supposed to say?” Vladimir said. He was the foreman of the station's night shift, and the main reason Erik had gotten them motivated to fix up the runway at all.

"Well, he's the fifth man to see this ghost wolf in five days," Erik explained. "It has to have some meaning, maybe in Russian folklore." They were sitting in the crew kitchen. The other members of the night shift were in the adjacent mess room, singing and eating cured ham sandwiches to make sure the vodka did not get to their heads before work.

"Look, Russians, we are a very superstitious people," Vladimir explained. "Especially the young generation, they all believe in spirits and all that shit."

"But why a ghost wolf?"

Vladimir shrugged. "I'm not superstitious, how should I know?"

"Well there seems to be some sort of collective hallucination happening with our men here, and I want to get to the bottom of it before it turns out to be something problematic." Erik took a loaf of bread out of the box and began cutting some off.

"Our men? I do not recall anyone from the night shift having seen any ghost wolves," Vladimir insisted. "Seems to me you should maybe tell the other foremen to stick to vodka when they take something against the cold, no?"

It was the middle of the night when an urgent knock on his door dragged Erik from a dreamless sleep. "You must wake! Vladimir say you must come!" Kotsja's voice was dulled, but loud.

"What's wrong?"

"*Yaponski* ship drive into dock!" Kostja sounded extremely agitated.

"They what?" Erik asked, unsure if he had understood correctly.

"They drive into dock, but not slow. Crash!" Kostja explained.

Erik sat upright in bed. He slipped on the tactile glove on his night stand, and projected a camera feed onto his retina. "I'll be out in ten seconds."

The scene was even worse in person than it had been on

the feed. The wedge-shaped Japanese icebreaker had lodged itself into the main pier, breaking the concrete structure in half with its reinforced black bow. There was an oblong hole in the starboard side, plastic crates and cardboard boxes spilling out of it, bobbing up and down in the freezing water. A boarding ramp had been extended onto the tilted deck, but it was entirely deserted.

Vladimir was standing next to the ramp, shouting orders in Russian, barely capable of overpowering the frigid wind. His normally grey woollen jacket was almost white with snow. The blizzard was already uncomfortable, but it would get much worse before it got better.

"What happened?" Erik shouted as he approached, Kostja in tow.

Vladimir angrily gestured toward the Japanese ship. "We hailed them on the water, they hailed back, then they break off all communication. I think *blyat*, something must be wrong, but they will fix it. Then I get a call from control tower, they say the ship is coming in too fast and is not decelerating." He drove his fingertips quickly toward his upheld palm. "A minute later we can see them, and they have not stopped. I call the tower again, they tell me there has been no response and no slowing down. Because I have a bad feeling, I tell the crew to get off the dock. Next thing I know, crack!"

"Were they drifting, or did they have the engines on?" Erik asked.

Vladimir shook his head. "Engines sounded like they turned off during collision, but it's impossible to tell with this *cyka* wind."

"Did you board?" Erik asked. It was protocol in such situations to board as quickly as possible in case there was an emergency on board that required assistance.

Vladimir nodded, a grim look on his face. "You should come see this."

A minute later, Erik, Kostja, and Vladimir were standing in the command bridge of the Japanese freighter. It was not elevated on a superstructure, but instead located on the gently sloping upper deck that could be accessed from the external deck.

Like all of the new Japanese Arctic vessels, this one could also function as a submersible.

Lying on the black linoleum floor between high tech screens and navigational equipment, were half a dozen Japanese, their faces perfect snapshots of pure horror. Their blue company uniforms were as torn as their flesh, steam rising up from their still warm blood spreading across the ground.

"What the hell." Erik stood at the edge of the dark pool, staring at the dead crew. "What happened here?"

"They look like they were mauled," Vladimir said matter-of-factly.

"Mauled by what? Were they carrying any wildlife?" Erik scratched his beard. "Is that even legal?"

"Cargo manifest says computers, phones, coffee makers, graphene sheets, and dried fish. Also some priority mail."

"I mean what kind of animal could even do something like this?" Erik asked.

"I don't know," Vladimir responded. "A bear, maybe? Somehow a polar bear got on board?"

"There hasn't been a polar bear sighted in three years," Erik protested. "And how would it get aboard this ship?"

Kostja murmured softly in Russian. "It was wolf. Ghost wolf!" he exclaimed, crossing himself.

Vladimir said something that did not sound particularly friendly in Russian, and Kostja responded, his voice shaking with fear. Then he ran out, screaming.

"Runs like a girl, that one." Vladimir shook his head.

"We best get out of here and start a proper search with weapons. If the bear is still in here, I don't want anyone else killed," Erik decided.

"We should probably also issue a warning for the whole complex, in case it escaped," Vladimir added.

"Good thinking," Erik said, trying not to think about the fact that he might be ordering the death of the very last polar bear on Earth.

Inside the base, things were tense. Though there were only a few people still up, mostly Russian station crew drinking vodka at the bar, Kostja seemed to have ignited an oil field. All except for the hardy men of Vladimir's night shift looked terrified, even if they tried to hide it. They actually believed that a ghostly wolf was roaming the island. A polar bear was bad enough, there was no need to add the supernatural to the mix.

Erik picked six men from the night shift, Vladimir included, and lead them downstairs, into the storage basement. Thin sheets of firn lay on the concrete floor of the hallway. Their breath condensed in the air. It was the kind of wet, inclement cold that penetrated to the bone in a way not even a blizzard could.

They stepped through a puddle as they walked past the heat pumping station, and finally arrived at a heavy door decorated with warning signs. Erik typed in a six-digit code and pressed his thumb on the print scanner. An off-tone klaxon resounded, and the door opened automatically.

Inside were enough weapons and protective gear to outfit a small platoon. Most were relics from decades ago, when the Ice Cold War had been in danger of heating up at all times, and every nation with Arctic interests was ready to defend their assets at a moment's notice. The Treaty of Auckland had put an end to that, but the weapons remained.

Erik handed out compact assault rifles, kevlar vests, and protectors for arms and shins. All of the equipment was adapted for use in the coldest of conditions. The guns had battery-heated barrels that could never freeze over, and the protective gear had latches wide enough to be strapped over a dozen layers of clothing.

Everyone with a retinal screen had software that could block out the noise of heavy snowfall, and they synced their feeds to the night- and heat-vision attachments on their rifles.

When the group came back upstairs, Clive O'Banyon was standing by the basement door. He was wearing a black sweater and cargo pants, and a hunting knife was strapped to his belt. Despite the late hour, there was no hint of drowsiness in his eyes. “It said employees only, so I thought I'd wait here,” he said, pointing at the sign next to the basement stairwell.

“Clive, I am sorry, but now is really not a good time,” Erik apologised. “You should go to your room and lock the door.”

The Irishman grinned. “I heard. *Ursus maritimus*, eh? I might be able to help with that.”

Erik shook his head. “Please, you are a paying customer, and it is my job to keep you safe from any potential danger.”

“Nonsense! We're all stuck on this station together, Erik. That means we all need to work together, too.” He tapped his hunting knife. “Twenty years ago, I was working with a team of scientists tasked with tagging and extracting DNA samples from all remaining polar bear specimens, in case they went extinct. It was dangerous work, but I can proudly declare myself to be somewhat of an expert on this particular creature.”

Erik considered his options for a moment. Clive looked competent enough, and he remembered reading something about an operation like this in his high school newspaper. It was common practice to this day to catalogue the DNA of disappearing species and store it in various gene vaults, so they could be resurrected in the future in case of total extinction.“Alright, follow me, I will give you weapons and armour.”

“No need, I have my own.” He pointed upward. “What kind of drones do you have?”

“Drones do not fly in these weather conditions,” Vladimir interjected.

“You don't have the right kind of drones, then.” Clive laughed, as though this situation was in any way amusing. “Luckily for you, I do.”

Even in the storm, the ladder to Martha Fredric's plane was surprisingly easy to climb. There had to be some hydraulics system in it, as it seemed unimpressed by the wind and the weight of the three men holding on to it.

Clive lead Erik and Vladimir into a small cabin, where the ladder was attached to a roll-up winch. A winding stairwell lead upstairs, into a roomy cockpit and radar room. Though the equipment was state of the art, everything was encased in chrome and wood, with leather seats and ancient lamps. If he hadn't known any better, Erik would have considered this a set for some kind of 1950es-revival adventuring film.

"Don't touch that door, please," Clive warned, not looking up from the console he was manning. "It is actually dangerous."

Vladimir was standing next to a heavily secured compartment door. Erik counted a whopping six latches and three separate locks.

"What is behind it?" Vladimir asked.

"Paying customer stuff." Clive spoke with humour, but insistently.

Before Erik could feel uncomfortable with the situation, a slight rumble went through the plane, and six video feeds appeared on a formerly black screen above Clive's head.

"I'll be sending an integration request to your control tower so they can keep an eye on things," the Irishman explained. "Should make the search a lot easier."

Through the feeds, Erik could see the drones hovering above the plane. They were heavy, battleship grey beasts of burden, probably larger than he was, and held upright by six propellers with blades the size his leg.

Clive opened a locker next to the secured door, and began putting on his own gear. It was far beyond anything Erik had in the weapons locker. A full-body Arctic ops combat suit, kevlar and graphene woven into its padding. The snow camo pattern shifted slowly around it in a seemingly random fashion, and Erik suspected it was capable of much more than that.

"What are you, some kind of mercenary?" Vladimir asked, a frown the size of Galdhøpiggen on his forehead.

Clive put on snow goggles, smiling. "Used to be. The good kind." A green light flashed in the corner of the goggles. They were obviously high tech, equipped with all number of functions and resolutions that Erik did not even want to think about. The Irishman put on a white beanie and pulled up his collar. "Shall we?"

Rationally, he could have sworn that it was only the wind, but Erik was sure that there had been an excited rattling on the other side of the door.

There was no bear to be found on the Japanese freighter, only more dead crew. One had been mauled as he walked down a hallway, two others in their bunks, and another in the bathroom. The various cargo holds were full to the brim, with no space for the storage of any large critters. Erik could not imagine a reason why anyone would want to smuggle a polar bear through the Arctic, and the fact that the world had not gone entirely mad gave him some peace of mind. It did, however, mean that the polar bear was somewhere on Graham Bell Island, and that caused all kind of concern.

"This bear is quite the surgeon," said Clive O'Banyon. He seemed remarkably light-hearted in the face of the scenery.

"How do you mean?" Erik asked.

"There's no paw prints anywhere. With these pools of blood you would expect at least a few. These cuts are eerily precise. It went straight for the neck, and then just left the bodies." Clive knelt down to the Japanese crewman lying on the bathroom floor. His jaw had been torn off, and his head was holding on to his body only by the spine. "Must have been a young bear, too. There's no good dental profile on these corpses, but the mouth is small for a polar bear."

"Please do not say wolf, I will shoot you in the face," Vladimir warned.

Clive laughed. "Don't be so confident you could pull the trigger faster than I could disarm you, mate. Now that you say it though, this may well have been an Arctic Wolf."

"There are no wolves in Franz Josef Land, least of all Graham Bell Island," Erik protested. "Have you been listening to the Russian sailors, Clive?"

"I'm afraid I don't even speak Russian, Erik," Clive responded.

"Some of us are very good at English," Vladimir noted.

"What do you find more difficult to believe? That a giant, not to mention extinct, bear climbed into this ship and killed everybody with surgical precision, or that a slim and cunning wolf, which has been seeing recovering populations throughout Siberia, did it?" asked Clive.

"If you put it like that..." Erik conceded. "But still, how would it have gotten here? And why would it be alone? And why would there be no paw prints?"

Clive shrugged. "I don't know, but we will have to find out, won't we?"

In accordance with the evidence, and a general lack of bear paw prints discovered by Clive's drones, which still seemed unimpressed by the increasingly violent blizzard, Erik lowered the alarm level slightly. To his irritation, the Russians found the idea of a wolf scarier than that of any polar bear, especially considering that there had been no wolf prints either, which Erik attributed to the fact that they would have been much smaller and more difficult to detect, possibly even filled in with fresh snow shortly after they were made. However, at this point, even the night shift was convinced of the existence of a ghost wolf.

An armed perimeter had been required for the workers to place graphene-lined cushions underneath the Japanese freighter and secure it to the dock. It was now no longer sinking, and could not be dragged out by wind or tide, but would remain there until summer, when it could be safely salvaged. So far, the Russians had refused to touch the bodies. If this persisted, Erik and Vladimir would have to move them into storage themselves. It was not about protecting them from the elements, but basic human dignity.

The blizzard had remained consistently annoying, but not too dangerous. According to the weather centre on Svalbard, this was about to change. They had been ordered to bunker down and get ready for a bad storm hitting them very soon. No emergency rescue operations could be mounted under these conditions.

The shutters of all windows had been closed, even the armoured ones at the control tower, and leaving the safety of the base interior required authorisation by a foreman for the crew, and Erik himself for everyone else.

He was finishing up his report for Sigmund Lied when Martha Fredric knocked on the door of his office.

"Ah, Martha." Erik smiled. "Are you here for your drones? I imagine you'd want them safely back aboard your plane before the brunt of the blizzard hits."

She shook her head, waving his words away. "Nonsense. Those dears can take much worse, and when the blizzard does become too much, they will descend and hunker down in the snow until conditions are clearer. I designed them myself, so I cam confident that they will work."

"Well we certainly appreciate them. They are very helpful for seeing dangerous weather approaching." Erik pushed aside the keyboard. "What can I do for you?"

Martha sat down in a chair, giving him a sharp, critical gaze. After a moment she said "I'm here to talk about your wolf problem."

"There is really not much we can do about it at this point in time, I am afraid." Erik was not about to put his crew in danger. "When the blizzard clears, we will search. Until then, it is not going anywhere. Frankly, I expect it to die in the storm."

Martha Fredric shook her head. "When the blizzard clears, everyone in this station will be dead."

"Excuse me?"

"Tell me, Erik, have you, or the people who work for you, seen anything strange over the past few days?" Martha asked. "Apparitions? Sounds? Sudden onset paranoia maybe?"

"Are you messing with me?" Erik asked.

"Quite the opposite. Clive was messing with you when he played games instead of being upfront about what is really going on here, and it's not a quality I appreciate in him." She slapped the armrests of her chair. "I've already talked to your crewmen, and what they describe is unanimous. You're dealing with a Lupus Spectre, an individual, for the moment."

"What do you mean 'for the moment'?" Erik asked. "And what the hell is a Lupus Spectre?" The woman sounded as crazy as Kostja.

"Lupus Spectres live inside blizzards. What your men saw was an outrider, a scout for the pack. He will already have made his report to the alpha. When this blizzard arrives, they will descend upon this station and feast like kings," Martha explained, keeping a straight face through all of it.

"You are not joking, are you? You really believe this." Erik leaned back in his chair, stroking his beard.

"As much as I love comedy, this is no joking matter. Lupus Spectres are dangerous creatures. The few cultures that have historically resided beyond the Arctic Circle know to fear the wolf as a harbinger of death, but we Westerners have only begun setting up shop here recently, and while blizzards were once extremely rare around these parts, now they are a frequent occurrence."

"You are talking about wolves living *inside* of a *storm*." Erik frowned. "That is crazy."

Martha shook her head. "Not wolves, spectres. They only look like wolves. Do not underestimate their intelligence, they may be primal beings without much in the way of sapience, but they are just as clever as humans."

"That makes it sound even less believable," Erik noted.

Martha sighed. "I seem to have misjudged you. You're not quite as sceptical a mind as I had hoped."

"I am very sceptical, especially of the supernatural." Erik could not help but feel a little offended.

"You've seen what the Lupus Spectre did to the crew of the Japanese vessel. Can you really believe that an actual wolf somehow found its solitary way up here from Arkhangelsk, over the unreliable ice, snuck aboard that ship, and killed everyone strategically?" Martha tapped on the armrest. "The Japanese rely on their trans-Arctic shipping routes remaining open all year, no matter what happens. That is why their ships are hermetically sealed submersibles. You may remember this, but some years ago, a Japanese freighter was en route to Dublin when Faroese pirates boarded it. Or at least they tried."

Erik nodded. He had indeed read about this in the news.

"They could not get inside the ship, and remained stuck on the exterior deck. Lockpicks, blowtorches, even explosives could do nothing but scratch the paint. The captain never even had to activate any special lockdown protocols. Eventually the pirates gave up and left."

"What does that have to do with our situation?" Erik asked.

"Do you not see? Only a being that is entirely unimpaired by walls could enter a Japanese freighter while it is in motion. And the walls of this base will not keep it or its pack out either."

"But why kill the Japanese sailors? They were going to

stay at the base anyway, it could have done this later. Vladimir said they were communicating just minutes before the crash," Erik pointed out.

Martha sighed again. "These are alien beings, Erik. I do not proclaim to have a full understanding of their psychology, but this is in line with how they have operated in the past. I have empathy with the idea that the questioning of your rationalistic world view is making you reach for straws, but now is neither the time nor the place."

"Why did it not attack you, then?" Erik was feeling a strange mix of amusement and fear that what this woman was saying might actually be correct. "They live in blizzards, they can clearly fly."

"We have methods. Our plane is not penetrable to them, and the scout would not have risked an attack so close to the base," Martha explained. "I know this sounds crazy and you do not believe me, but it is imperative that you at least trust me."

"So we put everyone on your plane, yes?" Erik was angry. "Then you lock us in there, take over the base, and demand a ransom from the company."

Martha took a deep breath, frustration clear on her face. "The plane does not have enough space for everyone. Not even close. It's large, but also quite full."

Erik paused. That put a hole in his theory, which had already failed to explain the deaths on the Japanese ship. "Say I believed you, which I do not, but if I did, what would you want me to do?"

An hour later, Erik was outside, wrapped in six layers of his thickest clothes. The blizzard had gone from grey seal to killer whale faster than he'd ever seen, and the frigid wind bombarded him with splinters of ice through the tiniest cracks in his armour.

Bending against the storm, Clive was ramming the last of six metal-and-plastic poles into the snow. Following right behind him, Martha was running three copper wires between the new pole and the last one. They formed a cage around Erik that was roughly the size of his office, and could easily be escaped by slipping through the wires. The side between the two poles that faced away from the base remained open.

"And this will hold it?" Erik asked. He was unwilling to admit to himself that he did believe Martha, at least a little bit. The things that had transpired were just too weird to be normal.

"I don't know, we've never done this before," Clive responded. The blizzard was too loud to allow for anything but shouting matches, so his voice was relayed through the speakers in Erik's ear warmers.

"We have done this before, and it does work," Martha reassured him.

Clive cackled quietly as he knelt down to stabilise the pole with a snow pile.

"As terrifying as they are, Spectres are easily frightened. That's why most kinds no longer exist: Humans drove them to extinction." Martha fastened the wires to the pole with quick, practised movements. The gloves seemed to be no hindrance at all. *"If we manage to kill their scout, the rest of the pack will avoid this place like a leper colony."*

"But if they are so intelligent, will they not see this trap for what it is?" Erik asked.

"They may be intelligent, but they are still driven by instinct," Clive explained. *"We just need to give the scout something that is irresistible."*

"You are planning to use me as bait." Erik had known from the beginning. If someone was needed in that role, it would have to be him. He was the manager of this station, and it was his job to protect its crew and guests. He would have allowed no other volunteers.

"It's going to be a little more difficult than standing around in here." Martha began running a wire from the top of the final pole and across the cage to the one opposite it. *"I assume you know how to move through a blizzard relatively safely."*

"The best way to that it is by staying inside," Erik said dryly.

Clive laughed. *"You're getting the hang of this."*

As Martha continued wiring up the top of the cage, Clive produced a black bag from inside his coat. Without warning, he popped it open, and threw the contents at Erik. A dark liquid that smelled of iron drenched his jacket, and it took him a moment to realise what it was.

"The smell of human blood will drive the Lupus Spectre mad," Clive explained.

"This is *human* blood?" Erik was terrified and disgusted at the same time.

"Don't worry, it's mine," said Martha.

Steam was rising from the black patches on Erik's jacket. He stared down at it, unable to think. "That thing will kill me," he finally decided.

"Don't think about it too much, that'll just make you afraid." Clive threw him a blue cone of plastic the size of a small water bottle. *"All you have to do is run fast and use this when it comes too close."*

"What is it?"

"A sound gun," Martha explained. *"Think of it as an anti-dogwhistle."*

"Remember to point it directly at the spectre's head," Clive added. *"In this weather the soundwaves will be weakened."*

"I am liking this less and less," said Erik, standing still in befuddlement.

"As I said, don't think about it too much. You might get cold feet." Clive patted him on the shoulder. *"This will be an adventure."*

Behind all the hats, goggles, and masks it was impossible to tell, but Erik could have sworn that Clive was smiling like a little boy on the morning of his birthday.

Even the white of snow, ice, and bright clouds before the aurora could not stop the creeping darkness. It was not too bad right outside of the base, but Erik had been wandering away from it for twenty minutes, and its bright lights were fading away in the blizzard.

Martha had spotted the ghost wolf through one of the drones' camera feed, and sent him off wandering in that direction. Clive had stressed that time was running out, and the rest of the pack would be arriving soon. Erik was not entirely sure how to make himself look "extra tasty," and he was also not sure if he wanted to.

There was a flicker before his eyes, a gust of white flakes twisting and twirling in the wind. It disappeared almost immediately, but it confirmed his suspicions. The blizzard was interfering with the wireless coverage, and if his retinal screens could not communicate with his office computer, the de-noising algorithm would lack the processing power required to do its job. He cursed himself for not having installed more routers over the island, assuming that nobody would be walking about during such extreme weather anyway.

It was important to keep moving. His many layers kept him reasonably warm, but standing still even for a moment while treading shin-high snow and fighting against the winds tugging at him could make it difficult to start walking again. Besides, his body heat and the permanent snowfall might make the snow around him melt and turn to ice. If the Lupus Spectre decided to attack then, it would take valuable tenths of a second to pull free, and he might not have those.

Another flicker. The snow had almost become a wall of white. Erik decided not to walk out further, and took a few steps in the direction of the base. The snow returned, clogging his field of vision for several heartbeats. When it faded away, a shadow was jumping at him.

It was a wolf, not so much made of shadow as it was darkness. The contrast was enough to make it visible, but some translucency remained. The Lupus Spectre was no bigger than a regular Arctic wolf. Its "fur" was shaggier, trailing off like smoke as the creature flew toward him. The eyes staring at Erik with murderous hunger were so utterly black they seemed to glow.

He jumped backward, stumbling in the dense snow. The Lupus Spectre was standing over him, it's cold breath sucking every last bit of warmth out of his face. In a panic, Erik used the sound gun in his hand. His heart was racing so fast it felt like his chest was about to explode.

The Lupus Spectre made no sound, but its dark form shivered, and then vanished, carried away by the wind. Erik pulled himself up faster than he would have thought possible and ran toward the lights of the base. Heavy clouds of breath condensed in the air before him. The snow flickered, and flickered again.

Sprinting with long, powerful strides, the adrenaline coursing through his bloodstream like boiling water through a dense pipe, he looked back, and saw the beast again. It prowled after him, paws sinking into the snow but leaving no prints. Somehow, the Lupus Spectre broadcast its internal conflict of hungry craving and fear of the sound gun.

Erik didn't care. He just wanted it gone. With a primal scream of fear, he aimed the gun at the spectre, and pulled the trigger. It stopped dead in its tracks, watching him as he kept on running away. Erik did not take his eyes off the beast, until it finally faded away again, and he turned his gaze forward, not stopping for a moment.

Eventually, when the lights of the station had become brighter, and the flickering of snow ceased, sense returned to Erik's mind. He slowed down, coming to a halt on a small outcropping of rock. His lungs hurt like they were freezing and on fire at the same time, his heart hammered incessantly, and his legs began to shudder.

He had shaken the Lupus Spectre. That was bad. That meant he would die, and so would everyone else in the station. He needed to get back out there, have the creature get his scent again, drive it wild with hunger. But what if it was too afraid of the sound gun? What if it had figured out that he was bait? What if he had already messed everything up?

"*Blyat*, Erik, you *mudak!*" Not three metres away, a large figure in a grey coat was stomping toward him. "*Pashol nahui* you complete idiot!"

"Vladimir? What are you doing here?" Erik asked. Nobody was supposed to be out here but him.

"Because I am looking for you, isn't that obvious?" Vladimir gestured around. "What the fuck are you thinking?"

"It really is difficult to explain." He had instructed everyone to remain inside the base while he, Martha, and Clive took care of business outside.

"*Cyka blyat*, those fucking Brits made you believe their bullshit, and now you are out here, killing yourself in a snow storm!" Vladimir hit the side of his head."How stupid are you?"

"I realise this may seem crazy, but-" Erik began.

"I talked to the men, this Fredric woman asked them about this ghost wolf business, and now suddenly you act like fucking Kostja Karpinski, except suicidal." Even under all the layers, it was easy to see that Vladimir was shaking his head. "I had them barricade the entrances. Whatever the Brits are planning, they will not do it just because you decided to sell your brain to some *gopnik*."

"No, listen, Vladimir, this thing is real! I have seen it!"

"*Cyka blyat*, stop it!" He raised a hand as though he wanted to slap Erik in the face. "When we get back I will call Sigmund Lied and have you sent to Norway for a fucking psychological examination. I cannot-" He never finished the sentence.

A shadow materialised in mid-flight, slamming into Vladimir and wrestling him to the ground.

"No!" shouted Erik, and jumped down from the rock, fiddling with the sound gun.

Vladimir cursed as he punched at the Lupus Spectre. The beast sunk its teeth into his neck.

Erik pulled the trigger, held it down as he shot waves of agonising sound at the ghost wolf. The creature jerked back, snarling soundlessly, and dashed away.

"What the fuck was that?" Vladimir shouted. "*Cyka!*"

Erik ran over to help him up. The Russian was holding his neck and breathing heavily. "That was the ghost wolf," Erik explained. "I don't know how, but it's real, and I am baiting it. Are you alright."

"I think," Vladimir managed, his hand still firmly on his neck. "Hurts like shit though." The heavy winter clothing seemed to have prevented the worst.

"We need to get out of here." Erik looked around nervously. "Can you walk?"

Vladimir did not respond, but began marching forward, toward the base.

Erik followed him, scanning the perimeter for the Lupus Spectre. He would have to return later, when Vladimir was safe, to play bait again. He could not risk one of his crew to die. They did not get very far.

After only a few steps, the Lupus Spectre slammed into Erik, ripping away parts of the outer jacket of his arm. He fell, and the sound gun slipped out of his hands. “No!” Before he was even fully down, he looked for it frantically.

A gust of wind above him, and a thump that slammed Vladimir to the ground. He shouted in anger and fear. Erik dug around the spot he believed the sound gun had landed, but came up empty-handed. Vladimir's screams turned to gargles.

Erik looked over as the ghost wolf was goring the throat of his friend, dark blood spurting onto the white snow. The sound gun was forgotten, and a realisation of his failure appeared on the horizon. Then, the beast looked at him with its pitch black eyes, and instinct took over.

Erik darted upward, sprinting at a speed he would have never thought possible, trudging through the heavy snow with the strength of a bear, burning reserves of energy he did not know he had. There was pressure on his calf, something pulled it backward. There was a rip, and sudden cold. Erik did not have to look back to know that the Lupus Spectre had torn away most layers of clothes down there.

He ran, barely considering direction, not thinking about what had happened, or if he even had a chance to escape. All he knew was that, if he stopped, he was dead, and dead was something he did not want to be.

He turned a corner around a small hill, and a mesh of wires appeared before him, fastened to a hexagon of metal poles. Some part of his mind knew that he had to run in there, and then he would be safe.

Gusts of impossibly frigid air hit his thigh every time the spectre snapped at it. Erik got into the final sprint. He had to enter that cage through the open side, had to get in there to be safe, to get away from the monster that was chasing him.

As he dashed past the poles, he stumbled and flew forward, landing face-down in the compressed snow, slithering on the thin sheet of ice that had formed there. There was a click behind him, and when he turned round frantically, he saw that

Martha, little more then a white shadow in her high-tech gear, had closed the cage behind the ghost wolf. The ghost wolf which was now standing right at Erik's feet, showing its teeth in a victorious grin.

There was a slight hum as an electric current ran through the wires of the cage, and the Lupus Spectre looked around, seemingly irritated. Erik's blood froze. This was not safety at all. He was stuck in here, with the beast, and it would kill him.

There was an explosion in the snow next to him. A humanoid shape emerged from beneath a cover of white like a vengeful demon. It had a long knife in its hand. The blade seemed to glow bright blue on its own.

The Lupus Spectre began circling, stepping over Erik's legs as though they weren't there. Its eyes were fixed on Clive, who mirrored the wolf's movements in a low stance, twirling the glowing knife in his hand. There was growling, and it took Erik a moment to realise it was not coming from the Lupus Spectre.

The beast and Clive jumped at the same time. They lunged toward each other, jaw open and blade swinging. At the last possible moment, Clive pulled back and held out his arm toward the ghost wolf. It bit down on it, so hard that the Irishman let out a grunt of pain. Then he drove his knife into the creature's belly, and sliced it open like it was made of butter.

The pathetic wince the Lupus Spectre gave did not make a sound, but Erik could *feel* it reverberate in the deepest recesses of his soul. Out of the darkness, faint, liquid light seemed to flow from the cut on the beast's belly, dissipating before it touched the ground. The creature deflated in a matter of seconds, the strong jaws sliding off Clive's arm. A small, glowing pool formed on the ground, but disappeared as soon as it was formed.

When all the light had left the Lupus Spectre, its body simply faded away like a shadow in the light.

"Let's get inside and wait out the storm," said Clive. *"I need a drink."*

Five days later, the skies had cleared, and Vladimir's body had been found. Some of the workers were recovering the Japanese sailors from their vessel, to be stored in an empty cooling room.

Erik was standing at the foot of Martha Fredric's plane. The aurora borealis shone mystically off its perfectly reflective hull. "And what am I supposed to tell them?"

"The very same scepticism you showed me will play to your advantage here," Martha said. She had one hand already on the ladder. "Just say you don't know what happened, and when you went out to find Vladimir you found him like that. They'll have about as much of an idea as you could possibly ever have."

"Though I would put money on them going with the polar bear theory," Clive added. He was drinking tea from a thermos flask. "They'll be clueless, but they won't blame you for what happened."

"What about you?" Erik asked. Their mysterious arrival and departure would not go unnoticed in any reports.

"We pay your company enough not to ask questions, and if they do, we will know how to answer," Martha reassured him. "What you really should not do is go around and tell people about Lupus Spectres. That will land you in a mental health institution faster than you can say 'unfit for duty.'"

Erik nodded, unsure what to say. "Thank you, I suppose."

Clive patted him on the shoulder. "Don't thank us, thank yourself. You acted like a bloody damn hero."

"Don't worry about us, Erik," Martha added. "Take care."

Before he could respond, she began climbing up the ladder, and Clive followed only a few rungs behind. Erik stood there wordlessly until they were both inside, and the ladder had begun retracting.

"They won't be able to taxi away if you stand there, Erik," the control tower said into his earpiece.

Erik nodded, and trudged away. He had a post-emergency damage report to compile.

Cleaning Up

By Gwydion JMF Weber

The road to the top had been a difficult one. Now that he was here, the Executive found that it had all been justified. Anything was worth it for even ten minutes of being the owner of this office. He looked out of the window, and watched the bustling of the metropolis in the afternoon sun. Tens of thousands of magcars levitated along tracks snaking up and around hundreds of skyscrapers.

The vehicles were manufactured by his company, as were the tracks. They had bought most of the architecture firms complaining that this transportation network would severely limit their design options, bankrupted others, and forced the holdouts to comply with their vision of the city with a series of expensive dinners for members of parliament.

Out on the sparkling sea, freighters the size of towns shipped containers with his company's logo on them to ports on this world and beyond. The Executive himself had orchestrated the privatisation and purchase of several major global ports some years ago, and made it so only company ships could be serviced there without a ridiculous markup.

The Executive swiped over the window, and the scenery changed. He was now no longer seeing southward, but to the west, where great mountains towered over even the greatest of buildings. The old observatory looked as pristine as ever, even though no observing had been done in that complex for over a decade. It had been his idea to turn it into a luxury hotel, and the research data proving that the science being conducted there was no longer worth anything had been easy to fake.

Out of sight, at much higher altitudes, his company's mining operation was pulling some of the most valuable raw materials known to man out of the ground. There had been environmental concerns at first, but proving that the species the activists considered threatened were already extinct had not been too difficult.

The Executive cracked his knuckles, and sat down at his workstation. Iris scan, DNA test, secret passcode, and brainwave analysis were the steps necessary to gain the kind of top-level access he had lobbied for back when he was only a desk jockey. Only the highest commander of the company got it, and it offered complete control over all computer systems, while at the same time being impossible to trace.

Nobody would ever know that anything had been done. It was time to get to work. He had cleaning to do.

First was a councilman he'd bribed. The man had been greedy, and not satisfied with fancy dinners and donations to retirement funds. The Executive respected that, but he had dirt on him, and was thus a liability. All he had to do was press a button, and the system made his car slip off the tracks and plummet to destruction. It made it look as though the councilman's chauffeur had committed suicide with his boss on board.

A journalist who was investigating said councilman's corruption was lured outside of his apartment by a call from his daughter, and crushed in the hallway by a fire door. The safeties had failed, and the exact mechanic responsible had been identified. There was a gas explosion in his home that night, eliminating him and his family as witnesses. No cause could ever be found.

A different councilman, young and idealistic at the time, had not accepted any bribes. So anonymous terrorists had kidnapped his wife, and he became the building code law's most vocal sponsor. Both the councilman and his wife were sucked out of their penthouse when a sudden pressure drop ripped out the windows. A tragic accident, as nobody saw the industrial drone that made the pressure drop happen in the first place.

The terrorists, who lived in the mountains, were killed when their explosives suddenly detonated on their own. Though they hadn't stolen them, reports of their theft were created and dated to months prior, to protect the company from blowback. Nobody should be able to claim that they sold weapons to terrorists, or that those weapons sometimes malfunctioned.

A murderer in a prison received a reliable message from an anonymous source. The paedophile architect that had so vehemently denied wrongdoing every time they had beaten him up was the man who killed his daughter all those years ago. In a rage, he killed the architect in the hallway before being injected with a tranquillizer dart by an automated turret. The dosage determined by the machine was too high, and the murderer was also killed. All records of any messages were empty.

In a distant country, a homeless man was accidentally beaten to death by a security robot. Luckily, the company manufactured no components of this robot, at least officially. There was a single off-brand chip installed in the visual cortex of the robot, but nobody could trace its production back to the company.

The fact that the homeless man killed was once the head of the city's port authority and vehemently opposed to its privatisation was a minor footnote in the news report, a curiosity that placed most of the focus on the fact that he had been ousted without pension for misappropriating funds in bad faith, a conviction he had always denied.

In a different distant country, a police officer obsessed with the murder of a lawyer that had remained unsolved for years fell into a hole. Just like that, the street swallowed him when a garbage hatch opened underneath him and he was disintegrated in the automated waste disposal system. Nothing like this had ever happened, nothing like this would ever happen again. The company had made that system totally secure, and nobody even suspected them.

While alive, the lawyer had worked for an advocacy group lobbying against the ridiculous markups the company was charging. At the time, he had been devising a strategy that would have demonstrated the illegality of what the company was doing to its competition in a court of law. His murder had sent a clear message, as had the destruction of all his hard drives and backups, but it had been clean, and could never be traced back to the company. Even the hitman had been eliminated.

The old scientist who used to run the observatory and was

now growing senile in a mental institution had an aneurysm and passed away peacefully. No autopsy would ever be able to determine that the nanobots that were keeping his blood flow going were manufactured by the company, as they all dissolved without a trace on command, and all paperwork of their installation was wiped from the databases of the company and the mental institution.

It was a trick the Executive had used many years earlier, taking advantage of the fact that almost all computer systems in the world were manufactured by a subsidiary of a subsidiary of the company. It was the same method he had used to manipulate the observatory's data in order to gaslight the old scientist.

Compounds that damaged brain tissue were delivered in the meals the old scientist got through a food company that could track where their product went, creepy messages were sent to subordinates, until finally his tailored medicine was laced with mild hallucinogens. The analysis machines monitoring the old scientist's blood never picked those up. They, too, were manufactured by the company.

Several kilometres inland, the manager of a chemical facility owned by the company found himself having an unexpected heart attack as his pacemaker failed. The man had grown old at a young age, always carrying around a secret heavier than he could bear. He'd been instrumental in creating the chemicals necessary to annihilate the endemic species around the area where the mines were supposed to be built.

The house of the environmental inspector who had declared the site free of dangerous toxins at the time was flooded with poison gas from his basement laboratory. After he was dead, the windows opened, and the gas dissipated into the air, never to be seen again. His son had been dying of an extremely rare disease at the time, and the Executive had offered him a spot in a top secret experimental treatment programme if the inspector faked the report. The boy had died. There had been no programme.

While training unarmed combat with a dummy bot, the company's security president had his neck broken. A terrible accident, but the machine would have been too stupid to actually do him any harm. As a matter of fact, he'd designed parts of it himself. Files from his personal and office workstations regarding an investigation into the death of the last executive were wiped without a trace.

All it took from the Executive was ten minutes of work. The system he had designed pervaded the entire company and all its subsidiaries, communicating across products, piggybacking on a software suite that nobody understood, because it had been grown by neural networks. It was clandestine, nobody knew of its existence. Imbued with superhuman problem solving capabilities, it required oversight from one person, and one person alone: the Executive himself.

There were no loose ends, no mouths that could talk, no soldiers that had issues pulling the trigger. Nobody could defeat it. Nothing was faster than the system, because the company owned the only one of its kind, and no one but the Executive even knew about it.

All these years he had played the game with paranoia, the fear of being discovered always gnawing at the rim of his consciousness. Now he was the Executive, and he was untouchable. He would never have to be afraid again.

The Flores Object

By Gwydion JMF Weber

Santa Cruz das Flores had never been such a busy town. A total of thirty-six different planes had landed in the past 24 hours, and all of them had been jets carrying officials from various international governments. That wasn't even counting the American, British, and Russian military planes that had been landing on the fleet of aircraft carriers crowded around the small vacation island in the Atlantic Ocean. The Portuguese government had been congratulated for their openness and cooperation by the international community, and placed in command of investigating whatever *thing* had just risen from the depths. The Americans had protested, as they were under the impression that this was an extraterrestrial spaceship, and they were, of course, entitled to first contact. Others had voiced their concern about touching the discovery at all, but they were a tiny, albeit vocal minority.

Portugal's "taking command" came in the form of General Luis-Alfonso das Pinas Almeida, a tall, serious man who wasn't wearing half the medals and decorations he could have pinned to his uniform. He was sitting in the dining room of the town's largest hotel, which had been cleared of the seating arrangements one might expect to find in a restaurant to make way for a roughly horseshoe-shaped conference space. It was the single largest room in Santa Cruz das Flores, and it was quite large for something in a town with barely more than 2000 inhabitants.

"Strike teams standing by for breach, Sir," said a radio voice coming from the command centre of the *USS Ulysses S. Grant. "We're waiting on your orders."*

Das Pinas puffed. It was as though they expected him to

be unfamiliar with military protocol. He looked into the round of scientists, engineers, commanders, and UN Ambassadors, all impatiently awaiting his next move. There was only one move he could make.

"Breach is go," the general declared in heavily accented English. His eyes were drawn to a huge flatscreen, where footage of the gigantic object captured by the cameras of military helicopters was displayed. It was a flat oval, at least if one could consider something that was over a hundred metres thick "flat", with a smooth, streamlined black surface, and a dome the size of a shopping mall protruding from the middle. Presumably, the dome was made out of some transparent material, but it was too densely covered in shellfish and algae to be anything but impenetrable. To everyone's surprise, the rest of the hull was untouched by marine life.

The first commando unit rappelled down from an assault helicopter, and others soon followed at different spots on the object. They were landing near what his scientific advisors considered to be "entry hatches", and from what das Pinas could tell, one did not exactly need a doctorate in alien spaceship design to determine where the doors were on this thing.

What he hadn't anticipated was that said doors would open without any struggle as soon as they were approached. Judging from the various helmet camera feeds displayed on an assortment of smaller screens, they all looked the same: A tunnel with an arched roof and shining, cobalt walls, segmented like an earthworm. The floor was tiled white, and it was soon apparent that these tiles were also the source of the soft, mint-tinged light illuminating the corridor.

The strike teams entered, and it wasn't long until they found something. The Russian team was first. A room, the door of which opened just as readily as the front gate had, almost presented itself to them. Inside, the only light came from their torch attachments, so das Pinas needed a moment to register what he saw. On four silver benches lay four corpses of dead humans. Three were women, the other was a man, and all of them were entirely pale, as though drained of blood. Their peaceful faces were almost as unnerving as their attire, which seemed to be made of rough hemp, and decorated with simple line patterns. One of the soldiers said something in Russian, and the attending Russian ambassador let das Pinas know that he was commenting on how short these people were.

The Americans were next, and their discovery had everyone in the little dining room frowning. Once again, it was a burial chamber, with four bodies on four silver benches. These looked distinctly Asiatic, and while three of them once again wore simple, primitive clothing, one man was clad in what seemed to be a suit of armour. One Japanese scientist gasped and said something in his native tongue, but das Pinas recognized one of the words – "Samurai".

A group with more contemporary attire was found by the Chinese team, who opened a chamber containing four young people with tattoos, facial piercings, and dyed hair. Their clothes were dark, and one of them was wearing a leather cloak.

A total of thirty-four such chambers were investigated, and inside was always the same thing. Four people, all from the same time period and geographical region, coming overall from vastly different places and eras of the world. Eventually, das Pinas ordered the teams to make straight for the dome, which he assumed to be the command centre. Over a hundred more doors opened for the soldiers, and the occasional glance into them suggested they were all the same as the first thirty-four. Zulu warriors, Celtic shamans, Polynesian fishermen, Victorian house servants, Hunnic riders, Aztec farmers. The variety was stunning.

It ended up being the French team that made it to the dome first. Despite being covered in sea life from the outside, the blue sky was visible from the inside as though there wasn't even a sheet of glass there. Standing inside the dome, pointing up at the sky, was the enormous statue of a golden person. It had no face or discernible sex, but it was definitely pointing at the stars.

Gasps and murmurs went through the room, followed by applause as people realized that this could be humanity's invitation to the stars. Talk of galactic federations, endless riches, and new technologies erupted as the other teams also entered the dome. But something did not seem right to Luis-Alfonso das Pinas Almeida. Something about the statue was just ... wrong.

They way it stood was not optimistic at all. There was no face, but the body language carried an obvious message.

"It is not pointing at the stars," he said, quieting the room with the weight of his authority. "It is saying 'look up.'"

A Letter To My Brother

By Gwydion JMF Weber

Forgive me, brother, for I have killed you. I wish it could have been avoided, but alas you are afflicted with the same curse I am, because we share the same blood, and that blood needs to end with me. We rule over a kingdom of suffering and slavery, sitting on a throne of woe, inside a castle built of lies. Neither of us are at fault for this. We were born into it, grew up surrounded by it, and were forced to play our parts in it. Only you didn't.

I know many people consider you brave for escaping this place, even though you were the crown prince. I know how the outsiders think of our kingdom. The things we do to our people, the unspeakable atrocities we commit to keep our grip on power, have a way of slipping past blockades and propaganda. I've always believed you a coward for leaving. I can understand your reasons, and I still love and respect you, but your place was here, with me, ending what our grandfather began.

I have taken up the mantle you threw away. Father is dead, and I am king now. You may have heard. I know all of his secrets now, have seen everything done in our name. The horrors our people suffer are beyond imagining, brother, worse than either of us could ever have come up with. It has to end, and you would be happy to hear that I have found a way. However, I don't think you'd like it.

Ever since our grandfather carved out this kingdom, it has been tied to our blood. It was one of his most important declarations: Only those descended from him could wear the crown, for only they were of the divine heritage. Our people, from the lowliest of servants to the highest of commanders believe many things about us, most of them lies created by those who ruled before us, and the one thing they believe in most is our bloodline. Therefore, to destroy this kingdom and end their suffering, we must end the royal bloodline. No one who could sit the throne can be alive. They must all be dead, and I must be the last to die, for only I have the power to make this come true.

This is why I had to kill you, brother. This is why I will have to kill your children. I will tell their assassins the same thing I told your assassins. I will demand they make it quick and painless, but if that turns out to be an impossibility, their deaths are of a higher priority. This is my life's work, brother. I have become a butcher of my own kin, methodical and strategic in my approach, ruthless in the execution. I doubt there is a hell for someone like me. A new one will have to be created, and if the gods are kind I will be the only one in it, forever.

I can hear your anger in my mind. I can hear you complaining about the stupidity of my plan, about all the unnecessary suffering it will bring. If you read this letter, you would tell me to simply declare the kingdom over, to free our people from the yoke of our family by making use of the divinity attributed to me. Maybe you'd be right. Maybe I could step out there, change this realm for the better, end the suffering, capitulate to the armies sharpening their blades at our borders.

But it might not work. We have uncles, cousins, and nephews. They are not like you and me. They believe in their own divinity, and have no plans to make the rule of our family end. While they may kneel at my feet and do my bidding now, there is no accounting for what they could do if they believed their power threatened. It is a risk I cannot take. All of them must die, just like you, to prove once and for all that our line is not descended of gods, but of petty men with no principles.

To tell you the truth, I am afraid of death myself. I know you would be seething at the idea that I will have a long life, immersed in the pleasures of absolute power even as an old man. It angers me as well that I am so weak, and I do hope to find the strength to end my life after my work is done, but I am afraid it will not happen. My plan is to disillusion the people with my actions, to teach them that I am not perfect by making mistakes, and to destabilize the kingdom before death comes to take me.

I know how dangerous it is. I know that, if I die without heirs, the kingdom will be torn apart by war. But if everything goes as I imagine it, nobody will be able to continue our tyranny, because nobody will be legitimate. Yes, there will be more suffering, but there will also be a future free from chains for the children of those now enslaved by the horror of our rule, and their children, and their children after them. It is a price I am willing to pay.

I am sorry to have killed you, brother. You could have had the life you wanted, and I took it from you. But please do not curse me for it. Curse our grandfather, for he was the one who set us on this path.

May you find peace in the afterlife.

Yours faithfully,

The King.

Lex Nocturna

By Gwydion JMF Weber

With agents of the Lex Nocturna in pursuit, there was no turning back for Janica. If they caught her, she would be vitrified on the spot. She slipped into the crowd crossing Charles Bridge, heading into the old town of Prague. It was a warm summer night, and the people around here were elated, some travelling between one party and another, others just getting started.

Red and green airships pushed around the sky, their glowing balloons decorated with Asiatic dragons. A docking tower poked out over the rooftops of Nusle district, laden with exotic shops advertising themselves with bright neon signs.

At first people had been apprehensive about the Vietnamese mercenaries and the mark they left on the city's skyline. Then everyone realised that they were much more effective at protecting Prague from the wyverns than the police (or the Lex Nocturna) had ever been. There hadn't been an attack in four months, and no casualties in a year. The creatures had learned, and kept away from the city now.

Janica moved quickly, but not too fast. She wanted to break out into a sprint, put distance between her and the agents behind her, but it would only have given her away. She had reason to assume they knew what she looked like. Even if they did, she was so average that they could have confused her with three dozen other women on this bridge right now.

She checked out the bridge tower for potential agents, but could not spot anyone. If she was lucky, the Lex Nocturna was still looking for her on the other bank of the Vltava. Maybe she'd even shaken them completely. Janica did not allow herself to get too excited. She was still carrying the mutagen.

Like a snake, she slithered through the crowds. Like a mouse, she disappeared through a hole in the wall, down a poorly lit stairwell, and into the catacombs. Laughter echoed from the ancient walls. Every few metres, battery-powered lamps had been drilled into the pallid rock. White light spilled out of the open door of an underground tattoo parlour.

Janica went the other way, following the distant sound of music. The vague jammering of electrocellos, the aethereal sounds of a Rhodes piano, and the rich tones of a hybrid guitar made for a rich texture of avant-garde entertainment.

She pushed past a group of partiers, much too drunk for this hour of the evening. It was much less crowded down here. If the Lex Nocturna caught her here, there would be no escape. She'd spend the rest of time as a glass statue in their palace, a warning to everyone who dared defy God's sacred order.

The music grew louder. Janica had been doing this for a long time. She knew her way around the catacombs. A woman in a fancy evening gown stood in the corner, smoking a cigarette by one of the air shafts. She wore a bejewelled mask.

Sounds of mingling, chuckles, quips, mixed with the music. More masked people in expensive clothes could be found, most of them chatting with glasses of champagne in hand. In the darker tunnels, the occasional two were losing themselves in the throes of passion.

In the antechamber to the lively ballroom, two men wore no masks. Their suits were also significantly cheaper than those of the other men around them. It was, however, not possible to look down on them. They were huge, with shoulders like bulls. Neither needed masks, as their faces were those of wolves already.

Their eyes were pale and intelligent, their beards dense and scraggly, flowing straight into their hairy chests without interruption. Their noses looked only vaguely human, and were made of the same dark flesh as a canine's snout. When one of them spotted Janica, he grinned, baring his fangs.

Without a word, he followed her into the ball room, one hand laid gently on her shoulder, pushing people out of the way with the other. The walls here were decorated with bones. Arches and columns were draped in femurs, while skulls stared down at the crowd of anonymous elites in wordless judgement.

The only ones not wearing masks were other wolf people. None were as tall or broad as the two brothers guarding the entrance, but they were still imposing figures. In the back room, one of them was dressed as sharply as the other guests. Tibor Vlkodlak was wearing a blue pinstripe suit, golden cufflinks, and polished leather shoes. His facial fur was scrupulously cropped into dark sideburns and a thick moustache.

“I thought you'd never make it,” he said, smiling his wolfish smile.

“I almost didn't. Lex Nocturna is on my trail.”

“Did you shake them?”

“Probably.”

“Well, it wouldn't matter if you didn't. There are so many rich and powerful people down here right now, they would not dare to make a scene.” Tibor held out his hand.

Janica produced the mutagen from her coat pocket and handed it over. “Don't be so sure about that. If the entire cabinet was in the same room as a mutagen they were after, they would blow up the entire building just to be safe. The Lex Nocturna thinks itself above the law.”

“It is, technically. Most laws, at least,” Tibor noted. He held the little corked flask carefully in his hand. “And you know, there is a good chance the entire cabinet *is* here right now, so we may be able to put your theory to the test.”

“Please, let's not. The worst that can happen to you is an internment camp. I'd be vitrified.”

Tibor laughed. “Come on, they know me. I'd be the statue right next to yours. But it is ironic, isn't it? My father fought against his fellow wolf chimerics in the war. Even though they looked the same as him, he hated them for who they worked for, what they believed. The people he liberated from the concentration camps did not look like him, but the sapiens were murdering them for what they believed. He returned to this country a hero. But now the sapiens want to put his offspring in the same kind of camps he liberated their parents and grandparents from."

"It's those damned wyverns, feral monsters. The Lex Nocturna can justify anything against chimerics so long as people are scared of them. And it's not like we can kick them out." It was a simplistic view, Janica knew, but frankly so was hating chimerics in the first place. So they had a few animal genes, they were still people.

"I don't see the Lex Nocturna protecting us from the wyverns, or paying the Vietnamese, for that matter. That is all the taxpayer's dime." Tibor beckoned for Janica to follow.

They walked through a series of quieter, darker tunnels of the catacombs. The floor was rugged, and the uneven walls cast ghastly shadows that drove more than one shiver down Janica's spine. She jerked back when one of them actually turned out to be a slim wolf man hiding in front of a heavy metal door.

Without saying a word, he opened it and the well lit laboratory on the other side illuminated his dark features. His fur was pitch black, and his face deformed in a way only a severe genetic dysphoria could be responsible for.

Daniel did not interrupt his animated chatter when his father entered the room. The young wolfman with the blond fur wore a filthy lab coat, and was much too caught up in discussing a series of diagrams on a chalkboard with his colleagues to notice Tibor enter the room.

The lab was not staffed by wolf chimerics exclusively. A Vietnamese woman consulting a medical volume in the corner had quite a bit of tiger genes, three young men working on some kind of distillation had otter features, and someone with grey skin, large ears, and a tiny trunk was among the discussion group. There were even a few sapiens in the room.

From the looks of it the place was in the basement of some old church. Dark doors of musky old wood lead to other rooms. Everybody knew that Tibor owned this laboratory somewhere, considering the range of genetic services he offered, but Janica had always assumed it was out in the country, where the Lex Nocturna had fewer eyes and ears.

She also knew from many evenings spent talking about the finer points of genetic engineering that Daniel was the head of the lab, not just because he was Tibor's son, but because he was actually qualified for the position.

Tibor cleared his throat. The room went immediately silent. Daniel threw his father a questioning look, then smiled when he saw Janica. “Ah, look who has finally made it!”

“Is this her?” one of the sapiens researchers asked. “The procurer?”

Apparently she had a nickname down here. The scientists all seemed to be looking at her with at least some degree of reverence.

“This is indeed my dear friend Janica, the one who has, I presume, just now delivered the final piece of our puzzle?” Daniel walked up to her excitedly. His eyes went wide when Tibor handed him the vial.

“You can't handle it like that, father. You need to be careful with it,” Daniel complained.

A scientist walked over quickly, holding open a padded box. Daniel slotted the vial carefully into a metal harness, then closed the lid. “Where did you get this?” he asked Janica.

“You know I can't tell you where I source my wares. But I have to be honest, I do not know what this is, exactly. Something very obscure, salamander-related, that's all. But you asked for it, and the Lex Nocturna wants it desperately, so I assume it is important.”

“Very much so. This is the missing link, the final piece of our puzzle,” He repeated. Daniel was a sucker from drama, but not very good at it. “With this, and a few more months of work, we can finally reverse-engineer how the Nazis made the first proto-wyverns. If we can do that, we can find out how the Russians made the second generation, and then we can fill in the gaps on our mutation table.”

“All this time you've been working on the genealogy of wyverns?” Janica asked. She was a bit disappointed, to say the least. This team had purified zygotes, allowing sapiens children to be born from chimeric parents, able to lead a normal life. Aside from their mysterious origins, wyverns were quite well understood.

“With all this knowledge, we will be able to develop better

weapons against them. We can finally exterminate the pest!" Daniel explained.

"I hope you're not saying what I think you're saying."

"But I am. We can tailor a virus to them that will render them all sterile in three generations."

"You do remember Cuba, right? The island that was completely depopulated twenty years ago? The island the was carpet-bombed with nuclear warheads to prevent the spread of a pathogen weapon originally designed to end a cat pest?" Janica recalled having this very discussion with Daniel a few years ago, and him agreeing that pathogen weapons were always a bad idea.

"This is different. It doesn't work the same way, not even close. This virus cannot kill anyone, we can account for mutational spread, and the organism it targets is a true chimera, not just a simple genetic graft. There's absolutely no risk of it jumping over to any other kind of animal." Daniel sounded hurt that she would suggest such a thing.

"You're making a huge mistake. This is dangerous," Janica was shocked to the core. How many mutagens had she brought to this project in the past months?

Tibor placed a hand on her back. "Time to go."

Janica spoke to the other scientists directly. "Stop whatever it is you're doing, do not be a part of this. This is way too dangerous!"

Tibor pushed her a little harder than he needed to, and lead her out the door.

"Why did you bring me down here?" Janica asked. She couldn't believe what she'd just seen.

"As a gesture of trust," Tibor responded. "I wanted you to see the good thing you have contributed to."

"You actually think this is a good idea?"

"I had my reservations, but these are some very smart people, and they managed to convince me. You said so yourself: The wyverns are the symbol that the Lex Nocturna uses to scare people of all chimerics. This is our way out, our way back to the surface, to society."

"What happened to purifying zygotes?" Janica demanded.

"And admit that our genes are inferior? It's a way to make

money, finance this much more important operation. I don't want to erase my people just so we can be free, Janica. I know you understand that." Tibor was almost dragging her through the tunnels.

"Not like this. There has to be another way." She picked up her pace, hoping that Tibor would loosen his grip. It only made him move faster also.

"There isn't, unfortunately." He opened another door and pushed her out of the restricted area, into a part of the catacombs she was familiar with. "Goodbye, Janica. You will find your payment in the usual place."

Before she could say a word, he closed the door again.

The tower was swaying gently in the violent storm. Groups of drunk Vietnamese sailors celebrated the fact that they weren't part of the airship crews today. Janica wondered if any of the ones who had shot down a black wyvern over the river three days ago were in this Bánh place with her right now.

She hadn't heard from Tibor or Daniel in almost four months. Every day she expected some terrible news about their virus in the papers, and for what? Yes, the wyverns were a symbol, but most people did not have a problem with chimerics, and they hated the Lex Nocturna. Even if all wyverns were destroyed, which Janica doubted would happen, the Lex would continue to hunt down chimerics. They were too powerful to be stopped.

Janica finished up her meat dumpling and paid, a small vial carefully rolled up in her 50 koruna bill. It contained a special mutagen isolated from the naked mole rat, which was protecting the daughter of a senior Vietnamese officer from cancer. She needed regular injections, as her body rejected the genetic material in regular intervals.

The woman behind the counter nodded and gave Janica her change of twenty-five thousand koruna. It had been difficult to find a source for the mutagen at first, but now that she had it the Vietnamese had become a regular source of good income. She felt bad about profiting off a little girl's lethal condition, but if she wasn't going to give her the mutagens, nobody would.

She took the narrow winding stairway down, always careful to keep her hand near the rail in case there was a particularly strong gust of wind. It was not at all necessary, just an irrational precaution from someone who preferred to be on the ground at all times. The Vietnamese knew how to build their docking towers.

When she stepped out onto the street, a man suddenly stood in her way. He wore an outmoded black suit and a clerical collar. A midnight blue ribbon embroidered with a silver crucifix was pinned to his chest. An agent of the Lex Nocturna.

A quick scan of her surroundings informed Janica that he had four colleagues with him, blocking all escape routes. Panic rose in her chest. She could already see herself being vitrified and put on display.

"Janica Palecek." The agent was not asking. "My name is Brother Slavoj. Don't worry, I'm here to talk."

"Somehow I don't believe you," Janica responded, attempting to push past him.

"No need to be afraid, it's daytime. We have no authority when the sun is out, as wills the Lord." The agent's grin told Janica all she needed to know. The sun had nothing to do with the Lex's authority. They became totalitarian cops from six in the evening to six in the morning, doing whatever they wanted. The other half of they day they were just quieter about it.

"What do you want?" Janica asked, still searching for an escape route.

"Simply for you to accompany me on a little walk. Not to worry, we will not leave the main road, there's always going to be a crowd watching." Brother Slavoj gestured down the street. It was full of wealthy young women shopping for clothes.

"Fine." Janica did not see any other option. "And to what do I owe this honour?"

"The bishop sends his thanks for your integrity in the affair of Minister Svoboda," the agent explained.

"I don't follow."

"Somehow you became aware of the fact that he had purchased a horse mutagen and informed the Lex Nocturna. He's being arrested by police as we speak, and will be surrendered to out custody for immediate vitrification by nightfall."

Janica needed a moment to remember what he was talking about. Of course, three weeks ago, a mysterious middle man of someone rich had given her a lot of money for a pretty basic mutagen. She couldn't help but feel a little bit of pride that it had gone to the Minister of Transport.

Still, she did not like the way Brother Slavoj was talking about it. "I did not tell you people anything about anything."

"That's true, but it's not what people will believe, your clients in particular." He grinned sardonically.

"If I were doing the things you are accusing me of, which I am not, you'd turn me into glass. Sabotaging my business seems like an unusual punishment."

"It is true that vitrification would be the appropriate punishment. Man should not play God."

Janica wondered how many mutagens the agent had been augmented with. The Lex Nocturna took care to make her agents look as human as possible, but anyone who had seen them in action knew that they were anything but. But then they *were* authorised by the big man himself.

"The appropriate punishment would be no punishment." Janica hadn't meant to say it. It just slipped out. For a moment she was terrified, but Slavoj's grin had not disappeared.

"You are free to disagree with the Lord. He does not require your approval to be right. However, your country signed a treaty with the Holy See. The Lex Nocturna protects you from the Devil's Wrath, and in exchange we have the authority to cleanse the world of ungodly beings."

Janica nodded toward one of the Vietnamese airships, pre-emptively cursing herself for her impending insolence."They seem to have stopped dying of the Devil's Wrath just fine without your help. All of Asia seems to have."

"Those who are in league with the devil will naturally not die of his disease. It's really not very complicated." Brother Slavoj sounded utterly certain.

"What do you want from me?"

"The bishop likes you, Janica Palecek. You may be a criminal, but you still have some level of morality. He believes your soul can yet be saved."

Janica grit her teeth. All this time she thought she had been operating in the shadows, yet it seemed that even the bishop knew her name. The idea did not sit well with her.

The agent proceeded. "Some of your friends, however, the bishop is none too fond of. You know a man called Tibor Vlkodlak, and you also know his son. We know that they are doing something dangerous, and we want to stop it."

"I know neither who nor what you are talking about."

"You've seen their laboratory. You know what they are working on. Considering your pharmacology degree, you of all people should understand how dangerous it is."

"I cannot point you to any such laboratory, as I still do not know what you are talking about." Janica could not shake the feeling that the agent would arrest her at any moment if she so much as hinted at an admission of guilt, daytime or no.

"There is no need for that. We've seen the laboratory too, at least what was left of it."

Janica stopped dead in her tracks. Had something happened to Daniel?

Slavoj's grin widened. If he'd needed any more evidence of her knowing full well what he was talking about, he had just gotten it. "Not to worry, they simply managed to flee before our raid. Nobody appears to have died, yet."

"Are you threatening me, then?"

"The Lex Nocturna does not make threats. We simply act. In fact, the opposite is the case. The bishop offers amnesty. Work, even, as a free collaborator of the Lex Nocturna. But most importantly, he offers salvation."

"I've done nothing wrong. I don't need your salvation."

"If not for your salvation, then for that of Olga Palecek."

Another wave of fear washed over Janica. "My mother has nothing to do with this."

"We have a branch office in Pilsen. If you reject the bishop's offer, they will receive orders to arrest your mother as a mutagen smuggler."

"My mother is a pious woman. She volunteers for the church."

“Glass statues make poor accusers. I'm sure she'd make a fine addition to the palace.”

There were two bishops in Prague. One of them was Czech, and preoccupied with the daily business of the catholic church. The other was Bishop Francesco Presutti, a middle-aged man, glib as an eel, running the countrywide operations of the Lex Nocturna. The Vatican selected only those reared under its own tutelage in Rome to be in charge of the Lex, and the Czech Republic was no exception. He greeted her on the palace steps, dressed in a simple white liturgical robe. Even though he'd never seen Janica before, he smiled at her as though she were an old friend.

The entire palace was built in a style evocative of the ancient cathedrals of Rome, but the fact that it wasn't older than ten years was obvious. High walls patrolled by uniformed guards with submachine guns gave the impression of a military fortification. The surveillance and security equipment was concealed just well enough to still be visible to anyone with a trained eye.

“Miss Paklinski, welcome! I have heard so many interesting things about you!” The bishop beckoned her inside.

Janica had always assumed that, if she ever got into the palace, it would be because she was about to be vitrified. Her body was convinced that this was now imminent, and logically she could not pretend like it was an impossibility. A pit of cold fear welled up in her stomach, and her legs were shaking.

Bishop Presutti lead her through a number of wide corridors, each lined with alcoves presenting a glass statue of some poor soul who had fallen victim to the Lex Nocturna. Janica had always expected at least a few of them to look stoic or serene, but all of their faces were contorted in terror and agony. There were no plaques, no names. Everyone in this macabre gallery was anonymous.

“You might be wondering why there are no chimerics among these sinners,” said Presutti, not having to look at her to know that her mind was preoccupied with the statues. “We do vitrify them, but they are shattered afterward, to be transformed into various items of glassware. They are not worthy of being displayed side by side with true humans."

Presutti's office was extensive, with numerous romanesque windows offering a beautiful view of the banks of the Vltava. A single glass statue stood in the middle of it. It was a man who looked remarkably similar to what might have been a younger version of the bishop himself, pleading for his life.

She was offered a seat on a couch. Presutti sat down opposite her, his smile unwavering.

"Tibor Vlkodlak. I want him, and you work with him."

"I do not know who you are talking about."

"Please, Miss Paklinski, you have nothing to fear from me. Yes, you are a godless woman who engages in the darkest of businesses, and you should be vitrified immediately, but I do not operate like other bishops of the Lex Nocturna. You appear to have at least some level of moral character, and you corner the mutagen market here in Prague. If I eliminate you, it is statistically likely that someone worse will take your place."

"So take them out as well," Janica heard herself say. Could she never just shut up?

To her surprise, Bishop Presutti laughed. "You sound like my colleagues. Bishop Assenza in Belgium had a ring of farmers who mutated their cows to produce more milk vitrified. The result was a milk shortage, but the mutagen trade continued. I am a student of economics, Miss Paklinski. I know that, for as long as there is demand for a product, there will be people willing to supply it. The best I can do is minimise the harmful effects. When humanity opened the Pandora's box of genetic engineering, we crossed that particular Rubicon."

"From what I have heard, Tibor Vlkodlak is a very moral person as well." Janica chose her words carefully.

"You are wrong. He is not a person at all. But for what he is he has always acted better than most, which is why he has not been vitrified in spite of his nature. But what he is attempting now is very dangerous, you know that."

"He wants to end the wyverns. A lot of people die because of them." She could not help but defend him.

"True, but his way of going about it is more trouble than

the potential benefit."

"Why don't you fight the wyverns yourselves? It is after all your stated mission to eradicate the evils of genetic engineering." It was not the first time in her life that Janica wondered how she had gotten this far in spite of being so utterly reckless with her words.

But once again, the bishop seemed amused. "Our Vietnamese friends do an excellent job of that already. We wouldn't want to interfere with their business. Besides, we are much too busy fighting the Devil's Wrath. You may not have heard of this, but there was another outbreak near Ostrava. We contained it, thank the Lord. But who knows what terrors a genetically engineered disease might bring."

Janica managed to swallow her remarks about the fact that the Devil's Wrath was itself genetically engineered. It was only proof that the bishop was right. It had started as an attempt to cure all infectious disease, but it had become the very thing it was meant to destroy. Millions had died during the last major outbreak at the end of the war.

It had killed the Nazi leadership, which everyone was happy about, and also Stalin and his cronies, which only slightly fewer people were happy about. But Winston Churchill, most of the Royal Family, and essentially all of the American government, congress, and senate had been wiped out as well. The world had still not recovered from the death of much of its leadership.

If Daniel's anti wyvern plague posed any such risk to the world, it had to be stopped. She hated herself for it, but Janica agreed with the bishop, logically at least. In her heart, Tibor and Daniel were heroes to a disenfranchised and oppressed people, individuals standing tall against the tide of the world, fighting to do good.

"What is it that you want me to do, exactly?" she asked.

"Obviously I want you to find out where Tibor Vlkodlak and his son are holed up. Ask around, look into your contacts, try to bring me actionable intelligence."

"You brought me into your palace in broad daylight. Everybody probably already thinks I am dead. If I walk out of here, nobody is going to trust me," Janica noted.

"Well, Miss Paklinski, today is your lucky day, because today is the day you become a living legend. In just a few minutes, you will be the very first person to escape from the Lex Nocturna."

Once again, Tibor and Daniel had been hiding right under everyone's noses. It had taken Janica over a month to figure out the location of their laboratory, and it hadn't come cheap. Yes, her escape from the Lex Nocturna had made her a legend in the underworld, but she was already well-known before that, and if anything it made even people who believed her story reluctant to work with her.

After all, the Lex would be looking for her more than anyone. Doing business with a person of such notoriety posed risks. She couldn't tell them that there was no need to worry because they were not looking for her at all. That would have destroyed the entire point of her deception.

But now she was here, the inconspicuous warehouse in the twelfth district up ahead. It was plastered with the logo of some big shot import-export company from America, but considering the situation overseas they had no option but to lease out their empty warehouses to interested parties for extravagant sums of money.

The building was encircled by three breaching units of the state police, all accompanied by agents of the Lex Nocturna. Brother Slavoj was with her on her perch, well hidden from potential onlookers. Janica sincerely hoped that neither Tibor nor Daniel were in that laboratory right now, or any of the other researchers for that matter. As much as she considered what they were doing dangerous, they were still her friends. Vitrification was a fate nobody deserved.

"They're going in," said Slavoj.

Janica expected shock and awe, flash and fire. Maybe she was too far away from the action, but she heard and saw nothing at all. The only sounds of the action were subdued voices speaking calmly and quickly through Brother Slavoj's headphones. Not even there could she hear the sound of gunfire.

The breach couldn't have been longer than a minute, but

Janica felt as though hours had passed by when Slavoj looked at her with a frown on his face. “They want you in there,” he said.

“And blow my cover?”

Slavoj conveyed her doubts over his walkie-talkie, but whoever was on the other end of that line seemed to have their mind made up.

Inside the warehouse, there was indeed a laboratory. It was fully equipped with everything from refrigerators to flask racks to machines that Janica could not begin to guess the function of. Aside from the head of a wyvern placed on a table in the very centre of the room, it was completely empty.

It wasn't just empty of scientists, it was also empty of science. There were no samples, no residuals, no writing on the chalkboards, nothing. Everything was in pristine condition. Nobody had developed anything here at all.

One of the Lex Nocturna agents was standing by the severed wyvern head, a blood-stained envelope in his hand. It seemed to had come from the creature's mouth. He handed it to her, and she noticed that it was simply addressed to *Janica* in elegant cursive.

She opened it with hesitation. The letter contained only a single word.

Traitor.

There was a flash, a loud boom, and a force that flung her high into the air. Something painful bored into her back.

When she woke up in the hospital bed, her entire body seemed to be on fire. A crucifix was the only thing on the sky blue wall ahead of her. Janica tried to scream, but all that came out of her throat was a weak croak.

She didn't know how long she tried to make herself known until a nurse came in. Judging by her headdress, woman was a nun in addition to her hospital duties. “You poor young thing,” she murmured. “Don't worry, I'll get the bishop.”

Some time later, Bishop Presutti was standing at the foot of her bed. He was smiling like a little kid. “Miss Paklinski, I was beginning to worry we'd never see you again.”

Janica attempted to ask what happened.

"Please, don't try to speak. Your larynx is still regenerating. According to the medicus you should be able to use it again in a week or two, but there is no telling how the regeneration process will have altered your voice. Hopefully quite a bit."

She couldn't say that she fully understood what the bishop was talking about.

"The laboratory was a trap, as it turned out. It was lined with explosives, and the trigger was inside the envelope, so it all went up in flames a few seconds after you opened that letter. Brother Klaus and Brother Slavoj shielded you from the explosive inside the wyvern's head. There are only a handful of survivors."

Janica tried to mover her arms, but found that she couldn't.

"Please, don't. Your body is experiencing severe changes at the moment, it should not be strained too much, says the medicus." Presutti pulled a hand mirror from a small cabinet by the window. "Please do not be alarmed, everything will be fine." Without awaiting a response, he showed Janica her new reflection.

This time, she screamed. What was looking back at her was no longer Janica Paklinski. It was the face of a black cat with vaguely humanoid features. The dark fur had not yet sprouted in many patches where her freshly grown skin was still visible.

Janica screamed until her throat hurt so much that she had to stop or choke on the pain.

Bishop Presutti seemed unperturbed by her distress. "We've turned you into a chimeric, at least superficially. The pontiff himself has authorised this, and the opportunity was simply too good to waste. The front of your body was essentially burned off completely, which made grafting and growing new tissue very easy. It is ultimately a reversible procedure, but I do hope it will last for many years."

Even if she could have spoken, there were no words in Janica's mind.

"Congratulations, Miss Paklinski! Not only do you have a new identity, and thus an intact cover, but in a few short months you will be the very first undercover agent of the Lex Nocturna! What a joyous day the Lord has blessed us with."

Janica wanted to disagree. She couldn't.

Their Lord and Saviour

By Gwydion JMF Weber

"They know about Jesus Christ?" Cardinal Di Franco asked, leaning forward in his armchair. The scarlet of his cassock shone against the royal blue leather of his seat.

"Well, the closest approximation would be *The Saviour*. They don't have a name for him, exactly," Father Pembe explained, an awkward smile on his face. He was the only person in the room standing, and though very much interested in communications, his interest extended almost exclusively to the scientific study of them, not public speaking.

Bishop Hueng was sitting in an armchair of his own, vehemently shaking his head.

"We, humans, are God's chosen people. One would expect to find the concept of a saviour in primitive extraterrestrial religions. Hell, we've investigated such faiths before."

"This is different," Father Pembe insisted. "The parallels go much further." He opened the next slide in his presentation. It was a picture of a village situated on the cusp of a snowed-in sierra and a wide, almost glowing yellow plain. The round huts were built of gold-tinted mud bricks, decked with roofs that were cones of giant, colourful tail feathers. The xenozoologists were calling the animal they came from *Peacock Mammoth*, though that did not quite capture the sheer size of the creature the inhabitants of this plain hunted. The next slide was a large building at the centre of town, an oval with painted walls and a carved lattice of bones covered with a weave of smaller feathers as its roof. There, at the top of it, was what could only be described as a cross.

“Everything in this culture is round. They have 360° vision. They understand round shapes better than anything. All of their art and architecture is smooth, streamlined, really. Only the cross has right angles. This is most definitely a Christian church.” He waved that picture away, and one of a small crowd in front of the church doors appeared. Two of the people were human, Father Lehmann and himself, both wearing filtration masks to protect themselves from the sulphuric air. The others were aliens.

Like humans, they were bipedal, with straight spines (or rather three thin spines instead of a single thick one), hands with opposable thumbs (or rather two double-jointed thumbs per hand), a mouth (or rather maw), and a powerful brain (or rather a sphere split into 4 even parts in their skull). On their skin they had yellow plates of thick cartilage, which became smaller and thinner at the head, where they gained various shades of indigo and blue. One of the aliens, taller than the others, had a chain around his neck.

“Is that...” Cardinal Di Franco leaned forward in his chair again.

Father Pembe nodded.

“It's a Rosary. There can be no doubt about it. It's made of bone, not wood, but that's mostly because there's no equivalent to trees in this region. But that's not all,” he added with a glance at the sceptical face of the bishop. The next slide was of the church interior, illuminated by the sunlight shining through the feathers in the roof. In the middle, there was a circular altar, above which a cross hung suspended from the roof. It featured a rather detailed depiction of a member of the alien species nailed to it.

“Incredible.” Cardinal Di Franco poured himself a glass of water. He was beyond awe.

“Incredible is exactly what this is,” Hueng commented. “Tell me, precisely when did their saviour visit these people?”

“From what we've been able to tell, and mind you, they have a very different system of timekeeping, it should have been around a hundred years ago. One of the town elders claims to have seen him as a youngster. They have the ten commandments, which translate to exactly our ten commandments in the right order, they have original sin, they have the story of the garden. It's a bit different, of course, not a garden at all but rather a park of fountains, and the fruit was water from a particular watering hole. Their version of Eve was talked into it by what amounts to a snake." A video of a creature appeared. Straight as an arrow, it was sliding down one of the icy mountain slopes before launching itself into the air and grabbing hold of an airborne critter. It then extended a parachute-like skin flap and sunk softly down to the plain below, devouring its meal. "It has no extremities, and it's quite opportunistic. If one accepts a non-literal interpretation of the Bible, these are the same concepts expressed in ways different species might understand them."

"Are there any differences in our faiths?" asked the cardinal.

"Yes, mostly deviations and alternative interpretations of similar concepts that would serve them better in their living conditions. Obviously most of the stories in history do not exist, and they have no Bible, nor a church as an organization, but these things emerged centuries after Jesus Christ lived on Earth, so if we're going by the century-theory, one might say they're still on schedule. But there is one major difference that struck us in particular." Pembe took a deep breath. "They have known about alien civilizations, because *The Saviour* told them. He said that he's visited many of them before, and that he would ascend back to the heavens to visit countless more."

"How convenient, that they come with a theological justification for your nonsense, Father Pembe," Bishop Hueng said, his voice thick with contempt. "I suppose they also knew you would come to visit them one day."

"They do speak of a return of *The Saviour*, as do we, but I do not believe myself to be that," said Pembe, slightly intimidated by Hueng. All of this was true, he had invented none of it. "The problem is that, the way the biologists see it, these aliens will never become a world-spanning species. They're too specialized on their comparatively small plains region, and have no intention of leaving into environments they are not adapted for. To be honest, they appear to be quite the anomaly in more than one way."

Cardinal Di Franco sighed, then hit a button on his

armrest. The window of the briefing room cleared a little, revealing the alien world beneath, packed in it's yellow-tinged nitrogen-oxygen atmosphere. The part of the single megacontinent on its surface they could see from this angle looked a little bit like a crucifix, Pembe thought.

“There is something you need to know, and it cannot leave this room.” The cardinal looked at both of them intently. “The reason why the Holy See financed a scientific expedition to this particular alien world happened on the Pope's behest. His Holiness spoke to me of a vision he had involving a group of people with yellow cartilage talking to a dark-skinned priest. He compiled the list of every single expedition member himself, because God the Father gave it to him. He believes that we must elevate this species so it may join our galactic community of the Catholic Church.”

Bishop Hueng laughed.

“I see what is happening here. You two are trying to establish for yourselves a little cargo cult at the expense of the Holy See. We all know his High Holiness wont live to see the coming decade, so why not increase one's chances of being elected his successor, Cardinal?” He slapped the side of his armchair. “You two thought that having me on the mission might increase your chances of being believed back home. People know I don't believe aliens can be saved. Maybe I would have disappeared on the way back, to make sure I couldn't change my mind.” He rose, straightening his robes. “That's not going to happen. I'll be taking the express shuttle home, thank you very much.”

With those words, Bishop Hueng Qing-Han left the briefing room. Sixteen years later, he would inherit the Holy See and become the new Pope, Pope Titus III, and purge the Roman Catholic Church of those who would accept extraterrestrials into their congregations.

Meanwhile, Father Pembe would become Pope Martin XI only a few years later. He was the first pope of the Catholic Church of the Stellar Peoples, whose heavenly halls would be a space station in geosynchronous orbit. Cardinal Di Franco would be known as Saint Alessandro, patron saint of alien worshippers, open-mindedness, and humility. It was not the first split in papal lines, and it would not be the last, but many hold that it was the most significant.

The Library

By Gwydion JMF Weber

The punch card felt strange in Ernestino's hand. The anachronistic slip of cardboard was unyielding, its perforations enigmatic, surrounded by the same air of surreality as the small woman who had given it to him in exchange for a packet of salted almonds.

He drew his coat closer against the cold wind blowing through the streets of Rome, and took a final turn left in a complex of concrete abominations. It was a dead end with a heavy metal door, more rust than steel at this point.

For a moment, Ernestino felt like an idiot. He was just some history student looking for volume 38 of Polybius' *Histories*, a book which, according to most sources, no longer existed. The only reason he was here was because he'd taken the advice of someone he'd never met before. Chances were he was about to get robbed.

But there was something about the punch card, and the woman herself, that he could not quite shake as being genuine. Who asked for salted almonds as payment for anything? Who used punch cards to get into places?

It took him a moment to find the tiny slit near the lock. After taking a deep breath and almost breaking into a chuckling fit, he inserted the punch card. It was pulled from his fingers with voracious force.

Some internal mechanism made the door click and clack. Then, with a groan, it pushed itself open, and the dusty smell of old books blew out of the darkness beyond.

Ernestino hesitated. This was his last chance to turn back,

the final opportunity to shake his head, give up on finding the book that didn't exist, and make do without it. But how could he do that?

His eyes needed a moment to adjust to the light of the gas lamps. The more he saw, the more he realised he had come to the right place. Shelves upon shelves of books, and not two of them identical in size, shape, or contents.

Some were squat and sturdy, stacked atop one another. One was tall and thin, almost concerningly so, poking up from the labyrinth ten metres or more, almost scraping the brick dome that was the ceiling. Though they were fitted with ladders, Ernestino was convinced that climbing up there would lead to a catastrophic collapse.

He took a few hesitant steps. The shelves were overflowing with books, tomes, even scrolls, ranging from pristine to ruined, slotted in with seemingly no rhyme or reason. How was he ever going to find anything in here?

The door fell shut behind him. Ernestino's heart skipped a beat. He scrambled back to it on instinct more than rational thought. Out of nowhere, a man appeared, a stack of books in hand, jerking back, almost falling. He let out a curse in what sounded like German.

“Watch it!” Franz shouted. The kid had dashed from the shelves out of nowhere. “Did nobody ever tell you not to run in a library?”

All he got was a perplexed look. Of course. The door. He repeated his question in the heavily accented and unlikely to be grammatically accurate Italian he was capable of.

“What is this place?” the kid responded. Heavens, a newcomer. Franz did not have time for this.

“It's a library, you idiot,” he grumbled, pushing past the kid and heading off in an unmistakable gesture that he had places to be and did not want to be bothered. It seemed as though the message had been too cryptic for the newcomer, as he followed Franz like a puppy dog, offloading a slew of questions that came too fast for him to even understand them all.

He didn't need to. Every newcomer had the same

questions, including Franz himself, once upon a time. He'd been among the quicker ones to learn that it was pointless to look for answers. The Library offered all kinds of knowledge, but on the matter of its own nature it remained silent.

"There's an information desk at the centre. All the books are indexed there. If your book is not in this room, it will tell you where you can find it," Franz explained.

The kid looked at the labyrinth of bookshelves ahead, daunted. "How do I get to there?"

"Just try, and you'll manage." Franz demonstratively picked up his pace. If he'd told the truth, that the maze was in a constant process of reorganising itself, that would prompt even more questions he had no time to answer. "Just follow your instincts and you'll make it," he added when the kid was still following.

Having finally shaken the newcomer, Franz walked through a tall archway and out of the room, finding himself in a corridor with spiral staircases going up and down on either side as far as the eye could see.

He took the seventh to the left downward, and found himself in his very own small but cosy reading room. Aside from the naked bulb hanging from the low ceiling, lighting was provided by battery-powered LEDs. The black walls were almost entirely hidden behind stacks upon stacks of books.

Franz put down his latest haul on the table, grabbed the top book, *The Star of Solomon* by Arthur C. Clarke, and reclined in the armchair that he had just found down here some years ago. The science fiction narrative was immediately captivating, and Franz was well over a hundred pages into it when he could have sworn that someone had just sprinted up the spiral staircase from his tiny room.

That had been a close call. Sang-mi had almost been caught by the German. She was surprised that he hadn't even so much as spotted her when she'd been cowering underneath his table. Usually he was out for much longer. She had not expected him to return so quickly.

But she'd made it, with the book she'd been looking for in

hand. She should have known that Odoric of Pordenone's journal about his travels in the Library would be among the tomes the German kept down there. Now all she needed was the key.

Without making a sound, Sang-mi hushed past the spiral staircases and to the revolving door at the end of the corridor. She made one turn, and it opened to a great hall of white marble, smelling of incense. Another turn, and it opened to a vast cavern where bats with glowing eyes hung from the ceiling. On the next turn, it opened to a lonely mountain top, devoid even of snow, with nothing but clouds to the horizon.

The final turn brought her where she wanted to go, a hallway done in an 18th century European style, the beige paint on the walls chipping off and falling onto the numerous stacks of books on the parquet floor. Behind the tall, narrow windows to the right, colourful fish swam through an expansive coral reef.

She took the third corridor branching off, walking through a dark tunnel of magazines until she reached a rounded archway opening to Song Dynasty palace tea room with a balcony overlooking the forests.

Some of the usual people sat in the usual places. One group in particular, three old men wearing era-appropriate garments, were being served tea by maids with wooden faces, never saying a word. They had been sitting there every time she entered this room of the Library in the three years she had known about it. Sang-mi couldn't even begin to guess how long they had been sitting there before that.

If she wanted to get the key, she needed to find the Librarian.

Sang-mi sat down on the balcony, and waited to be served. The colours on the face of the waitress who brought her tea had faded, making what had once been a smile look like the grin of a serial killer.

Grimacing with anticipation, Sang-mi downed the disgustingly bitter brew in only a few swallows. It was better to get these things over with as quickly as possible. Charleston, the man who had taught her this trick, always carried a bottle of stevia drops with him in case he needed to locate the Librarian in this teahouse. Like all men, Charleston used clever tricks to disguise his weakness. Sang-mi did not believe in such luxuries.

Gently, she began shaking the cup with a little tea left in it, watching the patterns that the black leaves swirling around in there were forming. After a few seconds she became frustrated, and shook a little harder than intended. Taking a deep breath, she started again, and a picture slowly coalesced.

The Librarian was nearby, but if her interpretation was correct, it would be difficult to sneak up on him. With a sigh, she put down the porcelain cup and made her way back into the corridor with the underwater windows. She took the next branch, entering a vast maze of red rock, the morning sun burning hot in the desert above. Shelves were carved into the walls, the books inside of them untouched by the weather.

It was easy to get lost here if one could not read the subtle markings etched into the stone. Even now she was taking wrong turns. The wind piped through the smooth tunnels and crevices, playing the landscape like a massive organ.

Short of breath and having begun to sweat in the heat, Sang-mi arrived at a small hole in the ground. Even for her it was barely large enough to slide into, and the small steps in the darkness required the precision of a ballerina.

Moments later, she stepped out of an open crate in the rumbling hold of a cargo Zeppelin. It looked like a thing straight out of a World War I adventure book, down to the vast ocean passing by through the windows outside. All the boxes, labelled in Greek or maybe Russian, were full of books.

Sang-mi moved without making a sound, her light steps masked by the rumble of the propeller engines. The Librarian was easy to spot. He was a decrepit old man, more wrinkles than face, white hair splayed in all directions. He was sitting on a stool, slim shoulders bent forward, hunching over an arcane tarot ritual.

Dangling from his crumbling leather belt, flashing silver, was the key.

The Librarian chose to ignore the thief as she made off with his key. Instead, he finished his solitaire tableau, packed up the cards, and rose. His bones cracked like he'd been sitting for a century. He had to stretch out his arms to get rid of the pain.

Ponderously, he walked into the cockpit to check the gauges and controls. He turned a lever or two to make sure the boat was driving steady, then walked back into the hold, where a chess set had appeared where his cards had been only moments before.

Sometime in the past or future, he had made another move just now, and was waiting for himself to respond. The Librarian took a moment to analyse the board, then made a move of his own. Considering how poorly his opponent was playing in this particular game, he had to be in the past.

The Librarian opened the outer hatch of the airship and stepped into a cold, shadowy library inside an ancient tower. A central ladder ran through it from top to bottom, with wooden platforms mounted at regular intervals to allow people access to the books, which were located on stone shelves worked into the walls.

Few readers came here any more. They all preferred the larger rooms, the ones with a lot of books packed tightly together, where they could find what they were looking for easily, without having to go through strange and dangerous rooms. Maybe the Librarian was getting old again, but he lamented this loss of a sense of adventure in the modern times.

After climbing up a few levels, he walked through a metal door and into the microgravity of a space station. The white tube was bright and sterile, and an astringent smell hung in the air. Terminals chimed as he floated past them, asking for input on questions of chemistry and physics. Others offered him helpful directions through the Library.

If it had been up to him, the Librarian would have never installed those terminals. They were convenient, yes, but they also strengthened the complacency the modern people had with giving their minds over to machines.

But the Library had a will of its own, and he had to come to terms with that. Looking through one of the portholes, he saw Earth, covered in a sheet of mother-of-pearl, and shook his head. What sublime hubris had created such a thing. He sighed. There was no doubt about him getting old again.

He arrived at the end of the tube, planted his feet carefully on the ground, then stepped out of the altar of a cathedral dedicated to no deity in particular. All the pews were bookshelves, laden mostly with religious texts or treatises on philosophy or theology.

As he shuffled over the cool stone tiles, the Librarian reminisced of simpler times. This was a good room. It provided ample space for material, quiet corners for reading, and it tied into a central theme.

The Librarian found an open travel chess board lying on a cluttered table. His opponent had made another move. Checkmate. He sat down and laughed. Maybe he wasn't in the past after all.

"Excuse me," a tall man with an Australian accent said. "Mister Librarian, I have something for you."

The Librarian looked at what he was holding outstretched in his hand and smiled. It was a book he'd never seen before.

On the inside, Charleston was giggling like a little girl. It wasn't every day one could surprise the Librarian.

The old man paged through then slim, black volume, looking over the alien letters. After a few moments, he started to laugh. "Oh what a scamp," he said, wiping a tear from his eye.

"What is it?" Charleston asked.

"It's a tactics manual for Go, published many years from now. Someone is joking with me."

Charleston smiled. He had found it on the steps of a museum in Hobart and figured it must belong here. There was a quiet understanding among those who frequented the Library that books which did not belong in the world should be returned.

"Mister Charleston, I have something you might be interested in." The Librarian lead him to a nearby shelf and produced a small paperback. "This is a cookbook written by Socrates, translated into English by Sir Ian Francis Burton."

"I'm not that much of a cook, unfortunately," Charleston responded.

"Well then you ought to become one, no?" The Librarian gave him a toothless smile.

His pager beeped. That had been quick.

Charleston excused himself and took off, moving through a cave of books into a rainy New York street with neither cars nor people in it. By way of an Italian butcher shop he took an elevator down into a clock tower.

There was a clock face on each of the four walls, every one of them transparent, and every one looking into a different world. Through the northern one he could see a vast, sandy desert, whereas behind the eastern one there was a port with ships made out of mushroom. To the south, Charleston could see an overgrown industrial landscape, and to the west was a rugged expanse of ice and frost.

Mister Li sat at one of the many reading tables, looking at Charleston with scorn.

"What happened?" Charleston asked.

"You said you were going to distract him!" The Chinese man's Oxford accent was flawless. Though he was young, he spoke with martial authority.

"That's what I was doing when you paged me." Charleston raised his arms defensively.

"Well Sang-mi ran into trouble. This is what happens when you get a Korean to do a job that requires brains." Mister Li slapped his hand flat on the table.

"I heard that." Sang-mi was coming up a stairwell, pushing a weeping young man in front of her with a very effective arm lock.

"Who is this?" Mister Li demanded.

"My problem. He was sniffing around the vault, practically ran into me."

"Please, I was only going where the reception desk sent me," the boy said in broken English.

"What's your name, young man?" Charleston asked.

"Who gives a shit what his name is?" Mister Li spat.

"Ernestino Padani, sir," the kid responded. "Please, I am just a student, I did not do what she says I did."

"I don't care." Mister Li rose. He had a pistol in his hand.

"Hold on there, mate." Charleston stepped in his way. "He's barely more than a child. You cannot disrespect the sanctity of the Library."

"You think I care about the rules that this abomination of a place has? There are secrets in here, national secrets of the United States, Japan, Australia, India, everyone. My government does not care how I get them, so long as I get them."

"And how do you think the great empires of the past fared in their attempts to outcompete their enemies with the knowledge contained within these halls?" The Librarian was suddenly standing in front of the northern clock face. He had desert sand in his hair. "How would you distinguish between documents which are real, and documents which do not apply to your reality?"

Mister Li spun around with trained precision and pointed his gun at the Librarian. "Stay back, ungodly creature."

"This place does not like being a slave to national interests, Mister Feng," said the Librarian.

"How do you know my name?" A moment of terror flashed over Li's face.

"I know many thing about you, Xia-Wen Feng, born on the 16th of August 1992 in Baoding, Hebei province. I know that your father was a school administrator, and your mother an army clerk before she became a housewife." The Librarian took a single step.

Mister Li pulled the trigger without a moment's hesitation. The bullet hit the Librarian perfectly in his heart. The old man looked down at the bloodless hole in his chest, then at Li, disappointment on his face. Then, he crumbled to dust.

The room was silent. Even the clocks seemed to stop ticking for a moment.

"What in all blazes did you just do, mate?" Charleston demanded.

Mister Li was about to respond when he caught fire. He dropped the gun, screaming in unspeakable agony as his body was bathed in flames. Charleston stepped back from the heat, worried he might catch fire himself.

The blaze was over as quickly as it had begun. Mister Li was standing there, unharmed. Not even his clothes were singed. But something about him was different, something in his gaze. Whoever he had been moments earlier, nothing of that person was left.

“I'd like my key back now, if you do not mind,” he said to Sang-mi. Even his voice was different somehow.

The thief hesitated, but ultimately obliged. She handed the Librarian the key she had stolen from him.

“Now I banish you.”

Sang-mi did not even have time to protest. She simply plopped out of existence as though she had never been there.

Charleston swallowed heavily. He was terrified of what would happen next.

“Mister Charleston, you've always had respect for this place. The fact that you can find new books means that you are special, and in light of the fact that you were coerced to do what you did, I will not banish you. You are, however, being watched.” He mimicked their gazes meeting with his fingers.

Charleston almost wanted to get to his knees. Being banished from the Library would be a fate worse than death. “Thank you, sir. Thank you so much.”

“Don't be sentimental now.” The Librarian smiled. “This young scholar seeks volume 38 of Polybius' *Histories*. You know where it is located. Redeem yourself by showing him to it.”

Soulsilver Pond

By Gwydion JMF Weber

The vapour hovering above the pool of soulsilver shone mystically in the few places where the sun made its way through the canopy of buildings overhead. Thick drops of it fell through the floor of a factory above, creating a river of magical sludge flowing through the rocks with an almost infuriating languor.

Down here, the pool was a location with a name to thousands of people. Eateries were named after its proximity to it, and those who were not were often described as 'the one by the Soulsilver Pond'. Children declared it their meeting point when they went out to play, as did young lovers in the late hours of the evening.

Meanwhile, to the owners of the processing plant above, the soulsilver was naught but a rounding error. A waste product in need of proper disposal, deserving only of the attention of pre-emptively bribed health inspectors. Who could exert ownership over something that was in their nominal possession, but which they did not care about? Conversely, who could exert ownership over something they cared about, but did not posses?

"Maybe someone bought the land that the Pond is on?" Connee suggested. She was staring at the shining liquid as though it would start revealing all its secrets if simply made uncomfortable enough.

"They don't sell plots down here, only structures," Hea answered, poking around in the soulsilver with her cyberarm. It was sprayed in almost the same pale blue as her skin, but didn't quite get there. "The ground itself would be owned by the city, which, as a corporate entity without singular consciousness, cannot assert itself as the 'owner' of this pool."

"Maybe it's the stockholders? One of them declares ownership, activates the soulsilver, and has the spirit within do their bidding." Connee was absent-mindedly playing with a tongue of flame flipping between her fingers.

"That's not how corporate ownership works," Hea dismissed.

"Well then I'm out of ideas. Unless it really is the owner of the processing plant, of course, but I doubt he even knows that he owns that factory." With a grumbling stomach, Connee turned her gaze to a nearby seafood shack.

Hea shook her head. "He owns the soulsilver, but not the ground it is on. And, as you said, he does not emotionally own the stuff."

"I mean, there's always-" Connee commenced.

"No. We are not doing your crackpot theories today. The spirit of a pool of soulsilver cannot, I repeat, cannot exert ownership over the pool it inhabits. Someone needs to consciously own and summon the spirit for it to even exist in the first place. Their minds don't work like those of people do."

"You've read three books on the subject, so you must be an expert." Connee shrugged. Without another word, she approached the takeaway.

"Hey, where are you going?" asked Hea.

"It's difficult to think on an empty stomach."

A few minutes later, they were dining on wok-seared kraken scallops with sautéed vegetables, garnished with a spicy and sour sauce that changed colours every blink of the eye. This time of the day, the place wasn't very busy, so they had the elderly lady working the kitchen all to themselves.

"Do the people down here have any unusual concepts of ownership?" asked Nea, bypassing subtlety.

The lady frowned. Her hands cut bell peppers, cucumbers and bananas with night-automatic movements. "Well, when you own something, it's yours." She seemed confused at the question.

"How about communal ownership?" came the follow-up. "You know, multiple people owning the same thing."

"Well, isn't that true for everything, really?" The elderly

lady slapped a large chunk of kraken meat on her cutting board and began slicing. "I mean yes, I own my business, and I own this shack, and I own the ingredients for the food I serve, but everyone has a liege."

This time it was Hea who frowned. Her species had never engaged in feudalism, and stuck to white-collar crime. Thus, she found it a difficult concept to grasp. Connee however knew exactly what the woman was talking about.

"And who is your liege, if that's not a taboo subject?" She'd encountered many a slum where the gangs preferred to work in the shadows, and nobody was allowed to tell anyone to whom their protection money went. Heck, she'd grown up in one of those places.

"Tarlan, of course." The old woman had a smirk on her face. "I'm surprised you haven't heard of him. He's the best liege of them all. I haven't had trouble with hooligans in thirty years thanks to him."

It emerged that Tarlan was indeed quite the Samaritan. They found him on a small platform, handing out an assortment of electronics equipment in front of a tailoring business. They looked like third-rate wares, and, judging by the strategic holes cut into the packaging, they were stolen.

He was a giant of a man, muscular to an almost comical degree. His eyes were of a deep purple, and his skin was a pale shade of crimson, suggesting a good amount of vatgrown ancestry. His bald head was covered in white scars, and his canines were sharp an overgrown, giving him a resting facial expression reminiscent of a wolf. But, in spite of his appearance, Tarlan exuded friendliness and compassion. He was quick to invite Connee and Hea inside, and offered them citrus water.

"It's not every day that people of such station visit me," he admitted, "but I feel honoured nonetheless."

"Who do you think we are, exactly?" Hea's question was heavy with suspicion.

"Researchers, of course." Tarlan sat a carafe on the table. "You're looking into Soulsilver Pond, and why exactly it has a spirit when it shouldn't."

Connee heard a click from Hea's cyberarm. It was a

familiar sound, and usually preceded a discharge of magical energy against someone who was a threat. If Tarlan noticed it, she could not tell.

"I have my eyes and ears all over this neighbourhood. There's a reason they call me 'liege'." He poured into three cups. "You can't just come in here, express interest in one of my greatest assets, and expect it to go unnoticed."

"So you are the one who is controlling that soulsilver spirit?" asked Connee, tensing up. This situation could go sour very quickly, and if Tarlan dropped his mask, she needed to be ready.

"How do you think a single man can defend such prime real estate from the plethora of gangs waiting at the gates?" Tarlan was still as relaxed. He was either oblivious to Connee's and Hea's sudden hostility, or he did not care. "I've controlled this spirit for a long time. I will continue to do so for many years to come. If you ask nicely, I can explain to you how I do it."

"You are mistaken, Tarlan. We are here for the spirit, but we are not researchers," Hea said. "We're Enforcers."

"A pity. Here I was, thinking that some actual scientists had taken an interest in my magic, and you turn out to be nothing more than some mercenary dogs from the Upper City." Tarlan's continued casualness had taken an eerie undertone. "I'll give you an opportunity to leave, and tell your handlers that you found nothing down here."

"How were you able to keep this a secret for so long?"

Tarlan chuckled. "It was never a secret. This is just the first time someone from upstairs has bothered to look. I suppose I finally took out the wrong guy."

"You used your spirit to murder a young man," said Connee. "You may consider yourself a good person, but that is unforgivable."

"Ah yes, I know the arsehole you speak of. He came down here, treated the place like his personal playground. His sins amount to much more than mine do, I can assure you as much. But, of course, nobody cares when people from the Lower City get hurt. Only when they defend themselves are they paid a visit."

"This conversation is concluded." Flashes of light sparked

forth from Hea's hand, coalescing from random jolts into complex, hermetic symbols.

"One thing we agree on." Tarlan smashed his hand on the table, bursting apart the cups and carafe. The citrus water streamed into a sphere floating in the air and froze.

In the exact moment Connee was ready to unleash inferno upon Tarlan, she was pulled back by an unseen force, dragged out of the tailor shop, and flung into the rocky plaza alongside Hea. Tarlan punched the frozen sphere, and it burst into a thousand daggers of ice headed straight for them.

They were caught by a barrier of pale, blue light emanating from Hea's palm. She wasted no time going on the offensive, barraging Tarlan with a series of magical bolts as he jumped out of his store like a maddened beast. He moved like a monkey, climbing the walls and rock pillars with ease, evading.

Connee launched discs of flame to where she anticipated he would go, but was thrown into the air after only three flicks of her arm. "The spirit!" she shouted, and Hea understood. The press of one button was all it took to activate the tiny charge she had deposited in the Soulsilver Pond earlier. The spirit, invisible around them, cried out in agony as the neutralising fluid corroded its soulsilver. Connee could feel the invisible structure around her writhe in agony, and its inhumane screams sent shivers through her bones.

Tarlan pounced on her, jumping impossibly far, arms outstretched. His teeth were now fangs, and he had claws where only moments ago had been fingernails. A blast of energy threw him off course, courtesy of Hea. In an instant, Connee was with him, hammering lashes of searing flame onto his exposed flank.

A series of quick, purposeful arm movements later, Hea had constructed an ethereal cage around Tarlan, who was howling in pain from his burns. All around them, the soulsilver spirit crumbled and dissolved as his home was destroyed. Some bystanders stared at them in shock, but most had nothing but anger an disgust in their eyes.

Connee and Hea both believed that they did good by locking away criminals like Tarlan. Seeing these people and the security he provided them, this was the first time they felt doubt.

Yamantau

By Gwydion JMF Weber

Born in the Yaroslavl town of Danilov, Yermolai Savelyovich Rebrov was 23 years old when he was reassigned to the Urals in 1975. Coming from an affluent household of party functionaries dedicated to maintaining the integrity of the Soviet Union, he was loyal to the motherland and had unshakeable faith in the ideals of Communism.

General Secretary Leonid Brezhnev read his name once on a list of young officers recommended for reassignment to a top secret installation that had brought him and many other Soviet leaders a number of sleepless nights. If one was prone to believing rumours, one might have believed that Stalin himself had been afraid of it.

It was an assignment that required the most loyal, capable, and dedicated people. The kind of person who believed in the wisdom of the party and its leadership, and would sacrifice everything for the Soviet Union, its citizens, and possibly the world itself. People who would have been useful in a great many positions, but were needed more urgently in the mountains.

It was because Brezhnev signed that very document that Sergeant Major Rebrov arrived at the foot of Mount Yamantau on a brisk spring afternoon, after an eight hour trip on the back of a military truck, together with 19 other men.

They were loaded off in the courtyard of a barracks complex built around a gigantic door leading straight into the mountain itself. The soldiers out here, who inspected the new arrivals one by one and verified their identities, looked at them with pity.

Three of the young recruits were pulled away. They were not meant to enter the complex, but become part of the outside barracks. Though they seemed disappointed, the other soldiers told them they should be relieved. They were the lucky ones.

An alarm sounded, and the great door into the mountain opened. It was thicker than Yermolai was tall, full of complex mechanisms and heavy locking bars. Machine guns were pointed at it from several towers.

An old man stepped out into the courtyard, flanked by four lieutenants. He wore the beige uniform and blue hat of the NKVD, and had the look of someone who had seen nothing but war in his long life. Even so, he stood straight as an arrow, bearing whatever burden was on his shoulders with the iron discipline of a seasoned military commander.

He introduced himself as Colonel Porphyry Emelyanovich Buzinsky, and commanded the recruits to follow him into the mountain. When they were all inside the garishly lit, downward sloping concrete tunnel, an atavistic kind of fear welled up in Yermolai's stomach.

It was impossible to judge the size of the underground complex, but the weight of it felt gigantic. A lieutenant lead them to a sleeping room, where each had been assigned a bunk. Nobody spoke. Silence had made this place its home. It seemed like steps did not make a sound on the linoleum floors of the long hallways.

When they had stowed their luggage, the lieutenant lead them into a dimly lit classroom. The chalkboard was obscured with a heavy curtain. Colonel Buzinsky was sitting behind a heavy desk, inspecting his new recruits one by one.

"I am a killer of enemies," the old man said when they were all seated. "When I was young, I fought in the Great Patriotic War, and killed over a hundred German Fascists. I was among those who liberated Auschwitz. It was a place of horror unlike any I had ever seen."

He rose from his chair and began pacing in front of them. "Every day I wish myself back to that place. Compared to where I am today, it was idyllic, peaceful, even cosy. Yes, you heard me right. I would trade this life away even if it meant experiencing the horrors of the war every day, and it would not be a difficult decision."

Yermolai frowned. Going to war the the glory of the Soviet Union, especially fighting an enemy as heinous as the Nazis, must have been a great honour. Only the weak were broken by the trepidations of war. But Buzinsky was a colonel. His wisdom had to be respected.

Instead of offering further explanation, the colonel pulled away the curtain, revealing not a chalkboard, but a window. Behind it, a handful of men and women in white lab coats sat in a canteen, eating borscht. They all had heavy bags under their eyes, their stares trailing off into the distance every few moments. None seemed to notice the soldiers looking at them. The window only went one way.

"I would like to direct your attention here." Buzinsky pointed at the left corner of the room, where a man who had just entered was pressing buttons next to an aluminium box. A few moments later, a light blinked green, and the man opened the box to find his own bowl of borscht inside.

"This is not a machine. There are cooks on the other side of that panel, and he has just communicated to them how he would like his lunch. It is imperative that he be unable to speak with them in any other way. To ensure this is our mission here."

The colonel pulled a canvas over the window, and a projector clicked on in the back of the room. A floor plan of the complex appeared, laid out in three concentric circles. The outermost was the thinnest. It was green, designated *Military Area*, and isolated from the next ring save for a number of locked doors.

The *Science Area* was blue, and featured many more rooms with cryptic designations, some of which were too small to read even for someone with Yermolai's excellent eyesight. They included things like *Stereophone Dimmer*, *Obesiance Chamber*, and *Albumen Sieve*.

The centre, occupying most of the base, was left entirely blank. *Subject* was wall it said.

"Our duty at this installation is to observe and monitor these scientists. They know we are here, and they know we are here to keep them safe, but they cannot talk to us, and we cannot talk to them. We make their food, clean their chambers, and sometimes go in to apprehend and pacify individuals who have lost their mind. But we cannot, under any circumstances, talk to them."

Yermolai felt the need to raise his hand. "Why is this, sir?"

Colonel Buzinsky's grin looked more like a snarl. "Because of their work."

Unsatisfied with the response, he raised his hand again. "What is their work, sir?"

"They do the same thing we do. Observe and monitor."

After a month of service, confined to the underground space of Yamantau Base, not having seen the sun in what felt like a lifetime, Yermolai was beginning to grasp the routines and practices of the complex. Even the simplest of tasks were fastidiously described in various manuals, and everyone with experience working here was highly scrupulous of following protocol.

Peculiar events were beginning to pile up. The first week, Yermolai was under the impression that one of his comrades in the sleeping quarters was a loud snorer. Every night, in his dreams, he heard calm, rhythmic breathing, and he wasn't the only one.

However, when he awoke early one night, at first suspecting that he had been roused by the snorer, he found that the room was as utterly silent. After a visit to the lavatory he had resumed sleeping, and the breathing returned.

One day, while mopping the floors, a fellow sergeant who had served here for some time told them to put their ears to the ground. Believing at first that it was some sort of chicanery, Yermolai obliged reluctantly. What he heard drove a cold shiver down his spine.

It was a slow, regular thumping, dulled by however many layers of concrete it was passing through. One of his comrades said it sounded like a heartbeat, but Yermolai could not concur. Hearts beat twice in any given interval, but this thumping only occurred once. He developed a habit of putting his ear to the ground from time to time. The thumping was always there.

Yermolai was rolling a food cart through the long tunnel leading to the northern monitoring post, where men with empty eyes and haggard faces listened to microphone feeds from the *Science Area* through heavy headsets, when he was told to breach containment for the first time.

An alarm howled, and a senior lieutenant ran past him, giving orders to stop pushing the cart and get geared up. Next to each of the doors into the *Science Area*, all of which were flanked by two guards at all hours of the day, was a locker with breaching equipment for up to twenty soldiers.

Yermolai put on a loose containment suit of brown plastic, donned sunglasses that blocked his peripheral vision, and inserted rubber plugs into his ears. Everyone in the breaching party of four was given a baton. Only the most senior officer received a small handgun, loaded with nonlethal ammunition.

When they entered the *Science Area*, Yermolai could hear the whining of atonal klaxons through his ear plugs. Heavy fire doors had blocked the hallways around them, as well as access to the individual laboratories. Under no circumstances could the soldiers know what was happening inside.

Scientists cowered in the corners, horrified looks on their faces. One came running, pointing them down a hallway. The lieutenant took the lead. It did not take long to find the reason for the alarm. Another scientist, a man in his forties with Siberian features, was standing at an intersection of two corridors, punching wildly in all directions.

His shouts cut through the klaxon and the earplugs, yet were too quiet for Yermolai to understand, if they were coherent at all. Quickly and with overwhelming force the soldiers subdued the man, administered a sedative, and slipped a straight jacket over him. When they had carried him back into the *Military Area*, he was put on a stretcher and thrown into a padded cell.

Six days later he was delivered to the surface in a body bag.

Yermolai inquired with one of the senior officers. It seemed that something like this happened half a dozen times a year. Sometimes it was one of the monitors who snapped, but those were usually easier to handle. The use of lethal force was authorised in such situations.

It was not the only time a person died. One morning Yermolai awoke to find his bunk neighbour, a young man from Moscow named Dmitriy, dead. His mouth was open in a silent scream, his eyes were bloodshot and wide open. Nobody had heard a sound that night, least of all Yermolai.

They were given an extra ration of good food that day, and told that Dmitriy had died of an unexpected heart attack. A bit of questioning revealed that unexpected heart attacks were a common cause of death in the Yamantau complex, and usually included symptoms such as sweating blood and having burns on one's internal organs.

It was after three months of service that Yermolai and his comrades were allowed their first visit to the surface. When he stepped into the barracks and smelled the fresh mountain air, he realised that he had forgotten what the sky looked like. They spent three days of leisure time with the soldiers stationed at the surface.

Though they were not allowed to discuss the goings on inside the complex, the recruits who had arrived with them and were picked for surface duty commented that they all looked half dead while fishing in a small pond.

When they went back into the mountain, Colonel Buzinsky was already waiting for Yermolai. "You have been asking many questions," he said in his sparsely furnished office. The only non-essential object in the room seemed to be a bronze-plated orrery, and even there Yermolai could not be certain it wasn't somehow important.

"I apologise, sir. If you wish me to stop I shall do so," Yermolai responded.

"Yes and no. You ask questions, but you are good with protocol. You do it in a manner that is not subversive, with consideration for operational morale. This makes you leadership material. It is important for people in senior positions to both think and follow orders, not out of fear, but because they understand the importance of command. I am promoting you to junior lieutenant."

“Will I get briefed on what the purpose of this base is, sir?”

“No. There are only four people alive who have a full picture of this, and I am the only one of them currently stationed here.”

It was disappointing, but Yermolai trusted the competence of the Soviet institutions.

Another three months later, after the next visit to the surface, he was promoted again to overseeing the monitoring room. He was without a headset, and it was explicitly not his duty to listen to the microphones inside the *Science Area*, but it was impossible not to hear a thing or two.

The first thing he realised was that the scientists were not speaking Russian. They weren't speaking any language he could classify at all. It included sounds that he'd never heard a human being make before, from hisses to whistles to grumbles. He asked one of the monitors if he understood what they were saying, and the man simply shook his head. Whether that was a no or a refusal to answer his question, Yermolai could not tell.

One morning he awoke to a gunshot. Considering it had come from the adjacent barracks, it should have been much louder than it was. One of the monitors had committed suicide. Colonel Buzinsky assured him not to worry, as this only happened to the monitors, never the other soldiers.

Yermolai did not feel reassured at all. The monitors were working under his supervision. He cared about the people under his command, even if he did not understand what they did.

For a week, the scientists seemed more agitated than usual. Through the one-way windows, Yermolai could see them shuffling about more quickly, exchanging concerned glances as they spoke to each other. Their chatter became quieter, more animated. One of them snapped and almost killed another. There was no way for them to know that one of the monitors had died, but they were reacting to it anyway.

Shortly after his first anniversary of being stationed at Yamantau Base, Yermolai ascended to the surface with Colonel Buzinsky. At first he thought a new batch of recruits had arrived, but waiting in the courtyard was only a tall, middle-aged woman smoking a cigarette. A new addition to the science team.

She did not salute but continued to smoke, looking at the mountain and the forests. When her cigarette was finished, she dropped the butt on the ground, took several deep breaths, and looked at the colonel with determination. “I need to remember what it's like.”

“You'll forget soon enough,” Buzinsky responded.

When the heavy door closed behind them on their way back down, Yermolai realised the truth. This woman knew what she was getting into better than he had. Once she put on that lab coat, she would never return to the surface again. She would be trapped underneath Mount Yamantau until the day she died.

A moment later, Yermolai realised that the same was true for him. He would see the surface from time to time, spend a few days out in the sun, but deep inside his heart he knew he would never be able to leave again. Whatever the work they were doing down here was, it was important enough to make loyal soldiers and intelligent scientists disappear forever.

It could only be of the utmost importance.

Sinbeast

By Gwydion JMF Weber

"Class 10? Are you fucking serious?" Bozeman asked.

"Competence has it's downsides, Joel," Cortez answered with a shrug.

"What if I pass?"

"And violate the Peterson Act? Face it, you're the highest-rated Hunter in three states. This is your duty as an officer of the court." Cortez was saying things Bozeman already knew.

"Can I at least get a hand?" he asked.

"Sessions is free, and he's got the rating. You sure you wanna split the bounty?" Cortez raised an eyebrow.

"Yeah, I wanna fucking split the bounty!" Bozeman hit the desk with his flat hand. "I'd rather be alive than dead and a few thousand richer. Jesus Christ Cortez, have you been in this office so long you've forgotten what's out there?"

Cortez made a gesture like a zookeeper calming a wild animal.

"Look, they executed the guy three days ago, his Sinbeast probably hasn't even formed yet. Who knows, he might end up being a Class 9, and then you'll still get paid for a Class 10! Isn't bureaucracy amazing?" He laid a sheet of paper on the table and handed Bozeman a pen. It was the contract on the Sinbeast of one Angelo Martinelli, issued by the Montana Office of Sinbeast Extermination.

"I die from this, my Sinbeast is coming for your ass, Cortez."

That night, on a small pier in the north of Canyon Ferry

Lake, Joel Bozeman and Anthony Sessions entered the police motorboat they had commandeered. The half moon was slowly rising above the mountains, and, aside from a few meagre clouds, the star-spangled firmament was clear.

"This is pretty okay, far as serial killer stomping grounds go," Sessions noted. "I remember Detroit was never as nice-looking as this."

"Well, at least we'll have some pretty scenery when we die," Bozeman said dryly.

"You sure he's gonna form as a sea monster?" asked Sessions.

"He stole rich girls on vacation and drowned them in this very lake. They called him the 'Canyon Ferry Lake Kraken'. So yeah, I'm pretty sure he's gonna form as a sea monster."

There was a moment of silence, and the only sound was the soft splatter of water against the hull of the boat.

"I fought a sea monster once," Sessions reminisced. "Gangsta kid, saw his brother get shot at Lake St Clair. Got real mad, went on a shooting spree against the people who did it. Died himself, of course. Not very strong, but slippery as hell, that one."

"He come back as a kraken?"

"Naah, just a water zombie. Scary eyes tho." Sessions took his binoculars to scan over Cemetery Island half a mile away.

Police radio started blaring.

"We got a big bogie, might be what you fellas are looking for," said the dispatcher with a voice much calmer than it should have been. Then again, she was sitting safely over in Helena. "To the west, first inlet below Cave Bay. We'll send a patrol car to help you guys out." Obviously this person had never even heard of a Class 10 before.

"Don't. Your officers are not trained for this. We'll take over from here," Bozeman responded.

"Alrighty then," was the answer. Sessions gave Bozeman a baffled yet somewhat amused look. Clearly, he had never dealt with a Class 10 either, and was underestimating the situation. The motor of the little police boat roared, and Bozeman gave it the spurs to cross the lake.

Their target became clear the moment they laid eyes on it.

A squat, shingle-roofed building, not quite as luxurious as the ones surrounding it. Then again, those weren't exactly villas either. The lights were flickering erratically, and the entire building was shivering as though caught inside an earthquake. Just a taste of what a Class 10 was capable of. Sessions had the house scoped in through his sniper rifle, but didn't see anything, and the jury-rigged sonar of the police boat caught nothing of interest going on in the water beneath them.

Carefully, Bozeman manoeuvred the boat to the shore and tied it to the rotten pier. He grabbed his HK416 assault carbine, loaded with silvered, depleted uranium hollow points coated in cyanide, and slowly made his way on land, Sessions in tow. Bozeman switched back and forth between the night vision and heat scan modes of his scope, and saw massive heat anomalies inside the house, which was shaking so violently now that he feared it might be ripped apart. Spots of extreme heat melded with areas of arctic cold, separating again as though the laws of physics didn't command them to merge.

The back door was open, and the second Bozeman stepped inside, the shaking stopped, and the temperature went back to normal. All the lights were turned on. The house was almost completely empty, not even any furniture around except for an old refrigerator standing in the middle of the room. The barrel of his gun pointed at the chrome-plated appliance, Bozeman opened the fridge, only to recoil at what was inside.

“Jesus, fuck!” he exclaimed at the sight of the severed head of a man in his early fifties.

“Oh shit, that's disgusting,” said Sessions, grimacing.

“This is something Martinelli pulled, one of his first murders,” Bozeman remembered. “He killed the girl's dad, then imitated his voice on the phone to lure her out to the lake from Great Falls.”

“He do that often?” Sessions asked, “lure folk in by imitatin' voices?”

“Shit.”

That exact moment, the entire house started moving. Bozeman stumbled and fell over. It was as though the entire hillside was being dragged into the lake, boat, pier and all, into a black gullet rimmed with razor-sharp teeth. The two hunters were slammed against the ceiling, then the floor, and when Bozeman came back to a few seconds later, it was dark, hot, and damp. The sound of wet flesh slapping on wet flesh was all around him, and the soft, warm ground was pulsating softly. The stench was disgusting. This was what a Class 10 looked like.

Calmly, has animal instinct of panic bubbling beneath the thin cover of his first-class professional training, he reached around to find his rifle lying next to him. Or no, wait, it was only the scope, ripped from the weapon, but still intact, and with some charge remaining in its internal capacitor. It was still in night vision mode, which was just as well because the switch was on the butt of the gun, and heat vision would help him little in here. He felt something soft touch his leg, like a tentacle, and, with a reflexive motion, pulled his machete and severed it clean. He held the scope over his left eye and looked around. He was inside some flesh-chamber, the tissue around him moving to the beat of some distant, gigantic heart. The way behind him was closed, and the way ahead was crawling with tentacles just like the one he'd just cut. This was going to be nasty.

Striking wildly with his machete at anything that tried to make a grab for him, he moved forward, down the slight incline that this flesh tube made. He could have stood up in here, but Bozeman proceeded ducked, some dark, primal fears deep inside of him clawing at the bars of their cages in the zoo of his mind. The zookeepers were drill sergeants, soldiers, and combat instructors, and not even their cacophony of angry shouting, words of camaraderie, and calm instructions was going to keep them chained up much longer.

He arrived at a small vortex of interlocking tentacles blocking the way. Bozeman put the scope in his pocket, grabbed the machete with both hands, and went wild on the things in the dark. A wail of pain went through the Sinbeast's body, and Bozeman grinned. Shouldn't have eaten a guy with a big-ass sword. When the path was clear, he stepped into a large, cavernous chamber the size of a small airplane hangar. This Sinbeast had to be destroyed soon, otherwise it would devour everything around the lake. A pool of stinking liquid covered almost the entire ground, barely knee-high as far as Bozeman could tell. On a small islet he could see Sessions, his extremities contorted in impossible ways, and his torso stretched to the point of almost ripping apart. He was bound by tentacles, and was quickly being broken down by the acidic liquid. A drop of it landed on the back of Bozeman's hand, and he shrieked in pain. It was like a sour fire burning through his skin.

He needed to find the boat. The boat was the only way to kill this thing. Retching from the smell, Bozeman looked around to find it leaning against the stomach wall, not far from were Sessions lay. Bingo. Keeping close to the shore, which was barely a foot wide, and careful to slice at any tentacles coming for his ankles, he made his way to the boat, tipped it over, and climbed inside. There, in the back, was a small metal box. Just what he'd been looking for. He pushed the boat back to the entrance, grabbed the box by the handle, and made his way back up the tube.

Sinbeasts defied logical physiology, but they did follow human imagination. If he was inside the thing's throat, he was also near the arteries, and the rest of the head. Inside the box were hand-sized C4 torches with spikes in the bottom. Grinning, Bozeman began sticking them in the walls of the chamber he'd woken up in. He was almost done with all of them when he heard the rushing of water coming from the mouth. The Sinbeast was trying to drown him. This would have to do.

“Fuck you, Cortez,” he said, and triggered the detonator.

First Awakening

By Gwydion JMF Weber

This wasn't her bed. This wasn't her apartment. This wasn't home. Instead of the lovely pumpkin-colour Lara had painted it with when she first moved in, the ceiling was grey. The walls were not that beautiful shade of azure that reminded her of the water in Greece. They were merely a different shade of grey. The mattress was not hard and unyielding, but perfectly matched her figure.

"Lara Emily Cespedes, please confirm your name."

Lara jerked up, looking around the room. Though there was no daylight, it was well lit. No dark corners, no speakers, no person.

"Lara Emily Cespedes, please confirm your name," the voice repeated. She couldn't tell whether it was a man or a woman speaking.

"That is my name?" she said, probing.

"I'm asking you," the voice said. "Is that your name?" it seemed to be coming from everywhere at once.

"Yes, it is. What do you want from me? Where am I?"

"You are aboard a seedship with no name. It is not necessary for you to know it. There are many more seedships than there are names," the voice explained.

"I'm aboard a ship?" Lara thought for a moment. Had she been drinking last night? Or was this a dream? It had to be a dream. A powerful, vivid dream, but, in the end, just a convincing hallucination. Then again, people who are dreaming rarely question the dreams they are in. "Where is this ship headed, then?"

“Its name is barely more than a number. It is protocol to let the colonists decide upon a name themselves, as it reinforces the sense of ownership of the new world they conquer.”

“Forget it, I don't care. Turn this ship around to Massachusetts, I have a thesis to work on,” Lara declared, slipping out of the strange bed. Unlike most mornings, she felt oddly alive, powerful even. The weirdness of the situation notwithstanding, she might have said that she felt great.

“I'm afraid that will not be possible.” The voice did not sound the least bit apologetic. “However, your virtual workspace has been transferred to your cabin systems, so work on your thesis can continue unhindered. However, you might wish to consult our library. The scientific knowledge in your simulation was a few hundred millennia behind on the topic of Genetics.”

“Come again?” Lara was too confused to even frown.

“The scientific knowledge in your simulation was a few hundred millennia behind on the topic of Genetics,” the voice repeated. It sounded exactly the same as last time.

“The fuck do you mean 'simulation'?”

“Indeed,” was the answer, as though that explained everything. “Your life thus far has been a simulation. Most characters and events in it are fictional, others are historical, with a few liberties taken where necessary. For example, when you reached maturity but still had not come to the conclusion that the world around you was a simulation, some famous individuals you admired hinted at the nature of your reality. Unfortunately, you did not pick up on the hints.”

“Wh-” she could not speak. The word “what” did not seem appropriate somehow. “I'm stupid?” she heard herself ask, unsure why this was the first question that came to mind.

“It is uncommon, but not unusual, for an individual to never realise that they are in a simulation. You will suffer no systemic drawbacks from this fact.”

“My parents? They're not real?” Lara could feel a gaping hole of pain open up inside her, but it was still covered with white linen, like a painting that was yet to be unveiled. She knew it was there, but she couldn't see it.

“They were. Your genetic material has been assembled

from two of the greatest individuals humankind has ever produced. Your mother was a molecular chef that revolutionised cuisine as we know it, not the manager of a roadside diner. Your father was a world-renowned neurosurgeon, not a small town veterinarian. The two never met in real life."

Lara felt – nothing. Where there had been a creeping feeling of existential horror, there was now nothing at all.

"What is happening to me?" she asked.

"In anticipation of how you might react to such a monumental revelation, you have been sedated for your own comfort. Do not worry, for you will be able to work through this trauma in time."

"But where is my mom? How was I born?"

"You were born in this bed. It is not a bed, but a unit that has formed, fed, and sheltered you for the past twenty-five years."

"Wait, why would you simulate the twenty-first century when the knowledge from back then was so woefully outdated?" There it was, the logical part of her brain, taking over full control.

"You have learned many skills in your unconscious mind, by way of dreaming. Sleeping and dreaming was invented to separate the conscious from the unconscious mind. Your waking time was to build your personality, and to make you familiar with the world."

"Well, I can never remember my dreams, so I guess all that futuristic knowledge isn't anywhere around here." Lara made a motion encircling her head.

"You will learn to meld your conscious and unconscious mind over the course of the coming year," the voice explained. "After this time has passed, deployment will begin, and you will have to build the basic infrastructure to refuel this ship and send it on its way, so that it may continue seeding new planets."

"So let me get this straight: My whole life wasn't real, I'm gonna become some superhuman überbeing over the course of the next year, and then I'm supposed to spend the rest of my life on some weird, potentially hostile alien hellhole?"

"No," the voice answered.

Instead of an explanation, Lara got a window. The entire wall to her right became transparent in an instant, and what she saw took her breath away. Down there, packed in a nitrogen-oxygen atmosphere, herds of clouds rolling over the continents, was a collection of familiar shapes and outlines. It was Earth, perfect and pristine, untouched by man, ready to be taken.

"This ship has been in orbit for thirty years. The world you will be colonising is one you are already very familiar with. You already consider it home. Now it is up to you and your peers to make it so."

A Merchant's Diplomacy

By Gwydion JMF Weber

The Brass Citadel was constructed atop a natural rock formation in the Acras Basin. Containing rare strata stretching over millennia of the world's history, the rock was of some interest to geologists, but the stronghold that ended up being erected there was not a scientific base. It hosted a research institute, famous for its cutting-edge petrological analysis laboratory, but its primary purpose was as a military surveillance hub that ensured the security of the many caravans passing through the region. Scouting planes took off from here to make the rounds, returning every few hours to refuel and switch crew, but never idle. Even during the most brutal of sand storms, the golden birds were flying, keeping an eye out for merchants in danger, signalling home for a rescue convoy to be deployed when necessary.

Despite its remote location, in a few short years, the Brass Citadel had transformed the basin from a marauder-infested wasteland into a paradise of profitable trade routes. The structure itself had become an oasis, and merchants used its central spire to find their bearings all over the treacherous desert. For traders, the Brass Citadel was a beacon. For Komanu Velkhas, it was the retirement he'd always wanted. Warm, sunny, not too stressful, and far away from the big cities while still supplying their comforts.

His office was located in the very tip of the main tower, just below the lookout cupola, with windows that gave a splendid, all-round view of the red rock desert. He was having a great day, sipping juniper tea while reading a novel from his personal library, when his secundant entered the room and bowed deeply.

"Komanu-hed, there is a situation that requires your attention," he said, not rising until Komanu was standing himself. "It is quite urgent."

"I thank you, Oreose-bun. What is this regarding?" The old man had never been one for ceremony, but he indulged his junior's deference to proper protocol.

"The Ghatak Trade Commission has arrived early, and they have clashed with the Royal Convoy of the Rhombey. I believe your presence might defuse the situation in the central chamber before it escalates into violence," he explained. The youth had an expression of guilt on his face. It was as though the Ghatak not respecting the schedule was somehow his fault. To Komanu's mind, that couldn't be further from the truth. Oreose Keetan was the person actually running the day-to-day operations of this place, making sure that the old war hero could spend his time enjoying the simple pleasures of life.

"I am grateful that you called for me. I shall be right down, Oreose-bun," said Komanu walking to his closet to don the uncomfortable items required for a full uniform. It was highly unorthodox not to be wearing them at all times, but after decades of service, Komanu felt entitled. His secundant bowed again, and took the lift back down.

Minutes later, Komanu stepped into the central hall. The room was ovoid, the bottom third filled with fresh water and inhabited by a variety of fish. A large platform was installed above it, connected to several corridors and doorways via bridges, and acting as the main hub for all foot traffic in the Brass Citadel. Oreose had not exaggerated the situation. On one side of the platform, the Ghatak in their moss-coloured robes were shouting abuse, fists raised, menacingly twirling their lightweight blades. Their pale, blue skin was covered in thin tattoos.

Separated from them by a cordon of Komanu's own soldiers, who seemed to be a bit overwhelmed by the circumstances, the stocky Rhombey jeered and beat their hairy chests. They were clad in golden jewellery, almost enough to make up for their lack of upper body clothing, and the domes of their bald heads were covered with ritual scars.

After observing for a few moments and finding himself unable to determine the wronged party on the spot, Komanu drew in breath and collected himself.

“Silence!” he shouted, the word resounding through the central hall like thunder. Even over all this raucous taunting, Komanu Velkhas' legendary voice was overwhelming. “The Brass Citadel is a place of peace and commerce. I will not tolerate this type of insolence under my roof. Oreose-bun, have these people separated and lead to opposite ends of the compound. Their leaders shall be sent to the executive conference room to talk this out with me.” Without waiting for a response, he brushed past the bowing Oreose, and took the lift back up into the tower.

Borao-Tan-Borao, the head of the Ghatak Trade Commission, arrived first. His fine, aristocratic features were underlined by his silvery voice. He seemed perfectly courteous, incapable of partaking in a confrontation as vile as the one in the central hall. Yet, Komanu had seen him there.

“It pains me that such clarifying conversations are necessary, Komanu-khat,” he said, his voice dripping with apology. Komanu found himself surprised at the fact that he was irritated by the Ghatak's improper use of the suffix. He was implying they were informal peers, while, in actuality, Komanu was his host.

“It pains me as well, Borao-don,” said Komanu, making a point of using the proper suffix, addressing Borao-Tan-Borao as a guest, “but it is necessary. I cannot tolerate such levels of animosity in the Brass Citadel.”

“Ah, you must excuse my impoliteness,” Borao-Tan-Borao conceded, “I am unfamiliar with the finer differentiations of your culture's language, Komanu-ta.” Komanu did not believe him. Before he could reassure the man that all was well, the sigilmaster of the Royal Convoy entered the room. Huutin the Quiet, he was called. A barrel-chested man with emerald eyes and a long, well-groomed beard, Huutin wore a light tunic with a very low neckline as a symbol of his status. His stentorian voice boomed through the conference room as he greeted them.

“Apologies for my delayed arrival, I hope you two have

not already conspired," he said. It was clearly a joke, but Borao-Tan-Borao could not help but take offence.

"Already with the accusations. Frankly I'm not sure why I must speak with this savage face to face. Being present at this location at the same time as him and his people is quite insulting. Which forces me to inquire as to why we were scheduled to be here at the same time in the first place," he said, not deigning to look at the Rhombey.

"You arrived early, and they had to leave a day late," Komanu explained. "We are well aware of the rift between your peoples, but unfortunately we cannot always accommodate it. It is uncommon but not unheard for Ghatak and Rhombey to share residence in the Brass Citadel, and never has it resulted in the threat of a brawl breaking out in the central hall."

"Please, Komanu-ta, you do not understand how disgusting the smell of Rhombey is to my people, and two days is not enough time to air it out." Borao-Tan-Borao wrinkled his nose. "I do not care what you do with mundane caravans, but we are the Trade Commission. We do not pass through here often, and we demand some respect."

"It is true, they only like the smell of their own," said Huutin the Quiet. "That's why they all marry their siblings."

"The bloodline must be kept pure. At least we do not eat our dead," Borao-Tan-Borao spat.

"Ha! It is a great honour to consume the flesh of a worthy opponent after slaying them," the Rhombey boasted. "It is an act of appreciation for the challenge he has provided, and the things one has learned from fighting him."

"Enough," Komanu declared. "I will not have this be a continuation of what happened in the central hall. I am here to help you lay your differences to rest, at least for the time being."

Huutin puffed. "As much as I look down upon this weakling," he said, pointing at the Ghatak, "I must agree that he is right about the importance of our caravans. It is acceptable for some lowly merchant to cross paths with the Gathak, but I am a confidant of the King. I travel across the great sand sea to negotiate trade with a distant land. The fees I pay are high, and the money this outpost will make because of my efforts is substantial. I expect special consideration to be taken in such a situation."

"As a matter of fact, our mission is to establish trade as well. The same argument should be made for us," Borao-Tan-Borao agreed. Komanu had to stop himself from smiling.

"Special considerations were made. Had your sandships not been carried by favourable winds, and had Huutin-don not run into unexpected problems, you would never have met," Komanu explained.

"Still, it is very tight scheduling," Huutin complained.

"I concur. Such oversight should not happen with our peoples," Borao-Tan-Borao added.

"And I take full responsibility for this. But for now, all you can do is coexist. The Citadel is large, your peoples will not run into each other, I assure you. Besides, the Royal Convoy will be leaving tomorrow, then neither of you will have to tolerate the other."

"I suppose it is an acceptable compromise," said Borao-Tan-Borao, flicking his fingers dismissively. "And please do understand this as a complaint against you personally, Komanu-ta."

"For the time being, yes. But this best not happen again," Huutin the Quiet decided. "This is, indeed, your fault."

A few minutes later, when Komanu stepped into his office, back to his juniper tea, he had a big smile on his face. Of all the weapons he had ever used, the prospect of profits was the most powerful. It could not only cut, but also mend. It was a welcome addition to his arsenal, and he had learned to use it as well as he could the pistol and the spear.

Yenma and Ser Wonfer

By Gwydion JMF Weber

"It's not easy being a knight, you know," said Ser Wonfer. "You have to be honourable every minute of the day, and loyal, too."

"I suppose you don't have an issue with the loyalty bit..." Yenma responded. She was looking forward to some alone time, away from her travelling companion, in this great castle.

"What's that supposed to mean?" Ser Wonfer tilted his head.

"Well, you're a dog. That's what that is supposed to mean," said Yenma. The wind on this bridge was cutting sharply through her gambeson, and it required significant discipline not to shudder.

"I don't see how that's a bad thing," was Ser Wonfer's response. "I can certainly track outlaws better than you, and I hear better, too. If anything, dogs make better knights than humans." His paws chattered over the cracked tiles like hale.

"It'll be interesting to see how you fare in a sword fight, then." With a frown on her face, Yenma noted that the soldiers manning the gatehouse did not wear the silver and burgundy chevrons of House Turell, but the pine green and pale orange stripes she vaguely attributed to House Bannard. Or was it House Tentre?

"I don't need a sword, I have sharp teeth, and a body made to attack a man's legs. You'll never find me surprised and without a weapon. Nor will you ever find me without a mount. I am my own mount." The dog hadn't yet noticed that these men wore the wrong colours. If all she saw were grey on grey patterns in the distance, Yenma might have problems with that too.

"Who is this at our gates?" asked one of the soldiers. He had impassive black eyes and a booming voice that was clearly audible even through the mountain wind.

"I am Yenma of Lothersby, and this is the venerable knight Ser Wonfer the Valiant."

There was laughter from the soldiers. "A dog who's a knight? A stranger thing I've never heard. What lands do you mark as your own then, Ser Sniffy?"

Ser Wonfer, ever the noble, ignored the insult with his head held high. "I am a travelling knight in service of the King himself. We are here to deliver a message from court, meant for the eyes and ears of Baroness Turell herself."

"Is it an eviction notice? 'cause I don't think she'll be leaving her tower anytime soon!" The soldiers broke out into roaring laughter.

Yenma rolled her eyes. "Is this, or is this not Baroness Turell's home?"

"Used to be," said the gatekeeper who had spoken first, "but it's not any more. She's still here though." He shrugged. "Might be she no longer lives. Folks say she stopped eating."

"We shall find that out personally," Ser Wonfer decided. "If you would be so kind as to open the gate now, we would much appreciate it."

"We don't take orders from a bloody dog!" the soldier complained. "You'll piss in every corner of the place, and then we'll have to smell it!"

"You will obey the orders of a knight!" A man emerged from the gatehouse. He was tall, broad-shouldered, with grey-blond hair and ice blue eyes, dressed in a fine robe of dyed wool decorated with intricate lacework of goldthread and gemstones. "I apologise for the indiscretion, Ser Wonfer. My lady, these raucous men are of the lowest standing. They know not how to spell the word manners, much less understand what it means."

"I've dealt with worse," said Yenma. "I've even had worse greetings at castle gates."

"I graciously accept your apology, my lord," Ser Wonfer said, bowing his head. "Your chivalry is much appreciated."

"Milord, we had no idea you were around," one of the soldiers said, almost kneeling.

"It should not require my presence to put some manners into you," the man castigated. "Now, allow me to introduce myself. I am Ser Colton Bannard, though you may also know me as Stormrider. Come, you must be exhausted from your journey."

"Colton Stormrider, of course! I've heard stories of your great deeds." Ser Wonfer was immediately swooning over their new acquaintance. "You are a shining example of a noble knight."

"I'm sure most of those tales were exaggerated to the point of being lies," Ser Colton conceded. He lead them into the great hall of the castle, and ordered a few dishes of food prepared.

"Not to be the one to break up this most humble of conversations, but we must speak to Baroness Turell. I would also like to inquire as to why it's your men, not hers, who are in control of this castle." Yenma didn't like this prattling about that Wonfer was prone to. There was something wrong here, she could feel it in the air.

"Of course, my lady. Unfortunately, the Baroness failed to pay her lease on the castle. She hasn't paid a single coin of copper in almost three years. Seizing it was our last resort, but it was necessary." Ser Colton's regret was mixed with a little too much righteousness for Yenma's taste. "She has been confined to her chambers, and is being supplied with the finest meals. It is a shame that she hasn't touched a single one for the past week, truly."

"We shall need to speak to her nonetheless," Ser Wonfer asserted. "The King's message is urgent."

Ser Colton Stormrider shook his head. "I cannot allow that. She is a captive of House Bannard, and, as a debtor, she is also a criminal enemy of the Crown. As her rightful jailer, I have the duty to approve all communiques."

"How does one simply 'seize' a castle like this?" asked Yenma. "Its position and defences are formidable"

"House Bannard built it. Of course we left in a few hidden passageways. It allowed us to take it without much bloodshed," Ser Colton explained.

"A very noble goal indeed." Ser Wonfer raised his nose

and sniffed the scent of the food being prepared in the kitchen. "Now, I am no lawman, but I will assume, by your honour as a knight, that your interpretation of royal law is correct. We shall relay you the message first."

"Hold on for a moment, Wonfer. I doubt this is legal, or in any way in accord with the King's wishes," Yenma interjected. "Knight or no knight, for all we know Ser Colton took this castle illegally."

"I understand your concerns, my lady. I swear by my honour that you will be able to relay your message to Baroness Turell, regardless of my judgement on it," Ser Colton Bannard offered. Yenma wasn't entirely convinced that this had not been his original plan all along. Making outrageous demands and then settling for what one wanted in the first place was a legitimate negotiation tactic. She herself had employed many times.

"It seems only fair," Wonfer said before Yenma could respond. "You certainly are as generous as the tales make you out to be. But first, let us eat. I can smell the honeyed duck, and my stomach is rumbling."

Baroness Turell displayed none of the grace and elegance she was fabled for. Instead of the regal hostess who had preserved her beauty well into old age, they encountered a haggard crone, clad in fine garments that seemed shabby all the same. Her hair was unkempt and filthy, her fingernails long and dirty, and her figure barely more than skin on bone. She dropped the little scroll with the royal stamp on it, then spat on the ground. "Take my castle," she said. "I no longer have need of it."

"But my lady, this is fantastic news!" Ser Colton seemed confused. "Your debt to the Crown has been forgiven. We are your only creditors now."

"At what cost, Ser Colton? My last living son, dead. Dead in a war that has claimed my other two boys already, a campaign for which my husband emptied his coffers to supply the King with armies. And for what? As that dolt on the throne grew richer and richer from the spoils of war, we had to sell our lands to supply more armies. 'It is our duty,' he'd always say. 'The King will repay us in time.' But instead, he started lending us money, so we'd spend it to raise new armies for him. The King never gave us anything. The debts he has forgiven, he owes me tenfold. He owes me a husband and three sons, yet he has someone else take away my home." There was no sorrow in her voice, only bitterness and hate. "I spit on the King, I spit on the Crown, and I spit on you, Ser Colton Bannard. I spit on you, your house, your honour, and your titles. You are an evil man, but you are too stupid to know just how evil you are."

A Special Kind of Hell

By Gwydion JMF Weber

It wasn't his first heart attack, and for a moment, as he was clutching his chest in agony, he thought that it might not be his last. He fell to the ground, writhing as his torso constricted under the pressure of a million black ropes. The kitchen knife he had been holding, a piece of carrot still clinging to its blade, slithered across the ground.

As the old man realised his impending demise, his last thought was of his great-granddaughter Kiri, three months old, and how he would not see her grow up. Then, after a final moment of painful euphoria, it all went to nothing.

It felt warm for a second. Then it was hot.

The old man opened his eyes, and the world came into focus around him. It had been there before, existed forever, but only now became visible. He was floating in an egg-shaped cavern, thick, black blood flowing from tiny holes in the jagged walls like putrid resin. Below his feet was lava, languidly bubbling, bathing the walls in an unsettling orange glow.

Standing on a rocky pulpit, its exact features hidden in shadow, was a creature that, despite the heat, drove a shiver down the old man's spine. Though it seemed hunched over, it was much taller than any man he'd ever seen. Its caprine legs seemed tense with force, capable of great leaps, and powerful muscles were visible down to the individual strand beneath its kidney-coloured skin. Long, white horns protruded from the being's head, which looked like a fleshless, deformed cranium. Fires burned in its eyes.

"Barnabas Mullins," it hissed. "I'm afraid you have arrived at your final destination." There was glee in its inhuman voice.

"No, this is not real," Barnabas decided. "This was never meant to be real. I am not in Hell."

The demon laughed. "Oh, but it is, and you know it is, because you know you are dead, and you know you are here."

"No! Fuck!" Barnabas punched the air. In his floating stasis, it was impossible to move around. He realised that his body was much younger than that of an 80 year old. He was young again, back in his physical prime.

He continued punching and kicking, rolled forward, backward and sideways, roaring at God and the universe. Thoughts he'd had early on in his life returned, and he mulled them over rapidly, arriving at the conclusion that setting up a world in which atheism was the only rational mindset, and then sending people to eternal torment for not believing, was utterly despicable. God was clearly worse than the devil.

"Oh, but he is not," the demon said. "You will come to see the error of that judgement soon enough."

"You can read my thoughts?" Barnabas asked.

"Why of course, Barnabas. What kind of theme park did you think we're running here. Hell is the place of ultimate violation! Your thoughts belong to us, not you." The demon stretched its neck and shook itself.

"This is not right! All my life I've been a good person, I've donated at least a million pounds to charity, I-"

"- fed the homeless from your own kitchen, supported your local businesses, gave liberally to those in need, never charged interest on your loans, and trained over a dozen world class chefs in your restaurants. You were a doyen of your field, Barnabas Mullins, and all of that was counted in your favour on judgement day." The demon stepped closer to the edge of the rocky precipice, telescoping its neck far longer than it should have been able to, bringing it closer to Barnabas, but just outside of his reach.

"But God is vain and wants to be worshipped, right?" Barnabas asked.

The demon cackled. "On the contrary. The big man

upstairs is fond of those who are good because they want to be, not because they fear hell, or crave heaven. Plenty of atheists up there, just not you." The demon chattered its teeth, shaking its head, neck coiling like a slithering snake. "No, you are here for the greatest of sins, and gravest of insults. You see, when the Heavenly Father chooses to take a person's life, that point in time is always carefully chosen. He expects you to trust him that it is your time to go. But you couldn't, could you? You wanted to cheat death."

It took Barnabas a moment to remember. Of course. The CryoLife contract.

"Yes, indeed." The demon laughed a guttural purr. "Not ten minutes after your heart went out they had you on ice. There was some brain damage, but the idea was that, once they had the technology to thaw you, they would also be able to repair it. But the body cannot live without the soul, Barnabas. When they finally began thawing people, none of them were truly alive."

Tears ran down Barnabas' face. He began sobbing uncontrollably, feeling the weight of the universe on his shoulders. "It's unfair!" he cried. "It's not fair how one thing, one decision, can damn you to Hell forever! There was nothing in the bible about this!"

"Well nobody ever said it was fair, did they?" The demon's neck retracted back to its body. It turned around on the precipice, and Barnabas was pulled toward it, landing on his feet behind the demon. The ground was sharp as a field of razor blades, cutting open his feet. Barnabas hissed through the tears.

The demon laughed. "You'll be in much worse pain soon enough, Barnabas. Don't be a ninny." It drew back a curtain of intestines, slick with blood and faeces, grabbed Barnabas' shoulder, and threw him into hell.

It was just another day. Despite his initial attempts, Barnabas had lost track of them. What was the point, if he was going to spend eternity in torment anyway? The last count he remembered was four-hundred-and-seventy-six. Much shorter than what his time down here had felt like, yet insignificant in relation to eternity.

The few moments of respite he had were a kind of agony in and of itself, allowing him to think about the pain he lived with at every hour of the day. Sleep brought only nightmares, some worse than the torments of the pit in and of themselves.

He was bound to a glowing pillar of ice, the chains around his wrists, neck, and ankles glowing with heat. The ice was dry, and burned his back with frost. Hot air blew onto his body from the front. It felt as though the temperature difference was tearing him apart.

Earlier that day, he had been inside a stomping press. It was a black box, devoid of light, and the ceiling crushed him against the ground at irregular intervals. The agony of being completely flattened over the course of slow seconds defied description, but the worst part was hearing his own bones snap. It was a kind of pain his mind could not fathom.

Later, a meat hook had been rammed through his jaw, and he was hung from a rack with a thousand other naked souls, roasting over open flames. Eventually, his own bodyweight would help the sharp hook cut through the bone and flesh of his jaw, and he would fall through the fire and into the embers, where ash would crawl into every orifice of his body, setting it ablaze from the inside, burning until he was nothing but a pile of ashes.

The ice pillar was comfortable, relatively speaking. He could observe the ceiling of the caverns, dripping with blood, and see the shadows inside buildings rising in the distance. There were dozens of ice pillars here, all with prisoners of Hell chained to them, presumably for the same ironic reasons as Barnabas. They were never able to communicate. Every time he tried to talk to them, his voice was stuck in his throat, and every time he saw one attempting to communicate with him, it seemed as though their experience was much the same.

Out of the corner of his eye, Barnabas spotted a group of Visitors. Figures in black robes, hoods drawn deep into their faces, walking across the galleries of freezing prisoners with wooden sandals, talking in hushed tones and strange languages.

Barnabas had no idea who they were, and no demon he'd asked had graced him with a response. But they were here, walking among the dead, people of all ages, skin colours, and sizes, gawking at their tormented faces. Sometimes he clung to the idea that they were themselves former residents of hell, who had served out their sentence and now lived a milder one, but it was more likely they were from Heaven, looking at the poor souls condemned to eternal damnation. Maybe they were just another form of demon, a torment for the mind, designed to give hope where there was none to be had.

As the group passed him by, one of them lingered. It was a young woman, her hood somewhat lifted, staring him in the face like only few of the Visitors ever did. But her expression was not one of glee or disgust, but something Barnabas thought might be relief. There was something in her eyes, those dark brown eyes, that was familiar to him. Maybe he had seen them here in Hell before, and she had indeed been absolved from her sins. If so, maybe he was soon to follow.

There were a hundred more torments before the young woman returned.

He was chopped into pieces by a giant, faceless butcher with a rusty cleaver, and fed to the pigs, feeling every iota of pain in every minute patch of flesh.

He was placed in a cage and prodded with spears by cackling goblins over and over, until there was nothing left of him but a pile of bloody bones.

He was weighed down and thrown into the bottom of a boiling lake, feeling his skin and muscle tissue flake off as he drowned for hours.

When the woman finally came back, Barnabas had all but forgotten about her. She was with a larger group this time, and had brought along someone else. A man, vaguely Asian-looking, but with blue eyes and a fuzzy blond beard, looked at Barnabas with scepticism as the young woman whispered to him. Finally, he nodded, and a smile flashed across the woman's face. They left again, following their group. For the first time during his stay in Hell, Barnabas was filled with genuine hope, and he didn't even know why.

He was roasted on a spit, stuffed with fruit, and fed on a

banquet to laughing demons, who dipped his legs in pure acid before chewing off his meat bit by bit with their razor-sharp teeth.

He was placed in the middle of an endless void, standing atop rotting flesh, feeling ill in every cell of his body. He walked for what felt like eternities, retching and vomiting uncontrollably.

He was decapitated, and his head was used as a ball in a strange field game the rules of which he did not quite understand. His extremities were used as bats, and his torso as a shield by what seemed to be a sort of goalkeeper.

This time around, the man came alone. He looked at Barnabas, tied to the ice pillar, with pity in his eyes. When the young woman arrived, he produced a pair of pliers much larger than his robe should have allowed for, and cut the chains binding his arms, legs, and head. Though the links were thick and the man not particularly tall, he cut them with little effort.

He produced a Visitor's robe much like his own and quickly draped it over Barnabas, who at first fell towards him, incapable of finding his feet. Finally, he was free, he thought. Finally, and unceremoniously, he had paid his dues. The torture was over. A mask was pulled over his face, but when he touched it a moment later, he could not feel anything but his own flesh.

He followed the man as he walked briskly to catch up with a group of Visitors who had passed his pillar before. It turned out that there were more than just a dozen, but hundreds, maybe thousands of people tied to the ice pillars. The Visitors, a small group this time, walked by them briskly, as if in a hurry, but not fast enough to draw attention to themselves.

After maybe an hour of walking, they arrived at a gate guarded by two massive demons armed with red tridents. They kept a close eye on the Visitors as they passed through a splendidly decorated stone archway, stepping through what seemed to be a rippling red liquid, disappearing into it one by one.

Barnabas stopped. Something in the back of his mind demanded he stay here, in Hell, because that was where he belonged. Whatever was beyond this gate was not meant for him. In fact, the slurping and sloshing liquid was, in many ways, scarier than the abyss itself. Just when he was about to turn back, the man pushed him, and he practically fell through the archway, into nothingness.

He awoke when the lid on his box was lifted, staring upward into the face of the young woman he had first seen so long ago. The bright light of the room she was in hurt his eyes. Barnabas drew in air reflexively, and felt pain in his lungs. For the first time in what seemed like an eternity, that was the only pain he felt. Compared to what he had experienced, it was barely a tickle.

Though he wanted to rise, the young woman gently laid a hand upon his chest, and he understood. His head was stuck in a kind of cold, metallic harness. There was a clicking sound, and suddenly he was free. She grabbed his shoulder and pulled up his torso, helping him out of the coffin.

Barnabas found himself inside a small room with flan-coloured plastic walls sloping at odd angles, illuminated by soft, indirect lighting. In his feet, he felt a sway and a rumble going through the room. This was not some building, but a vehicle.

Looking down his body, he realised that he was still young, much like in Hell. It seemed different somehow, firmer, more solid, less like an illusion. He realised it only in retrospect, but there had been something fake about his body back in the pit.

He turned around and watched the young woman close the lid of the box. It was a little larger than person-sized, like a sarcophagus, a golden cross embossed on the cover. It was plugged into various ports and tubes at the bottom, but most sockets remained empty.

Barnabas wanted to ask what it was, but could only produce a weak croak. His throat was parched. The young woman rose and handed him a glass of water. Her expression was a mix of elation and deep sorrow.

The water was sweet and refreshing, washing away what felt like sand grating in his throat, invigorating him. Barnabas expected to want more, but when the glass was empty, he handed it back, satisfied.

The moment he looked into the young woman's eyes, he remembered. They were his son's eyes. His granddaughter's eyes.

His great-granddaughter's eyes. “Kiri,” he wheezed. Speaking was difficult.

“Yes, it's me.” She said, smiling. “I don't remember you, but you must remember me.”

“I remember, “ Barnabas stopped, recalling memories from a time so long ago it seemed unreal to him. “I remember holding you a few days after you were born. You grabbed my beard and held on with a kind of force no newborn should have had.”

Kiri laughed. “I'm glad to hear I was always like that. Once I grab a hold of something, I never let go.”

Barnabas felt his knees getting weak. His legs gave way, collapsing like a house of cards, and he fell backwards into a chair. The padding was cool and soft.

“I was in Hell,” Barnabas muttered. The things that statement entailed ran through his mind. The cosmological implications, the realities, the consequences. If Hell was real and he had escaped, what would God do when he died again?

Kiri nodded, slowly. “Yes, you were. But you also weren't.”

Barnabas squinted, looking at her. “What do you mean?”

“Come, this will be easier if I introduce you first.”

Kiri lead him through a long, narrow hallway. Several doors branched off to their left, but none to their right. At the end, the cap-door slid open gently, and revealed a room that Barnabas immediately recognised as a cantina. There was a large serving counter to the left, and four long, cream-coloured tables with benches to the right, beside a large, gently curved window pane. It took Barnabas a moment before he realised that the blue beyond the glass was not the sky, but the sea.

“We're under water,” he said matter-of-factly.

“Yes. This is the *Swift Celerity*, named in a time where such redundancies were considered funny and ironic. I own a third of it, and so I am one of its three captains,” Kiri explained.

“You own a submarine?” Barnabas asked.

“It's more than just a submarine. Just a few hours ago it was a spaceship, dropping at high speed from a chandelier city suspended from the trans-polar orbital ring.” Kiri gently touched the glass. “Right now we are in the middle of the Indian Ocean.”

“Orbital ring? What do you mean?”

“A ring that goes around the Earth. There are eight of them, and each has vast solar arrays and entire cities hanging from them.” She paused. “It's where they kept you.”

“Hell? In space? I thought it was supposed to be deep underground.” Barnabas felt as though he was moving through sludge in his brain.

“As I said, that wasn't really Hell. It was a virtual reality construct, built to look and feel just like it. It is operated by a group of Post-Christian Pan-Abrahamists that dominates that specific chandelier city. They call themselves the Disciples of the Cocytus. In their mind, all those who had themselves frozen before a certain, in my opinion arbitrary, deadline are sinners, and need to be punished.”

Barnabas had to sit down on one of the benches again. “Why would they do that? That's absurd.” He stared at the floor for a few seconds. “I'm a good person,” he finally said.

Kiri shook her head. “You know how the people of your time looked back at slave owners? That is how many people of today look back at your generation. Even though you knew better, you ravaged the ecosystem of the planet for your own vanity, unwilling to give up an ever-increasing amount of luxuries, dooming future generations. You used to kill and eat animals, execute people with little evidence, and treat the poor as your personal playthings.”

“People don't eat meat any more?” For some reason, this was the only question that came to Barnabas' mind.

“We do, but it is grown from stem cells. No living creature has to die for it,” Kiri responded.

“I would have happily done that, but we didn't have that technology back then.” Barnabas felt overwhelmed by her accusations. “And what do you mean executing people? We abolished the death penalty in the sixties, and I drove an electric car almost all my life.”

“Now imagine a slave owner telling you that they needed the cheap labour back then, they eventually outlawed it, and he only reluctantly participated in the practice anyway.” Kiri gave him a serious look. “My crew and I are some of the few people who understand that people are a product of their times, and to see those who tried to live the best way they could as good people at heart. Most others would look down on you if they knew when you were alive, as some even do with me. Others would try and punish you for crimes against the planet, humanity, or whatever pet concept they believed marginalised in the twenty-first century.”

“How few people are we talking about here that don't want to see me suffer eternal torment?” Barnabas asked. He detected a hint of humour in his own voice. That was probably good.

“Maybe ten billion.” Kiri shrugged. “As I said, very few.”

Barnabas laughed. “Ten billion? By Gordon's Forehead, that has to be pretty much everyone.”

Kiri squinted, then relaxed as realisation crept across her face. “There are currently three-hundred-and-fifty billion humans alive in the solar system. We are very much a minority forced to cling to the fringes of society.”

Barnabas felt his mind falling backwards. His head was spinning, trying to imagine the absurdity of more people than had been alive during his lifetime being considered a minority. “How far into the future are we?” He finally asked.

“Far. I myself am over five-hundred years old. I am one of the oldest people alive.”

Barnabas' breath fell short. He began hyperventilating. The weight of these revelations seemed heavier than the existence of Hell. Kiri put a hand on his shoulder, and after few moments, he'd calmed down again. “I've been in Hell for five centuries?”

Kiri shook her head. “Barely a decade. There's a lot of frozen people from your time period, and the Disciples of the Cocytus bought up many cryopreservation companies before anyone ever learned about their plans. Only a fraction of the people they have were actually restored to life and inserted into the simulation.”

Barnabas almost jumped off the bench, pacing up and down the room. A second earlier, he'd barely had the strength to support himself. Now it was like his body was charged with electricity.

This was all a bit much. He had expected to wake up at some point in the future, young again, possibly even venerated as a piece of living history. The idea that he would be considered scum had never even entered his mind. It certainly should have.

He looked out of the window, into the darkening waters of the ocean, trying to find something to hold on to, but coming up empty. "What do I have left?" he finally asked. "I mean I had restaurants, book royalties, the cryogenics corporation was meant to maintain a fund for me."

"Your inheritance has long been dispersed," said Kiri. "You have descendants everywhere. The old house in Cornwall, where you died, my grandfather lived there for a while. I remember visiting, but my parents sold it. Too many old memories, and it had fallen into disrepair."

Barnabas wanted to complain that they would have forgotten him so quickly, but remembered that he had done much the same thing with his own father's residence in Notting Hill after the old man had moved to Bermuda.

"I know your restaurants continued to be quite successful, but these things come and go. Any self-respecting book on the history of modern cuisine has a page dedicated to you, but that is about the extent of your legacy."

Barnabas jerked backward. For the briefest of moments, his own reflection in the glass had become the face of a demon. He fell, looked around. The world was pressing down on him. The serving counter became a torturer's rack. The ceiling lights turned into open flames. The hum of the engines transformed into the growling of hellhounds.

Kiri's hand touched his shoulder, and everything returned to normal. "I spent a decade in Hell," he said. Back when he had been alive, no person would ever have been able to experience what he had gone through. The human mind was not meant to withstand that kind of trauma.

"That's true, but it was not real. Remind yourself that it was all virtual, and that it's over now, forever," said Kiri.

"Are there others like me? People who have been saved?" Barnabas asked.

"From the Disciples of the Cocytus?" Kiri grimaced. "Not

many. They have very tight security up there. We are lucky that they need tourists to maintain their operation. Many of those whom we have saved over the years are … broken.”

“There must be a self-help group of sorts, right?” Barnabas felt himself grinning, but did not know why. “I mean, this is the future, you must have the best drugs and therapists.”

“We do, for the torments of life. But this virtual Hell they created...”

“Why did you go to the trouble of rescuing me?” Something inside him was certain that he would have been happier in Hell, not knowing the truth of this strange new world. “It must have been dangerous.”

“I could say that you're my blood, and many cultures still value that, which would not be wrong. But there is another reason,” Kiri admitted.

“What?” Barnabas had no idea what that meant. Kiri's words were barely more than sounds to him right now.

“I think this would be easier if you met the other captains.”

A few minutes later, two other people entered the mess hall. One of them was the man who had accompanied Kiri on her visits, and who had rescued him from the virtual world. Barnabas noticed that his blue eyes had two pupils, and there were several skin-coloured plastic panels on his bald head. He was dressed like an ancient Greek philosopher, but his toga was made out of a material that shimmered like mother-of-pearl.

The other was a woman with blue skin that looked as though it had a texture like the shell of a peanut, and vivid orange eyes. Sawlike bony protrusions covered her cheeks, fluttering gently. She wore a practical one-piece overall that was made from something Barnabas assumed to be comparable to neoprene, and seemed to have neither breasts nor any significant behind.

“You already know Gossamer,” Kiri said, gesturing toward the man. “He is a virtual reality specialist. I think you would have called him a 'hacker' if he had been alive during your time.”

“This is Rha-Kom. She is from Ganymede.” Kiri touched the blue woman's shoulder as she said this.

Rha-Kom then grabbed Barnabas' shoulder, and looked him in the eye.

I would like it known that I strongly objected to your rescue. Bringing the ties of brood into this may muddy our message, and I was not willing to risk that. Alas, I was overruled. The blades on her cheeks vibrated as her words atonally resounded in his head, but her mouth remained closed.

"We are currently on our way to Salongo, a city with considerable diplomatic influence in the Earth System." Gossamer spoke with a rough, guttural accent Barnabas could not place. "They are currently hosting a conference on sapient rights, and we are part of faction that wants to introduce a resolution that would stop what the Disciples of the Cocytus are doing."

Kiri nodded. "In most jurisdictions, the dead have rights. The most common one is that their physical bodies cannot be destroyed if steps toward preservation have been taken, followed by it not being possible to seize their property without proper recompense," she explained. "In order to do what they do, the Disciples of the Cocytus have the minimum amount of rights for the deceased. We want to introduce a resolution that makes it illegal to insert cryopreserved deceased into virtual reality environments without their informed consent. This conference will lay the groundwork for when this is actually proposed at the United Nations."

"The United Nations still exists?" Barnabas asked. Maybe this world was not quite so different to what he remembered.

"The United Nations is the precursor organisation to this current organisation's precursor organisation. I just wanted to put it in terms you could relate to," Kiri elaborated.

"At this conference, we need you to present evidence as to what the Disciples of the Cocytus are doing," said Gossamer. "They make no secret of their motivations, but visitors only ever get to see the mild tortures. We believe that the horror of your experiences will sway a lot of people."

"I have no physical evidence." Barnabas felt the ground under his feet heat up and grow blades. He looked down, a wave of terror rolling over his body. The floor was normal, and the hallucination stopped. "There is no evidence," he repeated. "All I know and remember is in my head."

Rha-Kom touched Gossamer's shoulder and looked him in the eyes.

"That will do," said Kiri. "You will have to voluntarily subject yourself to a mental trawl so we can present your memories to the assembly."

Gossamer nodded at Rha-Kom, then turned to Barnabas. "You will experience some of the things you experienced in hell, going back to the most precise version of that memory in existence."

Barnabas stepped back. They wanted to put him back there. It had been a trick from the beginning. If he did this, he would be back in Hell, and the demons would laugh, because he had gone of his own accord.. "No, never. It's pointless anyway!" he blurted. "If I'm not the first person you've rescued, surely you have presented the memories of others, and nobody listened to you then. Why should they listen to you now?"

There was a short silence heavy with meaning.

"They broke during the trawl, which is something that happens when you imagine complex lies during the process." Kiri looked out of the window, into the ocean. "The Disciples have a method of making the memories of their Hell function as lies. We do not have the strongest of reputations when it comes to telling the truth because of that."

"So you pulled me out there knowing I would go mad?" The air seemed to be stuck in Barnabas' throat for a moment. He pushed himself against a wall, horns growing out of the heads of the three captains, their faces shifting to sadistic grins. One of the demons reached out for him, grabbing his shoulder.

It was me who insisted we use you for a trawl. Do not blame Kiri, she did her best to spare you this fate, but considering the risk every one of us and our crew would be taking you were not a resource I was willing to spare.

The illusion was shattered. Despite her harsh words, Rha-Kom's touch was soothing.

"This is madness, probably quite literally for me." Barnabas pulled away. "Please just leave me alone, I can't talk to anyone right now." He stormed off, through the corridor, and into the room that contained his coffin.

Though the box was an element of the very same Hell he had visited, it felt more familiar, safer, than what was to come. He did not want to be trawled, and he did not want to relive his torments. All Barnabas wanted was to sit in the corner of this room, and do nothing at all.

The engines soothed his mind. After a while, not even the occasional shimmies could disconcert him. Barnabas hadn't the slightest clue as to how much time he had spent down here. He wasn't even sure how many meals he had consumed.

Upon closer inspection, it had turned out that the coffin contained a tube with a mouthpiece that delivered a kind of green jelly in regular intervals. It did not take a genius to realise that this was how it kept people fed while they were inside, and considering that he was in perfect physical shape, probably a lot better than he had ever been during his twenties, it was quite nutritious. A healthy body was apparently indeed a healthy mind, even in virtual reality.

The coffin itself was connected to a tube of roughly the same size in the wall, and since Barnabas could not find a tank, he concluded that the crew of the *Swift Celerity* was continuing his supply of food, but was unwilling to disturb him.

The jelly was mostly tasteless, with a vague hint of umami. Barnabas was getting sick of it. He'd been sick of it from the beginning, really, but the thought of leaving this room and going to the mess hall for some proper food was still more terrifying to him than the notion of sitting in this chair forever.

He'd tried to stay awake, but fallen asleep twice. Barnabas had never been very good at remembering his dreams, and this time around it was no different. All he knew was that he'd woken up screaming and drenched in sweat both times.

The days he spent riding a never-ending sinus wave. There were periods of down time where he simply lay on the floor, his mind a fog of ashes. But occasionally he would touch the flames that were tearing it apart, and that was when Hell returned.

It was never anything specific. There was no visual or tactile element to his experiences. Sometimes he smelled burnt flesh or tasted rotting faeces, but only for brief moments. Barnabas was not experiencing memories, but pain, disgust, and humiliation in their purest forms.

Whenever it ended, it felt as though that part of his mind had been consumed by the fire, and he was now wandering its remains, barely able to remember the torment he had just experienced, or how long it had lasted.

He hated both parts of the cycle, but in one he was too weak to even rise, and in the other he was convulsing in agony. At times he felt like was standing inside himself, observing as a rational mind, but unable to help.

There was a knock on the cabin door. Barnabas did not know if he wanted to open it. If he did, he did not know if he even could. After a few moments, it opened on its own, and Kiri looked down on him, a sad smile on her face.

“I'm not going to ask you how you are feeling, because I know.” She spoke softly, as if being careful not to startle him. “I've seen this phase before. It's not pretty. But we are arriving in Salongo, and there is something I want to show you.”

There was a part of his mind that had been bored with all the lying around and doing nothing at all, and now it was the first to react and take control of his body. Barnabas jumped to his feet, full of energy, but feeling as though he was carrying a boulder. The muscles in his face did not respond to anything. He could neither smile nor frown.

Kiri lead him through the narrow corridor and into the mess hall. Though the sea outside was darker than it had been a few days ago, the ground below was well illuminated. Hundreds, thousands, of little chambers were sitting in the sands, coffins like the one he'd been in, status lights blinking. They were arranged in circular patterns around central towers, where countless tubes and wires emerged to supply them with food, oxygen, and access to their simulation.

“This is Saint Hallvard's Necropolis,” Kiri explained. “It is operated by an order of monks that have made it their mission to combat the Disciples of the Cocytus by showing greater virtue. Most of those people were cryopreserved, like you. Because they died before biological senescence was cured, the monks do not believe they should be a part of the modern world. But they don't experience Hell. The Order of Saint Hallvard simulates Heaven instead."

As the *Swift Celerity* moved forward, the clusters of coffins continued. There seemed to be no end to them. "They believe that not prolonging your life would be the same as murder," Kiri explained. "And as you will never be able to enter the afterlife if you live forever, they have taken it upon themselves to recreate Heaven on Earth. Many consider them to be the antithesis of the Disciples of the Cocytus, and they're not wrong. They're very transparent, and display their work openly. They do not allow visitors, but are financed through donations."

"Why are you showing me this?" Barnabas asked.

Kiri sighed. "The Archbishop of Salongo has offered you entry into the Kingdom of Heaven. He is a supporter of our cause, and wants you to be trawled at the conference. Gossamer believes he has found a method of circumventing the Disciples' memory encoding."

"What if I refuse?"

"The Archbishop's offer stands nonetheless. He won't force you to go through any undue suffering, but you need to understand that, either way, it's a one-way ticket. Once you enter their simulation, you will never be able to leave." Kiri looked down at the necropolis with melancholy. "I resisted the idea, but frankly it would be selfish of me to force you to stay here. With what you've gone through, I'm not sure you'd ever find a place in this world. I can't keep you just because I want a piece of the world I knew when I was young to be around."

A tear rolled down Barnabas' cheek. He found himself smiling. "I'll do it," he decided. "I will subject myself to this trawl, Kiri. And then we'll see."

"Are you sure?" she asked.

"You literally saved me from Hell. This is the least I can do. This and a fine gourmet meal for you and your crew."

Kiri laughed. It was a short, joyful chortle. She looked at her great-grandfather, a little girl in spite of her age. "Thank you," she whispered, then shuffled away.

Barnabas had expected the trawling machine to look like some kind of medieval torturing instrument standing in a dimly-lit parliament of steel and concrete. Instead, it was little more than a chair with a filigree headpiece attached sitting in a small, round room. Water was streaming softly over the polished bronze walls, and planter boxes stood on either side of the door.

The doctor, a soft-spoken man with dark brown skin and radiant yellow eyes, had introduced himself as Avenato, and was wearing what looked like a mixture of a light blue uniform and a navy lab coat. “I will be in here with you, if you wish, to ensure your mental safety.”

“So you're not actually the one performing the trawl?” For some reason, this mattered to Barnabas.

Avenato shook his head. “My colleagues are in the adjacent room, and they will administer the procedure, with the assistance of Gossamer. There is also a team of independent experts that will verify what they are seeing.”

“Witnesses? Like at an execution?” It made him uncomfortable.

Avenato looked confused, then gave him a reassuring smile. “That reference is so old, it's not even in most history books. The witnesses are there to make sure the results of this trawl are given credence. We don't like being accused of lying.”

Barnabas nodded. He was feeling nothing at all, and at the moment that was probably a good thing. “Let's get this over with, before I change my mind.”

“You are a strong person, Barnabas,” said Avenato. “You'll get through this, and I will see to it that you do.”

Barnabas took a deep breath, leaned backward, and closed his eyes. “I hope you're right.”

Hell was back. The transition had been abrupt, and not at all gentle. He had expected the room to crumble and fold back, or for the door to open and him tunnelling through, but now he was simply here, naked, tied to the ice pillar again.

Barnabas realised immediately the mistake he'd made. He was staring into the face of a demon, the very first demon he had met, the fires in its eyes flickering with glee only a hand's length from his face.

"Glad to see you've chosen to return, Barnabas. I'd been getting worried you'd lost yourself in your fantasy." Its face came closer, breath smelling like sulphur. "I've been trying to get through to you, and it seems like I succeeded."

"That was no fantasy. You're the fantasy," Barnabas croaked. He was having a difficult time believing his own words.

The demon cackled, retracting its face from him and gesturing around the ice pillars in a sweeping motion. "You humans never fail to amuse." Its spine swung around, skull still staring at him as the body was turned away. "All your life, every night, you dreamt. You dreamt in here, even. Do you know why?"

"The science is still out," Barnabas said quietly.

"There is no science, Barnabas, you know that. Deep down, you know. I, for instance, do not dream. I do not dream because only the children of God dream. The entirety of the universe is God's dream, and Hell is Lucifer's dream. When they taught you that God is in everyone, they meant it. You have a little piece of God in you, and that is the piece of you the dreams up these pathetic, temporary little worlds with no rules or meaning to them."

To his surprise, that gave him a little hope. "The place I was, the real world, it wasn't fleeting. It was real, it had fundamental laws, and it worked perfectly fine."

"Oh yes, you unlocked your piece of the divine, that is true." The demon turned back toward him fully. "You built your own little world, allowed yourself to be carried into it. You're an old soul, Barnabas. You've a few tricks up your sleeve. What you need to remember is that I have more, and every time you retreat into your little fantasy, I will get you out just when you feel secure in your reality again. If you don't come running back first."

"Why would I come back here?" Barnabas demanded. The demon's explanation did make sense, but his negotiation was new. It gave him the slightest shred of confidence that maybe, just maybe, this was not real after all.

"You're here now, aren't you? You came back because you chose to, because you know that this place is where you belong." The demon chattered its teeth. "And every time you leave again, after you come back, the punishments you have already endured will be child's play compared to those you will suffer."

Maybe it was a self-destructive streak he never thought he'd had, but Barnabas said "I don't believe you," and spat squarely in the demon's face. It was a lie, but the demon did not seem to care.

"Alright then. I'll let you off easy this time, just the regular Hell routine."

"And why would you do that?" Barnabas asked.

"Because unlike God, I am merciful." He laughed.

It was at that moment Barnabas realised that Hell was not real.

He was sat onto a throne of spikes, sinking slowly in agony, as though pressed ever deeper into the contraption, until finally someone else was sat down on top of him.

He was attached to a wheel and driven for hours over a field of searing hot razor blades. Imps greased the wheels with pure acid, and a giant wrung him from time to time before pulling him back on the wheel.

He was encased in a sea of molten lead, the metal entering every orifice, cooling solid, expanding, and bursting his body apart.

He was set ablaze in a lake of gasoline, thrashing and flailing in ever hotter flames, until the fire was stopped when a bucket of magma was poured over his head.

He was locked in a pot full of shit, piss, and vomit, and left to stew inside it over an open flame for hours.

He was flayed and thrown into a desert made of salt, his skin regrowing, locking the salt underneath, constantly burning his skin. It hurt so much that he scratched it all away, exposing it to even more grains.

When he was finally brought back to his ice pillar, it felt like weeks had gone by. All of those tortures he had experienced before. All of those tortures had been so unspeakable that they were difficult to even remember. All of those tortures had not been real.

Barnabas fell asleep, ready to wake in the real world.

"And we're done," Avenato said softly the moment Barnabas opened his eyes. "You did splendidly. A whole minute of trawling, with those kinds of memories. Excellent readings, too. You're a hero, Barnabas."

Barnabas took a deep breath. It was over. It was finally over. "Thank you," he said.

"Oh no, thank you," Avenato insisted. *"You will return to Hell, Barnabas. You cannot escape me!"*

Barnabas was shell shocked. For a moment. "What the bloody hell did you just say?"

"I asked if you'd like a glass of water." Avenato smiled, but Barnabas could have sworn that his eyes flickered like fire for a moment.

The Value of Land

By Gwydion JMF Weber

There had never been much of a point to the idea of building the flood wall in the first place. Yes, the tide was rising, but why erect this magnificent structure all along the coastline? Why not focus on the urban centres? Were the vineyards, golf courses, and parks so much more important than the lives of people in other parts of the country? Had the aristocrats of the West Coast truly been so callous as to build this massive dam where it protected nobody instead of helping those who couldn't afford any protection at all?

In the coastal cities of the entire continent, hundreds of millions had died, but not a single tree on the beach had been touched by a droplet of sea water in Oregon. To add insult to injury, the Flood Wall Foundation had bragged about investing in the Gibraltar Dam also, which had driven the sea level up by another metre or two, and protected the holiday resorts of the global elite in the Mediterranean, all the while the rest of the world drowned even faster.

And for what, really? The sudden lack of people had reduced the species' carbon footprint significantly, and the sea levels had gone down again, almost to pre-melting levels. Now the grandchildren of the same aristocrats that refused to help the needy back in the day were developing the new seaside property, some of which they had inherited from the purchase of worthless underwater mortgages, back when everybody thought the new sea level would stay this way.

Here he was, at the southern end of the West Coast Flood Wall, looking at the San Diego sunset, pondering the things he had always avoided digging into. Coulton Lee was not a bad person by any means. He was just a guy who worked for a guy, who worked for another guy, who just so happened to work for the richest woman in the western hemisphere. From the giant walker towing boats by the fishing wharf, to the office space in the city's highrises, to almost all of Baja California to the south of here, everything belonged to her. Much like her peers, she had done nothing to deserve these things. Much like Coulton's peers, he had no choice but to do her bidding.

"What do you even do?" asked the kid who had driven him out here, sitting behind the wheel of the 4X4 pick-up truck.

"I assess land value and give recommendations as to how much money should be offered to make the most efficient purchase," Coulton answered. There was no reason to lie to the boy.

"So why are you here then, and not out there, looking at the land you're supposed to assess the price of?"

"Because I'm not an adventurer, and I'd like to hold on to my life for a little while longer. The people down there know what's going on, and they don't like being staked out. If our offer surpasses whatever the Mexican government has assessed the value of the land owned by their citizens to be by twenty-five percent, they will use eminent domain to seize it and sell it to us, no questions asked," Coulton explained. "They're in too much debt not to do it."

"Are you sure your boss can afford that?" the kid inquired.

Coulton puffed. "It's pocket change for her."

"So why doesn't she just pay some huge sum that's guaranteed to be enough?"

"Because that would be a waste of money," said Coulton, not without a smirk on his face.

They listened to the waves slapping gently against the rocks in silence for a few minutes.

"Why would someone even want to buy the entirety of Baja California?" the kid wanted to know. He was a nosy one.

"The plan is to kick the population off her private property and turn it into a kingdom under the warm sun. Vancouver gets cold, and it's full of people." Coulton leaned back onto the hood of the car. “She'd rather share her personal domain with a fleet of robots and a bare minimum of servants than deal with the outside air being cold for half the year.”

“Would Mexico even allow that?”

“She owns half the Mexican debt, which not only gives her political clout, but is also the beauty of the whole scheme. She pays them money, which she then gets back.”

“It must get awfully lonely out there,” the kid mused.

“Hey man, I just work for her. I don't have to understand why she does what she does.”

There was the sound of a petroleum motor in the distance. Coulton rose to see a red quad bike make its way across the rocky beach. The driver was clad in heavy gear, his face hidden behind an orca-shaped helmet, teeth and all.

“Finally!” he exclaimed, tapping his wrist watch when the vehicle came to a halt next to them. “You're late.”

“So is your girlfriend mate, and it's not your doing,” was the muffled response from the driver. He opened the breast pocket of his leather jacket and produced a datastick. “This is it. Two years of dangerous fucking work, getting shot at by angry Mexican farmers for taking pictures of their houses.”

Coulton accepted the device, a smile of happy anticipation on his face. “Thank you very much, my friend. I'll authorise payment immediately.”

“You're not gonna check it, mate?” The driver sounded incredulous.

“I've worked with you and your team often enough to know the quality of your work. Consider this an advance of trust. Besides, I need to get back to the airfield.” Coulton typed a seven-digit code into his comlink, and a million dollars were transferred to the driver's digital wallet.

“Pleasure doing business,” he said, turned his quad bike around, and drove away.

Half an hour later, Coulton was rolling onto the tarmac of a private airport, an ultrasonic VTOL waiting for him. Men and women in dark business suits were standing by. Security goons, his welcoming committee.

“Well kid, this is where I leave. See that bald guy? He's

the one who pays you." Coulton pointed at the leader of the security team, who was approaching the driver's window. "'til next time."

Coulton did not look back when he heard the gunshot that the security leader executed the kid with. The boy was never intended to get paid, or even survive. None of the security people even knew the plan for Baja California. Hell, they barely knew what Coulton did for a living. Just someone from the home office in Vancouver, coming down south for some reason or another. All they had to do was watch his plane and kill his driver.

Coulton Lee was convinced that he wasn't a bad man. At least he had told the kid all the secrets the world wouldn't know for years. He hadn't been the one who pulled the trigger, nor had he been the one who ordered his death. He just turned a blind eye, because what else was he to do? Much like Mexico, someone much wealthier than himself owned his debts, and one of the things he'd given up to repay them was his conscience. It was the only way to survive.

Weird Witch

By Gwydion JMF Weber

Few places in the world were as beautiful as the foothills of Colorado in late summer. The dry brown of the mountains was mellow and calming, the deep green of the trees was full of promise, and the yellows of the grassy fields were invigorating.

Ryan was tearing through up road on his trusty quad bike, a mighty plume of dust trailing behind him. The lively green of Kravchenko's plantation was calling for him. The sweet embrace of Mary Jane, as his father would have called it.

Cori gestured for him to slow the fuck down as she opened the front gate. Her black hair was tied up in a ponytail that reached almost to her beautifully round butt. Her face was a perfectly ambiguous mix of black, white, and native American. Blue eyes, sultry lips, and eyes with epicanthic folds made for a perfectly unique person, like someone born in the future, at a time where race had become irrelevant.

Ryan pulled straight into the central yard, where two sedans, four pick-up trucks, and a dozen motorcycles stood in disarray. Kravchenko came out of his container office. He was a 40-something Ukrainian guy wearing jeans and a faded polo shirt. He was slender, almost gangly, and his triangular face looked as though it had been designed in a wind tunnel by race car engineers.

"Ryan, my favourite friend, how are you doing this fine evening?" Kravchenko's accent was as thick as the fat on a good steak, and though his friendliness was always somewhat exaggerated, it was genuine.

"I'm doing fine, thanks for asking. How's the weed

coming?" Ryan shook Kravchenko's hand.

"Very good, very good. Next harvest will be excellent, your customers will be pleased. How is the dispensary?"

"Can't complain, though a lot of my peeps have been complaining that your stuff flies off the shelves too fast. Your strains have been out of stock for a week." Ryan took the can of Mountain Dew that Kravchenko offered him from the fridge.

"I have very high quality standards, my friend. Just yesterday I burned a kilo of *Crimean Invasion* because it was not up to snuff."

"Well, that's not the one people are most interested in. They don't like feeling like they are in a warzone, so if you could breed that out and keep that salty factor in, my mom would be very happy. She makes like a kind of pasta with it, it's pretty good." The pop left a sticky taste in his mouth. Ryan looked at the can in his hand. Diet.

"I am an artist, you know that. I don't make this stuff so people can get high, I craft experiences, allow them to feel things, see the world as it truly is," Kravchenko insisted.

"It's just weed, man. I know you're into all that third-eye stuff, but my customers just wanna get high." Ryan took another sip, out of respect for his host more than anything.

"How can you be such an expert yet know so little about the real world, yes? You've seen what my product can do." Kravchenko smiled. They'd had this conversation a million times.

"Yes, that 'whole package' shit, the qualia of an experience that weed should not be able to give, that's what you do best, that's what people pay the big bucks for. You're the only one who does it, and instead of making stuff that feels like a ten hour orgasm, you produce strains that can cause literal PTSD."

"I told you to warn people before they buy my grass, friend. And if you think seeing your family slaughtered by Russian insurgents will leave scars, you should know that a ten-hour orgasm is even more traumatic. It would be irresponsible of me to sell such things."

Ryan waved the words away. "When will you send me new stuff?"

"I am packing several boxes of *Chernobyl* right now, but

that will be shipped up to Denver, special order. Next week you will receive a shipment of *Theotokos' Kiss*."

Ryan gasped with relief. Finally one that people were actually looking forward to. It was some of the best weed he'd ever smoked. "Wait, then why did you call me here?"

"I have to show you something." Kravchenko beckoned for Ryan to follow him into one of his greenhouses. That was where he bred his experimental strains. As always, they looked perfectly ordinary. Anyone able to figure out the Ukrainian's secret stood to make millions.

The weed smelled musty and cold. The plants were so dark that they were almost black. Ryan recognised the strain immediately. "Really, man? Last time I smoked this stuff it was like taking actual psychedelics. Every time I think about it I get the creeps."

"Yes, of course you remember that *Baba Yaga* that my cousin Koshei sent me. You probably also remember that I had difficulty growing it here."

"Which I am very happy about, honestly. If I put that shit under a microscope I would probably find mushrooms." Ryan shook his head. He hadn't smoked weed for a month after his *Baba Yaga* experience.

"Well, this is not *Baba Yaga*. The problem was the terroir, no? *Baba Yaga* grown in the old country is suffused with the spirits of that place, but of course here in Colorado we have different spirits, which is why it did not grow." Kravchenko gestured around to several Slavic and Native American totemic fetishes distributed across the greenhouse.

"It was a very difficult process, taking the *Baba Yaga* and making it absorb the essence of this place, soak up the spirits like a sponge. They are not used to this kind of thing happening here, the spirits. I had to import soil from Ukraine, mix it with local soil, get a bunch of shamans to do rituals." Kravchenko picked up a dark bud lying loose on a table. "This is my final product. I call it *Weird Witch*, because I like alliterations."

"Well man, thanks but no, thanks. I'm not smoking that crap again, and anything I don't smoke, I don't sell. You should ask one of those hippy-stores, there's plenty of them and they are into all that same spirit-world bullshit." Ryan could feel the experience of the *Baba Yaga* creep back into his mind. He tried to shake it off.

"Please, do not insult me. Those people do not understand the reality of the spirit world around them. They are nothing but religious fanatics, I am an atheist. We wouldn't work well together." Kravchenko put the bud back down on the table. "You are a businessman. You have the best shop in town, possibly the whole state. Expand your mind a little bit, and you could reach whole new levels of success."

"Sorry man, I'm just not interested." Ryan shook his head.

"Hey Lesh, one of the guys has been asking for you at the creekside field." Cori had come into the greenhouse without making a sound.

"I heard nothing." Kravchenko grabbed at his belt, but stopped when he didn't find what he was looking for.

Cori had his walkie-talkie in her hand. "We have these for a reason, man. You can't just fucking leave it lying around all the time."

Kravchenko gave Ryan one of those *women* looks that Cori surely would not have appreciated. "I'm sorry, my head is all over the place sometimes. That is why I let you run things."

When they were outside, the Ukrainian produced a pre-rolled joint from his breast pocket. "If you're not going to buy my *Weird Witch*, at least smoke some of my weed so your trip wasn't for nothing."

"Are you kidding? I'd drive across the whole state just to get a glimpse of this piece of primo ass." Ryan nodded toward Cori.

"Wow, total panty dropper, that line. How stupid are the chicks you usually fuck for that to work?" Cori walked off, not giving him another look. Her round butt looked at him though.

"So take it, my friend." Kravchenko was still holding the joint.

"I really don't wanna smoke your *Weird Witch* shit either," Ryan insisted.

Kravchenko shook his head vehemently. "This isn't *Weird Witch*, this is *Theotokos' Kiss*, from the last batch. I always keep some stashed."

"Well in that case, don't mind if I do." Ryan snatched the joint and carefully put it in his cigarette case.

"Remember, don't smoke and drive," Kravchenko said. "Unless it's to come back here and smoke some more weed with me."

"I'm not an idiot, Kravchenko. See you round man."

Ryan was sitting on his balcony when he lit Kravchenko's joint. Aside from the crickets and some indistinct pop music playing in the distance, the street below was quiet. He'd gotten a real Mountain Dew from the fridge to wash away the sticky taste of stevia.

It burned nicely, and Ryan enjoyed the smell as he took a deep drag. Some people would have told him to slow down, but he was a professional. His tolerance was so strong that it ruined the high on weaker strains.

The last rays of sunlight kissed the peaks of the mountain range. The air was fresh and warm. Ryan took another drag, and then another. Something was wrong with this joint. He wasn't feeling shit.

He paused for a moment, but dragged again before it could burn down too fast, then again for good measure, and then again because why the fuck not? The sunlight elongated, billowed like waves. Ryan wondered if light could be like water, eroding away layers of sediment from rock to form mountain ranges.

Birds rode the light waves like they would an air current. Fish joined them, absorbing the last of the sun's warmth before descending to the ground for the night. Ryan took another hit. The joint was no longer burning.

"Fuck." It was hitting pretty good, too, so he put the rest away for a rainy day, apologising for having doubted the joint's potency, then laughing at himself for talking to a fucking joint.

It was cold. He looked at the thermometer, but that hadn't really changed. It should still have beem nice and balmy, and in a way it was, but it also wasn't. This was not so much temperature as it was … something else. It just felt cold, and it was coming from the walls, the street, and the lights.

Inside it got slightly warmer, especially around his terrarium. His gecko stared at him, an alien kind of intelligence in its eyes. It knew that he was stoned, that he knew the fact that it could see him, and know that he was stoned.

Ryan went downstairs and into his backyard. The plants radiated a comfortable warmth, exactly the kind he was looking for. They stood out against the cold walls and fencing, and, like the ground, they were warm and alive. He could feel worms wriggling through the soil, roots and fungi channelling nutrients from one plant to the other, water rushing on the molecular level.

It was when he could see the spirits of the cicadas that Ryan realised Kravchenko had not given him *Theotokos' Kiss*. He recognised the clouds swirling above, the hands of unreality getting a hold of him. It was different than *Baba Yaga*. This shit had to be *Weird Witch*.

He looked at the clock. Only fifteen minutes since lighting the joint, which meant it wasn't peaking yet. It would not be easy, but he could still get to Kravchenko's grow and beat this shit out of him. You don't lace a joint with psychedelics, especially not twice.

Even with the motor running hot, driving down the road on his quad bike felt like sitting on a block of ice. It wasn't physically painful, and, as the city turned into the occasional house on the side of the road, everything around him got warmer. When he went off the blacktop road, the swirling dust made the bike more comfortable.

A large boulder followed him with its tiny eyes, breathing softly. Smaller rocks hopped around outside of their bodies, not having made peace with the fact that they could not physically move. The mountains, old and wise, observed hos journey with subdued curiosity. They knew something was different about him.

In the distance, a pack of coyotes ran in fear of Ryan's quad bike, herded by a twisted shepherd that had given up on sheep because they always got eaten. It was dark now. The dirt road lacked in street lamps.

Ryan did not need the headlights, though. It wasn't that the world around him was glowing, but he could see the life in it, the souls of the stones and the bushes, the grass and the puddles. He drove carefully, of course. He knew that he was high, and it would impact his reaction time. His perception simply wasn't off.

He passed through a grove of dancing trees. Giant amoebae swam underneath the earth, kissing their roots, exchanging life. They were part of a much larger network of souls, minds so alien they eluded him, yet he knew that, if he could only touch them, he would understand them all the same.

Everywhere in the soil, the gods of the trees travelled along narrow paths like leviathans squeezing through a tubular labyrinth. Humans thought of them as huge organisms, networks spanning the ground for miles and miles, but those were only conduits for their mighty, ancient souls.

Ryan evaded a rabbit crossing the road. He could see its path clear in front of him long before it ever appeared, feel its curiosity and fear. It wasn't a sudden movement, he simply knew where to drive so as to not hit it. When he saw it miss his rear wheel by mere inches, he could feel its gratitude.

Kravchenko's grow appeared in the distance, glowing like a sea of beacons. All the spirits of the land congregated there, caught in an endless celebration. Some were related to the ones he had already seen today, others were dark and foreign, yet strikingly familiar. Some did not get along, especially the ones which overlapped in purpose, but generally the mood was elated, and everyone was happy.

At least that was the closest thing to it. These spirits did not feel happiness in the same way he did. It was more like contentment, mixed with many of those emotions one could not explain while sober, and especially not while high.

The gate to the grow stood wide open. That was strange, but Ryan had other things to worry about. Kravchenko was going to have some justifying to do.

Green spectres turned around to him on the sides of the road, smiling, and throwing ghostly petals at him. Everything was so warm it should have been hot, but instead it was comfortable. Ryan felt like he was a part of that warmth, and the hotter it got, the better he would feel.

Only one car and a single bike were left standing in the

open parking area. Kravchenko was nowhere to be seen. Ryan got off his quad bike and looked in the cold, dark container office. The fridge with the diet pops was buzzing, but there was no Kravchenko.

A single look at the greenhouses sufficed. There was only one place that crazy Ukrainian could be. “Kravchenko you fucking asshole!” Ryan screamed as he opened the door to the *Weird Witch* greenhouse.

Dark hands dragged him inside. It wasn't what it had been a few hours earlier in here. The outside was crowded, but this place was packed more densely than the space should have allowed, and Ryan was immediately caught in the current of the spirits.

They touched every droplet of his soul, infused it with their power. He felt terror, love, agonising sadness, and unfathomable ecstasy. Memories of lands near and distant, thousands of years of them, flashed before his eyes in mere moments. The rise and fall of forests, people, towns, and lives, from the insignificant to the grandiose.

A newborn became a teenager, an adult, a shaman, a decrepit crone, until it finally dissipated into the land, having lived, loved, cried, and experienced. The ancient gods consumed the soul, and it changed them, like every other soul did when it returned to the place from whence it came.

Rivers eroded the land, floods killed burrowing creatures by the billions over eternal timespans. Death and life spun around each other so fast that they soon became the same entity, reaching out to him, dragging his soul away from his body with gentle words and strict commands.

Something grabbed hold of him, cradled him in its arms. This was more than just a spirit. It was a real entity of flesh and blood. Cori laid him on the ground outside the greenhouse, concern on her face.

Except it wasn't her face. It was a thousand different faces, faces of perfect beauty all of them, as seen through the eyes of a thousand different men and women. Her real face glowed flaming orange behind the ever-changing mask.

Ryan tried to reach out to her, explain what was

happening. "*Weird Witch*," was all he could croak. Cori shook her head. "Fucking Lesh," she mumbled, then grabbed her walkie talkie. "Listen up asshole, Ryan is here, and he's melting."

There was no response.

Ryan felt himself shaking, not just physically, but in his very soul. It was like he had forgotten where he as a person ended and the world around him began. Everything was connected, everything was water, and the water inside him was separated from the outside only by a thin membrane, like a jellyfish.

He could let himself go with the flow, drift away on the current, become spread in all directions, dissipate back into the world. Voices whispered to him in strange languages, all encouraging him to let go and become a part of them.

"Leeeeeeeeesh!" Cori roared. The ground vibrated with the thunder of her voice. It dragged Ryan back to reality, where he realised that he was terrified. He was dying. Whatever had been in that joint, he was not handling it well. Something in his brain was shutting down, and it would take the rest with him.

"What is it?" Kravchenko appeared in his peripheral vision, only he did not look like the Ukrainian he knew at all. Instead of hair, he had a dense nest of brambles laden with pinecones on his head. He had a long, moss-covered beard. His pale green skin was speckled with patches of old wood, and his shining, yellow eyes burned with power.

"You tricked him, didn't you?" Cori asked.

"I had to open his perception to the real world. This man deserves to know the truth."

"He walked into the *Weird Witch* greenhouse looking for you. I barely got him out in time." Cori was radiating pure wrath.

"That was a mistake. He should not have done that. He is not ready for it."

"No shit, Lesh. And he should have known this how, exactly? God damn it you moron. He could sink our whole operation because you couldn't keep your fucking quest of enlightenment to yourself."

Ryan's soul was being dragged in all directions, spreading apart like melted cheese. He could feel the waves of the spirit world grab a hold of him, bending him like a piece of paper, trying to take him away.

“Okay, Ryan, stay with me, focus on my face.” Cori looked him right in the eyes. The features he recognised returned, that perfectly racially ambiguous creature. She was doing it on purpose so as to keep him grounded in reality, he knew.

“So … beautiful,” he whispered.

Cori smiled. “I know, it's what I am.”

Kravchenko stood behind Cori. A squirrel scurried from his beard into his hair. “Give him this.”

“This is diet Mountain Dew you dumb fuck. Are you higher than he is right now,” Cori threw the can away, but Kravchenko's arm grew several inches in an instant, and he snatched it out of the air.

“He is drawn to the spirits of nature, this stuff is as unnatural as it gets. Why do you think I keep it around?” He handed the can back to Cori.

“You want him to evict himself from his own body? Because that's how you make that happen.”

Kravchenko's hair brambles rustled as he shook his head. “Trust me on this.”

Cori clenched her jaw, then opened the drink and put it to Ryan's lips. The can and the pop were cold as ice, colder even. The membrane around him froze, locking the substance of his soul inside his body. He was in agony.

“I'm gonna drive you home now.” Cori picked him up and carried him to the car. Ryan did not even question how a woman half his size could carry him with such ease.

Ryan woke up with a headache. He'd never had a headache from weed before, but what he'd been given yesterday had clearly not been just Mary Jane.

A gallon of water and a warm shower later, he was able to function enough to make himself some bacon and eggs. After breakfast, he went outside to find that his quad bike was standing at the exact same spot he had left it yesterday before he lit the joint. There was a moment of doubt, but Ryan realised that there shouldn't have been. Kravchenko had still laced it, and that was fucked up.

He started the motor and drove out to the grow in the late morning sun.

Cori gave him a concerned smile as she opened the gate. Kravchenko was sitting in a plastic chair among the cars, eating a fruit salad. When he saw Ryan, he was surprised. “My favourite friend, what brings you here today?”

“You laced my joint, asshole.”

Kravchenko shrugged. “That bud was stored for a while. Maybe some mushrooms grew on it. I most certainly did no such thing.”

“That shit seriously fucked me up, man! I *drove* out here! You know how dangerous that is?”

“And you drove back home again? You should have made yourself known, I would have put you up in a tent or something. That's very dangerous what you did there, friend.” Kravchenko ate a slice of apple.

“What the fuck are you talking about? You *saw* me!” Ryan made a fist. He wanted to punch Kravchenko in the face.

“I do not remember seeing you around. Maybe it was only dream, yes?”

Ryan took a deep breath. He was experienced enough with psychedelics to know that such a thing was definitely possible, he just found it hard to believe. On the other hand, what kind of evidence did he have?

“We're gonna talk about this laced joint business, Kravchenko.”

“Please, let's. You want some fruit?”

For the briefest of moments, as though it had been in the corner of his eye, Ryan could swear that a squirrel just ran up Lesh Kravchenko's sleeve.

A Good Place

By Gwydion JMF Weber

There was peace in this place, the old wizard found. He was standing on his eastern balcony, suspended above the steep cliffs and roiling sea. Gulls laughed as they soared along the tan rocks, and wild sheep wandered lazily across the green plains. In the distance, a parade of dolphins jumped between the turquoise waves.

The old wizard took a deep breath of the brisk sea air, smelling the salt and the earth, the memory of fallen rain. He took a drag from his pipe, the seagrass in it foaming like the crest of a wave. The invigorating power of the deep ocean rumbled in his lungs for a while, and the smoke he blew out turned to water as it left the confines of his balcony.

A steaming mug sat on a table next to the old wizard, the ceramic goblins on it toiling around like children on the playground. The hearty beverage within tasted like apples, cinnamon, and the dreams of a true optimist. He added a little goat's milk with honey and tasted it again. This time it was perfect.

When he was finished enjoying the ocean, the old wizard walked into his living room, the glass pane folding away like a curtain as he passed. A pyramid made of cut amethyst and the size of a human head hovered over a granite podium, spinning languidly. Oh how he had coveted this item.

Many years ago, when the wizard had been in his physical prime, he had lead an expedition to a distant island on a foreign world. Everyone had told him the legends of the place were untrue, that they were little more than sailor's yarn, and that his journey was dangerous to the point of suicide.

The only captain who would sail for him did not have a face, as it had been stolen from him, and the same fate had befallen all of his crew. The journey was arduous, and plagued by problems. Mutiny was almost inevitable when they reached the shore of the island, and managed to get fresh coconuts and citrus fruits from its sweltering jungles.

When they had encountered monkeys with scarlet fur, the wizard had been disappointed. But when one of them burst into flames as it attacked a crewman encroaching on its territory, it became clear that there was much truth to the legends. The monkey was killed, and its fire died, but there was not a single scorch on it.

They found the pyramid in the mound of a great volcano, spewing red lightning onto anyone who dared stand on the rim. Recovering it had posed difficult, and required the construction of an ever larger conductor, but they had managed to cut it off from its source of power, and load it aboard.

As he walked toward the kitchen, the old wizard stopped in front of a door he hadn't seen the other side of in weeks. It was black, heavy, and made of metal. With a smile on his face, he stepped through, and into a room that seemed at first utterly dark.

A narrow copper bridge lead him to a large platform illuminated by the starlight his eyes were slowly calibrating themselves to. There was nothing beneath the platform, the bridge, or the door. Everything was floating in the void, infinite in all directions.

He sat down by the vast telescope array in the middle of the platform, turning levers and dials to move it. Peering through the lens, he focused on a group of seven suns that had a bilious green lustre to them.

The old wizard had won them in a card game from a man with the face of a lion, a wanderer of many worlds. He'd been a young man back then, with a small purse, a narrow mind, and a big mouth. He and the lion man had been the only two players left from a table of seven, and the wizard had been winning. He bet everything on his final hand, so taken was he by his youthful greed.

The lion man, unable to match the bet, had pulled a bottle with the seven green stars out of his bag, and kept the rest of his coin. It had been a tense game, and nobody had ever found out that the young wizard cheated.

Realising that he was still holding a mug in his hand while grinning at the stars like a moron, the old wizard left his stellarium and walked into the kitchen. There, he leaned on the counter and looked into his garden. From here, he could only just see through the surface of his pond, and into the world beneath it. It was a reef, illuminated by a fictitious sun and glowing anemones, inhabited by shoals of colourful fish, shimmering sea snakes, and pallid merfolk.

He had constructed it on one of his sojourns to the great cities, when he had lectured at a prestigious university, already an experienced and respected man in his field. There had been a woman that every man coveted, so smart and beautiful had she been. The old wizard, wanting to impress, had created the reef and its inhabitants in his apartment's swimming pool.

The woman had not reciprocated his interest, painful as it had been, but when the old wizard moved to this place, he had taken the illusion with him. It was a pain to bottle and install here, in his rural garden, but with a few adjustments and a little trickery, he had managed to pull it off.

It was good, being here. He was in a good place. The old wizard took a deep breath that ended in a sigh, and looked out into the distance, vast plains to the left, and cliffs of the sea to the right. Maybe in a century, the world would call to him again, but today the old wizard was happy to sit in peace and reminisce. He was, after all, not running out of time.

Made in United States
Orlando, FL
16 February 2024

43747923R00168